To the loving memory of my father

BITTER ALMONDS

LILAS TAHA

ISIS
LARGE
PRINT

First published in Great Britain 2015
by
Bloomsbury Qatar Foundation Publishing
Bloomsbury Publishing Plc

First Isis Edition
published 2016
by arrangement with
Bloomsbury Publishing Plc

A catalogue record for this book is available
from the British Library.

ISBN 978–1–78541–200–4 (hb)
ISBN 978–1–78541–206–6 (pb)

Published by
F. A. Thorpe (Publishing)
Anstey, Leicestershire

Set by Words & Graphics Ltd.
Anstey, Leicestershire
Printed and bound in Great Britain by
T. J. International Ltd., Padstow, Cornwall

This book is printed on acid-free paper

CHAPTER
ONE

Jerusalem
1948

They told five-year-old Fatimah not to turn around, but no one told her to close her eyes. No one told her not to listen. She pressed her face against the window, a rag doll forgotten in her lap. Quiet rain speckled the cold glass, and a flickering street lamp cast broken yellow beams on the desolate street. Fatimah sat mute, comforted by the soft drizzle, and watched the scene behind her unfold on the reflective pane. If she sat very still, they might forget she was there.

Her mother pushed aside the midwife's fussy hands and scooted her huge body to the edge of the bed. Grunting, Mama got to her feet. She yanked at the collar of her cotton gown, ripping the front buttons and exposing her sweat-drenched chest. She spread her legs wide apart. Fluids trickled down and dampened the hem of her gown and the faded rug.

"Get back on the bed," the midwife instructed in a raspy smoker's voice.

"I can do this," Mama panted. "Baby is coming. I can feel it."

"Do as I say." The midwife brought her wrinkled face close to Mama's. "Your baby needs help. You will not be able to push it out by yourself. You've been trying all day, and the night —"

The door flew open. The next-door neighbor, Subhia, walked in. She closed the door and rolled up her sleeves. "How can I help?"

The midwife slid her hands under Mama's arms and attempted to get her back on the bed. "Come. Help me before it's too late. Lift her legs."

"We should've taken her to the clinic." Subhia bent to hold Mama's feet. "Now it's too late. Everyone in the village has left."

"She's stubborn. If she had done what I said, this baby would be out by now."

Quick knocks shook the wooden door. The women froze.

"We have to go." Subhia's husband urged from behind the closed door.

"I can't leave her now, Mustafa!" Subhia shouted over her shoulder.

"The gangs are bound to head this way. I'm not waiting any longer. The children are in the truck. I'll make room for the women. Hurry!"

Subhia gripped the midwife's arm. "What do you think?"

"We can't even get her back on the bed." The midwife shook her head. "And I'm not leaving her. Go with your husband."

With a loud cry, Mama squatted, bringing down the two women beside her. She gripped the edge of the bed and held her breath. Her face turned crimson and her eyes welded tight.

"Stupid woman, stop pushing. It's not time!" the midwife yelled. "You'll hurt yourself."

"I don't care. The baby is here!" Mama screamed the words. She then screamed for her own mother. Screamed for her dead husband. Screamed for God to help her, to protect her baby, to end her misery. Screamed until her voice failed her.

For a brief moment, a suspended instant in time, all the noises of the world disappeared. No raindrops tapped the window in front of Fatimah's face. No women frantically bellowed instructions to her mother. No panicked neighbor banged on the door. Only one sound could be heard.

A gasp.

A cry.

Fatimah ran to Mama's side, forgetting to remain invisible. "A boy?"

The women ignored her.

"Oh, Mama, look at his hair," Fatimah whispered, surprised by the wispy red fuzz.

The midwife wrapped the baby with a towel. She placed her lips over his nose and mouth and sucked hard, her cheeks sinking deeper in her bony face. She pulled back, spat on the soiled rug and repeated the process several times. She thrust the baby into Mama's trembling hands.

Another knock shook the door. "Subhia, please. We have to leave now."

Mama touched her lips to the baby's forehead. The simple movement drained whatever energy she had left. Her head dropped back on the bed's edge, eyes closed. "Take him," she mouthed.

Fatimah smoothed back hair off Mama's damp forehead. "I will help you take care of him, Mama."

Subhia cradled the boy, her eyes searching the midwife's face, grim and ominous.

"I'm coming in!" Mustafa shouted from outside.

The midwife snatched a blanket off the bed and covered most of Mama's body.

Mustafa stormed in, took his wife by the shoulders and pulled her to her feet. "Get in the truck." He knelt on the floor. "Grab whatever you need. I'm taking you out of here."

"Go. Take Fatimah too. I'll stay with her." The midwife swatted away his hands. "Take your family."

"I'm not leaving you two behind. There's no one left. You'll tend to her on the road until we get to the next town. If it's safe, I'll find a doctor."

"She will bleed to death if you move her."

"And you will both die if you stay. You heard what Stern and Irgun gangs did in Deir Yassin. They butchered people, women *and* children. They will do the same once they get here. Now stop talking and get moving, old woman."

Subhia settled on a pile of blankets in the truck bed. She had the baby in her arms. Her three-month-old son, Shareef, slept in the arms of his eight-year-old sister, Huda. The plastic tarp shielding them from rain sagged in the middle and rested on Subhia's head.

Fatimah squeezed her little body next to Huda's and placed Mama's head in her lap.

The midwife climbed in. She worked on getting Mama into a comfortable position.

"Did you remember to lock the door?" Subhia asked.

"I did." The midwife patted her chest. "I have the house key here."

"We'll be back in a couple of weeks." Mustafa slammed the truck tailgate. "Once this is over."

CHAPTER
TWO

Damascus
Ten years later, 1958

Fatimah balanced a laundry basket on her head, gathered the hem of her long dress with one hand and climbed the stairs to the roof. She pushed open the metal door and walked out to a bright day. Sagging ropes crisscrossed the wide open area. She used every inch of the clothesline to hang her wet load, working as fast as she could, humming all the while. She had other chores to take care of, but doing laundry for the big family was a full-day chore. This was her sixth and final load. She had started at dawn and now the midday sun would finish the job. She flipped the empty basket to drain the water and stretched her back.

A boy shouted a series of profanities from the street. Fatimah knew that voice, but she ran to the railing to check anyway. Her brother stood in the middle of a ring of boys, all older and bigger than him.

"Omar!" she yelled. "Meet me at the bottom of the stairs!"

Omar looked up and scowled at his sister for interrupting the scuffle. He pushed past the throng of boys, heading for the entrance to the three-story apartment building.

Fatimah's running footsteps echoed in the stairway. Omar waited for her at the last step. Taunting boys' voices came from behind.

"Saved by big sister!"

"We're not going anywhere, Omar!"

"A real man finishes what he started!"

"What do you need, Fatimah?" Omar's tone showed his impatience.

She shook the front of her dress to keep damp spots from sticking to her legs. "I heard what you said. How many times have I told you not to use that kind of language?"

"I was trying not to use my fists."

"You would have, had I not interrupted, right?"

He shifted his weight from side to side. "Sorry for cursing."

"What were you fighting about?"

He shrugged, failing to look innocent. "Nothing."

Fatimah had her suspicions. Her brother stood out like a sore thumb. Everyone in the neighborhood knew he was not Uncle Mustafa's blood relative. At least she had the same coloring as his children. Fatimah blended in. But her brother had fair skin, golden red hair and blue eyes. Omar carried himself differently than other boys. He walked with a purposeful stride, furrowing his brows as if concentrating on something in the distance. Rarely smiling, he projected the image of someone in pursuit of a mission.

For reasons unknown to Fatimah, an annoying old woman used to call him "the Englishman," and the nickname had stuck. Her brother hated it, and she knew it was the reason behind almost every fight he got into. Most likely the cause of this one. She stepped closer to brush dirt from his collar.

"Look what you've done to your school shirt. Go upstairs and take it off so I can wash it and have it ready for tomorrow. How many times have I told you to come straight home and change?"

"One thousand." Omar managed to turn the dutiful answer into an accusation.

Fatimah ignored it. "And what happened to your hair?" She extended her hand to flatten strands shooting up like antennas on top of his head.

He ducked and ran his fingers through his hair. "It's windy today."

"Wait a minute." She narrowed her eyes. "How come you're out of school?"

"Don't you know?" Omar clasped his hands together. "Jamal Abdel Nasser arrived today. Here in Damascus!" His voice rose with excitement and cracked on the last word. He cleared his throat. "Nasser will declare his leadership of the unity with Egypt. Other Arab countries will join the United Arab Republic." He inflated his chest and straightened his back, concentrating on a spot behind her left shoulder. "We will return to Palestine."

Omar's enthusiasm bounced off the walls around Fatimah, his face full of elation, a sparkle dancing in his sky-blue eyes. She tried to maintain a stern expression. "So school let out early?"

"People are gathering in the streets around Al Diafeh Square to see President Nasser. I'm going there." He paused, and pointed back with his thumb. "Once I'm done with those guys."

Fatimah wished she could go with him to see the famous leader. Over the past couple of months, Nasser's presence in Syria was all everyone talked about. Nasser's nationalization of the Suez Canal two years earlier had brought on the triple aggression by Britain, France and Israel to force his hand. His persistent defiance until foreign troops withdrew from the Suez Canal and Sinai ignited Arab nationalism everywhere, turning him into a great hero. Omar was not alone in his idolization of the daring leader.

Fatimah held Omar's elbow. "Get as close to the president as you can. I want details."

Omar's mood shifted. He knotted his brows and drew a long breath. "Soon, we will return to our father's house."

Something in his tone gave her pause. Something serious, making him seem older than his ten years. What was going on in that boy's head? He had never mentioned their father's house before. But again, a fever had gripped the nation, causing people to stay up nights. Was it hope? Had her brother caught it? Glued to the radio almost every evening, he listened to broadcast messages from Palestinian refugees in Lebanon and Jordan enquiring about relatives dispersed in other refugee camps. Omar never said a word, but she knew he waited to hear news about surviving members of their family. How could one tell a boy he was the only male survivor? That the continuity of the Bakry name rested on his shoulders, and his alone?

She pushed the idea to the back of her head. "Where's Shareef? Shouldn't he be out too?"

Omar turned and cast a quick peek outside. He thrust his chin. "Shareef's over there."

Fatimah stepped around him to see for herself. The neighborhood boys were waiting for Omar; Shareef was standing outside their circle. She raised her index finger in Omar's face. "He had better not get hurt. You know how much it upsets Mama Subhia. You always get him in trouble."

Omar's face reddened, as if someone had lit a match under his cheeks. "I can't help it if he follows me around all the time."

"Yes, but you're supposed to watch out for him. Shareef is not as strong as you are."

"He's the older one." Omar crossed his arms on his chest. "If anything, he should be protecting *me*."

"Really? Three months' difference?" Fatimah softened her tone. "When did you ever consider him older? You order him around as you please. So next time, send him home before you start a fight, all right?"

Omar raised his brows and opened his mouth to say something.

"And you shouldn't fight at all," she rushed in. "There are other ways to resolve problems."

A boy's voice called for "the Englishman" to come out and eat his words.

Omar placed his hands on her shoulders. "Don't worry about Shareef. I won't let him get hurt."

He tossed her a rare smile. It went straight to her heart. What would she do with this boy when he turned into a man? Good thing he didn't smile much. Girls would melt at his feet, and he would be fighting grown men.

"Don't ruin your shirt. I expect you inside in exactly five minutes. You need to change before you go to the square." She tapped his shoulder. "Don't use your sharp tongue or your fists."

"What does that leave me to fight with?" Omar headed back to the street.

"Think, Omar," she yelled after him. "Use your head."

He did. He walked straight toward the biggest boy in the group and with one head butt knocked him off his feet.

CHAPTER
THREE

Three years later, 1961

When it came to taking care of Mama Subhia's five children, Fatimah's maternal nature was second-to-none. The children preferred her loving and quiet disposition to their own stern sister, Huda. Struggling at school, Huda had given up after tenth grade and stayed home. The old midwife took her under her wing, teaching her the ins and outs of her trade, helping her gain a midwife certification when she turned eighteen. Huda became the aging midwife's right hand and was often called upon in their Palestinian refugee community. Her job made a small dent in the financial burdens of the family.

Fatimah filled the void of the big sister at home and managed to get her high school diploma at the same time. Uncle Mustafa encouraged her to enroll in nursing school, told her he would find a way to pay for it too. But Fatimah knew they couldn't afford it. With Uncle Mustafa working at the wool factory and Mama Subhia busy having babies, Fatimah had postponed or abandoned some dreams.

"What do you mean you found a job?" Mama Subhia asked one evening.

Fatimah walked into the room with a tray of Turkish coffee. She sat on the bed, careful not to disturb baby Salma sleeping by her mother's side. "Um Waleed told me she needed a helper a couple of hours in the evening." Fatimah kept her voice hushed. "It's not far from here."

"Um Waleed, the dress maker at the end of the street?"

"You know her. I'll be back in time to help you put the children to bed, so it shouldn't be a problem."

"But *habibti*, you don't even know how to thread a needle." Mama Subhia's use of the loving word in her motherly tone never failed to make Fatimah feel special.

"Um Waleed said she will teach me. Besides, she needs me to iron the outfits when they're done and do simple mending jobs. She'll pay me for each piece I finish." Fatimah leaned forward and stressed her words, "Just think about it. I'll learn a trade and make money at the same time."

Mama Subhia shook her head. "We don't expect you to make money. If you go to nursing school, you will have a degree and a better paying job."

Fatimah lowered her eyes to her coffee cup. "You know that won't happen, not any time soon anyway. I'm no better than Huda, and she's working."

Baby Salma made a noise in her sleep only her mother could understand.

Mama Subhia placed her hand on her baby's belly and caressed it. "Huda was never interested in school. We had no other options for her. And without Omar, I can't get Nadia to open a book. The way she depends on him worries me. She'll turn eleven soon, no longer a little girl." Mama Subhia placed her other hand on Fatimah's cheek. "You're smart, *habibti*. You can make a future for yourself."

Fatimah gazed into Mama Subhia's eyes and felt her warmth spill over. Without an ounce of hesitation, this woman had taken them in after their mother died on the road during their escape and given them a home, treating them like her own children. Sometimes a little better. She owed her a lot, and Omar owed her his life. She could not burden this family with her schooling, and she needed to find a way to cover Omar's education as well.

"A few more years and Omar will graduate from high school. I have to think about his future." Fatimah drained her coffee cup. "If I start working now, I'll be able to save enough to get him enrolled in the university."

The baby demanded their attention with a loud cry. Mama Subhia lifted her to her shoulder and patted her back. She kept crying.

"Besides, there's Shareef to consider," Fatimah continued. "Uncle Mustafa has enough on his plate. Let me help. I will prepare a bottle." She hurried to the kitchen, hoping to relieve Mama Subhia of her baby's cries. She had been unable to breastfeed since she had given birth to her son, Shareef. High fever had gripped

Mama Subhia for weeks, and the midwife forbade her breastfeeding him. The same had happened with her daughters Nadia and one-year-old Farah. The family had needed to buy expensive formula for each child, including Omar. All the more reason for Fatimah to find a job, lend a helping hand. Fatimah went back to the bedroom and handed over the warm bottle. Sucking sounds soon replaced Salma's cries.

"See how you're helping?" Mama Subhia smiled down at her baby. She tilted her head and narrowed her eyes. "Isn't Um Waleed's son one of the teachers at the boys' school?"

"Waleed? I think he's the history teacher. Why?"

"Waleed and his mother are good people. This might not be such a bad idea after all. Let's discuss it with Mustafa when he comes home."

"It's the first Thursday of the month." Fatimah hid a smile behind her hand. "Uncle Mustafa will be late tonight." As long as she could remember, Uncle Mustafa's sole recreational time was spending one evening a month at the café with his friends, listening to the enchanting voice of the legendary singer, Um Kulthoom, on the radio. People planned their schedules around the first Thursdays of every month. Almost no one missed the exhilarating nightlong event.

Mama Subhia handed over the baby to Fatimah and scurried to her feet. "I can't believe I forgot to turn on the radio. The concert is about to start." She headed to the living room. "I'll talk to Mustafa about your job tomorrow. Set a plate of almonds for him to enjoy in the morning." Winking at Fatimah, Mama Subhia turned on the radio. "Eating almonds takes him back to Palestine. It will help put him in a good mood."

CHAPTER
FOUR

Mustafa shuffled through the door and headed straight to the bathroom. He stripped and placed his dirty blue uniform in the hamper. Working on the main floor at the wool factory meant he brought home fine fibers on his clothes, body and hair. He needed to make sure they didn't get carried off into the air his family breathed.

Scrubbing his skin clean under hot water, a series of violent coughs gripped him. He leaned a bony shoulder to the wall and watched blood swirl around the drain.

"Are you almost done?" Subhia's voice came muffled from behind the door. "Supper is ready."

Mustafa closed his red eyes. "Two minutes." He hoped his voice carried a measure of strength.

Small particles had collected in his lungs, taking up space where oxygen should go. That was how the doctor he had seen earlier in the month had explained it. A man like him had no place in the stifling atmosphere of the wool plant. A farmer should be in open fields, sweating under the sun, breathing fresh air. Mustafa had brushed aside the doctor's senseless cure. He worked while many refugee men couldn't find jobs, had a roof over his family's head, almost enough to eat. He could handle a few coughing fits every now and then. Besides, there were no orchards of apricot and plum trees to nurture in this crowded city.

Dressed and feeling a little better, he sat at the head of the table. His children were already in their designated seats chatting about their day, except for Omar. Mustafa sighed.

"Where is he?" He directed his question to Fatimah, who was bouncing baby Salma on her lap.

"He went to the bakery on the corner. He should be here any minute."

Subhia passed a bowl of yogurt. "We ran out of bread. Omar volunteered. Let's get started. I'm sure he's already on the stairs."

Everyone got busy spooning food onto their plates. Omar's distinctive knock — three rapid beats — sounded at the door.

"Why doesn't that boy just walk in?" Mustafa mumbled under his breath. "Why does he need to ask for permission every time?"

Subhia placed a calming hand over his knee under the table. "Omar is being polite," she whispered.

"This is his home," Mustafa tried to whisper back. "How many times have I asked you to make that clear to him?"

"He's almost fourteen." Subhia brought her voice even lower, making sure the others didn't hear her. "He's growing up. If it makes him comfortable, where's the harm?"

"Shareef doesn't knock before he comes in, does he?" Mustafa dropped a dollop of yogurt on his plate. "Omar should feel just as comfortable."

"Yes, well. We have to accommodate the boy's nature, Mustafa. I hung a heavy blanket as a divider in their room. Shareef and Omar on one side, the girls the other." She patted his knee again. "It's better this way."

Eleven-year-old Nadia slid from her seat and went to open the door. She lifted her arms and hung on Omar's neck, her usual way of greeting him. Since he had shot up in height quite a bit in the last couple of years, it was easy for him to circle her waist with one arm and carry her to her seat as she squealed and giggled. He placed the flat pita bread stack he had in his other hand on the table. "They ran out of today's rations in the bakery. I had to go to the one two streets over. I grabbed the last stack." Omar moved to his seat next to Nadia and dropped down. "Sorry for being late, Uncle Mustafa."

Mustafa was tired and couldn't help being irritated. Was it Omar's tardiness that caused his nerves to flare, or something else? He couldn't put his finger on the issue. He nodded in acknowledgment and helped himself to a healthy serving of *ma'loubeh*. The main dish of rice and cauliflower was missing a main ingredient — meat. Again. It was near the end of the month. Subhia stretched his paycheck as far as she could, which meant no meat or chicken dishes the last few days.

Out of the corner of his eye, he noticed Nadia poking at Omar's shoulder in an obvious attempt to get his attention. Omar, however, fixed his eyes on his plate and ignored her. She leaned closer and whispered something in his ear. Omar arched his eyebrows. The two of them seemed to be in a world of their own. The

19

bond between them had always been strong in a strange way, and somewhat amusing to watch.

Huda, who had been spooning food into little Farah's mouth, suddenly snapped. "Stop that. Leave him alone, Nadia." Huda's way of conversing was to issue orders.

"I wanted to know if he brought me the latest issue of The Five Adventurers Series like he promised." Nadia sounded scared. "I finished my homework."

"You're not a child anymore, so stop acting like one," Huda continued in the same commanding tone. "Let Omar eat in peace. Don't bother him."

Omar lifted his eyes. "She's not bothering me." He turned toward Nadia. "I'll go over your homework after supper. If you did it right, I may have something in my jacket pocket for you."

Nadia's face brightened with a huge smile. "The Missing Necklace Secret issue?"

Omar nodded.

"Bribery? Is that how you've been getting her to study?" Huda's sharp tone could have cut through the bread in Omar's hands. "Filling her head with nonsense from those silly translated books?"

Omar lashed out. "At least she's trying."

The spoon in Huda's hand dropped on her plate. "What's that supposed to mean?"

Omar looked her in the eye. "Just because you lacked the ability to stay in school doesn't mean Nadia has to follow in your footsteps."

"And you have taken it upon yourself to teach her?" Huda curved her lips in a sideway smirk. "I wonder

20

where you got that smart brain of yours." She motioned with her hand toward Fatimah. "Your sister barely made passing grades."

Omar's face reddened. "The key word is *passing*. You know, the opposite of you failing?"

"Shut up!" Spit droplets shot out with Huda's words.

Fatimah sucked in a sharp breath, drawing her brother's attention.

Omar pushed his plate forward, mumbling under his breath, "Here we go again."

"How dare you speak to me like that?" Huda continued her verbal assault. "You forget your place, Omar. I am the eldest here and I will not have you —"

Mustafa smacked his palm down on the table. "That's enough!"

Water splashed from glasses. Huda bit her lower lip to keep quiet.

"Omar is doing a fine job keeping Nadia on track," Mustafa chided. "I would like to finish this meal in peace. Huda, I expect you to act your age. Apologize to Omar. Let's get this nonsense over with."

"It's fine, Uncle Mustafa," Fatimah said. "Omar knows Huda doesn't mean it. No need for apology or anything like that." She shifted her eyes to Omar. "I'm sure he didn't mean to upset Huda, right Omar?"

Omar nodded once.

"Here." Fatimah scooped a couple of spoons of rice onto Huda's plate. "You hardly ate anything because of Farah. You worked all day, you must be exhausted. Did you deliver a boy or a girl?"

Mustafa admired Fatimah's ability to control the boy with her soothing tone and diffuse the situation with razor-edge Huda. No one dared talk back to Huda except for Omar. Her sour personality intimidated her siblings and kept them at bay. She had never taken to Omar in particular. Old enough to remember the circumstances of his birth, Mustafa suspected Huda saw Omar as an intruder into her family. She got along fine with Fatimah because her easy-going nature never posed a threat to Huda's authoritative character. But Omar stood in Huda's face every chance he got, shielding the others from her criticizing tongue as best he could. Even Shareef cowered behind Omar. Mustafa didn't want to admit it, but he privately acknowledged that his blood son lacked Omar's backbone.

He shifted his gaze to Shareef, quietly observing the altercation. Both elbows on the table, Shareef kept his head down, his eyes darting between Omar and Huda, a worried look on his face. If only God could switch Huda's personality with Shareef's. Then Mustafa might handle the disease eating his lungs a bit easier, knowing the family would be under his son's charge once he was gone. Mustafa shook his head. What was he thinking? Too early to ponder the grim matter of his demise. He was still able to work and provide for his children.

Taking a long gulp of water, he studied his children's faces. The water settled in his stomach like a chunk of cement. Reality dictated he should look upon strong-willed Omar — not Shareef — to take the responsibility of caring for the girls, as hard it might be for Huda to accept.

He resumed trying to swallow his substance-lacking meal. Everyone's nerves had been put to the test over the past few days. The dissolution of the unity between Syria and Egypt had hit hard. The United Arab Republic had lasted barely three years, but that was long enough for an ambitious boy like Omar to feel the disappointment and taste the bitterness of deep loss.

Omar had reasons enough to lose patience with Huda. She had dropped out of school and made it her business to demean everyone who hadn't, and she was quick to blame him for whatever mischief Shareef fell into. But the real reason lay in her obvious resentment of his presence. Huda had made sure Omar knew the reason behind her elation at the prospect of liberating Palestine, as the charismatic president Nasser had promised in his fervent speeches. It meant Omar would connect with his roots and get out of their lives. She never came out and said it, but the boy was smart and had a sensitive nature. He knew how she felt, all right. It didn't matter anymore. Nasser's promises had disintegrated with the undone unity, along with everyone's dreams of returning to their homeland.

Mustafa wiped his plate clean with a piece of pita bread. No matter what he and Subhia did, they could not soften their eldest daughter's heart toward this orphan. Deep down inside, he couldn't blame her. He didn't need to be an expert to know the atrocities Huda had witnessed on the road the night they fled home must have ruined her young soul.

Women and children cramped on wagon beds, cars or trucks, old people balanced on the backs of horses and donkeys, families scurried on foot. Stories of the massacre in Deir Yassin and neighboring villages had rolled like a boulder down a mountain, horrific details told by the few survivors adding to its momentum. There was no way he could have protected Huda from seeing the carnage of that hideous crime. He had taken the road through the neighboring village of Ein Karim, searching for his brother and his family, praying to God they had fled to safety.

Mustafa's hand paused mid-way to his mouth. He had not been able to stop, not even to bury the children. So many bodies had been thrown in the streets like garbage, dogs biting on them. Returning the pita bite in his hand back to his plate, he glanced at Huda. It seemed like the stench of death had clung to her nose since that day, stamping her face with an expression of disgust. What kind of nightmares did she suffer? She was eight at the time. Maybe she irrationally blamed Omar for delaying their departure and subjecting them to that horror. Who knew what went on in her head? If she softened her attitude a little, she might attract a fellow who would help her heal and start her own family, perhaps bringing her a measure of happiness. She was nearly twenty-one and time was running out on her.

"*Alhamdulillah*. Can I get up?" Omar asked, interrupting Mustafa's thoughts.

"You go ahead, *habibi*," Subhia answered.

Omar left the table, taking his plate to the kitchen.

Nadia followed like a shadow. "Will you check my homework now?"

CHAPTER
FIVE

Four years later, 1965

On the rooftop late at night, seventeen-year-old Omar stood contemplating the city below. Fatimah referred to this solitary time-out as brooding. He increasingly sought the brief isolation, needing to separate himself from the busy noises downstairs. Sharing a room with everyone and keeping his sanity was a challenge. He used to be able to shut them out and lose himself in a book, but he had become more restless. Sometimes, he had to sneak out before Shareef took notice and followed him.

Fatimah helped create distractions, asking him to walk her home from Um Waleed's place and then telling everyone she had forgotten something and he had to return to get it, letting him take off on his own for a while.

Filling his lungs with cool air, Omar gazed upon the city lights in the distance. He sat on the railing, dangled his feet and swung his long legs back and forth. He checked his watch and decided he had at least ten minutes in this bliss before he had to return home.

Home. He sounded the word in his head. He had never known any other place, yet calling this home stopped short from warming his heart. Something was wrong with him, for sure. This was his family, no matter who had given birth to him. But something was missing. A lot of things were missing. A plan for his future, for a start. It was time he thought about what to do when he got his high school diploma.

He drew up a list titled "Priorities" in his head. At number one, finding a job to relieve the burden weighing on Uncle Mustafa's shoulders. The man shrank in size with each passing day.

He should ask Fatimah to help him approach Mr Waleed through his mother. The history teacher could put in a good word for him at any of the local newspapers. Knowing people in the business, he might be willing to open a door for him. Maybe they could give him a job in typesetting, or distribution. It didn't matter. It would be better than working at the wool plant. He could ask Marwan Barady for a job at his store. His best friend wouldn't hesitate, but seeking a favor from him should be his last resort. Everyone knew work relations ruined good friendships.

A cat jumped on the railing, startling him. He ran his hand on her back and pushed her closer to his side. The feline obliged. Stretching along his thigh, she rested her head on his knee. His fingers played with her warm ears.

University would have to wait. He pushed the word down to the bottom of his mental list along with dreams of working with President Nasser's team of analysts. Fanciful ambitions had no room in his world. Securing Fatimah's future took precedence. She would turn twenty-three this year. She couldn't possibly continue to work as a seamstress forever. And there was no way he would let her end up like Huda, stuck in time with no prospect of improvement. Not if he could help it.

"If only Huda would get out of her way," he spoke to the cat. "She's overshadowing her, you know? Keeping Fatimah one step behind. And Huda isn't going anywhere."

The cat purred, stretching her legs further and hooking her front claws in the fabric of his pants.

"Do you think I can get Mr Waleed interested in Huda?" Omar asked aloud. "He's a bachelor. They're close in age." He shook his head. "No, I like the man too much to inflict Huda on him." He lifted the lazy animal with both hands to his lap. "Let's talk about something else, shall we? Nadia's sexy friend, Sameera, for example." He looked around, checking he was alone, and brought the fur ball's head closer to his face. "What? I know she's fifteen, but have you seen her body? And that smile. Pearls for teeth, my friend."

The cat extended her tongue to execute a circular sweep of her face. "You should stop by the living room window tomorrow afternoon, say around three, to see her. I promised Nadia I'd help the two of them prepare for their English exam."

"There you are." Nadia's excited voice came from behind.

Omar almost dropped the cat. "I didn't hear you come up here." He turned his flaming face away.

She lowered herself to the railing beside him. "Who were you talking to?"

He placed the cat in Nadia's lap. "This one is a good listener."

Nadia inhaled with joy. She babbled nonsense to the cat in a high-pitched voice. She had a smile on her face that was almost permanent, her cheerful mood infectious. Puzzled by the strange sounds she was making, he couldn't help comparing her to Huda's depressing nature. "What are you doing?"

"Speaking cat."

"I hope I didn't sound like that." He swallowed, worried she might have heard what he had said about her friend earlier.

Nadia shrugged. "I didn't catch everything you said." She let the cat jump back to his lap. "Something about Sameera and the English test?"

Omar cleared his throat. "Yeah. I was thinking about your class tomorrow. Sameera really needs to pass that test, right?"

Nadia turned sideways to face him and winked. "I know you like her."

Seeing parts of Nadia's body hang over the edge made him nervous, and he no longer worried about her catching on to his embarrassment. He wrapped his fingers around her arm and pushed the cat aside.

"Be careful, Omar," she said, her voice dove-like. "Sameera has three brothers."

He swung his legs to solid ground and pulled Nadia to her feet. "So they sent you after me. It's time to go back down." They walked side by side toward the entrance to the stairway. "Don't worry. I'm not going to do anything to set Sameera's brothers on me." He flexed his arms. "Besides, I can take them all in a fight."

Nadia placed her hand on his chest. "Don't be stupid. You're not a superhero."

Something gripped Omar's stomach. He saw in Nadia's brown eyes genuine concern and affection. Home. This *was* home. "I think it's time you graduate to reading the classics. No more adventure series for you." He tried to keep the emotion sparked by the strange realization from spilling over in his voice.

Checking himself in the mirror one last time, Omar tucked his blue-and-white-striped shirt in his pants, ran a hand over his hair and left the bathroom. He headed to the dining table, which also served as a study area.

Nadia was flipping through her English book. She lifted her head. "Finally. I thought you would never leave the bathroom." She grinned. "Sameera will be here any minute."

Omar pulled out the chair at the head of the table. He would have Sameera take the chair to his right, across from Nadia. That way, he would be close enough to accidentally touch her arm or, if he played it right, bump her leg with his knee during their study session. The plain tablecloth would provide enough cover. He rested his back and crossed his arms, glancing at his watch.

Fatimah worked in one corner of the room, needle and thread going up and down in her hand with fascinating speed. The younger girls sat on the floor close to Fatimah's feet, playing with dolls. They had been told to keep their voices down since their mother was taking a nap.

Omar closed his eyes, wishing they had an additional room away from everyone. Their bedroom was off limits this afternoon. It would be ideal to study there, to close the door and have relative quiet. But Mama Subhia would not allow it. Improper, she had scowled, for Omar to be alone in a room with Sameera. Nadia didn't count, Mama Subhia had insisted when he pointed out they would not be alone.

Shareef closed their bedroom door. He walked over to sit in the chair Omar had designated in his head for Sameera.

"What do you think you're doing?" Omar arched one eyebrow.

"Joining the class."

"You don't have an English test." Omar tried to keep the agitation from showing on his face. "You don't even have English this year."

Shareef glanced at Fatimah. "All the more reason to refresh my memory." He drummed his fingers on the table. "It'll help with my French class."

Omar took a deep breath. So that was how Shareef wanted to play it? He too had his eyes on Sameera? Exhaling, he unfolded his arms and waved a hand toward the chair on Nadia's left. "Fine. As long as you move over there."

30

"Why?"

"Because this way you two will be on one side of the table and I won't have to keep turning my head to get your attention. Now move." Realizing he must have sounded rough, he added, "Please."

The doorbell rang. Shareef jumped to his feet. "I'll get it."

Omar half rose from his chair, then forced himself to sit back down.

Sameera floated into the room. Angels' feet didn't touch the ground, did they? Chestnut curls cascaded down her back and bounced around her perfect face. A fitted pink dress hugged her well-proportioned body and left little room for imagination. Directing her eyes at Fatimah, she chimed, "Good afternoon."

Omar stretched to his full height, his heart racing. He heard music. Violins, to be exact.

Fatimah lifted her head and welcomed Sameera, then went back to her work. Nadia greeted her friend with a quick hug.

"Please come in," Shareef addressed someone at the door.

A young man in his early twenties stepped in, keeping his eyes to the ground.

Sameera introduced him. "My youngest brother, Ahmad."

The boys shook hands.

Fatimah left her corner and approached with a welcoming smile. "We're happy Sameera could study with Nadia and her brothers. I'm Fatimah."

Avoiding eye contact, Ahmad placed his right hand on his chest, giving her the signal that he would not shake her hand if she extended it. She didn't.

Omar narrowed his eyes, annoyed by Ahmad's attitude. So he was one of those religious fanatics, refusing to shake hands with women. But Sameera didn't even wear a head cover. Didn't guys like him force their sisters and daughters to wear the veil? Omar had engaged in a couple of arguments with one of them at school. Physical arguments.

"Sorry to intrude like this." Ahmad cleared his throat. "I wanted to make sure my sister made it here in time."

"Of course." Fatimah's tone remained polite.

Ahmad turned toward Omar and looked him straight in the eye. "And I wanted to meet you."

Omar nodded, uncomfortable under the man's steady gaze. Ahmad's stance seemed to rather say, *"And I wanted you to meet the person you'll be dealing with if you misbehave."*

Ahmad didn't even look in Shareef's direction. Had he decided Omar was the potential threat to his sister? The unspoken warning flattered him in a twisted way. Would he do the same for Nadia if they were put in a similar situation? Of course. Only he would stay with her, monitoring every move the boy made above *and* under the table. He cleared his throat. "We should be done at seven. Would you like us to walk your sister home? Or should we wait for you?" There, that was the best he could do to reassure the man nothing bad would happen to his angelic sister.

Ahmad turned his head in Fatimah's direction, but didn't lift his eyes to her face. "If it's not too much trouble, I would like to come back at seven. Would that be all right?"

"No trouble at all."

Ahmad excused himself and left. Nadia motioned for Sameera to sit at the table. "Is there something wrong with your brother's eyes? He didn't look at any of us girls."

"Ahmad is the most religious of my brothers. It seems annoying sometimes, but he was actually showing respect." Sameera sat in the chair Omar had pulled out for her. "Especially to Fatimah." She squinted at Omar before he took his seat. "Ahmad is sweet. You'll see that once you spend some time with him."

Omar had no intention of spending any time with Sameera's brother. He slid Nadia's book closer and flipped through to the assigned section. Better concentrate on proverbial wisdom and grammar.

As the class got underway, Shareef's attitude shifted. The often quiet, almost invisible Shareef talked non-stop and made jokes. Funny ones. Shareef's confidence grew with each smile Sameera threw in his direction. Even sweet Nadia noticed the change in her brother, winking at Omar to let him know it.

At one point, Shareef left his chair across the table from Sameera and slid onto the one next to her, pointing at a sentence in her book. Or he pretended to, at least. It was obvious he was completely taken by the girl. And she encouraged him, paid attention to him. A first for Shareef.

Why did Shareef have to follow Omar's every move? Why couldn't he find his own girl? Omar could insist Shareef return to his seat, but that would dampen everyone's mood. It would also draw Fatimah's attention. He could say something to embarrass Shareef or belittle him to shake his confidence. That would be cruel. It would upset Nadia. He could follow through with his plan and see how Sameera would react to his "accidental" touch. Would she shift her attention to him instead?

While he contemplated his best move, a warm sensation snaked up his calf. He shot up in his chair, covering his surprise with a forced cough. His eyes darted to Sameera. She had her head buried in her book next to Shareef's. Was this a mistake? Did she cross her legs and brush his by accident? Did his leg extend too far to her side, and she couldn't avoid bumping it? Should he apologize? She didn't seem bothered. Did she notice, even? What was so damn interesting in that book? He should make a joke or something to get her attention since she seemed so taken by Shareef's silliness.

Nadia asked a question. He gave her an answer, not sure if it was the right one, his mind losing focus.

Sameera lifted her head and flicked back her hair with delicate fingers. "What time is it?"

Without taking his eyes off hers, he answered, "Past six."

Her lips parted in a smile, showing those dazzling pearls. "Good. We still have time." She touched

Shareef's arm. "Do you think you could get me a glass of water?"

Shareef was on his way to the kitchen before she had finished her words.

Lifting her body off her chair, Sameera stretched across the table to reach Nadia's book. "Let me see how you spelled that."

The snaking sensation returned along Omar's leg, a bit slower this time, creeping past his knee. He coughed again, drawing Sameera's eyes to his. He arched his eyebrows.

Her foot tapped his thigh twice.

Pushing his chair back, he rose. "Excuse me." He went into the bathroom. That was clearly not a mistake. So Sameera was no angel. She was that kind of girl? She played with one boy above the table and another under it? No wonder her brother hovered over her. He shook his head. What a fool he had been, thinking she was as innocent and pure as Nadia. Marwan had warned him about girls like Sameera, but he hadn't quite understood their danger until now. His good friend faced those sorts of girls in his store and had talked about their inventive ways to get his attention. Omar splashed cold water over his face. Poor Shareef. He had no idea what was in store for him. Should he warn him? Or show him what Sameera was truly like? If only Nadia weren't there. Whatever move he could make to expose her friend's readiness for boy games would embarrass Nadia, and he was not going to risk that. Let Shareef reach his own conclusions for a change.

Returning to the living room, he sat as far from Sameera as possible. He planted his feet under his chair and locked his elbows on the table, abandoning his plan to get close to dangerous Sameera. He concentrated his teaching efforts on Nadia. Would he get dragged into a confrontation with Ahmad anyway if Shareef got carried away? Not that Sameera might mind. From the way Shareef kept fidgeting in his seat, Omar suspected her feet warmed Shareef's legs at least three times before the clock struck seven.

Ahmad returned on time and escorted his sister home. Shareef disappeared into the bedroom as soon as they left. Fatimah called Nadia from the kitchen to help her prepare for the evening meal.

Omar went out to stretch his legs. On his way down the stairs, he saw Uncle Mustafa dragging his body up the steps.

"Where are you going?" Uncle Mustafa coughed to the side.

"For a walk."

Looking unable to stay on his feet a minute longer, Uncle Mustafa pointed a finger at him. "I need to talk to you. It's important. Don't be late for supper."

Omar hurried to the man's side, grabbed his elbow and helped him along. "I don't have to go."

Uncle Mustafa stopped and shook his head. "No, you go on ahead." He placed a hand on Omar's shoulder, catching his breath as if he had just run a race. "I need to eat and get some rest. We'll talk after supper." He held the railing and resumed his efforts, leaving Omar behind. "It concerns Fatimah."

CHAPTER
SIX

Omar stopped, one foot on a step and the other hanging midair. Something must have forced its way down his throat and wrapped itself around his guts. He leaped over several steps to block the front door before Uncle Mustafa could open it.

"What about Fatimah? I just left her inside."

With a calloused thumb, Uncle Mustafa smoothed the frown knotting Omar's brows. "You worry too much, son. We'll talk after supper."

Circling the neighborhood twice convinced Omar he had wasted enough time for Uncle Mustafa to think that he would return with a clear head. Truth be told, his mind had raced from one bad assumption to a worse one with every step he took. When he couldn't shake the apprehension building inside, he headed home and braced himself through a torturous meal until Uncle Mustafa was ready to talk.

Seated on a wooden chair in the small balcony off the living room, Uncle Mustafa sipped hot tea and nibbled on roasted almonds. The door opening to the balcony was solid wood. If one kept one's voice down when the door was shut, the balcony provided a decent private area, sheltered from the rest of the family and from passers-by on the street. Uncle Mustafa and Mama Subhia used it often to discuss matters out of earshot.

Uncle Mustafa motioned for Omar to take the other chair, offering him a handful of almonds. "If I close my eyes on a quiet evening like this, I imagine myself at my orchard in Palestine."

"Is that why you love almonds so much? They take you back home?" Omar studied the old man. Uncle Mustafa had not summoned him to talk about almonds.

"Nothing comes close to the rich taste of almonds from the old almond tree in my orchard. Come the first signs of spring, it was the first tree to flower, before the apricot and plum trees." He popped an almond into his mouth. "One way to distinguish bitter almonds from sweet ones. By taste." He filled tea glasses and handed one to Omar. "Haven't had a single bitter one yet. This is not good."

Crunching almonds and sipping tea, Omar tried to follow the man's logic. "The bitter almonds make you savor the sweet ones more."

"You're catching on." Uncle Mustafa placed his tea glass back on the small table. "Your history teacher, Mr Waleed, stopped by the plant today to talk to me."

"I didn't do anything. Haven't had a fight at school all year." Omar set down his glass and crossed his arms on his chest. "I thought we were going to talk about Fatimah."

"We are." Uncle Mustafa gave a quick nod. "Waleed asked for an appointment to bring his mother over one evening."

Omar shook his head. "I don't understand. I'm sure Fatimah didn't do whatever Mr Waleed claims she did." He unfolded his arms and leaned forward. "I like the man. I think he's nice enough, but he has no business getting his nose in Fatimah's job with his mother. The women should work it out between them, don't you think?"

"It's not about Fatimah's work." Uncle Mustafa took another sip of tea. "Waleed wants to bring his mother to ask for Fatimah's hand."

The thing that had been gripping Omar's insides all evening suddenly let go. A wave of relief washed over him. "Yeah? That's great news."

Uncle Mustafa tilted his head to one side. "You think so?"

"Mr Waleed is a decent man. Fatimah spoke highly of him the few times she mentioned him to me. Why? Do you know something I don't?"

"You know him better than I do. He's good to his mother. That's a solid indication of a kind man. We have to ask about him outside the school circle. You know. Who his friends are, if he owes money. Things like that." Uncle Mustafa put his elbow on the balcony railing, rested his head on his open palm and winked at Omar. "Of course, the first one you should ask is Fatimah."

Omar thumbed his chest. "Me? Why? What do I know about these things? Mama Subhia should talk to her."

"We love Fatimah like she was our own." Uncle Mustafa lifted his gaze to the star-dotted skies, as if speaking to God. "But I don't want her to feel pressured in any way."

"Pressured?"

Rising to his feet, Uncle Mustafa draped his arms on the balcony railing. The muscles in his bony jaw pumped.

Omar narrowed his eyes. The man was stalling. He pushed his chair back and stood next to him. "What's on your mind?"

"I don't want her to think we . . . want to get rid of her." Uncle Mustafa leaned his face closer to Omar's. "You're the only one who should talk to Fatimah about this. Find out if she's willing to give the man a chance. She'll be honest with you."

"And if she says yes?"

"We'll ask about him. If he proves to be the good man we think he is, she will have our blessings."

"What if she refuses him?"

"Then I'll know she made the decision on her own. You have to be very careful when you talk to her, Omar. Make sure she understands Subhia and I would love to keep her with us as long as she wants." He placed a warm hand on Omar's arm. "Both of you, son."

Words stuck in Omar's throat. Uncle Mustafa was saying one thing, but his tired eyes portrayed a different message. He couldn't quite read it. "I'll talk to Fatimah."

Uncle Mustafa returned to his chair. The muscles around his mouth relaxed, his lips sagging in a sad smile. "Good. I told Waleed they could visit this Thursday at seven, after *maghreb* prayers. Make sure you're ready for him." Reaching over to the teapot, he refilled their glasses. "Now let us pray a woman goes into labor that evening so Huda won't grace us with her charm."

CHAPTER
SEVEN

On their way home from Um Waleed's place the following evening, Omar took Fatimah through side streets, telling her he needed to pick up something from a friends house when she objected to the detour. He wished he could treat her to a cup of tea at a nice café, but he had no money.

They walked down narrow alleys paved with old bricks from the Ottoman era. If he ignored the sagging electricity cables haphazardly hanging over his head, he could swear they leapt back in time. Everything around them looked and smelled ancient.

The small arched wooden doors that protected entry to big houses retained the metal hand-shaped knockers in their centers. Marwan lived in one of those houses; a mansion was a better word to describe it. Omar had no idea huge traditional Damascene homes lay hidden behind such small doors, complete with inner courtyards with hexagon-shaped fountains at their centers and marble-lined walls. Whenever he visited Marwan, he had to hunch his shoulders and lower his head as he entered the low door, a physical reminder to be humble to the hosts.

They turned a corner. Omar had to step in front of Fatimah to maneuver around a couple of people drinking from a wall-mounted faucet. The small fountain, surrounded by white ceramic tiles decorated with verses from the Qur'an, invited passers-by to pray for a deceased loved one each time they drank.

Slightly above eye level, wooden window shutters with intricate designs protruded about half a meter from the walls. The *mashrabiat* concealed the inhabitants inside from curious eyes while letting sunlight and sounds of everyday life drift through. How would it feel to be part of a multi-generational family like the ones residing in those houses? He didn't even know his parents. Fatimah was his single connection to his *real* family. It was his duty to make sure she was happy. He better not mess up.

They came upon a small public square with patches of grass. He had to contend with the limited privacy of a bench under a street lamp.

"What's on your mind?" Fatimah asked as soon as she sat down. "We're obviously not heading to a friend's house. Are you in trouble?"

"I'm not going to dance around the subject." Omar sat next to her. "Tell me about Waleed."

Fatimah's face paled, her eyebrows knotted, and her smile turned into a frown. "I don't like your tone, brother. What are you implying? I work for his mother and sometimes I run into him when he comes home on my way out. That's all. If any of the neighbors said anything different, they lied."

"I'm not implying anything," Omar backtracked, realizing he must have touched a nerve. What did he know about an opening to this delicate issue? He cleared his throat and tried again. "No one dares say anything bad about you, Fatimah. That's not what I was trying to get at."

"What then?"

"I already know you think he's a nice man, but do you see yourself . . . living in his home?"

She sprang to her feet. "What are you talking about?"

Omar held her hand before she moved away. "Waleed asked permission from Uncle Mustafa to approach you about marriage. I'm trying to find out if you're open to the idea."

Fatimah pulled her hand out of his. "Oh, I see." Sitting back on the bench, she tucked her hands under her thighs. "Tell him he's wasting his time."

"Why?"

"We are not home, Omar. I will only settle in Palestine. I dream of us living under one roof in our father's house."

He smiled. "I have that dream too. With your ten children crowding the place in my version."

She rocked back and forth in her seat, keeping her head bowed. "I'm serious."

He searched for a way to lift her mood. "Let's make a deal." He touched her shoulder to entice her to look at him. "I will do everything I can to get us back to our home in Palestine, and you work on having those ten children in the meantime."

Fatimah's face contorted to cover a smile pushing through against her will. "I'm not thinking of getting married."

"To Waleed in particular?"

She shook her head. "To any man." She lifted a hand to ruffle his hair. "I can't believe I'm having this conversation with you."

Omar let her have her way and didn't try to duck. "I'm not a boy anymore."

"When did that happen?" she teased. "It makes me feel old."

"Old enough to be pursued." He leaned sideways and nudged her with his shoulder. "You like Waleed, don't you?"

Fatimah raised her eyebrows.

"Want me to tell you how I know?" He tried to keep his tone light. "You think he's smart, educated, kind-hearted and respectful. Oh, and I remember you telling me something about his looks. What was it?" He scratched his head. "He's a combination of me and Shareef. My height and Shareef's eyes or something like that."

"What?" Fatimah hid a smile behind her hand.

"No? Wait a minute. It'll come to me." He lifted his head, pretending to wait for inspiration. "My hair and Shareef's hunched shoulders. No that isn't it. My feet and Shareef's pointed chin."

Fatimah punched him in the arm. "Stop that," she giggled.

He snapped his fingers. "I remember now, you think Waleed looks like that heartthrob actor, Omar Sharif."

She burst out with a healthy laugh. "That's it!"

Omar clasped his hands under his chin. "Give him a chance?"

Fatimah's laugh died down, her voice became serious. "There are more important things to think about."

"Like what?"

Tucking her hands under her thighs again, Fatimah lowered her head and studied her feet, remaining silent.

"Don't you want your own family?" Omar pressed, trying to understand.

"Someday, maybe. When the time is right."

"And when would that be?"

"When you have your university degree and your future is secure." She lifted her head. Her big hazel eyes enveloped him with her warmth. "I saved enough money for the registration, I think. I will keep adding new clients from other neighborhoods to cover more. But you have to get an evening job."

He studied his sister's kind face. It wasn't Huda who was stopping her from moving ahead. It was him. He was the dead weight anchoring her down. Fatimah's obsessive concern for his future prevented her from thinking of her own. He heaved a heavy sigh. In the back of his mind, he must have known that. It felt good to blame Huda, anyway.

"I was planning to tell everyone soon, once the papers were signed." He tried to put a buoyant spring in his voice. "I already found a job. It would pay for my education. You don't have to worry about that anymore."

Her skepticism was hard to miss. She straightened her back and narrowed her eyes. "Where? What kind of job?"

Omar rose to his feet. "I'll tell you about it once everything is confirmed." He extended his hand. "Come, let's go."

They snaked their way back home. He managed to draw out Fatimah's impression of Waleed, finding it somewhat favorable. He kept steering the conversation away from his potential job every time she tried to ask, bringing up anything he could think of that might pertain to a man's character, letting her reserved excitement of being pursued by Waleed come to the surface.

By the time they joined the rest of the family, Fatimah had agreed to let Waleed court her for a time before she made a decision, given the approval of Uncle Mustafa and Mama Subhia.

The following morning, Omar snuck out of the house earlier than usual, making sure to leave Shareef in bed, probably dreaming of dangerous Sameera. He had enough bus fare to take him half way to his destination. Walking the rest of the way, he checked the roll of documents under his arm a couple of times, worried he was missing something. He arrived a good half hour before the doors opened and used the time to meticulously read through each page. Given his circumstances, this was the best he could do to ensure his sister's freedom. As soon as a uniformed young man swung open the main gate, Omar marched into the recruiting office. Presenting his documents, he signed over his body and soul to the military academy.

CHAPTER
EIGHT

A flurry of activity took over the two-bedroom apartment all day Thursday. The girls washed and scrubbed anything with fabric in its composition, from the sheer beige curtains to the well-worn rug and everything in between. The boys did the heavy lifting, moving furniture pieces while the girls swept tiled floors, dusted every flat surface and even ran wet cloths over the walls. Shareef was then sent out to buy one of the desserts served on such an occasion, *kanafeh*, a tray of melted sweet cheese topped with crispy shredded pastry. Mama Subhia had dug into her emergency stash to pay for it, refusing to let Fatimah cover the expense. She directed everyone with an efficient manner; the girls were dressed in their finest and ready for their evening guests in good time.

Nadia was set to watch her younger sisters in the bedroom. The three of them were not allowed to leave until they were called by their mother. Fatimah was to be stationed in the kitchen. When it was time to offer Um Waleed and her son the welcoming Turkish coffee, traditionally served five to ten minutes after their arrival, Fatimah would indicate her willingness to hear their proposal with her coffee service. Mama Subhia made sure to remind Fatimah, for what seemed the hundredth time, that she should start her service with the women, leaving her suitor to the end.

Two dining chairs were added to the living room. Mama Subhia would take one armchair and Uncle Mustafa the other, Omar to his right and Shareef to his left, leaving the sofa for the guests.

It seemed God had heard Uncle Mustafa's prayer, sending a neighboring lady into labor. Huda's services were called for around noon. She stormed out after subjecting everyone to her critical opinions of their hard work, finding fault in Fatimah's assigned chore in particular. Mama Subhia explained away Huda's behavior as being her normal stressed self, but everyone knew jealousy drove her crazy.

By the time Shareef returned with the *kanafeh*, the girls had already taken their stations and the adults sat stiffly in their designated chairs, waiting for the doorbell to ring.

Omar went into the kitchen to give Fatimah the dessert tray while Shareef dressed. She wore a pleated green skirt and a white blouse. Her wavy black hair rested on her shoulders.

He greeted her with a kiss to the cheek. "You look amazing."

"I'm so nervous." She inserted the tray into the warm oven. "I can't believe you talked me into this."

He waited for her to face him again and placed both hands on her shoulders. "Just be yourself. Waleed is no stranger. You know him. You have talked to him many times."

"Not like this." She shook her head. "Not while Uncle Mustafa is watching."

"Don't worry. You probably won't have to say anything. Let him do all the talking." Omar gave his sister a quick hug and left the kitchen. He walked into the living room just as the front door opened.

Huda walked in. "I made it back in time," she told a stunned crowd. "I saw them up the street. They should be here any minute."

Mama Subhia ushered Huda toward the kitchen. "Stay here. Help Fatimah."

Waleed and his mother arrived.

Mama Subhia glared at Waleed, studying him from head to toe while he and Uncle Mustafa exchanged the usual greeting pleasantries. Omar winced, feeling sorry for the man under the microscope. Seeing his teacher dressed in a suit like that made him realize Waleed really did resemble that actor, with his square face, dark eyes and thick black hair.

Omar glanced at his watch, counting the minutes down until Fatimah was allowed to join them. He wanted to go check on her, worried Huda might say something to make her more nervous. But he couldn't leave yet. It would be considered rude.

"So you're Fatimah's blood brother?" Um Waleed asked.

"I am."

"You don't look alike at all. Do you have the same mother *and* father?"

"They do," Mama Subhia answered before Omar could say anything. "Their mother was my dearest friend."

"And the father?"

"The Bakrys were our neighbors in Jerusalem," Uncle Mustafa interjected. He glanced at Waleed and nodded, giving him the signal to change the subject.

Waleed straightened in his chair, fixed his eyes on Omar and started what seemed like a well-rehearsed speech.

"My mother and I have come this evening to respectfully ask your permission to pursue your honorable sister with the intention of marriage."

Omar held Waleed's gaze, hiding his surprise at being the one addressed, rather than Uncle Mustafa, and at Waleed's formal tone.

"I've been your teacher for the past three years. I hope you've had a chance to know the kind of man I am." Waleed cleared his throat. "I can provide a decent living if Fatimah is willing to live with my mother . . . with your approval, of course." He gestured toward his mother. "My father passed away five years ago."

"*Allah yirhamuh.*" Everyone mumbled the typical prayer asking for mercy on the deceased man's soul.

"Our family," Waleed continued, "the Najads' are from Nablus."

Mama Subhia drew in an audible breath. Everyone's eyes shifted to her. She coughed into her handkerchief. Omar could tell she forced it. What had the man said that surprised her? He looked back at Waleed.

Um Waleed shifted in her seat. "I have come to know Fatimah well in the past three years. Allah has not blessed me with girls, but I love Fatimah like my own daughter. I will make sure she is happy with us."

Waleed ran an index finger sideways in his collar, swallowing several times. "I try my best to attend Friday prayers and I don't have any debts. I deal with the butcher, Abu Nawaf, at the south corner on a regular basis. Most of the grocers on Mehyi Eldeen Street know me. They will give honest answers to your questions."

He produced a piece of paper from his jacket pocket and placed it on the coffee table. "You can also ask about me at this newspaper press. My eldest uncle works there."

Omar blinked. So that was how things went in situations like these? He hadn't been to the cinema much, but the way they showed these instances in the films was less severe. His articulate teacher was a nervous wreck. His face gleamed with sweat, his leg pumped up and down at maddening speed.

Was he supposed to say something now? Omar glanced at Uncle Mustafa for guidance. The man stared back at him. Omar shifted his eyes to Shareef. He had his head down and his hands clasped in his lap, apparently finding them captivating.

"You are from Nablus, you said?" Mama Subhia rescued him.

"Both parents. My late husband's family too." Um Waleed inflated her chest, pride clear in her voice.

Tilting her head closer to Um Waleed, Mama Subhia said in what only could be understood as an apology, "I wish I had known that before."

"Don't worry about it." Um Waleed patted Mama Subhia's hand. "I'm sure it's very good."

Omar didn't know what to do next. What had happened? What kind of secret code were the women using? If Uncle Mustafa would say something, he could follow his lead. Was it time for Fatimah to come in with the coffee tray?

"Omar, is there anything else you would like to know about?" Waleed asked, looking a bit more controlled.

If they deemed him the central figure in this play, then he would speak his mind and ask about what truly mattered. Rules be damned. "How do you feel about my sister?"

Waleed blinked a couple of times. "I admire her manners."

Fatimah's footsteps came from behind. Omar gave Waleed a firm nod to indicate his approval of his answer.

Fatimah walked in, carrying a polished brass tray. Short coffee cups rattled on their saucers.

Waleed stretched to his feet and buttoned his jacket.

Uncle Mustafa spoke at last, making the official introduction of Fatimah's suitor. "Waleed Najad, history teacher. You have met before."

Fatimah served coffee as directed, starting with Um Waleed, then Mama Subhia, Uncle Mustafa, the boys and ending with Waleed. She placed the tray on the coffee table and sat between Waleed and his mother, crossing her legs.

Mama Subhia cleared her throat.

Fatimah uncrossed her legs and put her feet together, shifting them slightly to Um Waleed's side.

Omar rolled his eyes. More secret codes between the women? God help him when his turn came to be in that spot. If it ever did.

Waleed stiffened next to Fatimah. Holding the coffee cup and saucer in his hands, he turned to face her. "How are you this evening?"

Before Fatimah could say anything, Huda entered the room.

Waleed rose to his feet again.

"This is my eldest daughter, Huda." Mama Subhia's voice elevated higher than usual.

Um Waleed placed her coffee cup back on the tray and stretched a hand to greet her.

There was no room for Huda to sit anywhere. Omar was about to give up his chair, but Shareef beat him to it. Huda smoothed the back of her skirt with her hands before she sat down, smiling and connecting eyes with Omar.

Something was wrong. Huda almost never smiled. Certainly not the way she was beaming this evening. Something sinister in the twist of her mouth puzzled Omar.

CHAPTER
NINE

Nadia paced the narrow space between the beds, chatting with her younger sisters to keep them occupied. She stopped in front of the full-length mirror mounted on the closet door and checked the front buttons of her yellow blouse. The top had made its way down to her from Huda, passing through Fatimah's teenage years. The silk fabric had lasted longer than it should have. The girls knew how to extend the lifetime of an expensive item like that. Nadia hunched her shoulders forward to lessen the stretch of the front panels across her bosom, realizing she had developed more than the others in that area. She should ask Fatimah to let the seams out a couple of centimeters.

"How much longer?" Farah asked from her corner on one of the beds.

"Soon." Nadia frowned. They should have called them in by now. What was taking so long? She turned and sat by the edge of the bed. "Now remember girls, we go in, we greet everyone and then we come back here." She adjusted the ribbon on Salma's head. "If they ask questions, your answer should be brief. I don't want us to take too much time."

"Why can't we stay a little?" Farah whined.

"Because that's not how things are done."

"But why?"

"There's no room for us."

"I can sit on the rug," Salma chirped. "I always sit on the floor when I play."

Nadia leaned closer and whispered as if telling them a secret. "It's not a time for children. The grownups need to get to know each other first."

Farah shook her head; soft black strands covered her eyes. "You're not a child like us. You're sixteen."

Straightening, Nadia examined her profile in the mirror again. Her sister was right, she sure didn't look like a child in this outfit.

Collective coughs penetrated the quiet atmosphere, followed by the clatter of dishes.

Nadia jumped to her feet.

"What happened?" Farah followed. "Why is Mama apologizing?"

"I don't know." Nadia approached the closed door. Should she go outside to see? Maybe they needed help. She turned to the girls. "Stay here. I'll be right back."

Taking a deep breath, she opened the door and stepped out.

Everyone was standing. Mama coughed non-stop, Um Waleed by her side patting her back. Fatimah held a glass of water, her face ashen and white. Huda was bent down, collecting pieces of broken coffee cups by Um Waleed's feet. The men shuffled from side to side, staring at each other, seeming confused or lost at what to do. Omar had his back to Nadia.

"I'm so sorry," Mama managed between coughs. "The first sip must have gone down the wrong way." She looked at Um Waleed's dress. "Did I spill coffee on you?"

Brushing the front of her plain gray dress, Um Waleed smiled. "Spilled coffee is a good omen."

Huda straightened. She headed to the kitchen, passing Nadia. Huda sauntered, her back straight, sandals clicking on the tiled floor, lips parting in a strange sideway smile.

Nadia froze in her spot.

Omar turned, following Huda with his eyes.

A cartoon character popped into Nadia's head, an angry worrier with steam blowing out of his ears. Omar's menacing look confirmed Nadia's suspicion. Whatever bad thing had happened was Huda's fault, and Omar knew it.

"We are in need of fresh coffee," Mama addressed Fatimah. "I'm afraid I spilled Um Waleed's cup in my coughing fit. Be a dear and help Huda."

Fatimah collected the remaining untouched coffee cups and hurried to the kitchen.

Nadia followed. "What happened?"

Huda stood by the stove, arms crossed on her chest, that strange smile stamped in place. "Fatimah made a mistake. The salt canister is right next to the sugar one."

Fatimah filled the coffee kettle with water and set it on the stove, her movements twitchy, lacking finesse. "It's a good thing Mama Subhia took a sip before Um Waleed did," she mumbled under her breath.

Huda opened the cabinet door above her head and brought down another set of coffee cups. "Yes, that was a good thing." Sarcasm laced every word.

Nadia grabbed Huda's arm and swung her around. "How could you?"

Huda pulled her arm out of Nadia's grip, throwing her off balance. "I didn't do anything."

Mama entered the kitchen. "You had better pray Um Waleed didn't pick up on what just happened." She shook a finger in Huda's face. "I've never been so embarrassed in my life. I want you to go in there and excuse yourself. Stay with the little ones in the bedroom. Nadia will help Fatimah with the dessert service."

Huda opened her mouth to say something.

Mama shook her head in silent warning. She stepped to the side of the doorway, directing Huda with a nod of her head to proceed in front of her out of the kitchen.

Nadia approached Fatimah and draped her arms around her waist. "Everything's going to be all right."

Fatimah wiped tears. "We will see." She stirred cardamom-fragrant coffee into the boiling water, watched it foam to the surface a couple of times, and turned off the stove.

Nadia pulled back and arranged the new coffee cups on the tray. "Left or right? I can never tell which way the handles are supposed to be turned."

Fatimah approached with the kettle in hand. "Your left. The guests should be able to hold the handles with their right hands."

"Why did you let Huda brew the coffee in the first place? Aren't you the one who's expected to do it?"

"I asked her to pour the coffee after I made it," Fatimah sighed. "She must have added the salt when I turned to fill the water glass."

Nadia leaned closer, stealing a look at the door. "Omar knows Huda is responsible."

"How do you know?"

"I just do. He will make her pay for this. Wait and see."

"No, he mustn't. And you will not talk to him about this foolishness. It's between us girls. Promise me."

Nadia heaved a long sigh. "You're too kind."

"I'm just trying to put myself in Huda's shoes. This is very difficult for her. She's the oldest." Fatimah held the tray. "Let's get this evening over with. We're about to serve the *kanafeh* experts what they will only find lacking. More things for Um Waleed to criticize."

"What do you mean?"

"They're from Nablus. Famous for their unparalleled *kanafeh*. And what do we decide to serve them?"

"Store-bought *kanafeh*."

"Not from one of the best dessert stores, either. Mama Subhia is beside herself. Now prepare the plates and follow me in ten minutes, please." Heading out the kitchen, Fatimah turned and added in a hushed voice, "Make sure you keep your shoulders hunched a little, maybe cross your arms over your chest. That shirt is too tight for you."

The dessert service passed without incident. Um Waleed was gracious enough to take one bite of her serving, make a half-hearted comment on how good it tasted, and set it down for the rest of the evening. Waleed devoured his piece while conversing with Fatimah by his side. Nadia balanced herself on the arm of Mama's chair, opting to keep her arms crossed rather than eating her dessert.

Toward the end of the visit, Um Waleed asked Fatimah, "Do you welcome my son's courting?"

Fatimah lowered her head, clasped her hands in her lap and kept quiet. Seconds passed in silence. Everyone stared at Fatimah, her face turning bright red.

"Silence is a sign of approval," Mama said.

"Shall we read the *Fatiha*?" Waleed's voice was reserved, but his enthusiasm to seal his proposal with a verse of the Qur'an showed clearly enough.

Expecting her father to respond, Nadia was surprised to see him staring at Omar instead. Poor Omar, he was beyond uncomfortable, the creases between his eyebrows turning white with his scowl. He hated being the center of this official business. Balancing his body at the edge of his chair, he looked ready to bolt out of the room. He cleared his throat.

Fatimah flashed him a glimpse and then returned her gaze to the floor.

Omar nodded. "Very well then."

Everyone put their hands together, flipped their palms upward, recited the *Fatiha* in unison, and wiped their faces with their palms.

Mama told Waleed he would be welcomed in the house every Thursday evening to spend time with Fatimah. Should they decide to go out, Waleed would have to coordinate with her brother and Shareef to be chaperoned.

Nadia thought the whole process unnecessary, even absurd. Fatimah and Waleed could always meet in his place when she went there to work, his mother a proper chaperone just as it had been so far. Nadia brought this up after everyone had left.

"It's important for people to see the couple with a member of Fatimah's family in public to indicate the official status of Waleed," Mama explained. "Should there be another young man thinking of approaching Fatimah, he would know to hold back and wait."

CHAPTER
TEN

Omar was in no mood to learn more about cultural traditions. His mind was racing and he wanted to confront Huda about her involvement in the theatrical performance of Mama Subhia. However, seeing Fatimah's face glow with happiness caused him to reconsider. He wouldn't do anything to dampen her mood.

"Girls' business," Nadia whispered in his ear as soon as the front door closed after the guests left. He didn't have to ask her. Nadia knew what was on his mind when their eyes met across the room. He bit his tongue to keep quiet, avoiding Huda by escaping to the roof.

To distract himself and relieve the angry energy pulsing inside, Omar paced the open space, dirty tiles under his feet and dark skies above his head. The physical examination at the military academy would take place next month. His friends who had signed up before him told him the exam was extensive and grueling. But he was in good shape. He would pass. He had to. Soon, he would have a place to stay, some income, modest though it may be, and a career once he graduated in two years. Not bad for a Palestinian refugee orphan boy. Not bad at all.

Fatimah would accept reality, once he gathered the courage to tell her. And he would. As soon as he passed the exam, his papers stamped. Since his food and lodging would be covered in the academy, he would be able to send Fatimah most of his cadet allowance. It was best to give his sister another source of income in case things didn't go well with Waleed and she had to stop working. But if what he saw on Fatimah's face tonight was any indication, Waleed had already entered her heart.

Uncle Mustafa would worry Shareef might also join the academy, following him as usual. If he did, Shareef would no doubt fail the physical exam and go to the university as planned. Now that he had some leverage with Waleed, he should ask him to help Shareef find a part-time job, perhaps at his uncle's press. If things worked out right, Uncle Mustafa would have his son under his roof and additional income.

Mama Subhia would encourage him with his plans, being the most practical in the family, understanding his reasons for taking that step. Huda would pack his bag the instant she heard the news. The little ones would hardly miss him, Farah confiscating his bed to separate from Salma. And Nadia?

What about Nadia?

Omar slowed his pace. He approached the railing and sat in his usual spot. What of sweet precious Nadia? His friends told him cadets got a break for one day every three months. Could she handle not having him around for that long? Could she manage school without his help? Nadia had come a long way: smart, observant, kind and . . . beautiful. If he hadn't been distracted by his anger earlier, he would have told her she looked nice tonight. Very, very nice. Freed of its usual braids, her dark hair reached the small of her back. Her tea and milk skin glowed, contrasted by her fitted yellow blouse.

What the hell? Where was his mind going?

He massaged his neck. School. He was thinking of Nadia's schooling. Shareef would be of no help, his attitude toward his sister one of tolerance, nothing more. Maybe he would step in and take charge in his absence? Become more attentive and helpful? Not likely. Shareef never showed interest in Nadia's schoolwork unless it involved Sameera.

How could he warn Nadia about Sameera? Nadia's innocence prevented her from seeing her friend's true colors. He should tell her not to spend too much time with the loose girl. He wouldn't have to explain why. Nadia wouldn't argue, trusting him. She always did. He damned himself for not letting her know she looked beautiful before he left the house. A clueless girl like Nadia should be reminded of her beauty, getting used to hearing it at home so she wouldn't be swept away by the first rake who said it. What was the chance of that happening?

His hands balled into fists. He relaxed his fingers and ran them through his hair. Shareef must pay attention, damn it. The way he carried on with Sameera. He had four sisters. Didn't he know whatever he did to someone else's sister would come back and bite him? A good number of fights in the neighborhood revolved around that concept. Always a spectator, never getting his hands dirty, Shareef hadn't learned that lesson. Every guy in the neighborhood knew Omar had no official standing as Nadia's brother, but they respected him, keeping a watchful eye on her. When a fool from another neighborhood had dared to follow Nadia on her way home from school, neighborhood boys had alerted him — not Shareef — to silence the vulgar boy. After that fight, the rest of the riffraff kept their distance. Once he was gone, who would watch out for Nadia?

Heaving a long sigh, he closed his eyes. Two years. A long time to be away from the family. Too long to be away from precious Nadia. She would be eighteen when he graduated. Who would tell her she was beautiful then?

His eyes flew open. What in God's name was wrong with him? Why was he thinking of Nadia in that twisted way? They weren't related by blood. Nadia was not his sister or half-sister. But like Fatimah, he grew up thinking of her as such. What was happening to him? Why now all of a sudden? What kind of pervert was he? He jumped to his feet and headed downstairs. God help him, he had a sick mind. He deserved to be thrown under a tank or something, the way his thoughts strayed. He had better pass that exam.

A month passed. Omar spent his days training in the streets. He improvised techniques with the help of his friend, Marwan. Most nights, he stayed wide awake, burying his head under his pillow, trying to ignore the fact that Nadia shared Fatimah's bed on the other side of the makeshift curtain divider. Every sigh, turn, or rustle of sheets tapped his senses, causing him to recite President Nasser's many speeches to himself. Speeches he had committed to memory. When that failed to distract him, he recited every verse of the Qur'an he knew by heart, the doors of hell squeaking open to swallow him.

One Friday afternoon, as soon as the men returned from communal prayer at the mosque, Omar told everyone he had been accepted at the military academy, passing the qualifying exam. Nothing went as he had imagined. Fatimah had a fit. He had never seen her behave that way before, yelling and screaming at him, accusing him of not considering her feelings, of throwing away a future she had worked so hard to plan.

Uncle Mustafa chided Fatimah for dismissing Omar's strong patriotic drive. He patted Omar's back, sat him down, and asked details about when he had to report, what kind of training he would be enrolled in, and what he would need to get started. Shareef claimed his father wouldn't permit him to join, so he wouldn't even try. Mama Subhia looked disappointed. She shook her head and withdrew into her room. The little girls cried and asked why he had to leave. They begged him to stay. Huda, the single person behaving as predicted, shot a sinister smile and walked out.

Nadia came up to him and slid her arm in his. "Let's talk."

Omar withdrew his arm the minute they left the apartment. She proceeded ahead, leading the way to the roof, but he suggested they take a walk instead. Once they hit the street, he directed her to the open square where he had once taken Fatimah. They walked in silence, passing closed shops and empty streets.

Nadia broke the silence. "How long have you been planning this?"

"A while. Everything happened fast, though."

"How long, Omar?" she insisted.

"About a month."

"Since Waleed's first visit?"

"A few days before."

Nadia stopped, tilted her head sideways. "Is this why you've been acting so strange lately? Spending a lot of time at the mosque and keeping to yourself when you're home?"

Omar remained quiet. What could he say? He was disgusted with himself. It seemed the harder he tried not to think of Nadia, the more his sick mind took him there. A mental image of Nadia's shapely body tortured him, mixing shame to its allure and painful repulsion at the same time. Like a thief hearing sirens in the distance, his heart skipped a beat every time he heard her voice or saw her heading his way. He had done his best to avoid her over the past month, and he had sunk deeper into misery. He couldn't even confide in Marwan, his one true friend. What possible words could he use to describe his fixation? He couldn't wait for the torturous academy exam, welcomed it. His noble reason for joining the military turned into a perverted drive taking hold of him. He couldn't escape it, prayed hard to be rid of it. Really hard.

"I would have kept your secret." Nadia touched with her delicate fingers the patch of skin that showed from her open collar.

Omar followed her fingers with his eyes. He would go to hell, no question about it.

"Besides, how come they accepted your application without Father's approval? Shareef said he couldn't do it by himself."

Taking a deep breath, he touched her elbow and nudged her to resume walking. "I'm not like Shareef."

"If anything, you're younger."

"Shareef is an only son. He is excused from military service unless his father signs him off."

"I don't understand."

"The military will not take the only boy in a family. It's the law. But an orphan is a ward of the custodian court. All I needed to join was a signed paper from a judge. It was easy. The government encourages us orphans to join."

Nadia stopped again. She laid a hand on his chest the way she always did to get his attention. "You have a family. We are your family."

Omar stepped back. "I'm not your brother," he blurted out.

"Stop this silliness. You know we all consider you one of us."

Heat crept up his neck, his heart thumping fast, his ears ringing. He shook his head. "Legally, I'm not."

"So what? Some judge allows you to throw yourself away like that and you think no one's going to care?"

"Throw myself away? Joining the army is a duty for me, a step toward liberating Palestine." He tried to control flaring anger and toned down his voice. "And army officials don't care as long as I'm legally signed. I'm just a number in their files."

Nadia stepped closer. The heel of her shoe caught between pavement bricks and she lost her balance, falling onto him. "*I* care."

Omar steadied her, wrapping his arms around her waist. And then he released her, as if he held pieces of glowing coal, almost shoving her in the process. He took big strides to pass her, hiding his flaming face. "It's final. There's no going back," he called out over his shoulder.

She caught up with him, a hand raised to her head, checking the ribbon holding her braid. "When do you have to go?"

"They give us fifteen days to get things in order."

"What are you going to do after you're done?"

"I'll be an officer. A good position to be in." He pointed at her feet. "Be careful. You're going to trip again."

"You're destined to be a teacher, not a soldier."

"An officer," he corrected.

She waved him off. "I don't see a difference."

"An officer commands a unit and trains soldiers." He glanced her way. "Some dreams were meant to stay just that. Nothing more."

They reached the square. Nadia plopped on the bench, huffing in clear frustration. She crossed her legs, then crossed her arms with a jerk. "I don't like it."

Omar remained on his feet. "You don't like me making a future for myself?"

"I know I'm being selfish. You won't be living with us anymore. Fatimah will marry and move out too. I'll be alone."

Were those tears shimmering in her eyes? Omar sat by her side, rested his elbows on his knees and fixed his gaze straight ahead. "You have your sisters and Shareef. He isn't going anywhere."

"Huda hates me. Farah and Salma are too young to understand me. And Shareef . . . he's not like you."

"You have your parents. You won't be alone. Besides, I'll visit every three months. I want you to get good grades."

"Who will help me with my homework?"

He leaned back, finding the perfect moment to say what was on his mind. "Anyone but Sameera." He put as much authority in his voice as possible.

She brushed the bangs from her eyes. "Is she all you think about now?" Nadia leaned closer, her long braid spilling over her shoulder. "You know Shareef is taken by her, if you go he will make her forget about you."

Omar examined his hands. "I'm not interested in Sameera anymore."

"Because of Shareef? Don't be a fool. She can't stop talking about you."

"You shouldn't spend too much time with her."
"Why?"

Taking a long breath, his eyes searched Nadia's face, close, smooth and trusting. "She's not good company."

70

Nadia drew back and raised her eyebrows. She stared at him, chewing her lower lip.

He tore his eyes away. He should have Fatimah explain things. Didn't girls talk with each other about these matters?

"Omar?"

He did not meet her eyes.

"I warned you about her brothers."

"I didn't do anything."

"Then explain how you found out she's not good company."

"It's not important how I found out. Will you trust me?"

"Of course I trust you." She left the bench. "It's Shareef you need to worry about. Not me."

"Shareef can take care of himself." He joined her and nudged her elbow to head back.

She slid her arm in his. "I don't blame you guys. Sameera is beautiful."

Pulling her arm closer to his side, he allowed himself one brief moment of satisfaction. Then he untangled their arms and patted her hand before he released it. "Not as beautiful as you."

CHAPTER
ELEVEN

Omar had but fifteen days to work things out before he sealed his fate in the academy. At Waleed's urging, Uncle Mustafa's insistence and Fatimah's approval, Omar set the date to sign her marriage contract the last Thursday before he had to leave. He did his homework this time, asking Uncle Mustafa, some of his friends, their fathers and the Imam at the mosque what to expect, how to conduct himself as Fatimah's single male relative. He hoped his attempt to take charge would impress his sister, softening her toward him and encouraging her to let go of her anger over his plans.

Waleed accompanied the men of his family, trustworthy neighbors and respectable acquaintances for the important male-only event. Again, Omar was at the center, receiving the official request for Fatimah's hand from Waleed's oldest uncle. He listened to men testifying, one by one, to Waleed's good character. Omar didn't need convincing. He and Uncle Mustafa had asked about him at the places he suggested, and then followed their own sources for a thorough evaluation. Omar had no doubt Waleed would take good care of his sister.

Going along with traditions, Waleed's oldest uncle asked Omar about the amount of dowry expected from his nephew. Omar specified a modest amount in the form of a gold Ottoman coin. He and Waleed had agreed to that earlier during one of his planned visits. Waleed opened a small jewelry box and passed it around for the men to observe the coin reach Omar's hands.

Glancing at his watch, Omar worried the civil court clerk appointed to register marriage contracts might not show up. When he arrived at last, the clerk launched into a long lecture about the sanctity of marriage, reminding the groom of his responsibilities and duties toward his wife. Half way through the intimidating speech, Omar expected Waleed to bolt for the door. As if the situation weren't heavy enough for poor Waleed, the old man had to lay out every warning possible, citing verses from the Qur'an and quotations from Prophet Mohammad about marriage. Showing patience and attentiveness, Waleed listened, nodding his head every now and then.

The clerk requested to talk to the bride in person.

Omar led the way to Mama Subhia's room where the women had gathered. The door opened. Mama Subhia and Um Waleed crowded the opening. They guided Fatimah out to the hallway, keeping the bedroom door open. Fatimah wore a soft pink dress. A rosy color highlighted her smooth cheeks. Her lips were a couple of shades darker. Something on her eyelids made her hazel eyes look bigger. Omar had never seen his sister with make-up before. He gave her a kind smile, then stepped aside, allowing the clerk to have a semi-private conversation with her.

"Are you Fatimah Bakry?"

"Yes." She handed him her identification card.

"Can you confirm to me your age?"

"Twenty-four."

"Are you willing to accept the marriage proposed by Waleed Najad, age thirty-two?"

Fatimah nodded.

"I need to hear you say the words, please. Speak up, daughter. Don't be afraid."

"Yes, I agree." Her voice came out low, yet clear.

"Of your free will? Have you been coerced in any way to accept this proposal?"

Fatimah shook her head. "I have not."

"Have you received your dowry of one gold Ottoman coin?"

Omar approached, handed over the jewelry box nesting the gold coin framed as a pendant. He returned to his spot a few steps behind the clerk.

The clerk examined the piece of jewelry, then handed it over to Fatimah. He wrote its specifications in his book. "Do you have any conditions to this marriage, daughter?"

Fatimah looked at Omar. She raised her eyebrows, clearly confused.

Omar heard some families imposed restrictions on place of residence or other trivial issues in marriage contracts. He saw no need to complicate matters. He shook his head.

"I have no conditions," Fatimah answered.

"*Ala barakatillah,*" the clerk said, stating his satisfaction and calling for God's blessings as they moved forward. "Where are the two witnesses? No blood relatives to either party."

Omar called for Waleed to bring over two neighbors. They presented their identification cards and witnessed Fatimah sign the contract, then Omar and finally Waleed. They added their signatures at the end.

The women put their hands to their mouths, wobbled their tongues and launched into high-pitched *zaghareed* of joy. Folkloric ballads rang through the house, Um Waleed's voice the loudest and most cheerful. *Kanafeh* trays poured out of the kitchen, original Nablusian *kanafeh* oozing with sweet syrup and made under Um Waleed's watchful eye. The servers were Omar's friends from the neighborhood, distributing plates along with bitter Arabic coffee brewed with lots of cardamom. The afternoon event ended with a wedding date set the day Omar came home from the academy on his first visit three months later.

Feeling like he had aged twenty years in the span of a few hours, Omar shook every man's hand at the door on their way out, thanked his friends for their time and promised to return the favor. Uncle Mustafa nudged him to invite Waleed to stay behind.

As soon as the front door closed, Um Waleed stepped out of the bedroom and ran to hug her son, crying and laughing at the same time. Her tongue swung in her mouth from side to side like a pendulum with lightning speed, ringing the traditional vocal cheer. Waleed kissed his mother's hand and touched it to his forehead. He repeated the act twice, asking her to bestow her blessings on him and his future wife.

Omar watched from his corner. A stab of jealousy anchored him to the floor. Whose hand would he touch to his forehead when his turn came? Mama Subhia dabbed at her eyes, the embroidered handkerchief hiding half her face. She stood tall, her back straight despite intermittent tears. A proud mother's stance.

The girls filed in. Like a hummingbird, Nadia fluttered around Fatimah, singing and fussing over Fatimah's dress, her younger sisters giggling behind her. Huda stayed a couple of steps away, her face solemn. Fatimah approached Mama Subhia. She held her hand, kissed it and touched it to her forehead, mimicking Waleed's actions.

"*Allah yirda alaiki*," Mama Subhia kept saying over and over again, asking God to be pleased with her.

Omar's eyes watered. He swung his head to face the wall. This couldn't be happening. He had just married off his sister, conducting himself in the manliest manner possible for someone his age. Why the hell was he about to weep like a girl?

To his relief, Uncle Mustafa ushered him, Shareef and Waleed out of the house, leaving the women to their celebrations for the rest of the evening. On their way down the stairs, they passed neighborhood women and friends starting to arrive, carrying gifts, plates of food and bundles of flowers.

Shareef became animated, jumping down two steps at a time, saying over his shoulder, "My friends are waiting for me."

Omar craned his neck over the railing and saw Sameera among the women entering the building. She took two steps to the side to let the women behind her pass, then turned around and walked out to the street, Shareef not far behind.

Exhausted and spent, Omar slipped into bed past midnight. His back and hands hurt from scrubbing the kitchen floor. After the party, everyone had done their best to clean up before they turned in. Omar had stayed behind, insisting on putting the kitchen back in order for Mama Subhia. The girls were tired, and he didn't want Fatimah to have to spend any part of this night on housework. Besides, he needed an outlet, something to slip him into sleep as soon as his head hit the pillow, escaping thoughts and reflections.

Omar closed his eyes. Fatimah had looked genuinely happy tonight, glowing. Thank God Huda hadn't tried anything to spoil the event for her. He had one more night left in this room, on this bed, so close to Nadia. No. He would not let his mind go there. Why hadn't he fallen asleep yet?

Shareef snored from his bed to his left. Omar flipped on his side, facing Shareef and giving his back to the dividing curtain and the girls' side of the room. His body relaxed and he started to drift off.

"Fatimah," Nadia whispered from behind. "I can't sleep. I can't believe you can, either. Do you think they have fallen asleep?"

"I don't know," Fatimah whispered back. "Let's see." She called Huda's name. No answer. She called Shareef's name. His snoring continued, uninterrupted.

Nadia called Omar's name. His eyes flew open. For some twisted reason, he remained silent and motionless.

"They're asleep." Fatimah's voice stayed hushed. "Are you still thinking about the party?"

"I can't believe you're married."

"Not for three more months."

"But under the eyes of God, you are." Nadia's voice rose a notch. "You don't have to wait for the wedding to go with Waleed, right?"

"I want a wedding. The white dress and the see-through veil and the cake. I didn't think about it before, but now I find it important. Don't you?"

Nadia giggled. "I dream about it sometimes. My wedding will be the talk of the town. White flowers everywhere. No colors. Only white flowers. And instead of the mesh veil, I will wear a hat made of flowers."

"A hat?"

"Fine, maybe not a hat. A crown. Yes, a crown. And the gown . . . sleeveless."

A slapping sound followed. Then hushed laughter.

Omar wished he could close his ears, put the pillow over his head or something. He remained on his side, afraid to make a move. Nadia continued with her descriptions, Fatimah making silly comments every now and then. They switched turns, and Fatimah went into her dream wedding. He was sick to his stomach for eavesdropping, but he had no choice. He didn't want to do or say anything that would interrupt the girls' talk. In time, their hushed voices lulled him to the brink of sleepiness.

"And in all of this, do you see a groom?" Fatimah asked.

"Oh, yes."

Omar's drowsiness drained out of his body and took a dive out the window.

"Tell me," Fatimah encouraged.

"Are you sure they're asleep?" Nadia sounded anxious.

"Yes, yes. They are." Fatimah sounded impatient. "Who's the lucky guy?"

"One of Omar's friends who helped serve tonight. I don't know his name, but he was one of the early ones to arrive and he was so sweet. I noticed him right away."

"What did he look like?"

"Kind of Shareef's height, dark skin, smooth black hair brushed to the side, and his eyes . . . long curly eyelashes."

Omar's mind displayed his friends' faces one by one, scanning for long curly eyelashes, a detail he couldn't imagine. Which one was he?

"While we were working together in the kitchen," Nadia continued, "we talked about things. You would never believe it, Fatimah, but he used to read the same adventure series I did."

Omar held his breath. Marwan. Goddamn Marwan Barady.

CHAPTER
TWELVE

Leaving the academy on his first break proved to be more complicated than Omar had anticipated. By the time he chased down the necessary signatures and multiple stamps, half the day had passed. Arriving home late, he found himself without a specific role as every arrangement concerning the wedding had been taken care of. The rooftop of their apartment building had been transformed into a wedding hall. Flower arrangements of all colors formed an elegant backdrop to the stage where the new couple sat. Strings of lights entwined with clotheslines dangled above their heads. A band in one corner moved happy crowds on the dance floor and between chairs. Waleed had spared no expense on the wedding.

Uncle Mustafa instructed Omar to sit unsmiling in one corner during the festivities.

"Are you serious? Why can't I smile?"

"You want to show Waleed's family you are happy letting go of your sister?" Uncle Mustafa sounded angry. "You can't do that. They need to know Fatimah has a strong family to answer to if they mistreat her in any way."

Omar obliged for the benefit of Uncle Mustafa and the people who held ancient traditions to heart. On a personal level, he didn't need to send a cloaked message. He had already warned Waleed in plain words when he put Fatimah's hand in his, "Mistreat my sister and I will ruin the lives of everyone in your family."

From his corner, Omar watched the crowd. He noticed things he could have done without. Things that wouldn't have hit him hard had he been occupied, mingling with his friends. Uncle Mustafa's ghost-like appearance, for one. He moved like a man in his seventies, not late forties, shuffling his scrawny bowed legs with his back bent, coughing into a handkerchief almost every time he exhaled. Good thing Fatimah didn't need his cadet allowance. Sending it to Uncle Mustafa instead was the right thing to do.

Omar's wandering eyes landed on Nadia. He willed them away to Mama Subhia, sitting to the side, conversing with a group of women. She stood out in her black and red embroidered Palestinian dress next to Um Waleed's gray dress. The few times he had seen Waleed's mother, she wore some shade of gray. This one a few degrees lighter, but gray nevertheless.

His eyes found their way to Nadia again. He hung his head and lowered his gaze to the floor. Don't look up, a voice in his head commanded. A hearty laugh echoed and he snapped up his head. Nadia was radiant in a simple ivory dress, hair mounted high on top of her head, making her appear taller, more mature. She moved on the dance floor with reserved awareness, her hand flying often to her hair, checking if the style was intact. Surrounded by her friends, she scanned the crowd, eyes bright with healthy vibrant energy. When they settled, her face flushed red. Omar followed her gaze.

Marwan Barady stared back at him. He raised his hand to his forehead, giving Omar a firm salute. Omar acknowledged it with a terse nod. Had Marwan blinked, he would have missed it. Maneuvering his way through people, Marwan pulled up a chair next to Omar.

"Congratulations, my friend."

"Thank you." Omar sat straighter in his chair.

"You're lucky. You now have a respectable teacher for a brother-in-law."

"Right."

"What news of our national hero, Nasser? I bet you get a lot of inside information at the academy."

"Nasser's threats to deny Israeli ships passage through the Straits of Tiran will most likely throw us into war."

"So it's true, then? Nasser will not let this go."

"The narrow sea passages between Sinai and the Arabian Peninsula are too vital." Omar tried not to sound like a teacher, but he welcomed the distraction. "If the Israelis decide to strike Sinai, we will join forces with the Egyptians to repel the aggression. Pave the way to Palestine. Get back what we lost."

"I heard the Soviets are sending us arms and tanks. You ready for war?"

Omar met his friend's eyes. "You bet."

Marwan extended his hand. "I think you were always ready."

Omar gave Marwan's hand a firm shake. "Thanks for the confidence."

"You were missed here."

"Trouble?"

"Nothing worth mentioning." Marwan pointed with his head in the direction of a couple of young men leaning against a wall in the background. "Blue tie over there mentioned Nadia to my cousin."

Omar zoomed in on Mr Blue Tie. "And?"

"Let's say he didn't dare talk about her again." Marwan folded his arms on his chest. "Don't worry. Like I promised, I got your back."

"I knew I could count on you." Omar interjected as much confidence in his voice as he could. His plan seemed to be working. Knowing Nadia's infatuation with his good friend, he had asked him to keep a watchful eye on her in his absence. Bound by an unspoken code, Marwan would have to stay at a respectful distance, honoring Omar's trust in him. At least she had chosen a decent guy, Omar pacified himself.

"I can't say the same thing about Shareef." Marwan paused, seemed to hesitate to go on. "I don't want to dampen the mood here, but something needs to be done."

"Same girl?"

"I heard one of her brothers ambushed him on campus. Warned him to stay away. It was all hushed, of course. Everyone thought they quarreled about money. But I know the full story."

Omar shook his head. "Idiot." He found Shareef skulking in a corner with three guys, strangers to Omar. "Who are they?"

"New friends from the university, I guess." Marwan leaned closer to whisper in Omar's ear, "I think you should let his father know at this point."

Omar scowled. "That bad?"

"All I can say is that you may need to arrange for another wedding soon." Marwan pulled back. "Before it's too late."

Omar's eyes darted back to Shareef. Could it be? What a goddamn idiot. "Your sources?" The muscles in his arms tightened with anger.

"My oldest sister. She's friends with the girl's oldest brother's wife. The women are keeping it to themselves at this point. My sister knows I care about . . . your family's reputation. That's why she told me."

"You sure about this?"

Marwan ducked his head, touching his chin to his chest. "I would ask Huda if I were you."

"Shit! That far?"

"Sorry, man. I'm not saying another word. God forgive me for bringing it up. I got young sisters of my own." Marwan stretched to his feet. "You will let me know if you need anything?"

Omar shook his friend's hand. The last thing he wanted to do was talk to Huda about something as delicate as this. Talk to Huda, period. He had managed to avoid her so far. Spotting her among the women, she looked subdued. To an ignorant onlooker, she gave the image of being sad about losing a sister. Omar knew better.

"It's not that bad," Nadia's voice sang by his side. Concentrating on Huda, he hadn't noticed Nadia approaching him from the side. "Fatimah will be just down the street." Nadia took Marwan's chair.

Omar held his breath for a few seconds. The perfume she used moved a deep spot inside him. "I know," he breathed.

"It's fine to smile, you know. Just don't show your teeth."

He stretched his lips to a wide smile, without cracking them open.

Nadia giggled. "On second thought, don't smile. You look ridiculous. Especially without your hair." She tilted her head to one side, a warm and wistful expression in her eyes. "I missed you."

"I missed everyone." Omar ran a hand over his shaved head. "I expected to see you at home when I got there."

"You were late. We had to be at the salon." She touched her hair. "You like my chignon?"

"It's very . . . nice."

"You're not even looking at me."

He glanced her way, raising his eyebrows. "Your grades?"

"Took a good dive." She poked him in the arm. "It's all your fault."

"How bad?"

Nadia nudged him with her shoulder. "Will you relax, please? My grades are not bad, just lower."

Placing a hand on her chest, she swung her head toward the band. "Oh, I just love this song. Abdul Haleem is a dream," she breathed, referring to the dashing young singer whose song the band was playing.

Taking advantage of her distraction, he drank in her beauty. How would she feel if the popular singer were actually present, singing the song instead of the band? She would probably faint.

Nadia swayed sideways, moving her shoulders up and down with the music and rubbing Omar's shoulder in the process.

God help him, he needed to move aside. He pretended to stretch his back to create some distance between them.

Oblivious, Nadia craned her neck closer to his face, peering past a couple blocking her view. "Doesn't she look fabulous?"

He followed her gaze to where Fatimah sat drowning in her multilayer white dress next to Waleed. "Absolutely."

"I helped with her make-up." Nadia drew back. "Do you like my dress?"

"You look fabulous, too." Allowing himself to gawk at her, he added, "You always do."

Nadia blushed. Her eyes flickered to his left and her blush deepened. Without taking his eyes off her face, Omar knew she was looking at Marwan in the far corner. He nodded his head in Fatimah's direction. "You think she's forgiven me?"

"The instant the door closed behind you, Fatimah prayed for your safety and success." Nadia dabbed delicate fingertips to her cheeks. "Made us all cry. Omar, the guy you were just talking to. Is he . . ." Nadia's words faltered.

"Marwan Barady? What about him?" He braced himself for what he had to hear.

"He's not with you in the academy, right? I've seen him around. Since he helped with Fatimah's engagement party."

"Marwan has a business."

"Where do you know him from?" She picked at an invisible thread in her lap. "Shareef said he didn't go to your school."

"Marwan's father passed away when he was fourteen. He had to quit school to help his uncle run his father's business and see to his sisters. Shareef doesn't remember him, I guess."

"Is he Palestinian?"

"Syrian." Unable to control his aggravation, Omar's left leg started quivering. "What's going on, Nadia? Did Marwan do anything I should be concerned about? Did he cross any lines with you?"

Blushing, she mumbled, "Oh, no. Nothing like that."

"What then?" He tried to soften his tone, and failed. Why did he push? Knowing what her answer would be.

Nadia half rose from her chair. "Never mind. Forget I asked."

He shot his hand to hold her arm. "Not so fast."

She looked down at him with watery eyes. Heavens, he was about to make her cry. Letting go of her arm, he urged, "Sit down, please."

She shook her head. To his dismay, Nadia placed both hands on his shoulders and leaned forward to whisper in his ear, "I think he's like Inspector Atif." In one fluid move, she straightened and dashed away to join her friends.

Omar blinked and put a firm hand on his shaking leg to make it stop. Of all the heroes in the Five Adventurers Series, she chose the protective Inspector Atif as her idol? Did she know Marwan was watching over her? Had his plan backfired? Maybe he shouldn't have kept Marwan at a distance, drawing her in with his mysterious presence. And what the hell was he? Atif's scrawny sidekick? When would this girl grow up?

Seeing Uncle Mustafa trudging his way over to him, Omar rose to his feet and closed the distance.

Uncle Mustafa laid a hand on his shoulder. "It's time, son."

The couple's entourage of family members and close friends started its way down the stairs. Holding Fatimah's hand in his, Waleed headed to his place amidst cheerful songs and spontaneous dances. Older people who hadn't joined the wedding celebrations looked on from open windows and balconies. At the entrance to Waleed's apartment building, Uncle Mustafa held Omar back from following the party up the stairs.

"Your job is done."

Omar's steps slowed. Shareef fell in line with them. Tugging at his arm, they half dragged him back to the house. "Tell me about your training," Uncle Mustafa prompted. "You've lost weight. They don't feed you well?"

"It's fine." He was reluctant to talk about the hellish three months in the academy they called training. His muscles had grown stronger, his skin darker from long hours of exposure and his attitude meaner and harder. Being in the academy was serious business. Turning boys into men was a brutal process, distinguishing those with leadership qualities a ruthless one. If Omar hadn't fit in with the family before he left to the academy, he certainly stood out now. Leaving Uncle Mustafa at home, he turned to Shareef. "Come, we need to talk."

CHAPTER
THIRTEEN

Omar talked Shareef into taking the bus to Qassyoon Mountain overlooking the city of Damascus from the north. The last stop on the bus route would be secluded this late at night, providing a private place where no one would hear their delicate talk.

On the way, Omar kept Shareef busy with questions about his studies and his afternoon work at the newspaper press that Waleed had arranged for him. He found out the family's financial situation hadn't improved: Shareef's extra income went into his own pocket, covering books and other study materials. Fatimah's pay had stopped since she had become Um Waleed's daughter-in-law. Whatever Huda brought in remained the only constant addition to Uncle Mustafa's wages. Omar's meager cadet allowance covered a couple of doctor visits for Uncle Mustafa.

Once they got off the bus, Omar found the perfect spot and turned to face Shareef. "Now that we've covered everything else, want to tell me about your love life?"

"That's why you dragged me up here?" Shareef's tone was incredulous. He shoved his hands in his pockets. "My love life is none of your concern."

"It is when it drags your sisters' reputation through the mud." Omar kept his tone hard and threatening.

"What the hell are you talking about?" Shareef took out a cigarette box and shoved the edge of a wrinkled cigarette between his lips. He struck a matchstick and cupped his hands around the cigarette. "Who dares say a word about the girls?"

Omar went straight to the point. "Anyone who will know what you did to Sameera."

Taking a long puff, the burning tobacco illuminated Shareef's face. His expression changed from defiance to anger to shame. Blowing smoke out of his nostrils, he furrowed his eyebrows, retracted his chin, and swiped his hand under his nose.

Good thing Shareef had a character that could be easily shaken. Omar knew how to manipulate him. Something he shouldn't be proud of, but it had served him well so far. "So it's true."

Shareef turned to walk away. "I don't know what you're talking about."

Omar clasped a firm hand on his arm, stopping him in his tracks. "You didn't think about that, did you? You didn't think word would get out? How your sick father would take the news? Your mother?" Omar brought his face closer, stressing his words. "What would happen to Sameera? What people would say about Nadia, her friend, for God's sake?"

Shareef swallowed. "How did you find out? Who told you?"

"Not important." He let go of Shareef's arm, found a big boulder, and balanced his backside against it. "The right question is . . ." He pointed a finger in Shareef's face. "What are you going to do about it?"

Shareef kicked pebbles under his shoes. "I don't think any of her brothers know yet. So I don't see why I have to do anything at this point."

"Really?" Omar shouted the question. "Is that how you see it?"

"One of her brothers warned me to stay away a couple of weeks ago." He spread his palms up and shrugged. "And here I am, staying away."

"After what? After you ruined the girl?"

"They don't know that. Besides, when they do, they can't openly talk about it, accuse me or anything like that." Shareef's voice quivered.

Omar stretched to his full height and advanced to tower over Shareef. "You will do the right thing. The honorable thing. You will marry her."

Shareef laughed out his words. "Are you crazy? I will not marry a loose girl like that."

"If you don't, *I* will tell her brothers. Set them after you." He poked Shareef in the chest. "And I will not be around to defend you."

Shareef attempted to shove Omar out of his way. "You would betray me?"

He stayed put. "I'll do whatever it takes to stop you from creating a mess for the family."

"Then you marry Sameera." Shareef flicked his cigarette to the ground. "If you're so concerned about her, go ahead. Marry her."

Omar stared with unblinking eyes. In his head, he counted to ten, trying to stop his fist from slamming into Shareef's jaw. "And you will not because?"

"I will graduate with a respectable diploma, a promising career ahead of me. I plan to make a good name for myself. Marry a girl who gave herself to me?" Shareef shook his head. "No way." He wiggled a finger in Omar's face. "Don't look at me like that. You're no better than me."

"No, I am not." Omar's voice rumbled deep inside his chest like a wave bringing forth the first tide. "I'm not going to have a *diploma*, or a father to boast about my success, but I never dishonored an innocent girl, Shareef. I warned you before I left. Told you to pay attention. You made a mistake, no one is perfect. I'm trying to help you here."

"I don't want your help."

He needed to change tactics, find another way to inflict pain, open Shareef's eyes to the reality of his situation. He adjusted his tone. "How would you feel if someone did the same thing to Nadia?"

"I would kill him." Shareef's answer came quick, like a knee jerk.

Omar raised his eyebrows. "You don't think Sameera's brothers would do the same?" He saw genuine fear in Shareef's eyes. He pressed on. "They wouldn't touch their brother-in-law, though. They would help him along to secure their sister's future."

"Even if they knew the truth?" Shareef's voice lost its edge, sounding skeptical.

"Right. By then you would be family. But if you don't marry her, and they don't kill you, they will ruin your future any way they can, I guess." He rubbed his chin. "Personally, I would take that route if, God forbid, I was in their shoes. I would not kill the bastard, but I would make it my business to hunt him down, spread vicious rumors about him. No honorable family would give him their daughter. No respectable establishment would hire him." Omar returned to his spot, leaning back. "Just think what kind of damage her three brothers could do to your future."

Shareef's eyes roamed around, the wheels in his head turning. "I guess I can marry her," he started, then returned his eyes to Omar. "And divorce her after a couple of months. That will take care of the problem, right?"

Omar jumped forward, clenching his hands into fists. Hearing his blood roar in his ears, he cursed under his breath, took several deep breaths and forced his legs to stay put. One step at a time. "That's one solution."

"What about my father? He will never agree to this."

"Leave Uncle Mustafa to me. I will talk to him." Checking the time, he started walking. "The last bus will be here in a couple of minutes. Better not get stranded."

"What about money? Where will we live? I can't support a wife. What about her dowry?" Shareef fired his questions, making his way to the bus stop.

Omar walked along, somewhat pleased with the outcome, no answers to Shareef's questions ready in his head. There were other matters he needed to take care of before he returned to the academy the following day. Two major conversations. One he could put to rest in a matter of minutes. The other, he had no idea how to start.

CHAPTER
FOURTEEN

Sitting at the center of the sofa in the living room, Huda faced the front door. Omar saw her silhouette in the dark the instant he came in. He whispered to Shareef that he needed a moment alone before turning in for the night, ushering him into the bedroom. Omar took off his shoes and went into the living room.

Huda sat at full attention, framed by the moonlit window behind her, dressed in the simple silver dress she had worn at the wedding. She had her back straight, knees bent at a right angle, feet touching, hands in her lap. Her face, expressionless. With her short hair and lack of feminine softness, she could replace one of his stern sergeants at the academy.

"I've been waiting for you," she whispered.

"I can see that."

Huda got to her feet and motioned for him to follow her to the balcony. "I know what you and Shareef talked about."

"His stupidity?" Omar tried to cover his nervousness. He wasn't ready for a confrontation with Huda yet.

She took one of the small wooden chairs. "So? What's he going to do?"

"The right thing, of course."

Huda nodded. "Good. I thought he might try to deny his involvement." She crossed her legs. "My opinion of the girl is not favorable, of course. But Shareef's carelessness should cost him."

Omar eyed Huda under the big moon, looming close, curious about their secret talk. Her attitude surprised him. He didn't expect her to be on board against Shareef, her beloved brother.

"What?" Huda glared at him. "You expected me to fight you over this?"

Omar straddled the other chair. "I had my doubts. We never saw eye to eye, you and I."

"Families confide in me, Omar. They let me into their homes and trust me with their most delicate matters. You think I would take something like this lightly? The girl should not suffer the consequences alone."

"We are talking about the same girl?" He better be sure there weren't others. "Sa —"

"Don't say her name," Huda silenced him. She glanced over the railing. "In case someone overhears us." Turning back to him, she leaned forward and whispered, "The girl who came to study here."

Fine. He would play along. "What do you have in mind?" Omar whispered back.

"You have a way with Shareef." She straightened. "How did you get him to own up to it?"

Omar draped his arms over the back of the chair and clasped his hands together. "Like you said, I have a way with him." No need to tell her of his threats. Like walking on a tightrope, he didn't want to say anything that might cause him to fall out of her grace. He needed her.

"I assume you have a plan?" Huda tapped her shoe. "Getting Shareef to do the right thing by the girl is half the battle. There are Mother and Father to break the news to. I'm not sure how they will take it." She looked Omar in the eye. "We are talking about their *son*."

There it was. The dagger mouth Huda had always sported in his face. She had it hidden under that cooperative attitude from the start. He took a deep breath. Let it pass, he told himself. Get back on the rope.

"I'm willing to talk to Uncle Mustafa in the morning. Try to convince him to at least write their marriage contract until Shareef graduates." Omar paused, raised his eyebrows. "Unless you want to take on that task?"

Huda shook her head. "I can't talk about . . . such matters with my father."

"That's what I thought. Your role is with Sa . . . the girl's family. Her father and brothers are in the dark so far."

"How do you know that?"

Omar flipped his palms open. "Shareef is still alive, isn't he? And the girl is not harmed?"

"Only the oldest sister-in-law knows. She confided in Marwan's sister, Rihab, asking her to talk to me." Huda narrowed her eyes. "Marwan is the one who told you, right?"

Omar nodded.

"I thought so when I saw you two talking at the wedding."

"You're good friends with his sister? Can you ask her for a big favor?"

Huda turned her head to the side, hiding her face from Omar's view. "I can arrange for everything through the women. The girl's mother will do whatever she can to get her husband to accept Shareef when he proposes." She faced Omar again. "I don't have to ask for favors. Once my name is mentioned, the mother will know the truth and she will comply."

Power. The word jumped into Omar's head. Huda's occupation as a midwife gave her power over families. It wasn't just her dry personality that kept people at a distance. It was the secrets she held. Did she know his secret? A chill went through his body.

"I can discreetly sell a few of my things and take up new clients in other neighborhoods," she continued. "Make sure you let Father know a modest dowry can be secured. If things work out right, the girl's mother will help from her end." Huda smoothed her dress over her knees. "No matter what you think of Shareef, he has good qualities going for him." She held up one hand and started ticking off one finger at a time. "A promising future once he gets his diploma, an easy-going nature, a good family behind him, a teacher for a brother-in-law." She stopped at the last finger.

Omar touched it. "And a sensible older sister."

Huda stared back, lowering her hand. "Do you think you can pull it off before you have to leave tomorrow?"

"Not enough time. I'll talk to Uncle Mustafa, set the wheels in motion. Shareef has to arrange for the formal visit as soon as possible."

"Eid is next week. Maybe Shareef can work something out right after the holiday."

"You'll let Mama Subhia know?"

Huda took a deep breath. "Yes, but after Eid is over. Let her enjoy it."

Relieved by the somewhat amicable encounter, Omar relaxed his shoulders. "Better to leave the others out of it."

"You mean Nadia?" Huda's voice again took on a sharp edge, adding more of a questioning tone underneath.

Tension returned to Omar's muscles. He clenched his jaw. Was she testing the waters?

"I don't want Fatimah to be compromised with her husband if word reaches them," he explained. "I don't want Waleed to think less of Shareef."

"And Nadia?" Huda repeated.

"Is too young and innocent to face this about her friend, soon to be her sister-in-law."

"Sixteen is not too young." Huda rose to her feet. "Your concern about us is very touching." On the threshold, she turned to look down at him. "For someone who is not our actual brother."

Huda's words were meant as a slap to his face, Omar was sure of it. Did she know they had the opposite effect? That they stoked the simmering cinders in his chest, igniting a raging fire? What more validation did his tortured soul need? He was *not* Nadia's brother.

100

CHAPTER
FIFTEEN

Marwan left the busy market mosque and stopped at a bakery to pick up lunch. He carried steaming hot *sfeeha* into his store and called his employees over to take their break. The smell of onions and pomegranate syrup wafted as soon as he spread stacks of the flat meat pies on a table in the storage room along with a pail of yogurt. He closed the door behind him and took his place at the front to man the store.

Normally he would give his workers a two-hour break, but it was the last day before they closed for Eid and Souk Elhamedieh was overcrowded with people looking for good deals to purchase last-minute gifts. The day's sales would top the entire month's revenue. Marwan welcomed eager shoppers and prepared to deal with bargaining women who tried his patience with their stubbornness. His merchandise of men and women's clothing stood out among his competitors because of its superior quality, and he knew women's eyes caught the distinction. They haggled anyway.

Needing a break mid-afternoon, he left his main assistant in charge and leaned onto the front doors to catch a breath of air. Schools had let out and the streets were filled with young girls in uniforms of gray skirts and white blouses. Young men trailed not far behind, throwing compliments to gain attention — a dance he witnessed every day around this time. The guys' efforts went unnoticed most days, however on rare occasions a girl would cast a quick look back, duck into one of the narrow side alleys, and a young man would break away from his herd to follow her. Sometimes, when traffic slowed into his store, Marwan would watch from a distance and challenge himself to spot the girl who would make that move. His success at guessing improved from year to year. Certain types of girls threw crumbs, and guys picked them up with painful predictability. Almost every young man he knew played that silly game. Never him, no matter how carefree he yearned to be.

A group of four girls coming down the alley caught his eye. Three girls flirted with their followers using not so subtle gestures, raising their voices with encouraging laughs, taking turns to whisper to each other, and lingering for too long by store fronts without going inside. The fourth girl walked a step ahead, clearly trying to separate herself from her friends. She clutched books to her chest and kept her eyes to the ground. Hair pulled tight into a ponytail exposed healthy natural beauty and her unsmiling face stood in contrast to her companions' painted lips and color-smudged eyes.

Nadia stood out, not just because of her raw, untainted beauty, but because of her modest and reserved behavior. Vibrant young energy simmered under the surface of that controlled posture. She turned the heads of older men, knowledgeable men who recognized a jewel when they saw one. And she paid no one the slightest attention, not the fools trailing her flashy friends, nor the admiring men she passed. Watching out for her from a distance during Omar's absence, Marwan doubted she knew he existed.

One of the girls caught up with Nadia and brought her lips to her ear. Nadia shook her head and picked up her pace. Marwan pulled himself to full height. Nadia approached. She seemed unaware of him standing a couple of steps before her. The other girl grabbed her elbow and forced her to stop.

"One last thing," the girl said and dashed into his shop. "I need a sweater."

Marwan stepped back so she wouldn't brush against him. The others hurried after their friend. Nadia remained on the sidewalk. She met his gaze and her cheeks flamed.

"Salam, Nadia. Do you remember me?"

She brought her books down and nodded. "Omar's friend."

He threw a threatening look at the bunch of guys several steps behind and waved his hand toward the store. "Will you come in?"

"Only for a few minutes." She went inside and addressed her friends. "It's getting late. You promised you were done shopping."

The girls kept Marwan's assistant hopping between racks to bring clothing down from high shelves and spread them on the counters. They made so much noise and commotion that other women left the store mumbling. Marwan gritted his teeth.

Nadia remained close to the entrance. A girl with blood-red lips draped a fuchsia sweater over Nadia's shoulder. "See? This shade of pink goes quite well with your complexion."

"It's lovely." Not letting go of her books, Nadia slid the sweater off and pushed it into her friend's hands. "Better on you."

"I know you can't afford it. I can lend you money. You must get it. You haven't bought anything for Eid yet."

Nadia's blush deepened and the tips of her fingers turned white around the books she held. "I'm not a little girl. I don't need something new for the holiday."

"I will buy it, then." Her friend spread the sweater over her chest and looked at herself in the mirror. "It does look better on me. My skin tone is rosier than yours."

Marwan cleared his throat and approached the antagonizing, rude young woman. "I'm afraid you have to find something else. This is the last piece and it's already sold." He took the sweater from her hands and passed it to his assistant. "You left this out by mistake."

Without hesitation, the assistant folded the sweater, tucked it on a back rack and apologized. Red Lips joined her friends further into the store to look for an alternative.

Marwan approached Nadia. "Is Omar coming home for Eid?"

"He called yesterday and said he wasn't granted a break." She knotted her eyebrows. "Can you believe that? It's Eid! Everyone takes a vacation."

104

"The academy has its own schedule. They can't let everyone go home at once." He shoved his hands in his pockets when he caught the others staring at them. "Does your family need anything?"

"No, thank you." She passed him. "I have to get home. Are you girls done?"

The one with smudged eyelids pulled on Nadia's arm. "Do you know him?"

He stepped closer and answered before Nadia could say anything. "I'm friends with her brother. And for that, you all get a good discount."

The girls snatched scarves, blouses, and cardigans off hangers and piled them on the counters with enthusiasm, as if competing in a race. They giggled and babbled about patterns, trendy colors and styles, making more noise. Nadia hung in the background, her hands occupied with her books. She met Marwan's gaze and quickly looked away. Her self-composed smile lit up his entire store.

Nadia walked into the house and took off her shoes, her feet in need of a hot soaking. The smell of freshly baked sweets filled the living room. She went into the kitchen. Mama was sitting on the floor with Salma and Farah. Oven trays filled with date-stuffed cookies were spread around them.

Mama lifted her head, sweat glistening on her neck. "Finally, you're here. Quick, come clean the kitchen. Your sisters made a big mess."

"If I had known you were going to bake ma'moul all afternoon, I would not have gone with my friends to Souk Elhamedieh."

"Huda was helping and then she rushed out for work, mumbling something about a new client not from around here. I expect she will be late tonight. Did you have a good time?"

"It was crazy crowded." Nadia changed out of her uniform and sent her sisters to play at the neighbors'. She got to work, ignoring her aching feet. Mama baked the last batch of *ma'moul* and went to wash, leaving her to clean greasy trays and flour-covered counters. She was about to sweep the floor when the doorbell rang.

A young boy stood before her, bundles of brown paper in his hands. "Delivery from Omar Bakry."

"Wait here." Nadia dashed to the kitchen, wrapped a handful of cookies in a clean towel and returned to the boy. She took his load and handed him coins with the dessert. "Thank you."

Mama came out of her room, showered and dressed in a clean dress. "Who was it?"

"Omar sent gifts, Mama. Can you believe it? He couldn't come, but didn't forget to send Eid gifts." Nadia unwrapped the top bundle. "Look at these shirts."

Mama held a shirt in each hand. "Perfect for your father and Shareef."

Nadia opened the rest of the packages one by one. "This blouse fits Huda, I think. Dresses for Salma and Farah. And this scarf must be for you." She opened the last gift. Her hands shook as she pulled out a fuchsia sweater. She dropped on a chair, her heart doing somersaults behind her ribs.

Mama fingered the items. "How do you think Omar managed this?"

Nadia blinked. "It's possible he asked his friend Marwan Barady to send them."

"Omar must have been saving for a while. He thinks of everything, that boy." Mama tried the scarf around her shoulders. "If Marwan picked them out, he has good taste."

Nadia buried her flaming face in the fine sweater. "Yes, Mama. He does."

CHAPTER
SIXTEEN

At the academy, Omar received word from Uncle Mustafa that Shareef's marriage contract was scheduled for the following day. Bringing Uncle Mustafa around to the idea hadn't been that difficult. The man knew his son's shortcomings, and though outraged by Shareef's callous misconduct, he didn't seem surprised. Omar didn't know how Mama Subhia took the news, however, having left right after his private talk with Uncle Mustafa.

There was no way Omar could ask for a day break. The reason wouldn't convince his superiors to give him an exception. The political climate was tense, and it reflected off every officer's grim face. Israeli raids across the West Bank, aerial clashes over Syrian territory, and threats to thwart Nasser's power had added to the tension, bringing the possibility of war closer to certainty. Everyone held their breath in anticipation. Omar was living on a different plain than the one Shareef occupied. His was filled with political analysis and patriotic discussions. War loomed and darkened his sides. Shareef's plain was anchored in normalcy. Marriage opened doors to life's natural cycle. Omar could not have felt more removed if he tried. Immersed in grueling training, he had to tell himself things would go as planned and waited to receive a reassuring phone call from Huda. When he was summoned into his supervising officers' quarters that Thursday afternoon, he was surprised to see Waleed waiting for him, permission for an emergency leave in his hands.

"What's going on?" Omar asked as soon as they left the academy.

"A disaster." Waleed walked fast, ushering Omar into a taxi. "Shareef didn't show up as planned this morning. All the men waited, even the notary clerk. But he is nowhere to be found."

"The goddamn coward," Omar exploded.

"I thought you might know where to look for him, who his friends are?" Waleed scratched his head. "I told your superior officer that Uncle Mustafa's health was bad and that he was asking for you." Waleed shook his head. "I wasn't lying."

"Have you taken him to a doctor?"

"He's bedridden, Omar. I brought the doctor to him. It's bad."

Pinching the bridge of his nose, Omar braced himself. "What did the doctor say?"

"His heart gave way when Shareef didn't show up."

"A mule. A goddamn mule." Omar spit out the curse, ignoring the driver's disapproving scowl.

"I had to leave to come get you. Your next-door neighbor stayed in case they needed anything." Waleed glanced at the taxi driver and lowered his voice. "That's not all. Sameera's brothers are searching for Shareef. You know what that means?"

Omar ran a hand over his cropped hair. "It means we better find him before they do."

"I can take a guess at the reason behind their outrage, something other than the . . . public humiliation?"

Omar nodded.

"You should have told me. I'm family now."

"A matter like that, the fewer people involved, the better." Omar didn't hide his frustration. "Besides, I didn't want Fatimah to know."

"Well, the whole neighborhood knows now."

Omar took in a sharp breath. "The girl? She all right?"

Waleed threw his hands in the air. "God only knows. I'm still hoping we can salvage the situation if we find him soon and come up with a valid excuse."

"Like he was hit by a bus?"

"Something like that. But it has to look convincing."

Omar slammed a fist into his hand. "Oh, it will be convincing, for sure. Once I lay my hands on the dumb ass."

Waleed's eyes scanned the street outside his window. "Where should we start?" His tone shifted, became business-like.

"Come to think of it, let them find him. The shithead deserves what's coming to him."

"I would agree with you if it wouldn't kill his father. Now, stop reacting and start thinking."

"Goddamn it!" Omar shouted. "We are on the verge of war and the egotistic rake is running after his

110

whims." He scooted forward and touched the driver's shoulder, directing him home. He turned to Waleed. "You should be by Uncle Mustafa's side. They need you there. I will look for Shareef. I think I know where to find him."

"And when you do?"

I'll hand him over to Sameera's brothers, Omar wanted to say. "Something will come to me." He prayed for this to be true.

Trying the couple of places Omar had in mind where Shareef usually hung around turned out to be a waste of time. He searched anywhere he could think of, starting with the main hospitals and police stations to ease his mind and clear his conscience. He then checked the library at Shareef's precious university campus, the mosques he seldom frequented, the secluded place on top of Qassyoon Mountain, even a few seedy cafés. No one had seen him. In some places, Omar was told three men also stopped by asking for Shareef.

Omar needed help. He headed to Marwan's place, hoping he would know who Shareef's new friends from the university were, and that at least one of them could have an idea where he was hiding. Besides, Marwan had a car, and Omar had run out of bus fare money.

Toward the end of the night, and after tracking down Shareef's friends one by one, Omar and Marwan were able to get a lead. A bar on the outskirts of the city.

Parking his car a distance from the White Tulip Night Club, Marwan turned off the engine. "I can't go in there."

A neon sign announcing the belly dancer Blazing Zahira glared in Omar's face. "I understand. Don't wait out here, either. Someone might recognize you. You have a reputation to protect." He opened the car door. "Go home."

"I'm not leaving." Marwan pointed toward a dark spot. "I'll park under the trees up ahead."

"I owe you." Omar got out of the car.

"Wait," Marwan called after him. He stuck his hand out his window and handed Omar a roll of bills. "In case they don't let you in."

Omar stared at him in confusion.

"You don't fit the type who frequents these places."

Omar looked down at his clothes. He was still in his green fatigues, his dirty, low-ranking, star-free cadet uniform. Not even an officer could afford a place like this. He tucked the money in his pocket, thanked his friend and headed for the door.

Marwan was right, Omar had to pay his way in. The stench of *nargileh* smoke hit him hard in the crowded place. Men gathered in groups in front of a stage, clouds of fruit-flavored tobacco smoke hanging over their heads. Fruit, and God only knew what else. He let his eyes adjust to the dim light and then inched forward. Loud *dirbakkeh* beats vibrated the floor under his feet. On stage, a couple of men created the throbbing rhythm by beating small drums balanced on their knees and tucked under their arms.

Meandering around, Omar searched for Shareef, pretending the stifling atmosphere didn't faze him, like he was a frequent customer. When the voluptuous Blazing Zahira came on stage, he stopped, found a dark corner and watched her move her body in ways that made him dizzy. He wasn't naive. Spending time on the streets with guys from all walks of life, he had seen enough pictures of naked women get passed around. But he had never seen a belly dancer, provocatively clad in a see-through red outfit, perform live before his eyes. Half way through her sensuous dance, he checked that his mouth wasn't hanging open and willed himself to continue his search. He finally spotted Shareef, sitting with a couple of men, drinking.

Omar studied his companions and decided they were intoxicated enough he could handle them with ease should they interfere.

Riveted by the dancer, Shareef didn't see Omar approach. He circled Shareef's arm and whispered close to his ear at the same time, "Come with me."

Shareef gaped at him with his mouth open, the strong stink of alcohol on his breath.

"Get the hell up." He tugged at Shareef's arm.

"What?" Shareef narrowed his red eyes, trying to focus. "What are you doing here?"

"Saving your ass." Omar used his other arm to pull Shareef to his feet. "Don't make a scene."

Stumbling through the crowd, he dragged Shareef with little effort and they made their way out. Blazing Zahira kept the men busy. No one seemed to notice Shareef's objections, not even his drinking buddies. The fresh air gave Shareef the strength to yank his arm from Omar's grip. The move, however, unbalanced him and he fell, his face hitting the pavement.

Good, Omar thought. One convincing bruise, more to come. He waited for him to get back on his feet and pushed him toward Marwan's car.

"What do you want from me?" Shareef shouted. "Where are you taking me?"

"You know where." Omar struggled to keep his voice low.

Shareef planted his feet apart and crossed his arms. "No, I am not going there. I am not marrying her." He swayed from side to side like a tree branch on a windy day.

Omar slammed his fist in Shareef's face hard enough to send him a couple of feet back and to the ground again. "Do you have any idea what you have done, fool?" Omar exploded.

Marwan jumped out of the car and ran to stop him from pummeling Shareef, who rolled into a ball and started crying. "This is not the place," Marwan urged. "Come. Get him in the car and let's get out of here."

They shoved a sobbing Shareef in the back seat and took off. Marwan checked his watch. "It's nearing midnight. Do you want to take him home like this?"

"No way." Omar shook his right hand, his knuckles hurt. "It will upset Uncle Mustafa even more." He opened his window and let the breeze cool his skin and nerves. "Besides, there's a chance one of Sameera's brothers might be waiting for him in the neighborhood."

114

"I didn't mean to humiliate Father." Shareef's speech slurred. He spit blood out his window. "How upset is he?"

"You almost killed him," Omar roared.

"It's all your fault."

Omar nearly jumped to the back. "How is this my goddamn fault?"

Shareef scooted as far away as possible. "I told you I didn't want to marry Sameera. You forced me to."

Marwan lay a staying hand on Omar's arm. "Let him be. He's drunk."

"Do yourself a favor, Shareef." Omar's voice vibrated like a lion's threatening growl. "Shut your mouth or I will shut it for you. Pray your father gets better soon."

Shareef walked his fingers on the bruise under his left eye. Resting his head to the side, he closed his eyes.

"So? What are we going to do?" Marwan slowed the car.

"Hide him somewhere. Until I can find a solution." Omar ran a hand down his face. "I need to go home. Check on Uncle Mustafa."

"I could take him to our warehouse. It's far enough from the neighborhood. I trust the night guard there. He will keep him under control." Marwan glanced at the rearview mirror. "I doubt he'll try to escape in the condition he's in."

"I hate to get you more involved in this mess." Omar exhaled his frustration and exhaustion.

Marwan raised his eyebrows. "You have a better plan?"

He shook his head.

"I didn't think so. Let me help. It's a good plan. Gives you some time to set things right at home. When do you have to report back at the academy?"

"Shit! Tomorrow at three in the afternoon." Omar rested his head back and closed his eyes. "I need a miracle."

CHAPTER
SEVENTEEN

Nadia opened the door, her eyes red. She threw her arms around Omar's neck and broke down crying. Omar placed one hand around her waist and walked her backward to close the door behind him. His eyes darted toward Uncle Mustafa's room, its door closed.

"How is he?" Omar whispered into Nadia's hair.

"Not good. I'm scared."

"He's going to be fine." Omar tried to sound convincing, wishing he had found a chance to change his sweat-stained and smoke-saturated uniform. He held her shoulders and eased her away.

Nadia hung her head. "He's been asking for you and Shareef. You didn't find him?"

Waleed walked in from the balcony off the living room and stood a distance behind Nadia. Omar glanced at him. "I did." He lifted Nadia's chin with his index finger. "Shareef is fine. Can I check on Uncle Mustafa first, please?"

"I'll tell Mama you are here." She headed to the bedroom.

"Give me a minute to clean up."

Waleed motioned for Omar to follow him to the balcony. "Well?"

Omar filled him in on what had happened then headed to the bathroom. While he was scrubbing his face and neck, he heard a soft knock on the door. He donned the fresh shirt he had brought in with him and opened the door.

Huda shook a finger in his face. "Don't lie to me. Where is he?"

Omar peeked past her, making sure no one else was there. "Safe and sound at a friend's place. Drunk as a mule." He passed her. "I will bring him in the morning after he sobers up."

Huda laid a hand on his arm. "Wait."

Omar's patience was running out. He was dead tired and hungry, consumed with worry and anger. He needed this night to be over. "What is it?"

"Mama thinks something bad happened to Shareef. Mother's intuition." Huda squeezed his arm. "Whatever you say, make sure you put her mind at ease. We don't want her collapsing too."

Omar nodded. Something had happened to Shareef, all right. He had been hit by a bus and lost his backbone. Omar headed to the bedroom and stepped inside.

Mama Subhia sat next to Uncle Mustafa on the bed, holding his hand. Her eyes were swollen, her face pale. Fatimah came over to give Omar a tight hug. She left, taking Nadia with her. Uncle Mustafa had his eyes closed.

Mama Subhia leaned down to Uncle Mustafa. "Omar is here."

118

Omar pulled a chair closer to the bed. He cradled Uncle Mustafa's other hand, frail and cold, the veins prominent, mapping his life's journey.

"My son." Uncle Mustafa's words fell from colorless lips.

"Shareef is fine. I just left him. He's worried sick about you." Omar's stomach lurched. Good thing Uncle Mustafa had his eyes closed. Made it easier to lie. "Shareef had a slight accident on his way over today."

Mama Subhia gasped, slamming her chest.

"But he's fine," Omar added. "A little bruised. He passed out and someone took him to a doctor's clinic. That's why we couldn't find him sooner." He looked at Mama Subhia and stressed his words, "Really, Shareef is fine."

"My son," Uncle Mustafa said again.

"I will take him over to Sameera's family first thing in the morning. Seal the marriage agreement." Omar patted Uncle Mustafa's hand. "Don't worry. Everything is going to be just fine. I'm sure once I explain things to her family, they will understand."

"My son," Uncle Mustafa repeated, his tone urgent.

Confused, Omar raised his eyebrows at Mama Subhia. She blew into her handkerchief. "I think he means you, *habibi.*"

Omar's throat closed and his eyes watered. He turned his head to the side and buried his face in the crook of his arm. He pretended to wipe his nose, stealing a moment to get a grip. Uncle Mustafa's fingers closed tighter on his hand.

119

"I'm right here," Omar managed to say.

"Take care of the girls."

"Yes, sir. I will," Omar choked. "I promise you."

Mama Subhia broke down sobbing. Omar got up and wrapped his arms around her. He spoke soothing words, telling her to be strong, that Uncle Mustafa would pull through and would need her by his side. Omar used words he never thought he would utter. Words like *ummy* and *aboy*, referring to Mama Subhia and Uncle Mustafa as mother and father.

Huda walked in and took his place. He retreated from the room, his heart about to explode.

Fatimah and Waleed sat side by side on the couch in the living room. Fatimah's head rested on her husband's shoulder, her hands clasped in his. "You must be starving. Nadia is making you a sandwich in the kitchen."

Omar nodded. He didn't need food. He needed to get out of there before he lost it, seeing everyone so broken. Goddamn Shareef. Goddamn him to hell and back. Entering the kitchen, he dropped his body on a chair by the side table. Placing his elbows on the table, he held his head in his hands. Shit. If he was going to break down in front of Nadia, then so be it.

Nadia touched his red knuckles where the skin had broken on Shareef's jaw. Omar lifted his head, but kept his eyes cast down.

"I know you're lying to them." She placed a sandwich plate on the table. "And I know you must have a good reason to."

He closed his eyes.

"Fatimah washed your uniform shirt." Nadia headed out of the kitchen. "I will let you eat in peace."

Early the next morning, Omar got into Marwan's car. He had fallen asleep face down on the table in the kitchen for a couple of hours. Massaging his stiff neck, he explained his plan.

"Waleed will head out to Sameera's place, hoping to convince her family that Shareef is recovering from a minor accident he had yesterday. I will meet Waleed in the café at the end of the street around ten to see if we have the green light to take Shareef over, have him sign the marriage contract and put this mess to rest."

"You think they'll go for it?"

Omar sighed. "They have no choice. They want to shut everyone up."

"How are you getting Shareef to go along with it this time?"

"Don't worry. I'll make sure he does."

"Is he right-handed?"

"Yes. Why?"

"Then make sure you break his left hand." Marwan met Omar's eyes. "So he can hold the pen."

Omar burst out with a healthy laugh. Marwan was proving himself to be the right man for this kind of mission. Marwan truly had his back. He had to admit, had Marwan not held Nadia's eye, he would have appreciated the gem in his friend with the weight it deserved. Instead he pulled back, ashamed of what he might reveal if he reciprocated Marwan's open goodwill.

"One more thing," Marwan winced. "You sent Eid gifts to everyone at home."

Omar's laugh died. "I did?"

"I acted on impulse when I learned you were stuck at the academy. Sent them in your name. I know I had no right, and I apologize. I'm telling you so that we are on the same wavelength should it come up."

Omar worked his jaw, trying hard not to read too much into Marwan's thoughtful act. "Everyone, you said?"

Marwan nodded. "Shareef included."

Omar rubbed his eyes. No need to make a big deal about this now. He had bigger battles to fight. "How much do I owe you?"

"You give Shareef what he deserves, make sure he can't wear the shirt he has on again, and we will be even."

When they reached the warehouse, Omar broke a couple bones in addition to the ones in Shareef's left hand. Every time Shareef wailed out, Omar told him they needed him to look like he had been pulled from under a bus. They fed him the concocted story with all its details. Omar left to meet Waleed as planned, and Marwan drove Shareef to a clinic in a nearby town, a half hour away from Damascus.

Waleed gave the thumbs up to move forward, having won over Sameera's elder brother. Close to Waleed's age and probably prepped by his wife through Huda, the man had an open mind and was able to convince his father and brothers to give Shareef the benefit of the doubt, aiming to protect the family reputation. Waleed had to invent another lie to answer the question of why Shareef hadn't phoned in his accident to either family. Omar never found out what nonsense Waleed came up with, thanking his lucky stars for his brother-in-law's imaginative mind.

After Friday noon prayer, Omar stood behind Shareef, a firm hand grasping his right shoulder while he signed the marriage contract. The whole ceremony was rushed. Sameera's father insisted they hold it at their local mosque, where every man in the neighborhood witnessed the event. Word got around about Shareef's accident and his poor physical condition. Eyebrows were raised at the unusually large dowry Sameera's father asked for. The fact that its payment was deferred for a later time also made big ripples in the gossip pond.

Some people said Sameera's father was gaining a fourth son, a respectable young man with a decent future ahead of him. And some admired the father for not burdening Shareef with an immediate dowry as a means of giving thanks to God for sparing his life after the accident. Others commended the family for hurrying the wedding, showing consideration toward Uncle Mustafa's delicate health. People speculated and then congratulated.

But Omar knew having the dowry deferred was like handcuffs on Shareef's wrists, a debt payable on demand. If not delivered whenever requested and Sameera's family went to court, Shareef would be jailed until he came up with payment. Shareef was locked in the marriage for a while. Unable to pay his debt, he wouldn't be able to divorce Sameera in a couple of months like he had planned. Her father had made sure of that. Omar didn't blame the calculating man. Served Shareef right for his reckless actions.

Satisfied that his main mission was accomplished, Omar took a solemn and subdued Shareef home. He checked on Uncle Mustafa, changed into his uniform, said his goodbyes, and made it back in time to the academy. He never imagined he would find the back-breaking training a welcome relief.

CHAPTER
EIGHTEEN

One year later, 1967

Standing at full attention in his crisply pressed uniform, Omar received his graduation documents in the private office of his general commander. A star pinned on his shoulder strip designated him Second Lieutenant. No ceremony. No proud family members around. He was granted a special leave five days before the rest of his class. Circumstances called for the exception. Omar had a funeral to attend. His superior officer had informed him of Uncle Mustafa's death that morning, giving him but few minutes to absorb the shock before his documents were stamped, including orders to report in two weeks for his assigned station.

Marwan was waiting for him outside the main gates. Accepting Marwan's condolences in silence, he shook his hand and got into the car. He stared ahead, hoping his friend would not try to engage him in conversation. Conflicting emotions competed for room in his chest, constraining his ribcage and making it difficult for him to breathe right or to work his throat to say anything. He had earned his star, but Uncle Mustafa was gone. What else was there to say?

"Waleed and Shareef are arranging for the burial before noon prayer." Marwan laid a hand on his shoulder. "They're waiting for you to be involved in washing and preparing the body. It was the deceased's wish."

Omar closed his eyes. The privilege of a blood son. An honorable duty, which explained the exceptional release he was given. Even after death, Uncle Mustafa proved to be a true father to him. Omar rested his head.

"It seems Shareef is too shaken to do anything useful." Marwan gave his shoulder a gentle squeeze before he dropped his hand. "My sister tells me ever since Shareef brought Sameera home, he has been acting a bit strange."

"I know." Omar's voice sounded odd to his own ears.

"Is that why you didn't come home on your breaks?"

Omar remained quiet. How could he explain that he felt Shareef didn't welcome his presence in the house? He watched every move his wife made around Omar, acting like a jealous, over-suspicious buffoon. Besides, there was no room for Omar to sleep. With part of the living room closed to create private quarters for the married couple, he didn't feel right about sharing the girls' room. Especially with Nadia having turned seventeen, and Huda sucking in her breath whenever she saw him. The one time he had come home, he had spent the night at Fatimah's place and then invented reasons to return to the academy earlier than scheduled. One day he would return to his father's house in Jerusalem and be done with this space hopping, landing out-of-place with each step he took. He heaved a heavy sigh. That day better come soon.

Marwan seemed to have gotten the hint from Omar's silence, and he stayed quiet the rest of the way.

At home, Omar threw himself into the process of preparing Uncle Mustafa for his burial. Joined by the Imam from the local mosque, Omar and Waleed followed his instructions on how to wash the body, where to start, what prayers to say, how to perform ablution for a dead person, and how to wrap the three-layered white linen shroud.

Shareef hovered around, observing the ritual and proving himself to be useless. Through it all, Omar escaped in his mind somewhere else, to an orchard carpeted with flowering almond trees. Before his eyes, Uncle Mustafa tended to his orchard with happy energy, not spread cold and still on the wooden table under his hands. From behind the closed door of Mama Subhia's bedroom, the sound of women's soft weeping drifted through the house and he latched onto Nadia's intermittent sobs. When it was time to take out the body, the house filled with men: neighbors, friends and co-workers. Shareef, Waleed and Omar carried the body on a stretcher down the stairs to a waiting van. They passed through throngs of men murmuring prayers and reaching out their hands to share the load part of the way in accordance with tradition.

The van crawled its way through the neighborhood. Men filed into cars and followed. Loud speakers mounted on top of the van broadcast the funeral attendant's calls for people to forgive the deceased, loving husband and caring father, listing Uncle Mustafa's qualities and good deeds. The calls invited anyone to whom the deceased was indebted to get in touch with his son for payment or to forego the debt altogether. Shareef sat in the passenger seat of the van to declare his position as head of the family. He remained distant from the crowds that gathered in the streets during the procession.

Omar walked on foot alongside the van most of the way. Some of Uncle Mustafa's friends grasped his hand and tried to give him money, claiming they were paying back their debts to Uncle Mustafa. But he knew there was no way Uncle Mustafa had loaned anyone money. He had none to spare.

Omar invited the men to the traditional main meal held after the burial. No one seemed to question his position in the family, dealing with him instead of Shareef. A blank expression was stamped on Shareef's face and Omar couldn't tell if he minded the crowds' misplaced attention, or if he was too self-involved to notice his marginalization. After the special prayer held at the mosque over Uncle Mustafa's body, the procession headed out of the neighborhood. Omar got in Marwan's car and they took off to the cemetery.

Three days of mourning passed like a blur. The family was almost never left alone. Women paid their respects from morning to late afternoon; men filed in during the evening. The next-door neighbors opened their home to accommodate the overflow of people, lining the walls with rented chairs. At night, everyone crawled into beds exhausted and emotionally spent. Omar slept on the sofa in the partitioned living room.

On the last night, after the house fell into relative quiet, Omar sought his favorite spot on the roof. He had managed to avoid a confrontation with Shareef so far, but it was time to have a serious talk with him to work out the details concerning the family's financial situation. Shareef's income from his part-time job wouldn't be enough to keep the family afloat, even with Huda's contribution. Now that he had graduated, Omar's salary from the army should cover most expenses, but he wouldn't receive it until the end of the month. He needed to check what bills must be taken care of before then, come up with a payment plan.

The door behind him creaked open, and he turned to see who had followed him.

Fatimah stood in the doorway. The stairs' light from behind cast her in a saint-like halo. "Mind if I join you?"

He motioned for her to come sit on the railing next to him. Taking off his jacket, he draped it around her shoulders. "There's a chill tonight."

"I don't feel anything." She sounded exhausted, defeated.

"What are you still doing here?" He rubbed her shoulder. "You should go home to your husband."

"I was at the neighbors'. Huda and I helped them put their house back in order. It's Sunday and they missed their church time because of us."

"The Rafids are good people. I hope we will be able to return their favors under better circumstances."

"One of their daughters is bound to get married. We'll step in then." Fatimah took Omar's hand in hers. "I know it's not the right time, but congratulations, Second Lieutenant." She squeezed his hand. "You made Uncle Mustafa proud."

Omar swallowed a lump. "Please don't do this now."

Fatimah lowered her head and whispered, "Someone has to say it. I'm proud too. And Waleed. He can't stop bragging about you to his colleagues at school."

He gave her a quick hug. "I appreciate it."

"Come home with me. Nadia told me you've been sleeping on the sofa. There's a private room waiting for you at my place."

As appealing an idea as it was, he wouldn't allow himself to impose on Waleed's home for two weeks without the man's clear invitation. There was Um Waleed to consider as well. Omar raised his eyebrows. "What about your husband?"

"Waleed insists. He would have told you himself, but he had to go home early and you were busy with the men." She furrowed her brows. "Do you really need an invitation from him?"

Omar examined his hands.

She nudged his shoulder with hers. "Or are you enjoying Shareef and Sameera's abuse?"

He blew out a long breath. "I know what Shareef is doing, unable to trust his wife. He thinks, like him, I lack morals."

"Shareef is stupid and Sameera is worse. She's been getting on Mama Subhia's nerves ever since she moved in. Bothering Nadia too. Forgot she used to be her friend."

Omar looked into the distance, a thousand questions in his mind. "How is she?" He started with the one he needed answered the most.

"Mama Subhia is strong." Fatimah missed his intention. "She's undone now, but she'll pull through. The death wasn't a surprise. We all saw it coming." Fatimah brushed tears from her cheeks. "I suspect now that Uncle Mustafa is gone, Mama Subhia will not have to tiptoe around Sameera. God rest his soul, he didn't want tension in the house. Watch and see, Mama Subhia and Huda will put Sameera in her place."

Lowering his voice, Omar tried again. "I haven't been able to see much of the girls. Are they all right?"

"The little ones are devastated, but I worry about Nadia the most."

"Why?" He gave up on covering his concern. "What's wrong with Nadia?"

"Nadia has always depended on you, Omar. Since you left, Uncle Mustafa tried to fill the void. They became closer. Now that he's gone, she has no one." Fatimah rose to her feet, pulling Omar with her. "You should spend some time with Nadia before you leave. Get her to open up to you like you used to." Fatimah patted his hand. "She adores you."

His cheeks heated. He bent down and pretended to fix the creases on his pants legs, hiding his face and his embarrassing reaction to Fatimah's innocent remark. What would Fatimah think of him if she knew the depth of his feelings for Nadia? Would she remain proud of him?

Omar spent his days running errands for Mama Subhia and the girls, making sure not to be in the house when Shareef wasn't there. He had to borrow money from Marwan to cover what was needed until his salary kicked in. The debt to Marwan weighed on Omar's shoulders, but he had no choice.

Gathering the courage to take Nadia out on a walk like old times was difficult. It felt wrong on many levels. Her unblemished innocence had disappeared, leaving behind a melancholic maturity that chipped at his confidence. He checked on the family every evening before he retired to Fatimah's place for the night. Seeing Nadia sad and withdrawn tore at his heart. She sat by her mother's side, not saying a word, refusing to meet his eyes when he took his leave at the end of the evening. Like him, Nadia was grieving the loss of more than just a father. She needed a compassionate shoulder, and Omar couldn't bring himself to provide one. He was leaving in a few days and she would experience another loss if he grew closer. So he kept a reserved distance, hoping it was the decent thing to do.

Every afternoon, however, around the time the school day ended, Omar stood behind a big tree across the street from Nadia's school and waited for her to come out. He allowed himself one convoluted pleasure, despicable and demeaning as it was: following her home and staying out of sight. He noticed small gestures and committed them to memory — the way she hugged her books to her chest, the swing of her hips while she walked, the blue ribbon with the white lace fringes she tied her ponytail with almost every day, the slight tilt of her head to the right when she listened to her friends, the frequent tugging at the top button of her uniform shirt — little details Omar thought were his and his alone.

There was no justification for what he did, no honor in his stalking, but he couldn't stop. He craved the uncensored sight of Nadia. Alone in his bed at night, he chastised himself when his imagination ran wild. He made promises to quit the secret chase, and then broke them the following afternoon. The will to stay away had no place in an infatuated man's heart.

The following week, during breakfast one morning in early June, Fatimah asked Omar if he felt ill, remarking on his diminished appetite.

"I'm just worried about what's coming." He gave her a valid reason, though not the only one. "Israel's threats to attack Syria are gaining momentum."

Waleed turned on the radio. The monotonous voice of a broadcaster reported news. "You think we're headed for war?"

"War is inevitable."

Waleed glanced at Fatimah. "Don't worry, Nasser and the Egyptian army will back us up."

"Will they send Omar to the front lines?" Fatimah's eyes darted back and forth between her brother and her husband.

Omar nodded. "I'm almost certain of that. Most of th —"

A loud beep from the radio interrupted him. The broadcaster announced an urgent statement to follow. Everyone dropped what they were doing. Their heads turned toward the radio, as if the reporter were going to poke his head out of the radio box with the breaking news.

Israel had launched a surprise attack on Egyptian air bases in the early hours of the morning.

Omar jumped to his feet. "Shit! It's happening already." He rushed to the radio and raised the volume.

Military statements followed one after the other, giving updates about the situation on the Egyptian front. Most of the Egyptian jetfighters were destroyed on the ground. A handful were able to take off. Egyptian army troops were deployed toward Sinai.

Omar paced the floor like a caged lion. After each update, he would burst out with a curse or a statement of his own.

Fatimah became obsessed with clearing the table, going back and forth to the kitchen, one plate in hand at a time. Silent tears flowed down her cheeks. On her last trip, Waleed grabbed her elbow and wrapped his arms around her. "Everything is going to be fine."

Fatimah shook her head. "I can't listen to this."

"We should do something, damn it," Omar yelled at the radio. "Support our Egyptian brothers." He went into his room and returned minutes later with his uniform on.

Fatimah blocked his path. "Where are you going?" she screamed, her face stricken by fear.

134

"Move out of his way," Waleed said, his voice tender. "Omar is an army officer. He's expected to report to his base."

Instead of moving aside, Fatimah threw her arms around Omar's neck. "No," she wailed. "Not yet. Not yet."

Omar unlatched Fatimah's arms and brought them down to his chest. "I must go." He gave her a tight hug, and then moved her into Waleed's arms. "I promise to come back."

CHAPTER
NINETEEN

During the following six days, the family gathered around the radio in Mama Subhia's house. Riveted, they followed reports of battle close to the Golan Heights at the Syrian front, of Egyptian troop movements in Sinai, and of the Jordanian efforts in the West Bank.

Out of respect for Mama Subhia's mourning period, Shareef and Waleed tried to contain their enthusiasm when statements came out reporting that the Egyptian army had passed through Sinai toward the Negev desert heading for Tel Aviv. Each evening, they joined men at the local café to follow news and discuss developing details. Men who had sons or brothers in the army gloated among their friends. Shareef joined in, boasting of his relation to Second Lieutenant Omar Bakry.

One evening, Shareef jumped atop a small round table and bragged, "I used to help Omar train at home before he even joined the military academy."

Waleed gritted his teeth and swallowed a nasty come-back. Shareef acted like he and Omar were the best of friends, pretending his selfishness and blatant animosity toward Omar for forcing him to salvage the family honor had never occurred. What right did he have to claim any of Omar's accomplishments in this war?

An older neighbor announced a round of free hot tea for everyone in the café. "My son is in infantry. I bet he's heading his troop and will be the first to set foot in Tel Aviv."

Another man shouted from his corner, "My nephew is with the air force. His jetfighter will fly over the city first."

Elation filled the air. Cheers could be heard from the streets at all times. People broke out in jubilant cries as news of the three Arab armies' advancement to liberate Palestine poured in. Waleed recounted some of the happenings in the café to Fatimah when he returned home, further fueling her hopes and aspirations.

Despite Fatimah's intense worry about Omar's fate, she couldn't help dreaming about moving back to their father's house in Jerusalem. She talked about it many times. Waleed was confident the joined forces of the three Arab armies would wipe out the Israeli army. He and everyone else. Military statements on the radio confirmed victory was imminent. Patriotic songs filled the air between updates. Um Kulthoom, the famous singer, ignited nationalistic ardor with her passionate voice and zealous words. Other entertainers pitched in, some adored by younger crowds, including the young singer Abdul Haleem whom Nadia worshipped. Every Palestinian refugee, young or old, rode the euphoric wave; they would soon return home.

★　★　★

Lounging in her husband's arms, Fatimah tilted her head and traced a finger along Waleed's jaw. "Do you think my father's house is still standing?"

Waleed murmured unintelligible words, struggling to stay awake.

Fatimah flipped to her side and kissed his chin. "Do you?"

He opened his eyes. "Don't know."

"I remember the way the house smelled at dawn. The fragrance from the orange and lemon trees in our grove mixed with thyme and olive oil. Every morning, my mother baked thyme bread for Father before he left to work in the orchard."

"Thyme bread sounds good right now." Waleed licked his lips. "Do we have any?"

Fatimah sighed. "I'll bake in the morning."

"Why not now?" He nuzzled her neck. "I'm hungry."

"I'm not fiddling in the kitchen in the middle of the night. What would your mother think?"

"My mother thinks I'm the luckiest man alive." He ran a hand up her leg. "Want to make me hungrier so it would be worthwhile?" His voice was husky and seductive.

Fatimah wiggled out of his arms and rested her back on the headboard. "I'm trying to tell you something. It's important."

Waleed's hand went under her nightgown. "More important than me?"

"You're impossible." She playfully kicked him away. "I'm serious. Will you listen?"

138

Waleed scrambled onto his hands and knees, bringing his head forward. "Listening."

She held his face in her palms. "Do you know why I asked you about my father's house?"

"You would have your home back, Fatimah. I promise to build it again if it's razed to the ground."

"Good." She dropped her hands to her belly. "Because I want our baby to be born on my father's land."

It took Waleed several seconds to process what she had said. When comprehension dawned, his eyes widened. He put his hand over hers. "Are you sure?" He choked on his words.

She nodded. "Three months."

Waleed jumped off the bed and ran out of the bedroom. "Um Waleed!" He called out for his mother. "I'm going to be a father!"

"If it's a boy, we will name him Fawzi, after my father, of course." Waleed informed Mama the following morning, handing her a plate of the best *kanafeh* dessert his mother had ever made.

Serving dessert in the morning was an exception, in celebration of the great news. It was also Mama's first outing while in mourning. Wearing a black dress and a white scarf draped over both shoulders, she beamed at her son-in-law. "Of course. And if it's a girl?"

"Mariam," Fatimah answered, her voice firm and unwavering. "My mother's name."

Giving up on using a fork, little Farah licked her fingers, producing unappetizing noises. "Fatimah, your father is dead too. Why not name your son after him?"

Fatimah gave Farah a motherly smile, soft and serene. "It's the son's right to pass on the name of his father, not the daughter's."

Farah turned to Sameera. "When you have a son, Shareef is going to be Abu Mustafa?"

Mama dabbed her eyes with her handkerchief.

Sameera patted Farah's head. "It won't be soon." Her words fell flat. A string of cheese dangled from her lower lip. "Shareef isn't ready to have children yet."

Innocent of the workings of Sameera's marriage, Farah tried to play with the cheese string. "Why not?"

Huda swatted Farah's hand away. "This is not the right conversation for someone your age." Huda's sharp voice added weight to the air in the room. "Eat your *kanafeh* and stay out of the adults' affairs."

"What was your father's name, Fatimah?" Unfazed, Farah ran her tongue up her wrist, following a drop of sweet syrup. "I don't think I've heard it before."

"Jamal. Jamal Ali Bakry." Fatimah's pride mixed with amusement in her tone.

"Omar will be Abu Jamal, then?"

Nadia followed the conversation from her corner. She lifted her head when Omar's name was mentioned. "Could we turn on the radio, please? We missed the nine o'clock news."

"Right." Waleed put his plate down. He turned on the radio, raising the volume all the way.

Um Waleed motioned for him to bring it down a notch. "It's the same news, anyway."

Waleed complied, but stayed by the radio, one ear to the news and the other to the women.

140

"May Allah bestow victory on our troops soon." Um Waleed raised her palms toward the ceiling. "When they reach Tel Aviv, I swear I will put henna on my hair and dance on the roof." She turned to Mama. "You will have to forgive me, my dear."

"I will stop wearing black and join you as soon as Omar makes it home."

Waleed's curse penetrated the women's talk, silencing Mama. He cranked up the volume.

News of a major setback of the Egyptian army broke in. Abdul Hakim Amer, the Egyptian army chief commander, had issued orders for a tactical retreat from Sinai toward Suez Canal.

Fatimah sprang out of her seat. "What happened?"

As if the broadcaster had heard her question, his heavy voice, lacking the luster and passion of the previous six days, continued with the bulletin. Having destroyed the majority of Egyptian jetfighters during the first aerial strike, Israeli air forces delivered a devastating blow to tanks and artillery on the ground, inflicting heavy casualties among troops.

Staring at the radio in disbelief, Waleed put his hands on his head. "God have mercy. This is a disaster."

More disturbing news followed. The same scenario happened on the Syrian front. Without aerial cover, Syrian troops faltered. The Golan Heights fell to the Israelis.

"Why the hell is it the first time we are hearing about this?" Waleed shouted at no one in particular.

Fatimah went to his side. "Is this true? Were they lying to us? Or are they lying now?"

"Maybe the BBC has better coverage." Waleed's hands shook while turning the radio dial.

A BBC reporter confirmed the alarming news, adding that Israel had taken over the West Bank and eastern Jerusalem as well.

Waleed slid to the floor, his knees unable to carry the weight of this tragic turn. Fatimah dropped down next to him. "This can't be," she wailed. "The past week lies? All lies?"

Um Waleed launched into a series of damning prayers, asking for God's wrath to descend on everyone responsible, blasting to eternal damnation the Israelis, misleading politicians, Arab radio reporters with their false propaganda, all the way to Jamal Abdul Nasser himself.

Mama fell into a state of catatonia, her eyes fixed on a point in the space between the radio and Fatimah's head.

Nadia wrapped her arms around her mother. "Omar will be all right," she repeated over and over, then nodded at Sameera. "And your brother, Ahmad."

Sameera broke down crying.

Huda, the first to recover from the shock, knelt beside Fatimah and urged her to her feet. "Waleed, help me take her to bed. This is not good for her."

Huda's commanding tone brought everyone out of their daze. In a strange way, there was something sensible in her aggravating voice. Her unflinching attitude solidified the revealed intelligence. Yes, this was happening. The three Arab armies were defeated.

★ ★ ★

142

Back at home, Nadia opened the door to let Shareef in, his face solemn.

"Everyone is in total shock. People are gathering in the streets. No one knows what to do." He dropped on the sofa and rubbed his neck. "I guess I better go to the bank. Withdraw as much cash as possible."

"Why?" Nadia asked.

"We have to get out of here."

She held on to the doorjambs with both hands. "I thought our armies were on the outskirts of Tel Aviv. You think the Israelis will reach Damascus instead?"

He nodded. "Their air fighters might try, and we don't have the means to stop them. What we heard on the news was all propaganda to boost morale."

"Where would we go?" Her voice vanished on the last word.

Mama marched into the room. "We are not going anywhere."

He jumped off the sofa. "I'm the man of this family. I have to protect everyone and I say we should head north, away from the capital."

Mama crossed both arms over her chest. "We are staying here until Omar comes back."

"There have been heavy casualties. Omar might never return."

Mama staggered a couple of steps back, Shareef's words landing like slaps across her face.

Nadia went to her side and held her in her arms. "You don't know that."

Shareef lifted his arms to his sides, then dropped them in exasperation. "I can't find out if he's alive or where he is. No one can. Sameera's brothers tried to find out about Ahmad. Nothing. Reports are coming in that bombing Damascus is imminent. The Israelis are coming. We can't stay here."

"Let them come!" Mama shouted, tears flowing down her cheeks. "We lost our home once. Let them try to take this one too, and let them see what will happen. Let them try!"

Nadia stroked her mother's shoulders. "Please calm down."

At that moment, Huda walked in through the front door. "I heard your voices from the street. What's going on?"

"How's Fatimah?" Mama asked, her voice raspy.

"Better. She will be fine once her nerves calm. Waleed should keep her from listening to the news. What's the shouting about?"

Mama swung a hand in Shareef's direction. "Your brother wants us to flee the city."

Shareef rounded on Huda. "Tell her. She won't believe me. They might drop bombs over our heads any minute now."

"That's true."

He turned to his mother. "See? We can't wait for Omar. God only knows what happened to him."

Huda narrowed her eyes. "If you want to run, then take your wife and go. I'm planning to volunteer at the hospital to help the wounded." She put a hand on Nadia's shoulder. "I came to see if you would like to join me? They need hands. I know you can handle it."

144

"It's the least I can do." Nadia kissed her mother's hand. "Your blessings, Mama?"

"Go." Mama headed to the door. "I will talk to the neighbors to gather blankets and other essentials."

Huda threw Shareef one of her dagger-like sneers. "They're calling for people to donate blood." She swept him with her eyes from head to toe. "You can spare some, I'm sure."

CHAPTER
TWENTY

Strong smells challenged Nadia to keep the contents of her stomach in check. Disinfectant odors mixed with the metallic scent of blood and threatened her willpower. Because she lacked medical training, she was assigned to one of the registration stations receiving blood donors at the main hospital in the city center. Stiffening her body in order to stay in control, she jotted down the names and ages of men filing in. The depressing news had aged their faces considerably.

Huda disappeared into the hospital to help nurses with the influx of injured soldiers coming in from the military hospital. Army doctors sent mild cases to local hospitals in order to manage the overflow.

Concentrating on her work, Nadia flipped to a new page in the register. Without lifting her head, she asked the same question for the thousandth time since she arrived.

"Name?"

"Marwan Barady."

Nadia's hand froze on the white page. She lifted her head. Omar's friend? He had his eyes on his wallet, taking out his civil registration card. A scowl creased his forehead. Handing his card over, he met her eyes.

"Nadia?" Surprise added a tremor to his deep voice. He looked around. "Are you here by yourself?"

Taken aback by his condescending question, Nadia wrote down his specifications in the register. "Huda is inside the hospital with the nurses." She gave him a defiant stare. "I'm old enough to do my share."

Marwan shifted his weight, embarrassed or impatient. She couldn't tell.

"Right." He held her gaze. "I wondered if Shareef was also here. I plan to go over to the military hospital once I am done to ask about . . ." He swallowed the rest of his sentence.

Nadia arched her eyebrows.

"To see if they needed help there," he continued. "I could take Shareef with me."

"It's best not to wait for Shareef. I have no idea if he'll show up." She handed him back his card. "Do you have relatives in the army?"

"Three cousins." Marwan nodded, twisting his mouth sideways.

What did he mean by that expression? If only she had more experience reading men. "I pray for their safe return."

"Thank you." He slipped his card in his wallet. "I tried to enlist, but they wouldn't take me."

Embarrassment. That was what she couldn't read on his face. He was ashamed for being young and healthy and not fighting alongside his cousins.

"I know. You're like Shareef, an only son." Nadia pointed to a curtain behind her. "You are needed here."

Marwan placed his palms flat on the table, leaning forward. "Everything all right at home, Nadia?"

His face too close to hers, her cheeks flushed and she nodded hurriedly.

"Your mother well? Anything I can do?" His tone sounded urgent and sincere. "Need anything?"

Something warm in his dark eyes made her reach out and touch the back of his hand. "When you ask about your cousins, will you try to find out about Omar too?"

Marwan straightened, pulling his hand back. He glanced at the group of men nearby. Raising his voice, he addressed the men, "I will ask about your relative at the military hospital for you." He returned his eyes to hers. "Please telephone my sister at home should your family need anything. You have our number?"

Nadia looked past him toward the crowd. The men, engrossed in war discussions, didn't seem to notice her interaction with him. "I believe Huda does."

Marwan rolled up his sleeve, gave her a hint of a smile, and disappeared behind the curtain.

That night, Nadia crawled into bed after she had bathed and sprayed her pillow with perfume. She needed to get the hospital smell out of her nose. She and Huda had the room to themselves. Mama had taken the little girls to her bedroom, giving them peace and quiet after the long, emotionally draining day.

Closing her eyes, Nadia thought of Marwan. His enigmatic dark eyes. His rough tanned hand. His pride. His concern. She had waited for him to return with news of Omar, but the day had ended without seeing him again. Shareef had shown up in the afternoon, giving blood and barely acknowledging what she told him about Marwan's efforts to find Omar.

Hugging her pillow tight, she thought of Huda sleeping in her bed at the farthest side of the room. On their way home, Huda had grown silent, a distant and strange expression on her face. Accustomed to seeing blood, it couldn't have been the shock of tending to injured soldiers. Something else had driven her deep inside herself, making her appear vulnerable. A first, as long as Nadia could remember. She didn't know how to approach Huda, comfort her.

Nadia flipped onto her back. She looked toward the window. On nights like these, when sleep eluded her, she would stare at the moon and let her imagination take her to faraway places. But tonight, the windowpanes were painted dark blue. Shareef had followed instructions broadcast on the radio for safeguarding homes from possible aerial strikes. But he had done a poor job, missing the corners, allowing the moonlight to filter through. She squinted to peek at the moon from one of the missed corners. The waning crescent was fading, despondent and sad. Everything around her was depressing, everyone dispirited and dejected. Even the moon had lost hope.

She concentrated on a darker shadow near the light fixture dangling from the ceiling. When Father passed away, Mama had told her younger sisters he watched over them from heaven. Was he watching over Omar too? Would he keep him safe? Bring him home?

Muffled hiccups drifted from the other side of the room. Nadia lifted her head. Sobs were coming from Huda's corner. Leaving her bed, Nadia walked barefoot to stand over Huda.

"Are you all right?"

Huda lay on her side, facing the wall. She shook her head and tugged her blanket tighter around her shoulders.

"Are you cold?" Nadia felt a chill travel down her spine, not related to the weather. Huda's crying became louder, clearer. Nadia lifted the edge of the blanket and slipped under it. She wrapped her arms around her sister. "I'm cold too."

In the early hours of the morning, a loud boom propelled Nadia and Huda out of bed. Nadia clung to Huda in the brief deafening silence that followed. Every muscle in Nadia's body froze, including her lungs.

Slapping her across the face, Huda shouted, "Breathe!"

Sirens pierced the unnatural stillness. They ran out and joined the others in the hallway. Shareef held Sameera in his arms. Mama kept the little ones by her side.

"What was it?" Mama hugged the girls closer. "Where did it strike?"

"I think the Abu Rummaneh area," Shareef said. "Possibly targeting the army headquarters."

Mama sat on the floor, pulling the girls with her. "Don't be afraid. Don't be afraid."

Banging on the door called for Shareef to leave the safety of the hallway. He returned a couple of seconds later. "The neighbor, Mr Rafid. Checking if we were fine." He plopped down next to his wife.

"What are you doing?" Huda barked.

"What?" Shareef stared at her with his mouth open.

"Get up!" She shoved his shoulder. "Go help Mr Rafid check on everyone. You're the only men in the building."

Sameera held on to Shareef's arm. "We need him here."

Mama rested her head back on the wall and closed her eyes. "Go, son. Let us pray no one is hurt from shattered windows or anything like that."

Shareef headed out after getting dressed, his wife begging him all the while not to go.

The phone rang. Huda answered it. Dragging Nadia by the arm, she headed to the bedroom. "That was Um Waleed. Get dressed. Waleed is on his way to walk us back to his place. Fatimah is bleeding."

Nadia ran to the bathroom with a bucket of soiled linen for the third time.

"How's Fatimah doing?" Waleed followed her, right on her heels. "What's happening?"

"I don't know." She removed the soiled cloth rags into a bag, then dumped the contents of the bucket in the toilet. Red water spilled on her legs and the front of her dress. Frantic, she splashed clean water from the sink.

Waleed grabbed her by the elbows. "Is this my baby's blood?"

"I don't know." Tears and sweat dampened her face.

"Is my baby dead?" His eyes bore into hers, cold and frightening.

"I don't know," she repeated, louder this time.

Waleed shook her. "Tell me something, damn it."

"I don't know anything!" she yelled. "All I see is blood, and they are too busy to tell me anything." She shoved him aside. "I have to get back."

Another loud explosion penetrated the air, knocking Nadia to the floor and throwing Waleed against the wall. He helped her to her feet and ran to the bedroom.

Um Waleed hurried to block him from coming closer to the bed. "Huda has the bleeding under control. We have to take Fatimah to the hospital." Um Waleed held his arms. "There's nothing more Huda can do."

"Get her ready." Panic laced Waleed's voice. "I will get a taxi."

"You're not going to find a taxi in this chaos," Huda said over her shoulder. She sat at the edge of the bed, facing Fatimah and keeping her back to Waleed. "And no ambulance will get here in time. They're heading for the bombed sites."

Nadia sloshed forward, the hem of her dress dripping water. "Marwan Barady has a car. I'm sure he will help."

"Yes, call him," Huda urged. "His number is in the little brown book in my purse. Waleed, get more blankets. Um Waleed, get me a clean gown."

CHAPTER
TWENTY-ONE

Marwan drove as fast he could, maneuvering his way through streets full of disarray and confusion. Cars hurried in the direction of the bombed areas, columns of smoke making the mark. People bustled, calling out for children to return home.

Waleed ran toward the main doors of the hospital with Fatimah in his arms, his mother and Huda trying to match his steps.

Marwan touched Nadia's elbow. "She'll be fine."

"I should go in with them." But Nadia didn't move her feet. Twisting her body sideways, she bent at the waist and retched by the back tire. After the convulsions subsided, she straightened, ran a hand over her hair. Most of her ponytail escaped the blue ribbon holding it.

"Huda was wrong," she heaved. "I can't handle it. Not the smell of blood. Not the sight of it."

"I'll take you home." Marwan guided her into the passenger seat, his hands hovering over her shoulders, not making contact. "Your mother is probably worried sick."

As soon as the car took off, an airplane crossed the sky in front of their eyes. Nadia doubled over, clasped her hands over the back of her head. "More bombs," she shrieked.

Marwan stopped the car. Another jet roared by. He craned his neck out the window. "Those are our jetfighters. Chasing the Israeli pilot away."

Nadia unlaced her fingers and lifted her head. "Ours? Are you sure?"

"Certain."

She straightened her back. "But they said on the radio we don't have any planes left."

"I guess some were spared. I saw one jetfighter in the air on my way over, and now those two." Marwan draped one arm over the steering wheel. "Not that it will make any godda . . . any difference now." He stared at the sky. "It's all over."

"Did you learn anything about Omar?"

"Omar's regiment was sent to the battle front with the first wave."

Nadia inhaled a sharp breath.

"I will keep searching."

"And your cousins?"

"Two are back already. They didn't get to do anything. The retreat happened before they made it to the front lines." He started the car again. "Still trying to find the third one."

"I want Omar to come home." Nadia's lower lip quivered.

"He will." Marwan breathed out his words, doubting he sounded reassuring.

She closed her eyes and shook her head. "I can't believe three armies lost the war in what? Six days?"

Her blue ribbon came undone, fell to her shoulder and slipped between the two seats.

Marwan's eyes followed the escaping ribbon. He inserted two fingers in the small space, extracted the ribbon and tucked it in his shirt pocket. Roaming his eyes over Nadia, he worried about her disheveled appearance: her hair a big mess, her dress soiled and stained, her white shoes caked with what must have been dried blood. He killed the car engine.

Nadia opened her eyes. "Is it not safe to drive yet?"

"Do you know if Shareef is home?"

"No idea. He went to check on the neighbors before I left. He should be back by now, why?"

Marwan averted his eyes to the side. "I can't take you home."

"Something wrong?"

"We should stop at my house first."

Nadia jerked upright. "Just who do you think I am?"

"My sisters will be there, I swear. I want them to come with us."

"Why?"

"People shouldn't see you leaving my car without a chaperone. Shareef in particular." Marwan dropped his gaze to his lap. "Sorry for being blunt, but I know how his mind works. I will not put you in a position where you would have to explain yourself to Shareef, or to anyone else."

Nadia put her hand on the door handle. "I don't believe this. We're in the middle of a mess and that is where your mind goes."

"Shareef is the one who will think that, looking for an excuse to get in my face."

"I don't see why he would. You helped him with his marriage, didn't you?"

"He doesn't see it that way."

"What do you mean?"

Marwan regretted his words the instant he uttered them, unsure of how much Nadia knew of his role in pushing Shareef to honor his obligation to Sameera. Help was not the right word. He did assist Omar in trapping and beating Shareef, if one wanted to be accurate. "No man likes to be indebted in such matters."

"I will never understand men." She pushed open the door. "I'll walk home."

"That solves nothing. You think I would have you walk alone in this chaos?"

Nadia placed one foot on the ground.

He grabbed her wrist. "Listen. You don't have to go into my house. Stay in the car. I will have my sisters come out to you."

She glared at him. "Let me go."

Marwan withdrew his hand and placed it on his chest. "You don't know the kind of man I am. Omar asked me to watch out for you while he's gone, and that's what I intend to do."

At the mention of Omar's name, Nadia paused. "Watch out for me?" She flung her hands in the air and burst out, "I'm not a child anymore."

"Precisely my point." Marwan's voice shook. He took a deep breath. "On my honor. I'm thinking of your best interest."

156

Hesitation seeped into her eyes. "How far is it to your house from here?"

"Half an hour, but with this mayhem, it might take longer."

"I'm sitting in the back."

Marwan parked the car at the opening of a narrow alley. He pointed down the way. "The car won't fit through here. My house is the second door to the right." He left the car. "I'll be right back."

A couple of minutes later, a tall girl carrying a large bag walked up the alley. She opened the passenger door and slipped inside, a gentle smile on her face. "Hello, Nadia. I'm Rihab. Remember me?"

"Huda's friend."

"We met at Fatimah's wedding." Rihab handed over the bag. "I brought you a wrap-around skirt. I hope it fits over your soiled dress." She signaled with her hand toward the house. "Want me to get you slippers?"

"Thank you, no need for slippers. This skirt is enough." Nadia lifted her hands to her hair. "I could use a hair tie. I lost my ribbon on the street."

Rihab dug in her purse and handed over a hair tie and a comb. "Hurry, Nadia. We have nosy neighbors."

Nadia wrapped the skirt around her waist, braided her hair and did the best she could to put her looks in order. "I'm ready."

Rihab honked the car horn twice. Marwan left the house, two girls ahead of him. The girls, younger than Nadia, introduced themselves before they joined her in the back. Marwan threw a quick glance toward Nadia

157

and then started the car. Rihab tried to strike a conversation on the way. Nadia remained quiet. She spent the time comparing Rihab's tranquil nature to Huda's abrasive one. Both women had the ability to take charge and solve problems, each in her unique way. What kind of woman was she turning out to be? A helpless one in need of someone like Marwan to watch over her? A pathetic weak woman?

Everyone climbed up the stairs to Nadia's apartment, Marwan a considerable distance behind the girls.

Mama opened the door. "*Alhamdullilah*. What took you so long?" She took in Nadia's strange appearance. "Huda called from the hospital about an hour ago. Said you were on your way here."

"My fault." Rihab placed her hands on her sisters' shoulders. "I made Marwan promise to come back home as soon as he dropped everyone off at the hospital. I was worried. It's a mess out there. How is Fatimah?"

"Better. The baby too. Fatimah might spend the rest of her pregnancy in bed, I'm afraid." Mama held Nadia by the arms. "What happened to you?"

"I'll explain later," Nadia whispered. "We should thank Marwan for his help."

"Where is he?"

"Behind us on the stairs," Rihab said.

Mama pushed Rihab aside and craned her neck out the door. "Come up, Marwan," she called out.

Marwan hurried his steps.

158

"Please, come in, come in." Mama gestured toward the living room. "This whole business is so upsetting. I asked Shareef to take Sameera to her family. I couldn't handle more of her crying. He should be back any minute now."

Salma and Farah came in. They greeted Marwan's younger sisters with enthusiasm.

Nadia ran into her room, changed her dress and shoes and came back out with Rihab's skirt in a plastic bag.

"We need to get going." Marwan took the bag from her hands. "I have to check on my store. Need anything? Do you have enough candles? Bread?"

"We have enough." Mama held Marwan's right hand with both of hers. "I don't know what would have happened to Fatimah if it were not for you. Thank you."

"No need. No need."

"Can the girls stay for a bit?" Mama added with a hopeful smile. "We could use some distraction."

Marwan's eyes met Rihab's. He raised his eyebrows. She nodded.

It reminded Nadia of the way Omar checked with Fatimah before making a decision. Shareef never did that with her or any of their sisters. A stab of jealousy mingled with shame in Nadia's chest. When would Omar come home?

Marwan headed for the door. "I'll be back in a couple of hours."

Nadia followed him. "I'm thankful for all your help." She opened the door.

"Let me know when Fatimah is ready to go home. I'll be happy to drive." Marwan stepped out and almost ran into Shareef.

Shareef darted his eyes back and forth between them. "Drive her where?" He thrust his chin toward Marwan. "What are you doing here?"

"Dropping off your sister." Marwan squared his shoulders and inflated his chest, his stance combative.

"The hell you were." Shareef's voice gained momentum.

Nadia grabbed Shareef's arm. "Come, meet Marwan's sisters. We all just got here." She pulled Shareef into the house. Before she closed the door, her eyes connected with Marwan's. He broke into a wide smile with a "told-you-so" expression clear on his face.

Late that afternoon, Marwan dropped flat on his bed. He rubbed exhaustion out of his eyes, telling himself he would rest for ten minutes before heading out again. He had spent most of the day at the military hospital, distributing supplies and talking to injured soldiers. He had tried to lift their spirits, but the reality they all faced couldn't be down-played. They had lost their healthy bodies, many of their friends, their pride and, most importantly, they had lost the war. Nevertheless, Marwan had tried his best to tell them they were welcome back, that the real culprits of this catastrophic failure would be held accountable. Words had bounced off the walls and landed void of real meaning on the soldiers' bandaged bodies. Marwan had kept at it, thinking that if he repeated his words enough times, he too might believe them.

He had asked about his cousin and Omar. One of the soldiers, blinded with a long scar across his face, told him he had heard Omar's name mentioned before he was transferred from Quneitra, the closest military hospital behind the Golan Heights retreat line.

Still on his back, Marwan checked his watch. Close to five. He should call Shareef to let him know the news, offer to take him on the two-hour drive. Setting the tension between them aside, he had no doubt Shareef would want to see Omar.

Rihab entered his room carrying a food tray. "You're not going anywhere before you eat something."

Ever since they lost their parents, Rihab had taken the role of a mother, taking care of his younger sisters and running the household, leaving him to mind their father's business. She set the tray on his desk and sat next to him.

"Can't you wait until tomorrow to go? You look terrible."

"I'll be fine." He stretched his arms over his head and arched his back.

"What is this?" Rihab pulled out the blue ribbon from his shirt pocket.

Springing upright, Marwan snatched the ribbon from her hand.

"It's a girl's hair ribbon. Nadia's?" Rihab's voice lacked the compassionate tone he was used to hearing.

"Is it? I found it in the car." He tried to sound truthful.

"She thought she lost it in the street. I'm sure it's hers."

Marwan rubbed the ribbon between his fingers a few times. He placed it on his nightstand. "Return it to Nadia next time you see her." He kept his eyes cast down like a boy caught hiding his sister's doll under his blanket.

"I'm not the one who found it." Rihab pushed off the bed. "If anyone should return it, it should be you." She walked to the door and turned on her heels. "I doubt she will miss it."

Marwan lifted his eyes. Rihab stared at him with such intensity he thought she might x-ray his chest to get to his heart. She knew. His sister knew he intended to keep the ribbon and she was giving him permission.

"You like Nadia, don't you?"

Marwan nodded, too self-conscious to say anything under his sister's scrutiny.

"Enough to think about a future with her?"

He jumped to his feet. "What else?"

"If that's the case, you should smooth things over with Shareef." Rihab's tone returned to its usual warmth. "He's the one with the final say. You must know that?"

Marwan cleared his throat.

"I'll pave the way with Huda. When you're ready."

He strode over to give his sister a hug. "Thank you," he whispered. "As soon as things calm down and it's decent enough to think of such matters. After Omar comes home."

162

Rihab left, closing the door behind her. He chose a book from his desk and tucked the ribbon between the pages, letting the end dangle to create a bookmark.

CHAPTER
TWENTY-TWO

"I know you resent me, Shareef." Marwan tried to cut through the thick tension hanging inside the car. An hour had passed since they left for Quneitra. Marwan's nerves burned with every cigarette Shareef inhaled, blowing smoke like a steam engine. "Can't you understand I did what I did to protect you?"

"You followed Omar's orders." Shareef flicked his cigarette butt out the window. "Yeah, I understand."

Marwan let the snide remark pass. Work things out with Shareef, Rihab had advised. "Look, we all do things we regret." Marwan subdued his tone. "You're an educated man, a university man. I haven't finished high school. Did the best I could with what I know." There, enough hot air to launch the pompous ass to the moon.

A slow smile spread across Shareef's face. He lit another cigarette. "Go on."

"I don't know in what shape we will find Omar." Marwan tried to bury his irritation. "For his sake, can't we leave what happened behind us?"

Shareef tilted his head upward, put his lips together and puffed, working his lower jaw like a fish out of water. Rings of smoke floated in Marwan's face. "Yeah, all right. Let's move forward." He waved his hand. Ashes from the cigarette between his fingers scattered in the air. "I'll consider this an apology then?"

Marwan gritted his teeth. So that was how the stupid man wanted to see it? How could this fool have a sister as sweet and sensitive as Nadia? He gripped the steering wheel until his knuckles turned white. Smooth things over, smooth things over, Rihab's voice kept repeating in his head. He gave Shareef a curt nod and mumbled under his breath, "Right."

Marwan and Shareef followed a uniformed male nurse down a long hallway in the small hospital. Pieces of chipped paint dangled from the walls. Cone-shaped light fixtures hung from the ceiling, casting the hallway with yellow light. They passed rooms on either side. Moans drifted from several rooms, making Marwan conscious of the scuffing sound his shoes made. Approaching the main hall, screams mingled with the moans.

With wide eyes, Shareef took one step back and cowered behind Marwan.

The hall housed twelve beds, six on either side of a narrow walkway. Oversized windows provided ample breeze. Flies buzzed around the ceiling light fixtures. The iron beds showed rust stains on their headboards. A white mesh tent shrouded a bed in the far corner. The nurse headed toward that bed. Marwan tried to make eye contact and nodded a quick greeting to the soldiers, those who were able to see him.

The nurse stopped a couple of steps short of the shrouded bed and pointed with his hand.

"Second Lieutenant Omar Bakry. Don't have him flip on his back. He must remain in that position." The nurse turned on his heels and left to tend a soldier at the other end of the hall.

Marwan was about to part the dangling mesh, but a soft groan stopped him short. It came from Omar, laying on his right side, his back to them. Leaving Shareef in his spot, Marwan walked around to face Omar. He entered the mesh tent.

Omar's eyes were shut tight, eyebrows furrowed, jaw clenched. Beads of sweat collected on his creased forehead. A blanket stretched up to his neck.

Marwan couldn't see what kind of injury Omar had suffered. "Omar," he whispered. "Can you hear me? It's Marwan."

Omar groaned again, more like a long deep moan.

Marwan signaled for Shareef to come around to his side. "Shareef is here too."

Shareef entered the mesh enclosure. "Can you open your eyes?" He mimicked Marwan's hushed voice.

Omar released another agonizing moan. His eyes remained shut.

Shareef touched Omar's shoulder. "Wake up." He patted him.

A scream exploded from Omar. Shareef stumbled back and out of the white enclosure. More screams followed, heart-wrenching, hair-raising screams.

The nurse came running. He fumbled with a syringe, pulled the blanket off Omar and injected him in his backside. "You will sleep soon."

166

Marwan couldn't believe his eyes. Omar's entire body was bandaged. Spots of blood seeped through in places on his left side and back. The stench of urine mixed with blood hit Marwan with a wave of nausea. He grabbed the iron headboard to steady himself.

Shareef put a fist to his mouth, walked backwards a few steps, then turned around and ran out of the hall.

The nurse adjusted pillows behind Omar's back to keep him from turning over. "If I had known your friend was going to act like a girl, I wouldn't have let him in."

"Was that morphine?" Marwan swallowed to keep his stomach in check.

"He's in tremendous pain. We keep him sedated." The nurse straightened, pulling the blanket over Omar. "There's no point for you to stay. He won't come to any time soon. Let's go."

Marwan exhaled. "Can you please change him first?"

"I'm alone here. He's a big man. Can't do it by myself. I have to wait for morning nurses to do it."

The short, stout nurse sounded offended, but Marwan didn't care. He wasn't leaving until his friend was tended. "I will help you. I've been volunteering at the military hospital in Damascus." Marwan reached into his pants pocket and extracted a roll of bills. "I know what to do." He raised his eyebrows at the nurse, a silent question mixed with an invitation. Marwan didn't mind going that route. Hospitals were understaffed and overcrowded. Nurses did their best, but some needed incentives.

The nurse took the money out of Marwan's hand and tucked it in his pocket. "These will buy cigarettes for the healthier patients." He went to a cabinet and came back with a stack of medical supplies.

Marwan helped maneuver Omar's body, trying to be as gentle as he could, while the nurse changed his dressings and soiled clothes.

"What happened to him?"

"An exploding tank shell sprayed his body with shrapnel. His comrades said he waited to the last minute, providing cover for his men to withdraw." The nurse shook his head. "Never seen an injury like that before. His body is like a sieve. He's strong, though. Doctors extracted most of the shrapnel."

"Most?"

"A couple pieces are next to his heart. He must regain his strength before going under the knife."

They tucked Omar under clean covers and turned to find Shareef standing at the entrance of the hallway, watching them. They passed him on the way to the front room.

Following, Shareef addressed the nurse, "When will he get transferred to Damascus?"

"Don't know. It's up to the doctor. My guess, not for a long while."

"It isn't easy to visit him here." Shareef shuffled his feet where he stood. "I've got classes in the morning and then work."

"I can make it," Marwan interjected. "Every evening."

The nurse wrote in a big register. "Not sure the other nurses will allow you to help like I did."

Marwan tossed the car keys to Shareef. "Give me a minute, will you?"

Shareef didn't ask why. Showing his eagerness to leave, he almost stumbled on a wastebasket on his way out.

Marwan placed his hands flat on the desk the nurse sat at. "When does your shift start?"

"Six. I'm here every day except Fridays."

"I will be here after six then. What's your name, my friend?"

"Abu Wisam."

Marwan winked. "What's your favorite brand of cigarettes, Abu Wisam?"

"Me? I don't smoke. But everyone seems to prefer Marlboro."

"See you tomorrow."

As soon as Marwan got in the car, he placed a hand on Shareef's shoulder. "Best not to give the women details about Omar's condition. Waleed either. He has enough to worry about with his wife."

Shareef jerked his shoulder away. "I didn't expect it to be this bad."

"No need to get them worried when they can't come see him. Injured and recovering well should be enough."

Shareef nodded. He tapped a new cigarette box with his index finger until a cigarette separated out. "Were you serious? Will you come here every day?"

"I run my own business. I can close the store whenever I want."

"But why would you do that? Having to see Omar that way. He won't know you're here."

"I want to make sure he's well taken care of. I don't want him to have the same fate as my cousin."

"I don't understand the need." Shareef shrugged his shoulders. "Your cousin died in the field. Not on a hospital bed."

Marwan gave Shareef a thorough once-over. He started the car and took off. "Don't think too much of it. You will never understand."

Rihab knocked on Marwan's bedroom door Friday morning. He closed the book in his hands and set it on his nightstand before he called for her to come in.

"Get dressed. You have visitors."

He swung his legs to the floor. "Who?"

She closed the door behind her. "Huda and Nadia."

He sprang to his feet. "What? Here?"

"In our courtyard."

He thumbed his chest. "They want to talk to me?"

Rihab nodded. "I told them you were asleep to buy you some time." She put her hand on the door handle. "Get ready and join us by the fountain for coffee."

Marwan hurried to his closet, changed his pajamas, and ran a comb through his hair. He checked his reflection in the mirror, tucked his shirt down his pants one more time, tightened his belt, took a deep breath, and left his room.

He walked out to the courtyard at the center of the house and stopped short. Nadia sat by herself on the edge of the fountain, her hand making circles in the water.

She stood as soon as she saw him. "Good morning." Water dripped from her hand.

"Morning." He cleared his throat. "You're by yourself?"

Nadia shook her head. "That question again?"

He winced, wishing he could take it back.

She wiped her hand on her black skirt. "Rihab and Huda are in the kitchen making coffee."

He strode to a table and chairs under the orange tree, lifted one chair and brought it over to the fountain. "Please, have a seat."

She stayed rooted in her spot, her eyes fixed on his. "My condolences about your cousin."

"At least we know what happened to him. Some families are still looking for their loved ones."

"Huda told me he had a young wife. Children?"

"One-year-old boy." Marwan motioned with his hand to the chair.

She approached, getting the hint he wanted to close the subject. "I've never been inside a traditional house before. This inner courtyard is amazing, and the fountain is very . . . serene." She took the chair and crossed her legs. "You're very lucky."

Marwan brought two more chairs, but remained standing. "My great grandfather built the house in 1870."

"Are the walls all marble?"

"That's why it's cool here in the summer, even in the middle of the day. Trees provide ample shade too." He held the back of one chair. "My grandfather had to improve on the kitchen and add electricity, but other than that it's still the same. I can show you around if you like."

Nadia fiddled with the top button of her white shirt. "Mind if I ask how many rooms?"

"Twelve." He pointed to the doors behind her. "The ceiling in the winter hall is carved from walnut wood and has the original inlaid pearl shells."

She twisted in her seat to look back. "And the window panels? Original colored glass mosaics?"

"Those on the right are replicas. There was an accident when I was a boy."

"An accident with a soccer ball, as I remember." Rihab approached with a coffee tray in her hands, Huda by her side.

Marwan greeted Huda, got another chair, and positioned it opposite to Nadia.

Huda pushed up her long sleeves. "I'll get straight to the point."

Having come across Huda many times during her years of friendship with his sister, Marwan was used to her blunt attitude. He waited for her to say what was on her mind.

"Tell me everything you know about Omar's condition, please. I know Shareef is holding back and I want to know the details. We need to prepare our mother and Fatimah for what's coming."

172

Marwan watched Nadia, her face losing its color. He cleared his throat.

"Don't worry, Nadia can handle it," Huda said matter-of-factly.

Throughout the week, Marwan had been helping the nurse tend to Omar's wounds every evening, and though the nurse insisted Omar was sedated, sometimes his screams filled the room. No way would he give details.

"How bad is it?" Huda pressed.

He took the coffee cup Rihab offered, thinking about putting Huda off her questioning, ignoring her sister's delicate nature. "Omar is getting better," Marwan assured.

Huda glared at him. "That's not what I asked."

"I heard you." Marwan maintained eye contact with her. "And I answered you. He is recovering well."

Nadia placed her cup on its saucer on the edge of the fountain. "I want to see for myself." She turned to Marwan. "Will you take me with you tomorrow?"

He shook his head. "Can't."

She tilted her head to one side, spilling her ponytail over her shoulder. "Please? Just once?"

"It's a military hospital. They won't let you in."

"But they allowed you, right? And you are not even a relative."

"I'm a registered volunteer. Military hospitals don't let women in." Marwan was pleased with the excuse he came up with.

"That's not true." Huda spoiled his brief satisfaction. "Sameera's mother visited her son, Ahmad, in the military hospital."

Marwan had to think fast. "It's different in Quneitra. It's a tiny hospital behind front lines, different than the main hospital in Damascus. They have their own regulations according to security needs." He addressed Nadia. "They might transfer Omar here after his last surgery. Shrapnel pieces," he caught himself. No need to tell them the surgery was near his heart. "Omar is well taken care of. I'm making sure of that."

Nadia leaned forward, a hopeful expression on her face. "Will you stop every day at our house after you have seen him to tell us how he's doing?" She glanced at her sister. "Mama is very worried."

Huda nodded. "It will ease her mind."

Marwan rubbed his chin. It sounded like a good idea, but how would Shareef see it? He held Nadia's gaze, hoping she would understand the reason behind his hesitation. "It's late by the time I get back. Not a decent time for a man to make a visit."

"I'll go with you." Rihab hid a smile behind her coffee cup. The amusement in her voice didn't escape her brother. "I would love the chance to visit with everyone."

Huda set her cup down. "It's settled then. We'll see you tomorrow. What time?"

Marwan left his chair. "It won't be before nine, I'm afraid."

"Sounds good. Time to go home, Nadia."

"Absolutely not." Rihab sprang to her feet. "We will have breakfast together. Marwan, did I hear you promise to show Nadia around the house?"

CHAPTER
TWENTY-THREE

Thirty minutes had passed since visiting hours started at the military hospital in Damascus, and Marwan still hadn't arrived. Nadia stood on the balcony, looking up and down the street for his car. He was supposed to take them to see Omar for the first time since his transfer out of Quneitra.

She went inside and grabbed her mother's hand. "Let's go. We can take a taxi."

Mama pushed off the sofa. "Sameera, stay with the little ones." She adjusted the white scarf draped over her shoulders. "When and if Marwan shows up, tell him we couldn't wait any longer."

"But I want to see Omar." Sameera's whiny tone sounded no different than the younger girls, only more annoying.

Her nerves frail, Nadia snapped. "Did your husband give you permission to go with us before he left for work?"

"That is none of your business," Sameera bit back.

Mama placed one hand on her belly, slapped the other hand over it and exhaled. "Well, did he?"

Sameera shook her head. "I didn't ask him."

"I would stay put if I were you," Mama said, her voice dry. "You know how my son gets when you don't tell him beforehand where you are going." She headed to the door. "I'm not in the mood to resolve another fight."

A car horn sounded from the street. Nadia dashed to the balcony and came back. "Marwan is here. Let's go."

Marwan apologized. "I had to take care of an urgent situation at the store."

Mama didn't waste time. She took the passenger seat. "Hurry, please."

He turned the ignition. "Where's Huda?"

"Work." Nadia slipped into the back seat. She stared out the window, her thoughts drowning Marwan's small talk. Her hands hurt from baking thyme and olive oil pies all day with her mother. Flexing her fingers, she tried to hide her apprehension.

Marwan lied. Every evening, he sat in their living room with his sister and lied about Omar's status, hiding critical details. Everyone knew it, except her mother. For her benefit they participated in the charade and didn't press Marwan to say more. Nadia observed Marwan's face in the rearview mirror. No matter how hard he tried, he couldn't keep his dark eyes from exposing the truth. Omar was in bad shape.

Shareef lied too. He lied about visiting Omar on Fridays. Nadia drew it out of Marwan one evening. Marwan thought Shareef visited Omar on his days off. But Shareef spent his weekends with Sameera's family. Shareef lied to his mother, his wife, his sisters, and to Marwan.

176

Nadia sighed. Did all men lie? Omar never lied to her, did he?

Omar was her rock. Everyone's rock. He must get better soon, come home. Things needed to fall into place, to where Mama didn't cry every night, to when life was tolerable, hopeful. Omar would know how to make Huda back off from nagging her about nursing school. Fatimah would smile again and look forward to having her baby. He would stop Shareef from acting like a tyrant with Sameera.

Marwan would have more reasons to come visit.

Nadia snapped out of her reverie when Mama slapped her hands on her lap. "Oh, Nadia. We forgot the thyme pies for Omar."

Marwan shook his head. "He won't be able to eat them anyway."

"Why not?"

"He's on a special diet. A liquid diet."

Nadia closed her eyes. What else had Marwan shielded them from? What shape would she find Omar in?

Propped up in bed, his back supported by pillows, Omar worried no one would come. He must have misunderstood Marwan, an easy assumption since his brain was muddled with drugs most of the time.

Breaking through a fog, his eyes strained to distinguish details. A nurse stood at the foot of his bed, her white uniform too bright. She held something shiny in her hands.

Dear God! Don't let it be another needle. Omar rubbed his eyes with his right hand. The simple move pierced his body with pain, like a sword shoved between his ribs. He held his breath until it passed, releasing a couple of inventive curses. He gritted teeth. "No more pain killers."

"You sure?" The nurse waved the needle. "Your family is coming today."

"Don't want them to see me drool like a baby."

"Better than dirty their ears with your curses whenever you move," the soldier who shared Omar's room said. "Take it, brother. You need it."

"Don't want it." As long as he didn't move, he should be fine. "Aren't you supposed to meet your wife in the courtyard?"

The soldier wheeled himself out of the room. "Suit yourself."

Missing the simple dignities he once took for granted, Omar sought the nurse. "Need your help again."

The nurse brought a portable urinal and waited by the bed for him to relieve himself.

Omar looked for a small measure of privacy. "Could you lower the shutters?"

The nurse fumbled with the window shutters and returned to Omar's side. She shoved the full urinal under the bed and rearranged the covers.

"Please take it out of here." Omar worried the stench of urine might linger in the room.

Fast footsteps echoed in the hallway. Marwan and Mama Subhia walked in, Nadia on their heels. Omar didn't have a clear view of Nadia's face, his eyes adjusting to the dimmed light.

The nurse mumbled a quick greeting to Marwan and scurried out of the room, leaving the urinal behind. Omar suppressed a curse.

Opening her arms wide, Mama Subhia hurried over. Marwan raised his hand to stop her. Too late. She threw her plump body into an embrace, wrapping her arms around Omar's neck.

"*Alhamdullilah*, you are home." She cried and laughed at the same time.

Omar closed his eyes and bit his tongue to keep from cursing out loud. By the time Marwan managed to pull back Mama Subhia, sweat had drenched him from the burning sensation engulfing his body. He turned his head away, taking quick shallow breaths, a useless attempt to control the pain. What an idiot he had been. Where was that nurse?

"What's wrong?" Mama Subhia dabbed at her eyes.

"Give him a minute." Marwan dragged the only chair in the room closer to the bed and offered it to Mama Subhia. "Here, have a seat."

"Maybe we should call for the doctor?" Nadia whispered.

Sounding scared, her voice brought Omar back from his misery. He turned his head to face them and plastered on a smile.

"I'm fine." He meant his words, now that he saw Nadia's captivating face, her eyes warm and caring. Yes. He was home. He inhaled a deep breath. Nadia's familiar perfume masked the smell permeating from under his bed. God must be merciful. He focused on Mama Subhia. "Why are you crying?"

"We were so worried." Mama Subhia sniffled. "Are they taking good care of you here, *habibi*? You're so thin." She frowned at Marwan. "I will bring lentil soup next time." Leaning forward, she half lifted her backside off the chair. "Where are you hurt? Show me."

Nadia placed a hand on her mother's shoulder. "Not now, Mama."

"Where's Fatimah?" Omar changed the subject.

Nadia and Marwan exchanged a quick look, a signal passing between them. Omar didn't catch its meaning. Secrets? Since when did Marwan and Nadia share secrets? Heat crept up his neck, anger driving it from deep inside his chest. He punctuated his words, "How's Fatimah?"

"She's going to have a baby." Nadia forced a smile on her face.

"Yeah?" Omar narrowed his eyes. "She coming?"

"Marwan didn't tell you?" Mama Subhia adjusted her white scarf.

Marwan raised his eyebrows. "Didn't think it was my place."

"What's going on? Tell me what, for God's sake?"

Nadia touched the back of his hand. "Fatimah's pregnancy is complicated. She's on bed rest until the baby is ready, that's all."

Omar clutched a handful of his bed sheet. Complicated like his mother's pregnancy with him? Did women take after their mothers in matters like these? Would Fatimah give up her life to have her baby?

"Waleed and his mother take very good care of her."
Nadia leaned closer. "I stop there every day, hoping
there will be something for me to do. But Fatimah
needs nothing." She squeezed his hand. "Really,
Fatimah is fine."

"Fatimah asked me to give you a hug on her behalf."
Mama Subhia tried to get up again. Both Nadia and
Marwan pushed her down this time.

Omar swallowed his fear. "How far along is she?"

"Five months." Mama Subhia spread her hands a
distance above her belly. "She's this big. Huda also
checks on her every day. Don't worry."

Omar darted his eyes between mother and daughter.
"You'll let me know? When her time comes?"

"You will be home by then." Lowering her eyes,
Mama Subhia became occupied with her handkerchief.
"Shareef wanted to come with us, but you know. He's
at work. I'm sure he will stop by on Friday as usual."

Omar frowned. Did she think Shareef came to see
him every Friday? He opened his mouth to set her
straight.

Marwan coughed into his fist.

Nadia squeezed his hand twice.

They were asking him to remain quiet. More secret
messages between those two. Where did this familiarity
come from? He didn't like it. Didn't like it one bit. He
rubbed his thumb over Nadia's hand, giving her a
signal that he had caught on. "How did you do on your
finals? Results out yet?"

She brightened the room with her smile. "I passed."

181

Omar frowned, an act requiring effort, for Nadia's smile was infectious. "I know you passed. I want to know how well you did."

Nadia tilted sideways and her ponytail brushed his shoulder. "Well enough to get Huda on my back about nursing school."

He tugged her hand to his side, trying to keep the closeness. "I don't think being a nurse is the right fit for you."

"I have tried to tell her, but she won't listen."

"Huda wants the best for you," Mama Subhia chided.

"May I ask what your plans are then, Nadia?" Marwan cleared his throat. "If not nursing school, what do you have in mind?"

"I'm not sure yet. Perhaps a degree in literature. I've always enjoyed reading the classics." Nadia beamed at Omar. "The ones translated by the Green Press, remember? You got me addicted to them. I don't know how you managed to buy the entire collection after it went out of print. You can't find it in bookstores."

Omar sought Marwan, secretly beseeching him to leave Nadia in the dark. What difference would it make if she knew the source?

Marwan didn't get Omar's silent message since his eyes never swayed from Nadia's face. "Now I know why Omar asked me to buy all those books from the bookstore next to my house when it closed."

A deep blush colored the roots of Nadia's pulled-back hair. "I must thank you, then."

"I have the rest of the collection. Two or three volumes, I believe. I could bring them over, if you like."

"Yes, please."

Omar pressed his head back into the pillow, inviting a painful squeeze to his chest. Nadia knowing the source of the books made a hell of a difference to enamored Marwan. His friend's glowing smile needed shutters. Omar let out a loud cough to cover his frustration. "I haven't paid for those remaining volumes yet."

"Consider them a graduation gift?" Marwan asked, still beaming.

Mama Subhia waved her handkerchief at him. "Thank you, but we cannot accept. I will cover their cost."

Nadia straightened. "Let's not bother Omar with this now." She placed her other hand on his forearm. "You concentrate on getting better."

Omar was better. Much better with Nadia giving him her full attention again. A degree of contentment settled over him. He glanced at Marwan. Time to address a pressing matter. "Will you give us a couple of minutes?"

"Sure." Marwan left the room.

"How are you managing? I never got a chance to ask Shareef. You behind on the rent?"

"Marwan brings your salary to me every month," Mama Subhia answered.

Omar blinked.

"Covers everything." She lowered her voice. For whose benefit, Omar had no idea. Nadia stood next to her. "I put some money aside for you. To get you started when you come home."

He glanced at his nightstand. In the drawer, a letter from the Ministry of Defense stated his salary was held in their treasury until he claimed it. No way would they release his salary to Marwan. Marwan must have given Mama Subhia his own money, fabricating this story to save her pride.

Throwing his head back, he released a long breath. The debt he owed Marwan dangled from his neck like an iron chain. How could he ever repay him?

For the rest of the month, the family visited almost every day. Shareef showed up a couple of times, stiff and distant, performing a duty, nothing more. Sometimes, Huda stopped by toward the end of visiting hours and left with everyone, Marwan the designated driver.

Seeing the fondness developing between Marwan and Nadia ate at Omar's heart. Nothing escaped his eyes. Not the stolen glances, the agreeing smiles when either one of them spoke, Marwan's nervous twitches whenever Nadia looked straight at him, nor the comfort with which Nadia moved around Marwan, abandoning a level of reserve, which was Omars privilege, and his alone. The contentment he felt whenever Nadia visited vanished, leaving uneasiness to flourish.

One clear afternoon, Omar paced around his room, able to stay upright without having to hunch his shoulders, tolerating the occasional sharp pang in his ribs. An irritation he needed to get used to, the doctor had explained.

His roommate discharged, Omar had the room to himself. He welcomed the solitude and privacy. Most of the beds in his wing vacant, he sometimes shuffled down the hallway, pushing himself to the limit, his body broken and his spirits defeated, needing to stay on the move yet going nowhere.

He stared out the window, his hands clasped behind his back. He thought of his bleak reality. The army hadn't discharged him, but what did they expect from him in the condition he was in? To push papers? To shine stars and eagles for the jerks who had brought him to this point? This was not how the war should have ended. He should now be standing in his home, his real home. His father's home in Palestine.

Like a trapped and injured lion, he needed to lash out at someone. Something had to be done. Someone had to answer for this catastrophe. Nasser's attempt to shoulder full responsibility was not enough. The Egyptian people wouldn't let him resign. Four days after the ceasefire, Omar lay mangled, soaking in his own blood. Marwan told him people had poured into the streets, shouting their support for Nasser, calling for him to retract his resignation. What was wrong with people? Who would be held accountable for the lost lives, the trampled dreams, the squashed hopes? Who could he blame for his misery?

Behind him, he heard Marwan walk into the room and plop down on the vacant bed. "Salam. You hear the news?"

Omar didn't turn around. "You alone?"

"Yeah. Running errands. I will bring everyone over later. Need anything?"

"Don't. Tell them you're busy today. Not in the mood for visitors."

"Nadia will be disappointed."

Omar turned to face his friend. "I'm sure she can handle a day without seeing me." He waited to see if his words hit a nerve. Omar was no fool. Marwan was the one disappointed about missing the chance to see Nadia today, not the other way around.

Marwan coughed and broke eye contact.

Disgusted for being angry with the wrong person, Omar felt sorry for Marwan. He had been a loyal friend, a compassionate and responsible man. And he was falling in love with Nadia. Seeing them together almost every day, the dreadful fact screamed at him. How could he fault Marwan for falling for his Nadia? How could he not?

Omar turned his back, hiding his face from exposing his conflicting emotions. "What news?"

"Nasser held Marshal Amer responsible for the fiasco. It's confirmed Amer killed himself before he was to be court-martialled."

"Was the Marshal responsible?"

"Nasser put his confidence in Marshal Amer. But it seems he wasn't up to the task of chief commander of the army. He was incompetent, deceptive in his briefs to Nasser about the Egyptian army's readiness. Soldiers were not adequately equipped. Most tanks in Sinai ran out of fuel, for heaven's sake." Marwan exhaled.

"Nasser was let down by his closest friend and relative. Can't imagine how he feels."

Omar put his hands on the windowsill, leaned his body forward until his forehead touched the glass. "We fought to the bone on our end."

Marwan approached, laid a hand on his shoulder. "No one doubts that."

"We were making progress and then suddenly the orders came to withdraw. I still don't know why."

"With the Egyptian army almost out of commission in Sinai, and with our feeble aerial cover, Syrian troops were exposed."

Omar straightened. "Bullshit. We were pushing forward. Securing ground in the Golan Heights. But the minister of defense issued withdrawal orders." He slammed a closed fist on the windowsill. "What the hell for?"

"No one dares to ask this question to Hafez Al Assad."

Omar swung around. "The Egyptians already ran their investigations and held their generals accountable. Even their president assumed accountability." Omar thumbed his chest. "When are we going to prosecute the person who screwed up on the Syrian front?"

"The whole situation is dubious. I wouldn't dig deeper if I were you. There are eyes and ears everywhere." Marwan held him by the shoulders. "It's time to think ahead now. Plan for your future."

"Right," Omar exhaled, snapping out of his melancholy. He shrugged Marwan's hands off, walked to the nightstand, and dug out the letter from his drawer. "Read this."

Marwan ran his eyes over the letter. "They awarded you another star?" He saluted Omar. "Congratulations, First Lieutenant Bakry."

"Keep reading," Omar demanded, his tone dry.

Marwan placed the letter on the nightstand. "Yeah, about that." He sounded embarrassed. "I was going to tell you when the time was right."

Omar scowled. "You've been giving my family money every month, the equivalent of my salary."

"A little less, I'm afraid." Marwan pointed at the letter. "I didn't know you got a raise."

Marwan's attempt to make light of the issue irked him. This was serious business. Suffering under the weight of a debt like that suffocated him, kept him awake at nights. "As soon as I get out of here, I'll collect my paycheck from the defense treasury and pay you back."

"You already have." Marwan stepped forward, his tone serious. "It's the least I could do, left here like an old man while you risked your life."

Omar stared at his friend, working hard at keeping moisture out of his eyes. "I appreciate your generosity, Marwan. And your sentiment. But I cannot let this be."

Marwan shook his head. "You don't owe me anything."

"We disagree."

Marwan exhaled in frustration. "Can we talk about this later then? Six months from now? Get better. Go

188

home. Take care of your family. Then we will revisit the money issue. Does that sound good?"

"I'll pay you in installments over four months."

Marwan nodded. "Fine."

CHAPTER
TWENTY-FOUR

Giving up her bedroom, Mama granted Nadia free rein to prepare the room for Omar. With the little she had to work with, Nadia used her artistic talent to transform the dull old ambiance into a lively warm one.

With Huda's help, they moved Mama's bed and dresser into the girls' room, squeezing the bulky pieces into the cramped space. Transferring Omar's bed over, Nadia positioned it at an angle facing the two windows to take advantage of the natural light filling the room most of the day. She stacked Omar's books on the wide windowsill, turning the otherwise useless space into a bookcase.

Nadia was in her element. She bustled about, cleaning, rearranging furniture and adding a splash of color here and there by hanging her younger sisters' drawings on the bare walls. Aiming to involve Fatimah in the activities while she was bed-bound, Nadia asked her to sew soft green drapes to replace the heavy beige curtains.

Everyone pitched in except Shareef and Sameera. Shareef made a fuss when he learned of the room switch and refused to lend a helping hand, complaining that he should have been given the option to move into his father's room. He stormed out of the house, accusing his mother of favoring Omar over him, her true son.

Sameera watched her husband's outburst from the doorway of her room, her arms folded on her chest. Leaning to one side on the doorjamb, she shook one leg, exposing her nervousness. The movements made her hips jiggle while she stood, as if she were dancing.

"I bet this was your idea." Nadia advanced on Sameera. "You're the one who put that nonsense in Shareef's head. He never talked to Mama this way before."

Sameera backed into her room. "You're wrong. Shareef has felt like an outsider for a long while." She raised her hand and pointed in the distance behind Nadia's back. "You all ignore him, talk about Omar day and night." Moving her head from side to side, she raised her voice. "Omar needs this. Omar needs that. Poor Omar. What can Omar eat? How will Omar bathe? When will Omar go back to work? Omar. Omar. Omar." She crossed her arms. "Well, what about Shareef, huh? What about the real man of this family?"

Dumbfounded by Sameera's verbal attack, Nadia didn't realize Huda had followed her into the room and closed the door. When Huda spoke, Nadia jumped in surprise to her ice-chilled tone.

"You will lower your stupid voice." Huda took deliberate steps toward Sameera, her stance menacing and dangerous. "I will not have Mama hear one drop of your poison."

Sameera stumbled backward and sat on her bed.

"Answer one question for me." Huda bent down, forcing Sameera to lean back. "Who's paying the rent here, where you and your husband live in comfort?"

Wide-eyed Sameera opened her mouth, seemed to change her mind and closed it again.

"Omar is paying for the roof over your head. Even from his hospital bed, he made sure we all have a home."

"Shareef studies and works all the time." Sameera's voice shook. "He does his share."

"If Omar didn't provide for the family, Shareef wouldn't have been able to go on with his studies, don't you understand that? Shareef would have had to work full time and kiss his university degree goodbye."

"None of you give my husband the respect he deserves."

"Respect?" Huda laughed out the word. She brought her face closer, pushing Sameera further back until she braced herself on her elbows. "If it weren't for Omar, you wouldn't be the *respectable* married woman that you are now. Shareef would have been dead. One or all your brothers would have ended in prison." She jabbed Sameera's shoulder. "So you thank God for Omar. You thank Omar for interfering on your behalf and taking pity on you, and you thank Mama for accepting you into this family."

Huda straightened, keeping her intimidating stare on Sameera's yellow face. "Respect is earned, *girl*. Next time you use your charms on your husband, remind him of those facts. Remind him that the man of the family is the one who *takes care* of his family, not burdens them with his selfish whims."

Squaring her shoulders, Huda nodded once. "Tonight, you will have Shareef kneel at Mama's feet. Show her how sorry he is for what he said." She snatched Sameera's hand and tugged her off the bed. "And you will apologize to Mama right now."

The following day, Huda, Nadia and Marwan helped Omar ease into the back seat of Marwan's car. Almost reclined, Omar left little room for Nadia to squeeze in next to him, Huda taking the passenger seat.

Omar tried to keep his legs from bumping into Nadia's. "Will Fatimah meet us at home?"

"She can't." Huda turned to raise her eyebrows at him. "I thought Mama explained Fatimah's condition to you."

Omar scowled. "Waleed told me she was getting better."

Nadia placed a hand on his bare forearm. He tried not to sigh. There she went again, absentmindedly touching him. She had done it many times in the past few weeks, sometimes without obvious cause or reason.

"Fatimah can't climb the stairs." Nadia's soft palm ran down his skin to the back of his hand. "She *is* better." Her delicate fingers entwined with his. "She moves about her apartment now."

Omar shifted his weight to his other side, allowing Nadia's hand to slip away. Did she not realize how flirtatious her touch was? When would this girl grow up? Open her eyes? View him as the man he was? She never touched Shareef in the same manner. He had been paying attention, keeping track when they visited. What was going on with her?

"I want to see Fatimah." He cleared his throat. "Can we stop at her place? Before we head home?"

Nadia scooted forward, put her hand on Marwan's shoulder. "That would be a great surprise for Fatimah. Can we?"

Omar caught Marwan's eyes in the rearview mirror, checking with him. Damnation. Marwan had the same thought, apologizing for Nadia's carelessness.

"If we make it a quick visit," Huda said, unaware of the dynamics around her. "Mama will understand. I will call her from Fatimah's place."

Nadia sat back, put her reckless hand on Omar's thigh. "Can you make it up the stairs?"

Omar nodded. He didn't trust his voice. Huda. He must have a word with Huda to explain the world of men to Nadia. But what did Huda know of men? Not much. Fatimah. She would be the perfect teacher for clueless Nadia. If he could articulate his concern to his sister without revealing his true feelings, and without coming across as a control freak like Shareef.

Draping one arm over Marwan's shoulders, Omar held the railing with his other hand. They took their time climbing the stairs to Fatimah's apartment. The girls went ahead.

"Don't get the wrong idea." Marwan halted his steps, giving Omar time to catch his breath. "About me and your sister."

194

"Nadia is not my sister," Omar stressed, compelled to make that clear. He nudged Marwan forward, trying to end this conversation.

"Well, yeah. You know what I mean." Marwan moved with caution. "Nadia is very innocent. She . . . she has become used to me, I guess. I don't encourage her. I want you to know that."

This was his chance. Omar could order Marwan to stay away from Nadia, faking the reaction of a jealous, hotheaded, ignorant, so-called brother. But therein lay Omar's problem. He was an honest man; his friend would see through his charade. And then Marwan would start to wonder, ask questions Omar wasn't ready to answer. By speaking up the way he just did, Marwan showed a solid character. How could he bring himself to deceive him?

Almost reaching the door, Omar stopped. He removed his arm from Marwan's shoulders and leaned his backside against the railing for balance. Taking a deep breath, he brought his body to its full height and endured a pang in his chest. "Your intentions?"

"Honorable, of course." Marwan didn't hesitate. "I know this isn't the right time. But I am ready to propose."

Omar gave a quick nod, meaning to be reassuring, but his head jerked to expose his nervousness. He must find out if Nadia's girlish infatuation had taken a deeper turn. "And Nadia? What does she have to say?"

Hesitation seeped into Marwan's eyes. "I wouldn't talk to her about it without your permission, my friend."

That summed up Marwan's character in Omar's mind. Traditional to the core, dependable to the tooth, chivalrous to the extreme. How could he deprive Nadia of an opportunity to be pursued by this good man? Omar shook his leg, trying to ease a cramp. His muscles tensed with apprehension. Fear. He had lost his parents, his homeland, his health, his friends, and his pride. God help him, was he to lose Nadia too?

Marwan wrapped a hand around his arm. "You need to sit down?"

He studied Marwan's trusting face. God may not be that angry with him, to grant him such a loyal friend. A moral man like Marwan could be kept away from Nadia. He waited for Omar's permission? Not in his most daring dreams.

Pressing a hand to his chest, Omar pushed off the railing. "Keep it to yourself for now. It isn't time to think about this yet."

The disappointment that poured out of Marwan's eyes added weight to the hook prodding in Omar's chest. What kind of man was he? To keep his friend in torment, his Nadia from knowing she was loved by a decent man? What evil lay inside this cursed heart of his?

The front door opened. Fatimah's body filled the opening. She called out to Omar, her voice enveloping him with its familiar serenity and affection. He didn't know how he managed the few steps that separated him from Fatimah, but the instant he reached her, he wrapped his arms around her huge body and didn't

196

want to let go. Fatimah loved him with unconditional, unwavering love. Did he deserve it?

The reunion unfolded by varying degrees. Fatimah's fragile state allowed Omar to keep her on her feet for a brief time, enough for him to recharge his emotional battery. They sat side by side on the sofa, holding hands and ignoring everyone else. Huda conversed with Um Waleed; Nadia and Marwan took opposite chairs.

Fatimah locked apologetic eyes to his. "I wanted to come see you at the hospital, but they wouldn't let me."

"Even if you could have, I would rather you didn't set foot in that hospital."

"Nadia kept me informed of all the details. Are you in pain now?"

Pain? He had forgotten about pain. "I'm fine." He nodded toward Huda. "Are you seeing a doctor?" he whispered.

"Waleed insisted," Fatimah whispered back. "Don't worry, Huda understands. Her services are still needed, but I plan to deliver in the hospital."

Omar squeezed her hands. "Good."

"I want you to be there. For Waleed. He's very scared."

"Of course." He worked his throat with difficulty. Waleed was scared? He was terrified.

Fatimah patted his hand. "Don't worry. It will be fine. I know it." She placed his hand on her belly. "God will help me."

Omar would make sure God didn't have another plan for his sister. What did it take? A seasoned doctor in the delivery room? No problem. More than one? He would manage that, no matter the cost. He would stop at nothing. He snatched his hand away. "Wow!"

Fatimah beamed with a wide smile. "You felt that? Baby is letting you know he loves his uncle."

"He?"

"The way her belly is low, and looks like she swallowed a soccer ball, means she is carrying a boy." Um Waleed nodded with authority. "If it's flat at the top like a shelf, then it's a girl."

Omar caught Huda rolling her eyes. "Of course."

Um Waleed shook a finger in Huda's face. "Mark my word. It's a boy. I told Waleed to buy a ram and get ready."

Fatimah tensed. "There's no need."

"Of course there is." Um Waleed's voice vibrated. "I will not have my first grandson join this world without one."

Confused, Omar swung his head to Marwan asking for help.

"The aqeeqa," Marwan clarified.

"It's good to follow traditions." Omar couldn't help but side with Um Waleed. "Slaughtering a lamb and distributing its meat to the needy honors the baby."

Um Waleed waved in Omar's direction. "See? Even your brother agrees with me."

Fatimah pulled on Omar's hand, showing her irritation. "Like Omar said. It's a social tradition, not a religious obligation. Uncle Mustafa didn't do it for any of the girls."

198

Omar shook his head. "Uncle Mustafa couldn't afford it."

"*Aqeeqa* is usually offered when the baby is a boy." Marwan averted his eyes to the floor. "My uncle did it for both his sons and daughter."

Um Waleed put a hand on her waist and tilted her hips. "Even if it is a girl, I want Waleed to distribute *aqeeqa* in her name. What do you want the neighbors to say about us?"

Fatimah glared at her mother-in-law. "They will say we are smart not to go into debt over an ancient tradition." She turned to Omar. "Waleed will be upset to know he missed you. Can't you stay until he comes home from work? Can't we eat together? Stuffed zucchini, one of your favorites."

Omar picked up on her desire to change the subject. "Don't worry about this now." He willed himself to his feet. "Mama Subhia is waiting on us."

Fatimah's hand still in his, he tried to pull her with him, but the effort hurt his ribs. He winced despite himself. Nadia came to his aid and helped Fatimah off the sofa. Fatimah wobbled in her spot and tugged on Omar's hand, causing him to bend forward. Sharp pain traveled down to his abdomen. Gritting his teeth, he doubled over and his head landed on Nadia's shoulder.

Nadia shot her arm to his back to steady him. "What's wrong?"

A groan escaped Omar's throat when the pain spread to his hips. Pressing both arms to his midsection, he twisted away and almost fell to his knees.

"What's happening to him?" Fatimah's voice shrieked with panic.

Marwan pushed past her and Nadia, slipped his strong hands under Omar's arms and eased him back onto the sofa.

Omar lay flat on his back, buried his face in his arms and held his breath. Clenching his jaw shut, he suppressed a nasty curse begging to give him false relief.

"Tell me. What can I do?" Marwan's tone was business-like and confident.

Omar dropped his arms and breathed. "Get them out of here."

"I'm staying." Fatimah tried to insert a pillow under his head. "I want to help."

Nadia wiped his brow with her hand. "Me too."

He opened his eyes to Nadia's petrified face. "Leave," he yelled, his control gone.

Huda pulled Fatimah away. "Marwan knows what to do. Come." She looked over her shoulder. "Nadia, you too."

Nadia shook her head, generous tears flowing, "No," she mouthed, her voice absent.

Omar snatched the pillow and pressed it to his midsection. "Get the hell out," he barked.

Marwan held Nadia by the shoulders and forced her toward the door. "Go."

The women rushed out of the room, closing the door behind them.

Marwan held his legs, preventing him from falling off the sofa while he twisted and withered. "Pain in your gut again?"

He slammed his fist to the back of the sofa. "Shit. Never this bad."

Marwan lifted his feet. "Bend your knees. The doctor said this might help relieve pressure."

He cursed out loud. Many times. Convulsions ground his insides, turning them into minced meat. Good to stuff Fatimah's zucchini. He let out a harsh laugh at the thought, his consciousness about to slip away. Sweat drenched his shirt, or was it blood?

Omar opened his eyes. "Where am I?"

"Fatimah's place." Marwan was balanced on the sofa's arm by his head.

"Did I pass out?"

"Yeah."

He tried to get his bearing. "Did I say or do anything I should apologize for?"

"Not to me, but the women got an earful of your colorful language."

Omar exhaled. "Shit."

"Listen. Best to take you back to the hospital. Have the doctor check you."

"He won't tell me anything I don't know. He already warned me of episodes like these."

Nadia's voice came from behind the closed door. "Can I come in?"

Marwan checked with him, raising his eyebrows.

Omar grabbed the back of the sofa. "Help me."

"Give us a minute," Marwan called out.

He sat upright, his shirt stuck to his skin, his armpits wet with sweat. Good thing he was scrubbed clean before he left the hospital. How bad did he stink? Hugging the pillow, he concealed his upper body.

Nadia walked in, carrying a tray with a water pitcher and a couple of glasses.

"Fatimah all right?" Omar tried to sound strong.

"Fatimah is doing fine." The glasses rattled in Nadia's hands, her face draining of color.

Did he look that bad?

"She's worried. Huda and Um Waleed kept her out of earshot." Nadia set the tray on the coffee table.

"Sorry about that," Omar mumbled.

"I told them I would get them once I checked on you." Nadia filled a glass and handed it to him. "How do you feel?"

Omar took short sips. "Better."

"What happened?" Nadia ignored Marwan, who poured himself a glass. She lifted a hand to Omar's forehead. "You scared us."

Drained of energy, he closed his eyes and dropped his head back. "Muscle spasms. Nothing serious."

"His muscles are scarred and weak," Marwan explained. "Once he regains his strength, the spasms will go away."

"You mean this could happen again?"

"Afraid so."

Omar opened his eyes, glared at his friend. "Don't scare her."

"No point hiding facts. Besides, someone at home needs to know what to do when you have another episode."

"I can do it. Teach me," Nadia said.

"No need." Omar's voice sounded more scared than angry. Have Nadia see him twist and cry like a baby?

Huda entered the room, followed by Fatimah. They hovered over him and kept him from stopping Marwan taking Nadia aside to teach her what to do.

Arriving home, Omar braced himself for Mama Subhia's warm welcome. He reveled in the genuine love she showed, put his agony behind him and tried to enjoy the attention. Tolerating her light embrace in the living room, he noticed a change in Nadia's attitude. She appeared nervous and apprehensive, fluttering around and biting her lower lip. He couldn't figure out what had fazed her. He also noticed she walked Marwan to the door and took her time to bid him goodbye.

Sameera lurked in the background, as if afraid to talk to him. Huda disappeared into the kitchen. And Mama Subhia went on and on about how much she had missed him, how thankful she was to have him with her again, and how the miserable outcome of the war didn't matter as long as he was safe.

Shareef walked in through the front door.

Mama Subhia sucked a sharp breath. "You're home early."

"Quick break." He extended a hand to Omar. "Good to have you home."

Omar shook his hand, had no clue why Mama Subhia's tears poured. She opened her arms wide to her son, and they embraced in that awkward position, Shareef almost folded in half. Nadia stood at a distance, the strange expression on her face adding to Omar's bewilderment. From her corner, Sameera observed with her brows knotted, mouth twisted to one side. Huda peeked her head out of the kitchen. The women seemed taken aback. If only he were in a state of mind that would allow him to analyze, evaluate and understand the undercurrents that were going on. But he was dead tired. A bed. He needed a bed.

Shareef took a chair. "Do you know when you're expected to report to your commanders?"

"Medical leave for a month." Omar suppressed a yawn behind his hand. "Hopefully the doctor will give me the green light."

"Prescriptions?" Shareef glanced at his watch. "I can get them on my way back from work."

"Already got them. Pain killers, that's about it."

Shareef turned to his wife. "Lunch ready? I have to get back soon."

Sameera hurried to the kitchen. It reminded Omar of his comrades obeying orders from their officers. How far had Sameera fallen from her angelic status? Unable to think straight, he closed his eyes and rested his head back.

Mama Subhia tugged on his arm. "Let's get you to bed."

Nadia hurried and opened the door to Mama Subhia's room. She stood by the entrance, wringing her hands. "This will be your room."

Omar checked with Mama Subhia. She gave him a gentle push. "Go on."

He took one step into the room, passing an anxious Nadia. "This can't be." He turned to face Mama Subhia. "I can't take your room."

"You can and you will." Mama Subhia pushed him further in. "It's the closest to the bathroom." She held his forearm and pulled, urging him to bring his head down. "It isn't the same without Mustafa, God rest his soul."

"But —"

She patted his arm. "I need to be with my daughters, and you need your privacy."

Omar straightened. "Thank you."

Shareef's voice came from behind. "Thank Nadia. She's the one who worked hard to get it ready."

Nadia lifted her eyebrows, questioning. "Do you like it?"

Seeing nothing but her adorable face, he mumbled, "Very much."

"I will see about lunch. You get some rest." Mama Subhia left the room. Nadia followed her. Omar met Shareef's clouded gaze. He brought his voice down a notch. "Don't take this the wrong way. I am very grateful. Is everyone on board with this arrangement?"

Shareef gave an awkward nod. "Like I said. Welcome home."

Omar's friends visited non-stop over the next several days. Young officers and soldiers poured into the house, their defeated demeanor distorting the grandeur of their otherwise impressive presence. Busy preparing coffee and tea trays, Nadia wondered if she would have admired the handsome men had they returned victorious. Instead, their pressed uniforms and political discussions annoyed her. They saturated Omar's room with cigarette smoke, reminded him of his failures and pushed him deeper into depression after each visit. Day after day, she watched him try to stay balanced and pull himself out of the despondent slump the entire country had sunk into.

Omar struggled with everyday tasks. Going to the bathroom, bathing, changing his clothes, and some days, keeping food in his stomach. Nadia would stand outside his closed door, unable to lend a helping hand, hearing him fumble and swear in frustration. He didn't allow any of the girls to help him, including her mother. Shareef was always absent and never offered his assistance when he came home. His callousness drove Nadia crazy.

To regain his strength, Omar employed the younger girls for his training. Salma and Farah lay on the bare floor, held on to Omar's ankles and allowed him to drag them around the room. He had tremendous difficulty at first, able to move them half a tile forward before he collapsed in pain. But he persevered, placing markers on the tiles as goals. For his arms, he carried around food cans, books and sacks of rice or bulgur. The girls challenged him to carry them as the ultimate goal. They giggled, encouraged and provided the right amount of incentives. Omar sweated, yelled and gritted his teeth in concentration. He kept at it, leaching one set target after another.

Marwan didn't visit as often as Nadia thought he might. Always coming in with a group of friends and leaving with them, he seemed to avoid talking to her, or even glancing her way. Not knowing what to make of his sudden disinterest, offended and disappointed, she acted in defiance and did her best to avoid running into him as well. On the days he visited, instead of taking the service tray into Omar's room as usual, she would send Salma in her place. When it was time for him to leave, Nadia felt the urge to use the bathroom. One time, Marwan left with the group he came with, then returned a minute later saying he had forgotten his keys. Nadia let him in and pretended to be busy. On his way out, he met her eyes. Something was wrong. Marwan's dark eyes screamed at her, asking for something. Understanding? Patience? What held him back? Who? Huda? Shareef?

One Thursday evening, while Omar's friends mingled in his room, devouring everything Nadia sent their way from the kitchen, Mama joined her by the sink.

"Um Waleed called. Fatimah is restless." Mama put a hand on Nadia's shoulder. "I think I'll go over there."

Nadia dried her hands on a towel. "I'm coming."

Mama shook her head. "Shareef and Sameera took your sisters with them to her parents' house, so they will be back late. Omar's friends will leave soon. He shouldn't be left alone."

Nadia nodded. "I hope Fatimah is all right."

"Don't tell Omar. No need to worry him."

"Will you call me to let me know?"

"I'm sure it's nothing." Mama headed to the door. "If Huda comes home soon, send her over."

A couple of hours later, Nadia closed the door behind the last visitor. She went back to the kitchen to put things in order, eager to get out of her shoes and clothes, and away from the sink. Her hands felt like she had spent the entire day washing dishes.

A loud crash sounded from Omar's room. Nadia ran over.

Omar was curled in the fetal position on the floor, twisting and moaning. Broken glasses and plates spread around him and under him.

Nadia rushed to kick sharp pieces away. "I'm here. I'm here." She squatted by his side.

"Goddamn it," Omar shouted and slammed his head on the floor a couple of times. The veins in his neck bulged out.

Frantic, Nadia wrapped her arms around him. "Please, stop moving. You will hurt yourself."

"Go away," he choked between gritted teeth. "Get out of here."

"I can help you." She snatched his blanket off the bed and spread it two-folds over the scattered glass next to him. "Can you get onto the blanket?"

Omar rolled to his knees and balanced himself with one hand, the other pressed at his midsection. Spewing obscenities Nadia didn't understand, he crawled to the blanket and flipped on his back.

"Sorry, I am so sorry," he half-mumbled half-screamed, folding his arms around his waist.

Nadia held his ankles, and like Marwan had instructed, stood straight, lifted his feet and placed them on her shoulders. "Bend your knees."

Praying she wasn't causing him more harm, she took small steps forward, stretching his legs higher in the process. His fists clutched the front of his shirt, and he huffed short quick breaths with each step she took. She noticed a number of small cuts on his nape, neck and forearms. Patches of blood spread on the fabric of his pants in multiple places, most around his left knee.

"Don't be alarmed." Omar closed his eyes, his voice weak and shaking. "I might pass out."

"You will not, Omar Bakry," Nadia yelled. "You will not scare me like that." Tears flowed down her cheeks, her nose ran and sweat dampened her forehead.

"Trying not to . . ." His voice disappeared, his head lolled to one side.

"Omar?"

He didn't respond.

She lowered his feet to the floor and knelt by his head, her hands hovering over his cheeks.

"Don't panic. He lost consciousness. That's all." She ran her sleeve under her nose. "Marwan said it might last a couple of minutes." Checking her watch, she contemplated calling Marwan. He would know what to do. But the hour was late, and he wouldn't get there before Omar came to.

Should she slap Omar? Splash cold water on his face? Wait for him to open his eyes? Sitting back on her heels, she surveyed his limp body. Damned if she was going to sit there doing nothing while he lay unconscious and bleeding.

She hurried to the bathroom, grabbed a couple of clean towels, filled a bowl with hot water from the kitchen, and went back to sit on the floor, using a pillow under her to protect against broken glass.

Starting with the cuts on his nape, she dabbed at the blood with a wet towel first, then dried the area, careful to remove any glass pieces stuck to his skin. Working her way down, she unbuttoned his shirt, took care of a cut on his neck, his shoulder, found a couple above his navel and tended them. Blood ran heavier on his arms, the cuts there deeper. Using her teeth, she ripped strips from the dry towel and wrapped them around the gashes as bandages.

"It's time to wake up now, Omar," she said out loud. "I want you to wake up now."

Omar didn't move.

With the back of her hand, she brushed hair strands off her face. "I can't stand the sight of blood, you know that?" She shook her head. "Definitely not going to nursing school."

Faint scars from his war injuries spread all over his left side. She ran her fingertips over the raised lines, then turned her attention to his leg. Blood soaked the area covering his left knee. She bent over and tried to roll his pant leg to expose the cut. The fabric wouldn't pass his calf.

"Of all the days, Omar. You chose today to do this?" She slammed her lap in frustration. "When no one is here but me?"

210

With shaking hands, she fumbled with his belt buckle and fly zipper, her eyes blurry with tears. "I can't believe I am doing this."

Determined to get the bleeding gash on his knee under control, she gathered her red skirt between her legs and straddled him, grabbed the sides of his pants and pulled to bring them down his hips. Once part of his underwear showed, she stopped, wiped more tears off her face.

"Don't you dare come around now. I will die of shame." She closed her eyes and tugged again.

"What do you think you're doing?" Huda's voice froze Nadia in place. Her eyes flew open. She swung her head around.

Huda stood in the doorframe, the look on her face too scary to decipher.

"Thank God you're here." Nadia let go of Omar's pants and got off him. "Help me."

Approaching, Huda's eyes ran over Omar head to toe. "How long has he been out?"

"Several minutes. I don't know." Nadia pointed at his knee. "See? He cut himself really badly twisting on the floor."

Huda grabbed a pillow off the bed, threw it down and knelt on it. "Well, for one thing, I'm not helping you undress him." She leveled cold eyes on her. "Surprised you managed to get this far."

She swallowed. "He is . . . he is bleeding. Has cuts all over."

"I can see that." Huda ripped apart Omar's pant leg from the thigh down, exposing his bleeding knee.

Nadia pressed the back of her hands to her flaming cheeks. "I didn't think of that."

"Bring me my bag." Huda's tone sounded threatening rather than commanding. With precise movements, she extracted a sizable piece of glass from Omar's wound. More blood gushed out. She used cotton gauze from her bag, grabbed Nadia's hand and placed it on the wound. "Apply pressure while I wrap a bandage."

Warm blood trickled between Nadia's fingers. She turned her head to the side and swallowed several times to steady her nerves.

Once Huda was done, she nodded. "There, this should hold."

"Oh God, I forgot." Nadia wiped her blood-stained hand on what was left of the towel, gathered Huda's things and stuffed them in her bag. "Quick, you have to go to Fatimah. Mama is there already. They need you."

Huda sprang to her feet. "She bleeding again?"

Nadia shook her head. "I don't know. Mama said to send you over as soon as you came home."

Huda pointed at Omar. "Keep him warm. Make sure he drinks plenty of fluids when he wakes up." She headed to the door. "And don't tell him I was here. I will never be able to look him in the eye again. Not after seeing him in that state." Huda slammed the front door shut.

Nadia blinked. What did she mean? What state? She studied Omar, his open shirt barely covering one shoulder, his pants half way down his hips, his thigh exposed by the huge tear in his pant leg. Almost naked, tight abs detailed, bulging muscles defined by damp skin, Omar could have jumped out of one of her adventure books. How come she hadn't noticed that before?

A sound emanated from Omar's throat.

Heavens, he was waking up. Fearing he might see her gawking at him, she rushed to drape a blanket over him. She took in the chaos around her. Shattered plates and broken glasses, crumbs of the baklava that had been served earlier in the evening, and drops of blood splattered everywhere. Taking a deep breath, she smoothed her hair and went to work.

CHAPTER
TWENTY-FIVE

Swooshing sounds penetrated Omar's dark world. He opened his eyes. Where was he? A crooked crack in the ceiling didn't orient his muddled mind. He turned his head toward the strange sound. A pair of shapely smooth legs blocked his view. He blinked, his eyes traveling up a woman's red skirt to her hips, swaying right to left. A dancer? Blazing Zahira? Was he in the White Tulip Night Club? He shot up to a sitting position. A blanket dropped off him, revealing his bare chest.

"What's going on?" His voice cracked, his mouth dry.

The woman turned, a broom in her hands. "You're awake."

Nadia? He scrambled to his feet; the blanket fell to the floor and his pants threatened to follow. He clutched the sides just in time, his mind racing to focus. "What the hell?"

"I did it."

His left knee buckled and he stumbled down on the bed.

Nadia's fingers fluttered over the top button of her blouse. "I have never been this scared in my life." She flattened her hand on her chest. "But I did it."

214

Omar stared at her, tried to gather the fronts of his shirt with one hand, the other not letting go of his wide-open pants. "What?"

"You were thrashing on the floor. Cut yourself everywhere on broken glass. I took care of your cuts." She let the broom crash to the floor and stepped closer. "And you know how I can't handle seeing blood."

He glanced at his bandaged arms and leg. Why was he exposed like that? God have mercy, what had he done? He worked his throat with difficulty. "I don't rememb —"

"Sorry about your pants." Nadia bit her lower lip. "It was easier to tear them." Her cheeks turned red. "Easier than trying to pull your pants down." She turned to the nightstand, hiding her face from his eyes.

He swallowed to wet his dry throat. Nadia undressed him? Like lightning, the thought shot energy through his half-naked body.

"You should drink." She handed him a glass of water. "You must have been carrying the service tray when the spasms happened."

"I remember trying to clean up."

She sat next to him on the bed. "You shouldn't have."

He pulled the blanket across his lap. There was no decent way he could zip his pants with her sitting this close, and no way could he walk to the bathroom in the condition he was in. He needed her out of the room. "Could you go get Mama Subhia, please?"

"She's not here. No one is."

He emptied the glass in one gulp.

"Don't try to help me again," Nadia whispered, her brown eyes wide and earnest, her lips red and moist.

Omar pulled the blanket higher on his waist. Shit. Where did his filthy mind wander? His body couldn't handle having Nadia this close without reacting like a love-struck schoolboy? Shaming him?

Nadia got off the bed and retrieved the broom. "Let me clean this mess and I will leave you to rest."

His movements stiff and painful, he placed the empty glass on the nightstand and stretched on his side, making sure the blanket covered him well. He watched Nadia sweep the room, her swaying hips stealing his breath. Like a bull fighting in its arena, Nadia in her red skirt became his matador. His exhausted and confused body reacted to every move she made, every twist of her hand, every flick of her hair, every tap and step. In the back of his dirty mind, crowds cheered Nadia on for the final plunge.

He closed his eyes. Blazing Zahira in her see-through dancing ensemble beckoned him with her liquid moves. *Dirbakkeh* drums beat in his ears, matching his racing pulse. The belly dancer had visited him often in his dreams, when he lay helpless in the hospital bed night after night. But she had Nadia's fascinating face, Nadia's tea and milk skin, Nadia's bouncing ponytail. At the time, he had blamed medications in his system for the scandalous visits. What excuse could he use now?

Nadia made a sound. A dainty low murmur.

He opened his eyes.

216

Reaching with her broom under one of the chairs, her posture allowed him a glimpse of cleavage.

Sweat drenched his chest and back. He was drowning, sinking to rock bottom. If only he could throw off the blanket. Or pass out again before his body pushed him to an embarrassing point.

"Leave," he managed the words, sounding rude and urgent.

"Almost done," Nadia sang. "I need to mop with water now." Giving him her back, she bent forward to collect a dirt pile.

Perfect. What a match for the perverted man that he was, turned on by a broom in Nadia's hand. He rolled to his other side with difficulty, looked out the window, studied the girls' funny drawings on the walls, his eyes searching to land on anything but Nadia's roundness. His skin on fire, his muscles tight with anticipation, he ached. A desirable, pleasing kind of ache, persistent, escalating, engulfing the dull sensation of his cuts, dousing his nerves. Diving further away from the surface of dignified composure, a groan escaped his throat.

"Can I get you anything?" Nadia's voice sounded closer, tantalizing, enticing, luring him to the brink of disgraceful surrender.

"I need you to leave now." Behind him, the mattress dipped with her weight. He held his breath.

Another sound emanated from her. A soft sigh.

He buried his face in his pillow. The bull yielded, teetered in his spot, about to fall.

"What is it? Let me help you."

Pulling the blanket over his head, he barked, "Get the hell out."

At the crack of dawn, before anyone awoke, Omar slipped into the bathroom and bathed, scrubbing his skin raw. The hot water scorched his cuts. He didn't care. His core dirty, he couldn't get clean enough. How was he to perform Friday prayers? Stand before God, shoulder-to-shoulder with pure men, after the night he had spent immersed in filthy thoughts? Bathing purified his body, but how could he cleanse his mind? Should he not go to the mosque? Claim he wasn't well? A legitimate reason, for sure. But his doctor frequented that mosque, and he was supposed to evaluate him. If the doctor didn't see him return to normal activities, he would postpone his reinstatement. God help him, he needed to work, get busy, leave the house, stay away from Nadia as long as he could.

Returning to his room, he rifled through papers and dug out the last letter he had received from the Ministry of Defense, summoning him to report to his division the following Saturday and view his medical report. A week. Omar had a week to convince his doctor he was well enough.

The phone rang. Who would call this early? He opened his door and hurried to answer the phone in the living room.

Nadia beat him to it, wrapped in her night robe, her hair loose on her shoulders.

"We'll be right there." She ended the call.

"Who?"

218

"Waleed." Nadia headed to her room, removing her robe on the way. "Fatimah was in labor all night. We need to go to the hospital."

Omar stumbled after her. "I'm going now. I can't wait for everyone to get ready."

"There's no one here. Mama and Huda spent the night with Fatimah." She closed the door in his face. "By the time you find a taxi, I will be ready."

Omar limped to the waiting area, following Nadia. They found Waleed pacing around the room. A couple of men sat in a corner smoking.

"They're all in there." Waleed pointed down a long hall. "Huda will come out to let me know as soon as there's news."

"Doctor Anwar?" Omar needed confirmation that the expert doctor he had recommended a while ago had been called in.

"Phoned him before we left the house. He made it here soon after we arrived."

Omar nodded. His contacts had come through. One of the soldiers in his regiment was the good doctor's nephew. Omar patted the wallet in his back pocket. The money Mama Subhia had set aside for him would come in handy.

"How is she?" Nadia asked.

"Calm. Really calm." Waleed rubbed his stubble-covered chin. "It's strange, you know?"

One of the men in the corner laughed. "Your first baby, huh?"

Omar scowled at the man shrouded in smoke.

"My fifth," the man said between puffs. "If she doesn't give me a boy this time, I'm going to find me a second wife." He spread his lips wide, exposing a rectangular gap between his top teeth.

Waleed struck a conversation with the man, asking him about his wife's four births in this hospital.

Nadia grabbed Omar by the elbow and steered him to chairs under an open window. He rested his arms on his knees and stared at the floor. Nadia took the chair to his left.

"I can't believe Waleed is asking this man about his wife like that." She crossed her legs. "It isn't decent."

"Waleed is nervous. Better he stays engaged." Omar glanced at the man. "Doesn't seem like the man is bothered by the questions."

"I still think it isn't right," she whispered. "Those are private matters."

Omar sat back. "Why didn't you tell me Fatimah was in labor all night?"

"You needed your rest. Mama told me she would call when it was time." Nadia waved her hand in the air. "And here we are." She rolled her shoulders and stretched her neck from side to side. "How's your knee?"

"Stings a little when I bend it." He studied her face, dark shadows under her eyes. "You're tired."

"I didn't sleep last night."

He cleared his throat. "Why?"

"I was waiting for Mama's call, waiting to see if you needed anything. I don't know. I just couldn't sleep."

He left the chair, folded his arms over his chest and leaned his back against the wall. He studied the other man in the corner, chain-smoking and following Waleed's conversation with the toothless father. Every now and then, the man's beady eyes would dart to his.

If Omar took to the cigarette like everyone he knew, he would smother his nerves with nicotine too. Fatimah better come out of this all right. She was strong and healthy, delivering in a sterile hospital, under the care of a real doctor. Times had changed since his mother birthed him. Fatimah's baby would not kill his mother. Tasting blood in his mouth, he realized he had been chewing the inside of his cheek.

"Where are your little sisters?"

"Shareef took them to Sameera's family. I called him last night and told him to keep them there."

Had Omar known they were going to spend the night alone in the house, he would have dragged himself out of there. Clueless Nadia didn't think about what the neighbors might say, but he did. There was no room for suspicion in matters like these. "You should have told me."

"When? While you were unconscious or after you threw me out of your room?"

"Thank you for your help last night. I know I didn't sound grateful, but I am."

Nadia twisted in her seat and glared at him. "You were angry, Omar. And . . . and rude."

Blood rushed to his neck. Taking deep breaths, he tried to keep his face from turning red. By the strange look in Nadia's eyes, he doubted he succeeded. He moved to sit by her side, pretending to check his shoelaces. "Sorry about that. I wasn't ang —"

"I don't understand men. You never act as expected."

"You girls are not that much better."

"Women."

Lifting his head, he paused.

Nadia inflated her chest and straightened her back. "You mean us *women*."

Sitting back in his chair, a long breath emptied out of his lungs. "Right. You women confuse us too." He did a double take. "Wait a minute. Who else acted unexpectedly with you?"

Nadia's cheeks reddened. She cast her eyes down to her lap and remained silent.

Alarm bells sounded in his ears. "Talk to me, Nadia."

She shook her head. "This isn't the time."

"What else can we do?" Masking his dread, he nudged her shoulder with his. "It will keep my mind off Fatimah."

Waleed plopped next to him. "God. I don't think I can handle one more piece of information."

Omar put a hand on Waleed's shoulder. "Fatimah has the best doctor in town taking care of her. Try to relax."

The chain-smoker ambled over, stood in front of Omar. "What's your rank?"

Omar rose and extended his hand. "Sec . . . First Lieutenant Omar Bakry."

The man squinted, his beady eyes turned to slits. He let Omar's hand hang in the air. "You say it with pride?"

Waleed sprang to his feet. "Now wait a minute here."

Omar stayed Waleed with one hand. He stepped closer to the man, the stink of nicotine stopping him from advancing further. "How did you know I'm in the army?"

The man lit a cigarette and blew smoke in Omar's face. "You are the Englishman."

Omar flinched. "No one has called me that since I was a boy. Do I know you?"

The smoker shook his head. "No. But I know you."

"If you did, you would know better than to call me by that name."

The man returned to his chair, leaving a cloud of smoke behind.

Omar advanced. "Who are you? What do you want?"

"It doesn't matter what I want." He sucked hard on his cigarette, its burning tip glowing in front of his beady eyes. "We will meet again, *Englishman*."

Omar balled his fists, his muscles ready for a fight.

Waleed held him by the arms. "Let him be. This is not the place."

"You hungry? I need to eat." Nadia tugged on Omar's hand. "Come with me to the cafeteria."

Omar dragged his eyes away from the man taunting him to Nadia's frightened face. Making a scene here would be stupid. He looked back at the chain-smoker.

A strange smile spread over the man's lips. He raised a hand to his forehead and saluted.

Omar gritted his teeth. Something was different about that salute, more like a signal. Who the hell was this man?

Nadia tugged again. "Please."

Sighing, he let Nadia drag him along.

When they were out of earshot, Nadia asked, "What's wrong with that man?"

"Like everyone else, he's disappointed with the war. Looking for someone to blame." To change the subject, he slowed his steps. "Are you going to tell me what's bothering you? Or shall I start making assumptions and worry about Fatimah and you too?"

"It's nothing." Nadia picked up her pace, passing him. "I'm confused, that's all."

He caught up, held her elbow and turned her to face him. "About what?"

"About who," she whispered, her eyes cast down.

His hand dropped to his side. "Who's confusing you?"

"Marwan." She flashed a hesitant look. "He is . . . different."

"Different how?"

"Distant. He's avoiding . . . us." She fiddled with her collar. "He used to visit with us all the time. Now he comes to see you, leaves without a word."

Omar resumed his walk, covering his relief by pretending to look for the cafeteria sign. "Marwan has a lot on his mind. Huge responsibilities, managing the family business on his own. His uncle bowed out after his son died. Left everything to drop on Marwan's shoulders."

Nadia fell into step with him. "Huda and Mama went with Rihab to pay their respects to his cousin's wife. Poor woman. Widowed at a young age."

"Many like her. You didn't go with them?"

"I couldn't on account of the little girls." She turned to face him, walking a couple of steps backward. "What about Marwan's other cousins? How come he has to bear the full burden by himself?"

"They're his cousins from his mother's side. No ties to his father's trade. They have their own businesses to run."

They reached the cafeteria, bustling with the morning crowd. Thankful for the interruption, he put the issue of Marwan to rest in Nadia's mind. He ordered melted halloumi cheese sandwiches.

"Five sandwiches?" Nadia raised her eyebrows. "You that hungry?"

"For the two men. They probably didn't have anything to eat, either."

"You're going to feed that obnoxious man?"

Omar twisted his mouth sideways and nodded. "Him too."

While they waited for the sandwiches to be ready, Nadia surprised him with a question. "You think Shareef told Marwan off?"

"What do you mean?"

"The other night, as Marwan was leaving, I could swear he had something to say to me, but he held back. It's no secret, Shareef doesn't like Marwan." Her fingers walked over the collar of her dress again: no button to check, but the habitual move exposed her nervousness. "Did Marwan say anything to you?"

"About what?"

"About . . . about his future plans?" Her voice sank in her chest.

Omar grabbed the bag of hot sandwiches off the counter and took his time paying. This was it. Nadia sought confirmation from him about Marwan's intentions. What was he to say? Marwan wanted to propose? Marwan had proposed, and he had put him on hold. What would she think of that? What would she think of him?

"Marwan is taking care of two families now, his uncle's and his dead cousin's. Not to mention his sisters at home. I doubt he'll be making plans for himself any time soon."

Something shattered in Nadia's wide brown eyes. A hopeful luster dimmed.

What had he done to his Nadia? What selfish heart did he love her with? Exhaling, he shifted the bag of sandwiches to his other hand. He spoke the truth, didn't he? Marwan's family obligations became more complicated by the day. How could he throw clueless Nadia into the mix? There. That was a noble reason justifying his decision to keep Marwan at bay. Damned if he felt better about it, though.

"You should think about your future, Nadia. Time is running out. Apply to the university if you aren't interested in nursing school."

"You should stand by your friend. He was there for you."

As if he had received a slap in the face, Omar flinched. "I know all too well what Marwan did for

226

me." He squared his shoulders. "I'm doing the best I can with what's in front of me right now."

Nadia's face dropped. "I didn't mean to suggest that you have forsaken —"

"I know what you meant." He cut her off. "Let's get back. I hope there's news."

Limping at a faster pace, he tried not to get angry. What right did he have to feel insulted by her words? She was right. He should help Marwan, though the stubborn man didn't complain to him about his circumstances. What could he do for him? He couldn't interfere in his family affairs, or help with his business. He could pay him his money back as planned. That was about all he could do.

Omar glanced at tight-lipped Nadia by his side, her head bowed, her steps in sync with his. He could give Marwan a sliver of hope. Let his heart settle, put his mind at ease, bring back that luster in Nadia's eyes. Like a merchant's balancing scale, Omar could lessen his friend's burden and amass his own at the same time.

Fussing and crying, his head held in a tight grip, the plump ram was half-dragged, half-urged up the stairs. Waleed held him by the horns. The butcher pushed his hind, using both hands. The butcher's boy enticed the ram forward by waving a bunch of grass in his face.

Neighbors and friends gathered on the steps along the way, cheering them on, repeating the same phrase over and over, *Masha'a Allah*, praising God for increasing his blessings on the young family.

Unable to help with the physical labor, Omar watched from the top step. He had been working all morning, getting Fatimah's kitchen ready for the ceremonial ritual. He had lined the floor with plastic sheets, set the biggest pots he could find on the counters and dangled a chain with a hook from a beam in the ceiling. He had managed the details with Marwan by his side, guiding him.

"You sure this is going to hold?" Marwan pulled on the hook with all his strength. "My uncle used a tree in our courtyard."

"It will hold." Omar positioned a huge brass pot beneath the hook.

"Rational people get a medium-sized lamb. What your brother-in-law did was foolish. This ram is as heavy as the both of us combined."

Omar laughed. "Um Waleed went with him to the shepherd's. She picked it out herself."

At the mention of her name, Um Waleed walked into the kitchen. "Everything ready? Where are the papers to wrap the portions with? I don't want to use newspapers. People deserve better than ink-smudged meat."

"The butcher's boy has a roll." Omar walked her back to Fatimah's room. "Don't worry, everything is taken care of."

Her back to the door, Fatimah sat in a chair facing the window. Huda stood by her side. Mama Subhia sat on the edge of the bed, Sameera to her left.

Huda raised her hand to stop him at the door. "She's nursing."

"I need the list." Omar lowered his voice. "Waleed thought you added more families."

Fatimah handed a piece of paper to Huda. Um Waleed snatched it out of her hand and gave it to Omar. Before she let go, she said, "Start with the neighbors gathering on the stairs."

"Of course."

"Bigger portions go to the needy families on this list."

"I know." He tugged on the paper.

Um Waleed didn't let go. "Keep the liver for us. Fatimah will need it to get her strength back."

"Got it." He tugged again, irritated by the woman. Did she own a single piece of clothing that wasn't gray?

"See if the butcher wants to keep the lambskin. If not we can send it to the tanner, make it into a rug."

"We are paying the butcher for his work." He tugged hard, fearing he might rip the damn list, but he freed it from Um Waleed's hand. "No need to give him the sheepskin." Omar tucked the paper in his pocket and returned to the kitchen. He found Shareef had arrived and threw him a quick greeting.

The butcher laid the ram on his side. The ram's legs thrashed. Waleed held his head down while Marwan struggled with his back legs.

"Why don't you tie them together?" Omar wished the animal would settle down.

"No need." The butcher ran his right hand from the ram's neck to his belly, smoothing the fleece. With a calm voice, he recited verses from the Qur'an and continued with the hand massage. Several minutes passed. The animal stopped resisting and his legs relaxed. The butcher motioned for Marwan and Waleed to remove their hands. They did. The ram remained still.

Repeating the lulling motions, the butcher asked in a hushed voice, "Name?"

His actions seemed to hypnotize the men around him, and no one answered. He looked at Waleed. "What's the child's name?"

"Fawzi."

"His full name, man." The butcher's voice remained calm, but a sense of urgency could be detected in his tone.

"Fawzi Waleed Fawzi Al Najad."

Replacing his right hand with his left to continue massaging the ram's neck, the butcher extended his right hand behind his back. His boy, no more than twelve, placed a big knife in the butcher's open palm.

"This magnificent lamb is to honor Fawzi, the son of Waleed, the son of Fawzi Al Najad." Tightening his grip on the leather handle, the butcher kept the knife hidden from the ram's eyes. He folded the ram's ears over his eyes and took a deep breath.

"*Bismillah Al Rahman Al Raheem*," he said in a steady voice, in the name of God, most merciful, most gracious. With one swift move, the knife sliced clean through the ram's neck, ending his life. Cradling the lifeless body, the butcher lifted the head. His boy inserted a pot under the deep cut to capture the gushing blood.

230

The men moved in silence, subdued by the heavy act of taking a life. They helped string the animal from his back legs on the hook. Blood drained into the pot. The butcher's knife went to work, skinning, gutting and cutting with obvious skill.

Waleed and Shareef took charge of distribution to the neighbors and of cleaning the kitchen after the butcher finished his chore. Omar and Marwan loaded Marwan's car with wrapped packages and followed the list, making sure to do the rounds as fast as they could while the meat was fresh. In his haste, Marwan drove out of character, his jerky movements leaving Omar nauseated.

After the last stop, Marwan asked, "Fatimah's place?"

Omar shook his head. "I'd rather not. They're probably still cleaning."

"How did you get Shareef stuck with that?"

"Um Waleed bullied him into it. I guess he couldn't come up with an excuse fast enough to get out of it."

"Home, then?"

"Can't," Omar blurted. Nadia was home. Better stay away. The past few days, he had tried his best to avoid her, and she must have sensed it, or something else had affected her behavior around him. He couldn't figure out if she was angry with him or if she was despondent because of what he had told her about Marwan. The brief instances they had run into each other, Nadia had gone out of her way not to look at him, finding things to occupy her hands. She had stopped her casual touching too. He had noticed that the most.

"You can't go home?"

Omar rested his elbow on the edge of the window, ran a hand through his hair. "I need a breather."

"I hear you. Come over. Rihab makes the best falafel sandwiches."

"Don't want to impose."

Marwan made a sharp turn. "Nonsense. Did you see your doctor yet?"

"Yeah, I saw the sadistic tyrant."

"He didn't clear you?"

"Extended my leave for three more months. Said I should stay home for the winter." Omar threw his hands in the air. "What the hell am I to do with myself for three full months?"

"Get a job."

"Doing what? I can't physically do a damn thing and I don't have a release from the army. No one will hire me."

"Come work with me. I don't care if you don't have a release."

"I will not get you in trouble, my friend." Omar slammed his palm on the dashboard. "I don't get it. If they're going to assign me to a desk job anyway, what difference does it make if I made a full recovery from my injuries?"

"Perhaps they have a higher plan for you in the army."

"I'm a Palestinian. I will never move up the ranks. This is it for me."

"You don't know that for sure."

232

Omar glanced sideways. Born to a deeply rooted Syrian family, Marwan would never understand the kind of limitations a Palestinian refugee like Omar faced. "You know what I'm thinking?"

"What?"

"I'm thinking about spending those months at Fatah headquarters in the Jordanian desert. I can train Palestinian militia at the Karameh refugee camp there. My skills are needed."

Marwan slowed the car. "Someone from the *fidaiyeen* contacted you?"

"A week ago. Ran into him at the hospital the day Fatimah delivered."

"He tried to recruit you right there in the hospital?"

"Nah. He sent me a signal. I met with him a couple days later. Seems I have a reputation." Omar folded his arms on his chest. "There is a place for me with the *fidaiyeen*. Fighters are joining in from all nations, not just Palestinians. We could repel Israeli attacks across the Jordanian border."

"You think you can disappear with the Palestinian resistance for three months and return to your post here? You're a fool if you think you can pull that off. They will never let you."

"They?"

Marwan raised his hand and counted on his fingers. "One, getting involved with the *fidaiyeen* means you will never be able to leave. They will own you. Two, the Jordanians will keep track of you wherever you go. Even though they're sympathetic to the Palestinian cause, they will not allow another army to expand on their

233

land." Raising his third finger, Marwan lowered his voice. "Three, the Syrians will consider you a deserter when you don't report back in time. You will never be able to show your face here again, and if you do, you will be caged like a dog."

Omar turned his head away. He shouldn't talk about his plan to anyone, not even to Marwan. Doing anything that would risk cutting ties with the family in Damascus was out of the question. He had promised Uncle Mustafa to take care of his girls. No force on earth would make him jeopardize that. But he also had a duty to fulfill. The man who recruited him had said he would be very helpful to the resistance movement with the kind of military training he had. Palestine waited for her rescuers, and he was no coward. No one would *own* him, not the *fidaiyeen* nor the Syrian army. He would have to sneak in and out of the Fatah militia camp on his own terms.

"You're right. I'm so frustrated. Trapped here behind red tape while my brothers are fighting every which way they can."

"You did your share."

"And I failed." He pointed at a corner. "Drop me off there, will you? I'll walk home. I need to clear my head."

"You and me both." Marwan pressed his foot on the gas petal, jerking the car faster. "It's settled. You're coming over."

Omar eyed his friend. Nadia was right. Something was off with Marwan. His casual talk seemed forced, distracted. Nadia was at the heart of the matter, no doubt. Omar pinched the bridge of his nose, resisting the obligation to give his friend a chance to get things off his chest.

They drove through the city in silence for a while. Disgusted with his selfishness, Omar finally prodded, "Everything all right at home?"

"Yeah."

"And your uncle?"

"Not doing well. He wants me to take his second son under my wing. Teach him the ropes, introduce him to the market."

"Take his brother's place?"

"Something like that. The boy is fifteen."

"You were a year younger when you took on your father's business. You turned out fine."

Marwan slammed his palm on the steering wheel. "But I lost the chance for a decent education. I will not let my uncle do that to Nader. The boy is smart, driven. He should have a better chance."

Omar motioned for Marwan to take a right turn after he missed the street they should have taken. "Is that what Nader wants?"

"Nader wants to please his father, carry on the family reputation. But someone has to look out for the boy. The Barady name is solid enough in the market, if I keep it up until Nader gets a diploma, he can take over his share then."

"Your uncle won't have it that way?"

Marwan shook his head. "My uncle is devastated by his son's death. Not thinking straight." He missed another street they should have turned into to go home. "My uncle wants . . . more."

Realizing Marwan wasn't paying attention to his driving, Omar pointed in the distance. "There, park the car. Your uncle wants payback?"

"After my father died, my uncle was everything for us. If it weren't for him, I wouldn't be standing on my two feet right now." Marwan brought the car to a stop with a jerk. "He could have taken over the business, covered our expenses, done his duty and no one would have faulted him for that." He exhaled long, struggling with whatever he was trying to say. "But he insisted I learn everything about my father's trade. He introduced me to the merchants my father dealt with, backed me up. He shaped me to be the man they wanted to do business with."

Omar couldn't put his finger on what was bothering his friend. "You owe him to do the same for Nader. I get it."

Placing his hands on the steering wheel, Marwan stretched his arms and dropped his chin to his chest. "More. He wants more. I can't refuse him." Lifting his head, he glared at Omar, his eyes intense. "Can you understand that?"

Omar nodded. "What can't you refuse, man?"

Marwan swallowed a couple of times, working his throat to get difficult words out. He shifted the car into gear and drove off. "Better get home."

Rihab's falafel sandwiches dripped with tahini sauce and hit the spot with Omar. He ate more than his fill, crunching pickled hot peppers between bites to enhance the flavor. The dripping sesame seed paste needed more lemon juice in his opinion, but he didn't say anything. They ate under the orange tree in the courtyard and Marwan seemed to relax. Encouraged by his lightened mood, Omar licked his fingers in front of Rihab, complimenting her for the fabulous meal. "That was the best falafel I've had in years."

Marwan watched Rihab go into the kitchen. "I will miss her."

"You're planning a trip?"

"She's getting married. Her wedding is at the end of the month."

"Congratulations, man. Huda didn't tell me."

"Huda doesn't know yet. The decision was made recently."

"When did Rihab get engaged?"

Marwan left the table, went to the fountain and washed his hands. "I thought you knew. Rihab has been engaged for the past year."

"I had no idea." Omar followed Marwan. "A year is a long time for an engagement."

"She refused to go ahead with the wedding on account of my younger sisters." Marwan dried his hands on a towel hanging from a tree branch. "Didn't want to leave them. Kept the poor man waiting all this time."

Omar avoided Marwan's gaze. Wasn't he doing the same thing? Keeping Marwan waiting for a green light from him? He took the towel. "Who's the lucky man?"

"A merchant's son from Aleppo. A decent man. But he's running out of patience. The girls are old enough not to need her mothering now, so we are moving forward." Marwan gave a half-hearted smile. "Though I fear Rihab worries about me the most."

"She will move to Aleppo?"

"Yeah."

Rihab joined them with a tea tray in her hands.

Marwan took the tray. "Thank you. We'll have it in my room." He poured tea at a small table in the corner. Omar walked around the room, studying the family pictures and paintings framed on the walls. Generations of Barady family members stared back at him with grainy gray faces. Aware of the absence of such pictures in his own life, jealousy poked his chest. He wandered over to the desk and checked a stack of books.

Marwan fell silent, heaving a heavy sigh every now and then. The spoon in his hand clattered without mercy against the sides of the short tea glasses, stirring sugar and spinning the wheels in Omar's head in search of a way to draw him out.

"So you're going to look after your sisters by yourself from now on?"

"I won't be by myself. My uncle solved that problem."

Omar's fingers paused between pages. "What do you mean?"

Marwan flung the sugar spoon onto the brass tray. "I can't say no to him." He shook his head, sounding defeated. "I just can't."

238

Omar closed the book in his hands. "What's going on? What does he want from you exactly?"

"God help me, Omar." Marwan lifted red eyes. "He wants me to marry his son's widow."

"Oh!" Omar blew a long breath. "I see."

Marwan dragged his palms down his face. "He thinks it will solve *everything*." His voice came out muffled and strained. He dropped his hands. "It will keep my cousin's share within the family without having to deal with fortune hunters who will go after the widow. Her boy will have a decent living until he can take over his inheritance. I will have help with my sisters while Rihab finally moves on with her life." He spread his hands wide. "See? Everything is solved."

Giving Marwan his back, Omar closed his eyes. He placed his flat palms on the desk surface, catching his breath. Could it be this easy? Getting Marwan out of his way, out of Nadia's life, without having to do anything? Was this God's way of showing him he wasn't forgotten?

Marwan's voice came closer from behind. "You know where my heart is."

Omar opened his eyes. A blue and white ribbon dangled from one of the books before him. He knew that ribbon well, the details of its white lace fringes imbedded in his memory. How had it come to be tucked in Marwan's book? How long had it been there? Had he asked for it? Had she given it to him as a token of her affection? How would she take this news? Would it break her young heart? Omar forced his throat to

239

work. One word came out, heavy with concern, with worry, full of bitterness and frustration. "Nadia."

"How am I to cherish a woman as a wife," Marwan choked, "when my heart belongs to another?"

Omar swung around, his pulse racing. How was he to answer that? And why couldn't he come up with something to ease his friend's agony? Must he? He could stand aside and let things unfold on their own. Allow his suffocating aspirations to rise to the surface and catch a breath of air at last.

"Talk to the widow. Try to make her understand." The words forced their way out of his mouth, overriding a voice in his head saying, *Let it be. Let it happen*.

Marwan dropped on his bed. "I tried. All she cares about is her son's wellbeing. I promised her, no matter what, I would take care of her boy like he were my own." He slammed a fist into his palm. "But my uncle won't have it. Says I have to honor the family. Keep the Barady name above everything. If she marries someone else, it would shame us among merchants to allow a stranger to raise our orphaned namesake."

"That's ridiculous. We don't live in the Dark Ages. You're a free man."

"Free?" Marwan shook his head. "I'm nothing without my family name. Our heritage goes back hundreds of years. I cannot ignore that."

Omar paced the room, trying to focus his thoughts; his feelings — a different matter. A moment ago, he was jealous of Marwan's deep roots, but now he saw they had turned into shackles around his ankles. "The widow has a say in this, right? And her family?"

"They left it up to her. But her father said he wouldn't stand in the way of another Barady member taking care of his daughter and grandson. Would be proud if it happened. And she . . . seems to agree."

"Meaning?"

"She doesn't mind this arrangement if I agree to it." Marwan twisted his lips in a sad smile. "She's under the impression I'm a good man."

The voice in Omar's head screamed for him to end this conversation there, to leave. But the miserable look on his friend's face nudged him to decency. "There must be a way to get you out of the picture without damaging your family image."

Marwan rose to his feet. "There *is*. I need your help for it to work."

"What can I do?"

"Go to my uncle. Tell him I had given you my word to marry Nadia. He wouldn't allow me to break an honorable promise like that." Marwan lifted his eyebrows. "Family reputation above everything else, remember?" Lifting his arms sideways, he inflated his chest. "I'll be released of my obligation to the widow with honor. She can choose whomever she wishes to marry. The boy will be raised under my care." He dropped his arms. "Problem solved."

Omar blinked a couple of times. "Aren't you forgetting something?"

Marwan nodded. "Nadia doesn't know about my intentions, I know that. Let me talk to her."

Omar looked away. What arrogance! Did Marwan think Nadia waited on a word from him? Her mind made up to accept his proposal? He pressed a fist to his midsection, recalling Nadia's questions at the hospital. He was the arrogant fool, thinking he could keep her to himself. Of course she wouldn't object to Marwan. Everything he observed in the past months confirmed her hopes to be his.

Marwan stepped into his view. "If you tell my uncle you postponed my official proposal because of all that happened with the war, he'll respect that even more."

Omar coughed into his closed fist, reeling himself in to face his cruel reality. No matter what he wished for, or did, he should at least give Nadia the chance to hear Marwan out. *If* she wanted to.

"My uncle thinks the world of you." Marwan gripped his shoulder. "A soldier like his son. He *will* listen to you."

"You know it's not up to me. Shareef has the final say."

"I think I've reached a level of acceptable civility with him. I haven't completely won him over, but I'm sure with your help we can convince him to go along."

Omar clenched his jaw. "You don't know what you're asking."

"I'm asking you to use your powers of persuasion."

"What if Nadia refuses you?"

Marwan sucked a sharp breath. His hands dropped to his sides. The hopeful expression on his face collapsed in front of Omar's eyes. Did he not consider

242

that possibility? Was he that sure of Nadia's feelings? What had she done to give him such confidence?

Marwan shook his head. "I have a feeling she will not."

Stifling a need to slam his fist into Marwan's audacious jaw, Omar turned and headed to the door, needing to get out of there before he lost his mind. "Let me talk to Nadia. See where we stand."

Marwan followed him, touched his arm, urging him to turn around. He thrust his hand forward. "Do I have your word?"

He had no choice but to take Marwan's hand and give it a firm shake. "We are men talking here, aren't we? I will get back to you in a couple of days." He pulled the door open with more force than necessary. "In the meantime, it's best to keep your distance."

CHAPTER
TWENTY-SIX

An urgent knock sounded at the front door. Omar sprang out of bed and rushed to see who dared bother the household after midnight.

"You the Englishman?" A tall, thin man asked in a hushed voice, his eyes darting down the stairwell and back.

"Who are you? What do you want?"

The man shoved a package onto Omar's chest. "Take this." He glanced over his shoulder. "You will understand."

Omar grabbed a handful of the man's shirt instead of the package. "Understand what?"

Shareef's voice came from behind Omar. "Who's there?"

The man pushed the newspaper-wrapped package against Omar's chest again. "Take it. Don't let anyone know. I was told to deliver this to the Englishman."

Hearing Shareef's footsteps advancing, Omar released the man, took the item and tucked it under his pajama shirt. The man hurried away and disappeared down the steps in the darkness. Omar closed the door and turned to face Shareef.

"Someone looking for Faisal Nabawi." The name popped into Omar's head from a movie poster he had seen on the streets. "You know him?"

Yawning, Shareef shook his head. "At one in the morning?"

"Some emergency." Omar headed to his room. "Told him he had the wrong building."

Shareef didn't waste time on the matter. He shuffled back, mumbling curses on the way and shooing his wife into their room.

Safe behind closed doors, Omar placed the package on his bed and unwrapped it. Two pieces of folded paper and a brown leather wallet fell out. He flipped open the wallet first. His face stared back at him: an identification card had his picture with someone else's name and specifications. He slipped out the card, examined it on both sides. Not a counter fake. Ziyad Nimir, twenty-six years old, born in Jaffa. He slipped the card back in the wallet and picked up one of the folded papers. It held a white travel document with the same personal details. Stamped on the inside, a visa to enter Jordan valid for two months.

Omar dug in his nightstand drawer for his ID card. Comparing the two, he concluded the new one was authentic. The last piece of paper in the package had a list of names, detailing his new family history. On the back, clear instructions on how to sneak into the Karameh camp once he crossed the Jordanian border.

Dropping the papers on his bed, he scratched his head. This was it, then? A new identity and a purpose? He sounded out his new name, Ziyad Nimir. Could he pull it off? Could he become this older man during the time he would spend in the camp, training militia who would trust their lives to him? To a fake from Jaffa?

He gathered the documents and surveyed the room, searching for a good hiding place. Under the mattress? Nadia changed his sheets, and she was thorough. She might pull them out while she maneuvered the mattress. In his drawer? It didn't have a lock. Between his clothes? The little girls sometimes used his closet for a hiding place when they played. Examining the books stacked on the windowsill, he chose three books at the bottom and inserted one document in each book. No one touched his books without his permission.

"Omar, are you awake?" Nadia's hushed voice came from behind his door.

He cracked the door open. "Everything's fine. Go back to bed."

"Mama is worried. She heard you and Shareef talking." Nadia tightened the belt of her night robe. "Who was at the door?"

"Someone had the wrong address. Tell her not to worry."

Nodding, she turned around. Dark strands cascaded down her back, free and unrestrained. Her hair brushed the light fabric of her robe when she walked.

"Nadia," he called out before she moved far.

Her abrupt turn threw her hair to one side over her shoulder. With questioning eyes, she raised her eyebrows.

He stepped out of his room, needing to get closer, wishing he could rub a lock of her hair between his fingers. "Want to go tomorrow to the university to check registration?"

Nadia's face, illuminated by the mid-month moon, brightened with a wide smile. "Oh, could we?"

"Get your papers ready."

He waited for her to go into the girls' room, not bothering to conceal his blatant admiration of her figure. Gliding away, her narrow waist accentuated the roundness of her hips. At that moment, half shrouded by darkness, he wasn't Omar Bakry, the shamed soldier of a failed army, or the chained soul indebted to his friend, or the deprived man stuck behind an uncontrollable heart. He was Ziyad Nimir, the disguised leader, the skilled officer, the healthy man who had the freedom to admire Nadia in the open, without contrition or self-condemnation.

On the small balcony, Omar sipped his morning coffee and waited for Nadia to get ready. He spotted Huda coming down the street, walking like a drill sergeant he knew. A teenage boy walked beside her. Omar checked his watch; it was nearing eight. She must have been at a delivery all night. The boy most likely had been dispatched by the family to escort her home, sheer pretense for the neighbors' benefit. No one dared point fingers at Huda for staying out all night. Her occupation gave her benefits other women in the community didn't have. Immunity.

Grimacing, Omar set his coffee down on the tray. Huda's mood was bound to be sour. More sour than usual. He had hoped to get Nadia out of the house without running into Huda, to spare Nadia her continuous nagging to attend nursing school.

Huda's sure footsteps announced her arrival, and Omar braced himself to hear her arguing with Nadia as soon as she entered their room. To his surprise, Huda joined him on the balcony instead.

"We need to talk." She took the other chair and peered into the Turkish coffee pot on the tray.

Omar poured her a cup. "Good morning to you too." He tried to smile, but decided not to. It might encourage her to stay, and he wasn't in the right frame of mind to handle whatever she wanted to throw at him.

"It's important. Very important."

"It will have to wait. I'm on my way out."

"When will you be back?"

He stretched to his feet. "Noon, maybe. I'm taking Nadia to the university." He glowered at Huda, daring her to object. "To start her registration process."

She put her cup down. "Good. She must enroll. Nadia should pursue her dreams."

For the second time this morning, Huda had surprised him. He narrowed his eyes. "I thought you were against it."

Huda shook her head, the look in her eyes difficult to understand. "I want her to have a diploma, to get a good job, to be independent." She averted her eyes to the streets below. "This world is too harsh." Rising, she gave him a gentle push. "Go. Take her. We'll talk when you come back."

Omar hesitated, alarm bells sounding in his head. What was wrong with strong-willed, abrasive Huda? Her attitude toward him had changed in the past couple of years. Life's cycle had seasoned her, made her more mature, abrasive none-the-less. What fazed her now?

Nadia called him from inside. He pushed Huda's issues to the back of his mind and escorted Nadia to the Registration Department at Damascus University.

On the way, Nadia talked non-stop about her decision to study English literature, stressing her desire to become a teacher. Omar couldn't find an opening to say what was on his mind. Nadia's excitement for getting what she wanted despite Huda's objections kept her bouncing from one topic to another, cutting him off whenever he saw an opportunity to say something. Her joy was infectious and he marveled at her ability to lift his mood. Before heading home, he took her through his usual route around the neighborhood.

Nearing the bench at the public square, Nadia's steps faltered. "You're not going away again, are you?"

"Why would you think that?"

"Last time you took me on a similar walk, you told me you were leaving to the academy."

Omar forced a smile. "I'll always come back. You can count on that." He cleared his throat. "But that isn't what I wanted to talk to you about."

She touched his arm and snatched it away almost immediately. "Tell me then."

Her awkward move confirmed his suspicions. Nadia had changed toward him too. If only he could figure out the reason behind it. He brought his voice down, "Are you angry with me or something?"

"What?" Her fingers flew to the top of her blue dress. The navy-cut collar didn't have buttons. "You made my dream come true today." She inserted the tip of her index finger under the fabric and moved it from side to side. "Can't you tell how happy I am?"

"Just making sure." He nudged her to resume their walk. She would turn eighteen on her next birthday. A necklace. He should buy her a necklace, something for her fingers to play with instead of collars and buttons.

"Are you?" she asked.

"Am I what? Angry?"

Nadia nodded, her large irises searching his face. Fearing she might trip for not watching her step, he held her elbow. "Can't you tell?"

She pulled her elbow out of his grip, plopped down on the bench, and crossed her legs. "How would I know? You've been acting very strange the past few days. I used to be able to catch your moods, but I can't anymore."

He joined her on the bench. "There's a lot on my mind."

"Talk to me. What are you waiting for?"

Sighing, Omar lifted his eyes to the clouded skies. Birds flew in circles in the distance. "If you'll keep quiet for a minute, I'll tell you."

"We used to speak with ease to each other. The war changed you."

He swung his head toward her. "Did you think it wouldn't? Grow up, will you?"

250

Flinching, she crossed her arms over her chest. "I have. *You* didn't notice."

"What's that supposed to mean?"

Biting her lower lip, she inhaled deeply. "You still see me as a little girl, in need of protection from everything and . . . everyone."

Omar tore his eyes away, concentrated on the soaring birds. "That's what I wanted to discuss with —"

"I can handle myself, you know," she interrupted. "I don't need you or Huda to solve my problems."

He adjusted his seating to face her. "What are you talking about?"

"Huda told you, didn't she?" She dropped her hands in her lap and examined her fingers.

At a complete loss, he opened his mouth to say that much but she cut him off again.

"She promised she wouldn't. But, no. Poor little Nadia has to be protected. Like I don't have the brains to make stupid people shut up. I'm not helpless." Her face turned red, her hands waved around at nothing in particular. "I know how to deal with this garbage. Once I find out who's spreading those nasty lies, I'm going to gouge their eyes out. Watch me. I *will* do it."

Omar grabbed her wrists. "Hey, hey. Calm down." Looking around, he lowered her hands to the space separating them. No one on the streets paid them attention. Not yet. He kept her hands in his, surprised to see this feisty side of her. Trying to remain calm, he controlled his voice as best he could. "I don't think I have the full picture here. What garbage?"

Nadia's lower lip quivered. "You know. The rumors some women . . ." She swallowed, tears gathering in her eyes.

Omar patted her hands before releasing them. He dug his checkered handkerchief from his pocket and handed it over, waited for her to blow her nose. So women gossiped about her and Marwan? He should have seen that coming. Taking a deep breath, he sighed his words, "It will all work out soon."

Nadia crumbled the handkerchief in her hand, keeping her eyes cast down. "I just don't understand how someone could think that about me and . . . you."

He jerked his head. "What did you say?"

She lifted wet eyelashes, tears running. "Everyone knows we are one family living together. So what if we are not related by blood. That doesn't mean we are doing anything wrong. I don't understand what changed all of a sudden. People are stupid and . . . and evil." Nadia broke down in audible cries.

Omar left the bench. The birds above his head screeched in his ears, deafening him. Or was it the sound of his blood boiling, rushing through his veins? His mouth went dry as a desert, his entire body tensed, gearing for a fight. He searched for something to strike at. Giving Nadia his back, he grappled for composure, afraid to make a scene and attract attention. Someone was using him to tarnish Nadia's reputation in the community. Why? Who? Truth be damned. The suspicion alone would be damaging enough.

Nadia touched his shoulder.

252

He swung around, knocking her hand away as if she had branded him with a hot iron.

"Huda was trying to find out who started the rumor. Did she tell you? Is that what you brought me here for?"

"We'll discuss it at home." He forced his voice to stay steady, but it vibrated in his chest and erupted with a strangled sound. "Coming here was a mistake." He let her walk home ahead of him and remained quiet along the way.

A loud commotion sounded on the stairs outside the front door to the apartment. Omar jumped over the remaining couple of steps and pushed open the door. It took him several seconds to understand the scene he had walked in on.

Mama Subhia bent over Sameera in one corner of the living room, fistfuls of Sameera's hair in her hands. Huda held her mother from the waist, trying to pull her back. Everyone was screaming.

Nadia closed the door behind Omar and stopped short.

Omar sprang to action. He pried Mama Subhia off Sameera and dragged her to a chair. Huda tried to keep her seated while he helped Sameera to her feet.

"Let me tear her apart, the conniving bitch," Mama Subhia yelled, her chest heaving with exertion and anger.

"Calm down, Mama. Your heart." Huda turned toward a stunned Nadia. "Fetch cold water."

Nadia ran to the kitchen and returned with a glass of water. She sprinkled water over Mama Subhia's face.

Omar didn't know what to do with Sameera, who was sobbing and clinging to his neck. Afraid she might collapse like a squid once he let her go, he allowed her to use him for support. "Someone tell me what's going on."

Huda fixed fierce eyes on Sameera. "She has been spreading lies about you and Nadia."

The glass in Nadia's hand crashed to the floor.

Omar unlaced Sameera's hands from around his neck. "Is this true?"

Mama Subhia slammed her chest. "From inside my house. No wonder women listened to this nonsense." She tried to push her body off the chair, but Huda held her back. "They heard it from this snake living among us."

"I said what I know," Sameera hissed.

Releasing her, Omar took one step back. "And what the hell do you think you know?"

Sameera ran hands over her hair, wiped tears dripping down her chin. "I know a lot." She pointed at the women huddled together. "They never accepted me into this house, thinking their precious Nadia was better than me. They despise Shareef for marrying me." She straightened her back. "I'm not stupid, or blind. I see how you look at her. I know that look."

"You know nothing," Omar shot back, his heart racing.

"I know you two spent a night alone." Sameera jutted her chin in defiance, challenging Omar. "Now, that's not a lie, is it?"

Nadia grabbed Sameera's arm and swung her around. "You are out of your mind."

"You think you are above reproach? All proper and innocent? Well, look whose reputation is in the dirt now."

Nadia slapped Sameera across the face with enough force that it caused Sameera to lose her footing and slump against the wall.

Huda lunged at her with both fists. Nadia reared for another slap.

Omar grabbed Sameera and shoved her behind him, offering his body as a barrier. Huda's blows landed on his chest; Nadia's nails scratched his neck.

"Everybody calm down." He held back Huda with one arm and Nadia the other, attempting to control the situation, hoping he would fail and let them tear Sameera apart. "You're upsetting your mother." He released them and they both went to Mama Subhia's side.

Crying, she slapped her thighs over and over. "We are ruined. Ruined."

"The night Fatimah went into labor," Sameera yelled at Nadia. "You called my family's house and asked us to stay there with the little girls, knowing your mother and Huda were spending the night with Fatimah." She cowered behind Omar's back. "You planned it so you would be alone with Omar."

Omar swung around, slammed a palm against the wall by Sameera's head. "Go to your room, woman," he barked. "Lock the door and wait for your husband."

Sameera's surge of defiance vanished in a heartbeat. She hurried away as instructed, bumping into furniture until she reached her room.

Omar slumped forward to land his forehead on the wall. His insides were twisting without mercy. He closed his eyes in anticipation of a possible spasm attack, welcoming it at this point.

Mama Subhia wailed behind him. "May God curse the day Sameera came into this house. May He show me the day she gets what she deserves for what she has done. And Shareef, I curse —"

"Mama, please," Nadia sobbed. "Don't curse your son."

Omar lifted his head, turned and leaned his back against the wall, needing it for support.

"No decent family will approach you now, Nadia. Or any of your sisters." Mama Subhia rocked back and forth in her seat. "We are ruined."

"Stop that nonsense, Mama." Huda knelt in front of her mother. "The lie didn't spread like the bitch designed. I learned about it from a woman I tended, and she knows the kind of people we are, never believed a word of it. She stopped it from passing her doorstep and agreed to help me flush out the instigator. I never imagined it would be Sameera."

Nadia sank down beside Huda. "You mean no one else knows?"

"I don't think so. I told you women are gossiping so you would be extra careful until I found the source."

"It came out of this house. Someone *will* believe it." Mama Subhia held Nadia's hands. "The damage is done."

"You need to rest." Huda got to her feet, pulling Mama Subhia up with her. "Help me, Nadia. Let's get her to bed." She raised her eyebrows at Omar. "We'll take care of things."

Before she let the girls escort her inside, Mama Subhia lifted disappointed eyes to Omar. "You promised Mustafa to take care of his girls. Now see what has happened."

Holding himself together by a thread, Omar went into his room. He lowered his body onto one of the chairs by the window, placed his elbows on his knees, and held his head in the palms of his hands. How could he have let this happen? He should never have returned home after he left the hospital. He could have rented a room somewhere close by, maintained a distance for people to see, or stayed at Fatimah's place. He knew something was off with the way everyone had behaved the day he came home. He knew, and he ignored it. Sameera had it in for him from the start, moving around him like a sneaky fox, watching, calculating, scheming.

He lifted his head, gasping for air. The windows were shut, Huda's attempt at keeping the neighbors out of earshot. How could he fix this? How could he keep his word to Uncle Mustafa? Redeem himself in Mama Subhia's eyes? Stretching to his feet, he tried to fill his lungs with air, trapped and powerless.

Nadia's intermittent sobs drifted from the girls' room. He took hold of the chair and threw it against the wall. The night lamp followed, then the nightstand it stood on. The contents of his drawer scattered across the floor. The bed was next. He flipped it over, then kicked the bottom over and over until his foot went numb. Everything inside his body hurt. But most of all, the pain from Mama Subhia's accusing words was the ultimate blow. Gulping for air, his lungs burned with each breath.

Huda stood in the doorway. "Are you done?"

"I need to get out of here."

She spread her feet apart and placed her hands on the doorjambs. "You can't leave now."

"Move."

"Shareef will be home soon. What do you think my selfish brother is going to do once he learns of this?"

"I don't give a shit." He shoved her aside and hurried to the front door.

"Knowing how Shareef feels about you, who do you think he's going to believe? Nadia or his wife?"

Omar's hand froze on the door handle.

"Are you really going to let Nadia face him alone?"

Omar let go of the door handle, balled his fists by his sides.

"I spared Mama and Nadia one crucial detail."

Omar swung around, his legs unable to hold him upright. "There's more?"

"Sameera claimed you had your way with Nadia that night."

A deep groan rumbled out of Omar's throat. He pressed his fists to his abdomen as if Huda had dealt him a physical blow.

"And that is exactly what Sameera is going to tell Shareef the minute he walks in." Huda folded her arms on her chest. "We need to contain him. Like Mama said. The damage is done. The snake has been planning this for a while." She unfolded her arms and pointed at the girls' bedroom. "Nadia is in there crying her heart out, Mama is almost catatonic at this point, and you want to smash furniture and leave?"

"Call Waleed. We're going to need him." Dragging his feet to the sofa in the living room, he slumped forward. "Tell him to leave Fatimah at home."

"I took the little girls over there this morning to keep them away from here. Fatimah will have to stay with them anyway."

Omar nodded. "Please open a window. I can't breathe."

CHAPTER
TWENTY-SEVEN

Trying to put his room back in order proved too arduous a task for Omar in the condition he was in. The surge of anger that propelled him to destruction put a lot of strain on his muscles, and he staggered at every move he made. His thoughts swept over events in disarray, jumping from past to present, lacking focus or reason. The unjust accusation leveled against him contradicted the guilt over the way he felt about Nadia, and his bruised honor blanketed every thought and sensation. He kept his distance from Nadia and Mama Subhia, suspecting if he opened his mouth, he would do more harm than good.

Huda withdrew with the women into their room. Not a sound drifted his way. The silence in the house cast an eerie vibe, the kind that descended after a thunderstorm, promising relief from the charged atmosphere. This one delivered none. Omar sat on his reassembled bed, faced the open door of his room, and waited for either Waleed or Shareef to walk in.

Waleed arrived first. Eyeing the destroyed furniture pieces piled in one corner, he scratched his head. "You had another episode? Do you need to go to the doctor?"

260

Omar pointed at a chair. "You need to sit down for what I have to tell you." He didn't waste time, or stumble on his words. He explained the situation in a straightforward manner, keeping his jumbled emotions in check as much as he could.

Waleed listened without interrupting, releasing a couple of sighs every now and then. "So what Sameera said was partly true? You two were alone that night?"

Omar placed his right hand on his chest and surged to his feet. "I was passed out half the time. As God is my witness, I never did anything to suggest any of this."

"You don't have to swear to me. I'm not doubting your honor or Nadia's. I just want to make sure I have all the facts." Waleed rubbed his chin. "I had no idea Sameera hated Nadia that much."

Omar dropped down on the bed. "I brought this on. I made Shareef marry her and bring her to this house."

"If you're going to think that way, then I'm as much to blame as you are. We need to think ahead. Find a solution."

"I will do whatever it takes."

"First, we need to control Shareef. We can't have him talk to his wife before we have a chance to fill him in."

Huda walked into the room and greeted Waleed with a curt nod. "What's the plan?"

"Don't let Sameera come out of her room." Waleed stuck an index finger in the air. "Not before Omar and I have explained things to Shareef."

Omar approached Huda. "How is Mama Subhia?"

"I gave her a pill to relax. She's calm."

"And Nadia?"

"I'm fine." Nadia joined them, her voice raspy and weak, her eyes red and puffed. She avoided looking straight at him.

He clenched his jaw, hoping to God she didn't blame herself. If only he could talk to her alone, make sure she understood she hadn't brought this on with her actions that night. Sameera would have found another excuse to attack her. He turned to address Waleed. "Please stay close to Shareef. Be ready to hold him back if he's stupid enough to lash out at the women. I'm not strong enough."

They passed the time in silence. Huda and Nadia sat side by side on Omar's bed, Waleed paced the room and Omar rested his back against the wall. He locked his eyes on Nadia's bowed head. When he heard Shareef's key in the door, he hurried to usher him into the room. Returning to his spot by the wall, he folded his arms on his chest and gritted his teeth.

"What's going on?" Shareef asked, his mouth slightly open as usual.

"We learned something outrageous that affects the family reputation." Waleed touched Shareef's chest. "Your reputation in particular."

Shareef raised his hands, palms out in a defensive move. "I didn't do anything."

"Your wife did."

"Where is she?" He turned to leave. "What did she do this time?"

Waleed sidestepped him to block the door. "We asked her to stay in her room."

"Move out of my way." Shareef half-laughed out his demand, not gauging the seriousness around him.

Showing her impatience and annoyance, Huda sprang to her feet. "Your wife has been telling women in the neighborhood Omar and Nadia are involved."

Shareef turned to face her. "Involved in what?"

"Sameera spread rumors they were together." Huda took a step closer. "That they were alone the night Fatimah went into labor. You took the little girls with you to your in-laws that night, remember?"

Shareef's gaze shifted to Omar. "I don't understand."

Omar unfolded his arms and stepped in front of Nadia, attempting to block Shareef's view of her. "Sameera is telling people Nadia and I shared a bed that night."

Nadia jumped to her feet and screamed, "She said what?"

Huda pushed her sister back onto the bed. "This is not the time to get hysterical."

Mama Subhia came into the room. Ignoring her son, she went straight to Nadia and took her in her arms.

Omar wished he could turn around to calm Nadia, but he didn't dare take his eyes off Shareef, who shortened the distance between them. His nostrils dilated, he brought his face close to Omar and arched his eyebrows. "Who is the lowly beast now?"

Waleed swung Shareef around. "Don't be a fool. You know it isn't true."

"We will see about that." Shareef shrugged his arm free. He yelled his wife's name at the top of his lungs.

Sameera sauntered in, her back straight, a smirk on her face.

Shareef grabbed her hand and jerked her forward. "Did you see them together?"

"They were too careful."

"Liar," Nadia screamed, her voice cracking with her sobs.

Emboldened by her husband's obvious suspicion, Sameera raised her voice. "Proof can be attained." A sinister look hovered in her eyes. "A simple examination. Isn't that part of Huda's job?"

Huda stumbled next to Omar. She ran her eyes over Sameera from head to toe with disgust. "How low will you sink?"

Omar's arms shook, a true beast inside him about to break free from his crumbling control. Sweat broke on his forehead. He roared at Shareef, "Take your wife out of here before she gets hurt!"

Instead of ushering Sameera out, Shareef left the room. She yelled after him, her eyes widened with panic, her voice piercing.

Waleed put himself between Sameera and Omar. "Calm yourself. Step back."

Omar turned his head to the side, clenching his jaw tight. He meant to get the bitch out of the room before Huda attacked her again. Did Waleed think he would raise a hand to the woman? Did none of the men in this family have a favorable opinion of him?

Shareef returned with a bundle in his hand. He placed it on the wide windowsill and unwrapped a green velvet cloth to reveal a copy of the Qur'an. He looked Omar in the eye. "Swear on the Qur'an you didn't touch my sister."

Sameera stepped forward. "He will lie."

"Shut up," Shareef spit. He pointed at Omar. "I know you don't take this oath lightly. If you are innocent, swear to it."

Mama Subhia went around everyone to face her son. "Why are you doing this?"

"You will soon know what kind of man your precious orphan turned out to be."

"How could you think that of your sister?"

"Contrary to what you believe, Mother, no one is perfect." Shareef pointed with his chin in Nadia's direction. "Not even her."

Determined to keep Shareef's fury focused on him instead of the women, Omar stepped between mother and son. "Call the neighbors to stand witness." His voice sounded strange to his own ears. Did wrath change a man's anatomy? Rearrange his vocal cords?

"Don't do this for my benefit, Omar." Mama Subhia placed her hand on his shoulder. "I accept your word."

Shareef thumbed his chest. "His word is worthless to me. Waleed is an acceptable witness."

"You're crossing a dangerous line," Waleed threatened. "I vouch for Omar's word without the oath."

"Let's get this over with." Omar moved toward the windowsill where the Qur'an lay, but Waleed stayed him with his hand. "Can you pray?"

He frowned, confused by his question.

Waleed brought his face closer and whispered, "Are you pure?"

Omar nodded, fearing his face might flush from Waleed's embarrassing check. Why did he have to ask? Upright men bathed to purify their bodies before dawn prayer every day. He was no different. "Of course." He clenched his teeth, absorbing another blow to his decency.

"Go do your ablutions like you're getting ready for prayer anyway." Waleed nudged him aside. "You are going to have to lay your right hand on the holy book for this oath."

Eager to get the matter settled, Omar went into the bathroom. Going through the repetitive motions of washing his face, arms and feet calmed him. Years of performing the purification steps five times a day in preparation for his prayers should have rendered the process ordinary, almost mechanical. But the weight of the task he was about to undertake made him cherish every drop of water touching his skin, cleansing his soul from within, leaving him serene and accepting. He understood Waleed's diligence and appreciated the opportunity he had given him to settle his nerves. The heavy act of swearing on the Qur'an indicated his word alone was not enough. Sameera had first attacked his honor, and now Shareef had cut deep into his worth as a man. None of it mattered. Nadia's wellbeing mattered the most. He would undergo anything for her sake.

Rolling down his shirtsleeves, Omar returned to the room and found everyone standing in a half-circle around a small table, facing him. The Qur'an, nestled in its velvety sleeve, rested at the center of the table. Nadia stood as far away from Shareef as possible. Omar connected eyes with her, and he tried to give a reassuring nod. The agonized expression on her face struck him harder than he expected, and his fury flared to consume his acquired serenity. He flexed his right hand, making sure his boiling anger didn't cause it to tremble. Shareef might take the shaking as a sign of shame or reluctance. He lifted his hand to his chest. "I am ready."

Shareef shifted in his spot. "Do it." The challenge in his tone lacked an edge, as if unsure how to proceed.

Omar placed his right palm flat on the Qur'an and steadied his gaze on Shareef. "I swear by the All Mighty God, I am innocent of what you are accusing me."

Sameera stuck her lips to Shareef's ear and whispered something.

Shareef shoved his hands in his pants pockets. "State the accusation."

Omar inhaled deeply, managing to stay collected. "I swear I did not take advantage of your sister."

Shareef bowed his head, breaking eye contact. "Did you dishonor her?"

"That is enough, man," Waleed intervened. "You got your oath."

Moving fast, Omar took hold of the Qur'an in both hands and hugged it to his chest. "As God is my witness, I never touched Nadia in any way that wasn't appropriate." He prayed Shareef wouldn't ask him to swear testimony about his recent nightly thoughts of Nadia. He lifted the holy book to his lips, kissed it and touched it to his forehead; he then repeated the act twice before placing it back on the table. Squaring his shoulders, he looked Shareef in the eye. "Are you satisfied?"

Shareef swallowed a couple of times, his Adam's apple bobbing with clarity, exposing his nervousness.

Nadia broke out of her spot and approached her brother. "Look at me."

As soon as Shareef looked at her, she spit in his face. He reared in surprise and raised a hand, about to strike. Omar grabbed his arm midair and shoved him backward until he slammed against the wall.

"Take your wife and leave this house," Mama Subhia said in a cold voice from behind Omar. He unintentionally relaxed his grip, unable to maintain a good hold, surprised by Mama Subhia's sharp tongue.

Shareef broke free and faced his mother. "You're kicking us out?"

"I don't want to see her face here again."

"This is my home."

"You are going to have to make another home for yourself." Mama Subhia's tone matched the hardened look in her eyes.

"You know I can't afford to rent my own place. I'm graduating at the end of the month. How am I to find a job if I don't have a place to stay?"

"You should have thought about that before you chose to accept your wife's lies and humiliate your sister."

Omar ran a hand through his hair. "If anyone should leave this house, it should be me."

"That would confirm the nasty rumors." Mama Subhia shook her head. "You must stay."

Shareef pointed at Omar. "So you choose him over me?"

"I choose to protect my daughter. Something you failed to do as her brother."

Noticing Nadia and Huda had fallen silent, Omar wondered if they agreed with their mother's decision. Flanked by her daughters, fierceness mixed with worry on Mama Subhia's face, a lioness standing guard over her weaklings. From where did she get this sudden harshness? Omar tried to soothe her. "We can fix this. You don't have to take it that far."

Mama Subhia took a deep breath. "Sameera must leave this house."

"Go pack your clothes," Shareef barked at his wife.

"Where will I go?"

"To the sewage hole you crawled out of." Huda spat out the words with enough force that they bounced off the walls and echoed around.

"Go." Shareef pushed Sameera ahead of him. "I'll take you to your family." He turned on his heels. "But know this, Mother. I will not come back."

"That would be your choice, son."

Storming out of the room, he shouted over his shoulder, "You will never see me again."

Waleed grabbed his arm in the hallway. "Go to my place. Fatimah will welcome you until things calm down here. Your mother is too upset right now. Give her a couple of days."

"I don't need your charity." Shareef pushed Waleed out of his way. "I'm done with this family."

"Don't be crazy." Waleed tried to follow him. "You can't cut ties with your mother."

"Let him go," Mama Subhia commanded before she collapsed on the bed. "I will not have him spend one more minute with us after he degraded his sister. Nothing will stop him from doing the same thing again. I have Salma and Farah to think about."

The front door slammed behind Shareef and Sameera. Mama Subhia's chest heaved for breath. Huda rubbed her hands. Nadia ran out and came back with a bottle of cologne, sprayed her hands and wiped her mother's face. Omar opened the windows, letting fresh air circulate through the room.

Mama Subhia waved off her daughters' hands. "We need to move fast to kill the rumor. Something to circulate among the women and take their minds off that nonsense."

"People will talk about you kicking out your son." Omar released a heavy sigh. "Because of me."

"Shareef chose his path and I don't want to hear another word about that." Using Huda's hands for support, Mama Subhia pushed herself off the bed. "I had to do it. People will know we don't tolerate Sameera's vicious lies. Now, think of a solution, please."

"Get them married," Waleed said from the doorway.

"Who?" Omar swallowed, unsure he understood Waleed's suggestion.

"You and Nadia. You know, sign a marriage contract. Let people know you are legally married under the eyes of God. It will silence everyone once and for all."

270

Omar's eyes darted to Nadia. She sat motionless, her face to the floor. He wished she would glance his way, give him a clue to her thoughts. But she didn't lift her head, and he didn't know how to respond, his heart caught in his throat.

"That wouldn't work." Huda stepped in front of him. "It would give credit to the possibility that something did happen between them." She focused her gaze on him. "Women will have a great time speculating about your relationship with Nadia all those years. It will feed the fire."

He tried to keep his face as expressionless as possible. Why did Huda say that? What sort of reaction did she expect from him? Did she know? A tough spinster who never showed interest in men herself, how could she figure out his obsession with Nadia? Had he been that obvious?

"Huda has a point. That wouldn't work." Mama Subhia brought her hands together and laced her fingers under her chin. "The women must be fed something more appealing to wipe out all doubt."

"Nothing more appealing than gossiping about whose daughter is getting married next, and to whom." Huda shrugged. "That's all I hear about from the women I visit."

"A powerful name." Waleed stepped forward. "We need a solid family name to throw its weight behind Nadia. Spread the word she is being pursued by a respectable, well-known family."

Omar turned toward the window, hiding his face from Huda's piercing gaze. Goddamn Marwan Barady.

His reputable family name would be the perfect silencer. And Marwan needed but a signal from him. If he had a tiny hope of Nadia refusing Marwan before today, that hope shattered to a million pieces. For the sake of her reputation, she would accept Marwan. And he would have to watch it happen.

CHAPTER
TWENTY-EIGHT

Positioning himself by the window, Omar leaned his backside on the windowsill and watched in silence as the others discussed Nadia's fate. She sat stone-like on his bed. Names were thrown around, of eligible men from the neighborhood or among Waleed's acquaintances, and ways to approach them. A couple of the suggested names caused him to cringe, since he knew a thing or two about the kind of men they were. He waited, unable to bring himself to utter Marwan's name before he had a chance to talk to Nadia in private. At least, that was the excuse he internally used to keep quiet. He feared if he opened his mouth, he would scream his lungs out for the way he felt. He waited for her to lift her head, to object or nod, to say anything. But Nadia remained distant and mute.

The more engrossed Mama Subhia, Huda and Waleed got in their planning, the more agitated and restless he became. Easing a growing cramp in his leg, he shifted his weight and released a frustrated breath.

Nadia shot to her feet, as if a switch had flipped in her head. "Have you all gone mad?"

Mama Subhia stopped mid-sentence. "What's wrong?"

"You have all gone insane, that's what's wrong." Nadia waved her hands in a wide circle. "This . . . this crazy plan you are cooking up for me. I'm right here. I'm not invisible. I have a say in this, don't I?" Placing her hands on her chest, her voice shook. "I just registered at the university. How could you think I would marry anyone now?"

Huda opened her mouth to say something, but Nadia ignored her, pointing at Omar. "And what about him? None of you said a single kind word to Omar after what he just went through. Shareef crushed his dignity, trampled his honor, and you all expect him to swallow his pride and stick around for my sake. You throw a ridiculous idea at him, then shoot it down because it doesn't serve my interests. What about his name? His reputation?" She turned to face Omar. "Why are you so quiet? Say something."

Taken aback by her concern for his feelings and her dismissal of the peril she faced, he moved fast to hold her elbow, and urged her along with him. "Let's talk." He threw a glance at the others before he left the room. "Give us a minute, please."

Nadia didn't hesitate and she matched his quick stride. He hoped for complete privacy, but with the recent accusation hanging in the air, he opted for the kitchen and kept the door open. Releasing her elbow, he took a step back and tried to keep his voice steady.

"I'll do whatever it takes to make things right for you. All you have to do is tell me what you want." He hesitated a fraction of a second before adding, "No matter how ridiculous an idea it may be."

274

"Can you believe that?" She rolled her eyes. "And I thought Waleed was a rational man, for him to suggest something so . . . so outrageous."

Omar cleared his throat. "Waleed means well. He's trying to help."

"I know. I know." Nadia slumped forward. "What are we going to do with this mess?"

"I'll support any decision you make, but before you do, you should know all the options before you."

"Weren't you listening? Apparently the only option I have is to pick a name from their magic hat."

"Marwan Barady is an option." The instant Omar uttered the words, the floor moved from under his feet. He dropped onto the nearest chair.

"You will not ask your friend to take pity on me, thank you very much."

"I don't have to. Marwan already asked my permission to propose to you." He raised a hand and indicated with his fingers. "Twice."

Nadia held the edge of the kitchen table. "Why do I have a hard time believing you?"

"I've never lied to you, and I wouldn't start with something like this."

"When did he ask you the first time?"

"The day I came home from the hospital."

"That was more than a month ago."

He held her gaze. "Right."

"So in the hospital the night Fatimah delivered, when I asked you about Marwan's future plans, he had already talked to you?"

He got to his feet, hoping his legs would hold him steady. "Yes."

Keeping her footing, she tilted her head back to look him in the eye. "And you kept it from me?"

Seeing the hurt in her big brown eyes, he braced himself for her tears to flow. "It wasn't the right time then. Not for Marwan. I told you about his family obligations."

"But you didn't tell me he was interested." She placed her hands on his chest and gave him a push. "Why?"

Her shove barely moved his body. A sadistic ache in his chest kept him standing firm, asking for punishment or simply more contact. Exposed, as if a bulldozer rolled off his body and stripped the flesh off his bones, he raced to find a coherent thought in his head. He had kept his word to his friend, hadn't he? He had let her know about Marwan's intentions. What was stopping him from telling her about his feelings? Would she still find Waleed's suggestion outrageous?

Nadia shoved him again, with more force this time, her voice rising. "Why didn't you tell me?"

Desperation drove him to recklessness. He held her wrists and kept them at his chest, trapping her against him and the table. "I had my reasons."

She tried to pull away.

He didn't let go. "Ask me."

"When was the second time?"

"Day before yesterday." He brought his head down until he felt her breath on his face. "Now ask me about my reasons to hold him off both times."

276

"I know why." She arched her back, creating more distance between their faces and thrusting her hips forward in the process. "You think I'm too young."

Cursing under his breath, he released her and she stumbled past the table.

"What's wrong with you?"

"Goddamn it, Nadia. Ask me."

"About what? You're not making sense." Confusion mixed with anger in her voice. The expression on her face shifted between bewilderment and fear.

His timing was wrong, as was the place. And he was going about it the wrong way. But he couldn't stop. Sameera's words of the special way he looked at Nadia and Huda's suggestive comments echoed in the back of his mind. Even Waleed's notion for them to marry didn't come out of the blue. Waleed must have sensed something. If they saw it, why didn't she? Like a drowning man grasping at anything on the surface to pull him out, he fumbled ahead. "How can you not know? Everyone seems to have picked up on it."

"I . . . I suspected Marwan's interest, that's why I asked you that day in the hospital."

He slammed the table with his palm, his composure reduced to dust. "I didn't mean him."

Nadia threw her hands in the air. "Oh, my God! You just said he was an option, didn't you?" She pointed at the door behind him. "Were you lying? Is that why you didn't tell them about Marwan?"

"I didn't say anything in there because the instant I mention his name, your mother and sister will salivate for the perfect solution he brings."

"So?"

"I want to know how you feel about him first." He crossed his arms over his chest, tightening his hold around his ribs, afraid he might crumble to pieces any minute.

"What do you think?"

"I'm not a mind reader. You have to tell me."

Her fingers flew to her collar. "Marwan is a good man."

"That's not what I asked."

"I . . . admire him. I always have." Her voice dropped to almost nothing.

He knew what was coming, and without a shred of sensibility, he asked for the torturous answer. Did one physically feel one's heart break? Why couldn't he take a full breath?

Waleed poked in his head from the doorway. "How is everything?"

Nadia walked past Omar, nudging his arm with her shoulder on the way. "We have a solution. Five more minutes, please."

Omar didn't dare turn around and let Waleed witness his undoing. Cold sweat dampened his nape and palms. He went to the sink and splashed his face with water.

"I need to get home soon," Waleed said. "Fatimah is waiting for me."

He heard Waleed walk away and buried his face in a towel.

"Who else did you mean, Omar?"

"Does it matter?"

278

"If it has to be this way, then I can't think of a better man than Marwan. Does he know about our ... problem?"

Throwing the towel aside, he watched the twirling water in the sink, his hopes going down the drain with it. "No."

Then it struck him. *Did* Marwan know? Through his sister, maybe? Was that why he had become persistent, asking for an answer soon, making it seem urgent? Was that his friend's way of giving him a solution without flinging the accusation in his face? Bile rose to his throat. He swallowed many times and faced Nadia. "He couldn't have known. No way Huda told Rihab, right?"

"But now that Shareef is out of the house, Marwan is bound to know. Besides, it's not fair to keep him in the dark like that."

"Sameera's family will not let her open her mouth. And Shareef is not stupid enough to tell anyone why he left."

"Was kicked out, you mean. There's no telling what Shareef may say or do anymore."

"I'll explain things to Marwan. It's better he hears it from me, anyway."

The tears he was bracing for flowed down her cheeks. He glanced at the door, making sure no one was there, then cradled Nadia's face in his palms. "Do you trust me?"

"You know I do," she whispered.

He waited for her to pull away, but she didn't. "I'll bring Shareef home and have him accept Marwan's official proposal. Is that what you want?"

"Just an engagement. I don't want to get married now" Her cheeks reddened in his hands. "Do you think Marwan would agree to that?"

"I'm sure he would." He dropped his hands to his sides. Rubbing his fingers together, he savored the feel of her smooth skin.

"How will you get Shareef to come back after what he did?"

"I have my ways. Don't worry. Your job is to convince Mama Subhia to accept him back. At least until we finalize things."

"And if Mama doesn't agree? Marwan can ask you instead?"

"It's not my place, Nadia. Shareef is your brother."

Her lower lip trembled. "But you will keep him from ruining things?"

"I'm not going to be there."

"Why not?"

"I can't."

She grabbed his arms with both her hands. "What do you mean? I need you with me."

Releasing a ragged breath, he pried her hands off him and gave her his back. This girl, woman, creature had no idea what she was doing to him. Be there? Watch Shareef give her hand to Marwan? Was she clueless *and* cruel?

"I have to leave at the end of the week. I've been assigned a special errand with the army." He headed to the door, hoping running away from her might make it easier to lie. "I'll arrange things before I go. Don't worry, Shareef will do fine. He will have no choice."

★ ★ ★

Tucking his new identity documents into his suit jacket, Omar walked out of the house late afternoon. He bore his new persona well, and used it to go through the motions of arranging Nadia's engagement. Omar Bakry no longer walked the streets. It wasn't him who entered Sameera's family home demanding to talk to Shareef in private, scraping whatever was left of his pride off the ground. It wasn't him who made an offer Shareef couldn't refuse, bribing him with a fat teaching contract in oil-rich Kuwait as soon as he graduated. And it wasn't him who pulled a favor from one of his street friends, now working at the Ministry of Education, to secure that contract. No, it wasn't him at all.

It was the mysterious fake leader, who had no ties to Nadia or her family.

He didn't have to say anything to Marwan's uncle. He sat in the old man's antique living room and nodded his head when asked if Marwan had told the truth of his commitment to Nadia. No one asked him to produce witnesses, or to swear on his honor, or to place his hand on the Qur'an. It must be nice to be trusted like that, to be treated like the man he once was.

Going along with tradition, he set the engagement date for Thursday afternoon. Two days. In two days, Nadia would be tied to Marwan Barady.

Good thing he wasn't Omar Bakry anymore.

Days melted into nights. Nadia went without sleep, unable to embrace the life that was about to descend on

281

her. Her eighteenth birthday would come in ten days, but she had grown years older in her mind. Sameera's vicious lie had the power to spin Earth faster on its axis, bringing on a new world — mean and harsh. Soon, she would be Marwan's fiancé — a dream she had yearned for before the world she knew stopped existing. How could she take that step when she didn't recognize the woman she had grown into?

Mama and Huda arranged for the big event, and despite the fact that it should be a men-only affair, they invited women neighbors to help them in the kitchen, claiming Mama wasn't well enough. They sent out her younger sisters to spread the word around the neighborhood. Waleed and Omar took over inviting the men on behalf of Shareef, who returned home like a triumphant king, leaving Sameera with her family. At least he spared the rest of them the unbearable confrontation with the snake. Mama insisted on that in order to accept him back into the house.

Omar spent his nights at Fatimah's and when he came home, he was either changing clothes to leave again or shoving papers into Shareef's hands. Nadia didn't know if he put Marwan in the picture like he promised, and when she caught him in the kitchen one morning, the look on his face scared her enough not to ask.

She tried to stay out of everyone's way, as if the whole affair didn't concern her. Something was wrong with her composition, for certain. When she told her close friends her news, their elation and excitement didn't rub off on her. When Fatimah fitted her for her engagement dress, she saw someone else in the mirror. Someone disjointed and broken, like a puppet pulled up by hidden strings. What was missing in this play?

Mama called her out to the balcony Wednesday evening. Dragging her feet, she slumped on the chair.

"Listen to me, Nadia. I don't want you to spoil everything we have worked so hard on. Now tell me, what's wrong?"

"Are you seriously asking me this question?"

"I thought you liked Marwan?"

"That's not the problem, Mama."

"What is it, then? You've been acting like it's going to be the end of the world for you tomorrow. You came up with this solution, remember?"

She rose to lean on the railing, facing the open skies. "I don't know what Marwan is thinking. Omar promised me he would tell him."

"Tell him what?"

"Oh, Mama. You know what I'm talking about."

Mama joined her at the railing and placed an arm around her shoulders. "He must have, *habibti*. Omar wouldn't hide something like that from his friend."

"How can we be sure?"

"Ask Omar when he gets home."

"Ask me what?"

Nadia did a swift turn. Omar filled the doorway, his face the same as that morning, dark and foreboding.

"Didn't mean to interrupt, but I heard my name? I thought you called me."

"I'm glad you're here." Mama pulled him to a chair. "Sit. Talk some sense into her, will you?"

He handed Mama the bag in his hand. "Roasted almonds." He kissed her forehead. "Uncle Mustafa would have approved of Marwan, don't you think?"

Mama clutched the bag of almonds to her chest. "I'm sure of it." She wiped under her eyes with the tips of her fingers and headed inside. "I'll make you something to eat."

Omar leveled his gaze on Nadia. "What's going on?"

Nadia took back her chair. "What did Marwan say when you told him about . . . the problem?"

He straddled the other chair. "He didn't say a word. Traditional men like him don't talk about such matters. He wouldn't even let me finish my words. He's making a statement with his actions, though."

She bowed her head. "What does that mean?"

"He's bringing close to a hundred men from the Barady family and their acquaintances tomorrow to ask for your hand. You know how impressive that is?"

She ran the back of her hand under her chin, brushing away unexpected tears. Why couldn't she hold it together anymore? And why wasn't she impressed? What was missing?

"You're crying? You should be happy. Families brag about the number of men accompanying a prospective groom, don't you know that?"

She shook her head. She didn't know and she didn't care.

"It shows the groom's good standing in the community and how much he values the woman he seeks. Shareef will have plenty to gloat about among his friends."

Lifting her head, she wiped away more tears. Why wasn't she happy, indeed? She searched Omar's close face for something that eluded her. Like the time she hid her valuable watch in a safe place then forgot where, she was plagued by the effort to remember. Restless now, she stared into Omar's bright blue eyes and found the hidden spot, but the item itself was lost to her. What was missing, Nadia? What was missing?

"I don't want to marry before I get my diploma. Did you tell Marwan that?"

Omar sat back. "I did. You'll have to discuss those details further with him."

A sense of urgency overwhelmed her, and she gripped Omar's knee. "But does he understand that?"

Omar shot to his feet, letting his chair crash against the railing. "What more do you want from me?"

Mama came back onto the balcony, carrying a tray of food and tea service. "Stop worrying, *habibti*. Everything is going according to plan."

He straightened the chair and offered it to Mama.

She spread hummus on pita bread. "Do you have to leave tomorrow?"

"Afraid so. I need to catch the three o'clock bus."

"And you can't tell us where this assignment is?"

"North, is all I can say."

Mama handed him the sandwich. "When will we see you again?"

"I hope to get reinstated here in three months."

Nadia held the teapot and filled glasses to the rim, her eyes blurry. Tiny tea leaves swirled around with the sugar spoon.

Omar. Omar was missing.

CHAPTER
TWENTY-NINE

Preparations were well underway for the important event on Thursday. Women from the neighborhood crowded the kitchen. Mama Subhia and the girls removed furniture to make room for the influx of men. Omar helped as much as he could, unable to find a legitimate excuse to stay away from the house. At two in the afternoon, he slung his duffle bag over his shoulder and said his goodbyes, kissing Mama Subhia on the forehead.

Nadia followed him to the stairwell. "I wish you didn't have to go."

He paused on the top step and pulled out a small box wrapped in newspapers from his pocket. "I have something for you."

"What is this?"

"To go with your dress. Sorry I won't be there."

"You don't have to give me gifts." Her voice shook.

He took her hand and closed her fingers around the wrapped box. "I want you to have this. Happy birthday . . . and congratulations on your engagement."

Nadia tore at the newspapers, lifted the cover off the small box and pulled out a chain holding a silver pendant. "Wings? You're giving me wings?"

"Angel wings." Backing away, he went down a couple of steps on the stairs. "And you've always had them." He pointed at the dangling pendant in her trembling hand. "That's to remind you how lucky Marwan is."

He turned and scurried down the steps, refusing to see more tears spill down Nadia's cheeks. The steps under his feet blurred. He ran a hand down his face and wiped his eyes. Damn!

Shareef met him at the bottom of the stairs. Omar thrust a firm hand to Shareef's throat. "You screw this up for Nadia, and you will wish you were never born."

Shareef's eyes bulged and he gasped for air.

Omar let him go and left the building. He zigzagged his way through narrow alleys. Hitting the main streets, he picked up his pace, jogging past people on their way home from work, eager to start the weekend. He approached the bus depot and sprinted, ignoring the fact there wasn't a certain time for him to report anywhere, believing the lie he used to stay away. He ran to the station then bolted through it, and kept on running past the bus stop and along the roadside leading out of the city center. Crunching pebbles under his feet, he ran until his lungs burned, pushing his healing body too far. Spasms took hold of his abdominal muscles, and he doubled over on the side, hitting the dirt.

He lay on his back and waited for the trees to stop twirling. The world spun like the wheel of a water mill. A bird soared in the sky, spreading its wings wide. He followed it with his eyes as long as he could.

Curious men approached. Rising to his feet, he hugged his duffle bag and went back to the ticket booth, ignoring their stares. He would travel to Jordan, join the Palestinian militia, and stay away as long as he could.

In the strange disciplined savagery of the militia training camp in the Jordanian desert, Omar worked through his frustrations. He grew his beard to look older and fit his new identity. He found his place with the mix of men, young and old. Angry men, eager to take back what was theirs. With his training skills, he gained respect from everyone in the regiment assigned to his command, and he formed a fighting force that was the envy of other factions in Al Karameh camp.

He found peace among the tenacity of freedom fighters and the unbound enthusiasm of warriors. Staying aloof, he formed no ties to any of the divisions in the camp, and by refusing monetary compensation from the Palestine Liberation Organization, he remained independent of political affiliations. Keeping his true identity a secret, he gained no friends and carved a revered presence by staying a mystery. The man who recruited him in Damascus never showed up in camp. No one knew the Englishman's real name, and Omar dug deep into the trenches of obscurity, burying his deprivation under layers of practiced hardness.

On the twenty-first of March, men talked about taking a break to celebrate Mother's Day with their families. He stayed put with his men and kept vigilant. Intelligence reports from Jordanian army officials warned of troop movements on the Israeli side of the border. He remained on edge.

Early morning, Israeli defense forces launched an attack on their camp. The Englishman was ready, his fellow fighters were ready, and the Arab world woke to a different war equation this time. Palestinian *fidaiyeen*, supported by the Jordanian army, repelled the attack and defeated the Israelis, captured armored vehicles, and inflicted heavy losses.

Victory how sweet the taste.

Dignity, how valuable the gain.

Winning the Battle of Al Karameh became the Englishman's identifier, an essential lever in the complexity of warfare. He had made his mark. He had made an impact. He mattered.

When the dust settled, Omar packed his duffle bag. One of his fellow commanders stormed into his tent. "I don't understand why you are leaving. The men need you. Look at what you've done in three months. Think of what you can accomplish if you stay."

"I have commitments."

"Your commitment should be to the Palestinian cause. We are stronger now. This is a historic chance for us. It will never happen again."

"I came to fight the Israelis. My mission is done."

"We all made sacrifices. Left our families and careers to take up arms. This is where we belong." The commander jabbed Omar's chest with his index finger. "This is where the *Englishman* belongs."

He sidestepped the commander and walked out of the tent. "I paid my dues and now I'm going home."

He had to return. If he didn't report to the Syrian army, he would be branded a deserter and would have to stay on the run. How would he see Nadia then? There were chains pulling on him, chains as strong as patriotic causes. Chains of the love he couldn't bury deep enough, shoot out of his system, burn to ashes, or blow to smithereens. Nadia was his cause, pure and simple. No one could shame him for it. He belonged in her world. Engaged to his best friend, married to a king, he didn't care. And he was the Englishman, the triumphant hero who would return home, his head held high this time. Would she take notice?

Closing the door to Marwan's car, Nadia dumped her stack of books on the back seat. "Where are the girls?"

"I thought I'd come get you first. Give us few minutes alone before we pick them up from school."

"What for?"

"The girls are always around. Your sisters, mine. I feel like we're babysitters every time we're together."

"Chaperones, or have you forgotten how cruel people are?"

"I would be happy with an adult chaperone, someone who gives us space every now and then." He stuck his index finger in the air. "And I don't mean Huda. She scares me."

"Well, I'm sorry my brother bailed on me and Omar is not around. I don't have eligible chaperones other than the girls."

Marwan blew a long breath. "People won't talk about you like that, anymore." He held her hand and brought it up to his lips. "It's over."

She snatched her hand away. "We can't just sit here alone in the car for everyone to see."

"You're being paranoid."

"Please drive."

"Fine." He jerked the car into traffic.

"I have three exams to study for, and an essay due on Tuesday. You will have to excuse me this weekend."

"I get it."

"Get what?"

"I understand, Nadia. You don't want me to visit today. You could just say that, you know. Say it clear and simple." He changed gears with the same intensity his voice carried. "Don't come over, or I don't want to see you, or I would rather be alone. However you want to phrase it. Just be straight about it, will you? Don't use excuses."

"I'm telling you why I can't afford to waste a weekend."

"That's how you see it? Wasting time — when you're with me?" His voice dropped, and she had learned over the past months, that was how Marwan showed his anger. He became subdued until he found a way to diffuse the situation. At times, she wished he would lash out instead.

Inhaling deeply, she tried to soothe him. "Don't read too much into this, please. You agreed to be supportive."

292

"I have been, don't you think? But I didn't realize you would rather be with your books so much instead of me."

"Of course, you wouldn't understand how important this is."

"Why? Because I didn't get to finish school? Is that it? I'm too ignorant to *comprehend*?"

"That is not what I meant." She couldn't help yelling and felt ashamed for losing control. "You're a man, an established merchant. You have everything set for you. You don't need more." She placed her hand on her chest. "I do. I *need* the security of a university degree."

"Security? You don't feel your future is secure with me?"

She dropped her hands in her lap. "You're getting it all wrong."

"That's Omar's influence, I know it." He screeched the car to a stop in front of the girls' school. "Let me tell you something. I do understand. I understand you made a promise to Omar to pursue your studies. But you also made a promise to me. I am not that selfish to ask you to choose between me and your diploma."

"What is it, then?"

"I would like to feel I *am* your future, and not an obstacle in the way. I need more." He ran his index finger along her jaw line. "I miss the way you used to look at me."

Salma and Farah ran to the car, Marwan's sisters right behind them. Grateful for the interruption, Nadia greeted them with more enthusiasm than usual. She threw Marwan an apologetic smile, faking it. He was right. She wasn't the same infatuated girl she used to be, dreamy and naive. She was a calculating woman now, a careful one. A woman who didn't have the safe haven of a father, or a sensible brother to lean on. And Omar was gone, forced away by Shareef's slander. Would Omar still have her back when he returned?

Omar was right. She was not ready for this. He had nudged her before the problem happened, had pushed her to think about a future independent of a man in her life. He had understood she needed more than what Marwan offered. She fingered the silver wings on her chest. When would Omar come back?

Marwan drove, the girls babbled in the back seat, and she drifted away. Why couldn't Marwan understand her point? She hated having to spell things out as if he were a foreigner, an outsider. No matter how hard she tried, her earlier childish infatuation wasn't maturing into a deeper connection with this noble man. He had earned her respect and admiration, for certain. But she had transformed into an emotional miser in his company, holding something back, something dear and special, raw and honest, defining the kind of woman she wanted to be. How could she explain that?

She glanced at Marwan, his profile rigid and tense. She could be submissive if she wanted. Have him come over this weekend, go along for the rest of the day, and then stay up all night studying. That would pacify him, wouldn't it? But why should she? It wouldn't be her, not her at all. Would he even pick up on it? Realize she wasn't genuine?

Omar would. In a heartbeat.

294

Once he arrived in Damascus, Omar reported to his command post and found he had two days to take his new station in Homs, a three-hour bus ride north of Damascus. Nothing he could do about that. He would have to settle for seeing Nadia and the family once a month on a weekend break. His next stop was Marwan's store, to make sure Marwan didn't tell anyone where he was. He intended for the meeting to be brief, to get his story straight before he saw everyone, and not give in to the yearning in his core for news of Nadia.

As soon as he walked in, Marwan pulled him into a bear hug, mumbling a prayer in his ear. "You're safe." Marwan pulled back, assessing him with his eyes. "You all right? No injuries?"

Omar worked hard on controlling his emotions. He didn't anticipate this warm concern, and he had no idea why he expected anything less from his best friend. "I'm fine."

Marwan closed the store and guided Omar to his desk area. "You did it. You redeemed our dignity. You, the *fidaiyeen*, and the Jordanians." Slapping him on the shoulder, Marwan's unreserved laugh reverberated through the store. "My God, you guys did it."

Omar shook his head. "I didn't do anything. I wasn't even there."

"Of course. But this is me you're talking to. Details?"

"I'm sure you heard the news reports. That's enough to know. To be frank, I couldn't wait to get out of there." He rubbed his neck. "It's all screwed up now. Tensions between Arafat and King Husain."

295

"Didn't I tell you? The Jordanians will not accept a growing Palestinian army on their land."

"I didn't train the *fidaiyeen* in that camp to turn their weapons on fellow Jordanians." Omar slammed his fist on the desk. "Those are good men, real fighters, caught in the middle of a skewed power struggle between leaders."

"President Nasser has been trying his best to resolve the situation between King Husain and Arafat. Our defense minister is not willing to involve the Syrians in this shameful conflict." Marwan removed newspapers from the desk drawer and spread them out. "Assad is at odds with the politicians since the defeat of the Six-Day War. They are trying to hold him accountable, but Assad has held them at bay so far." Marwan snapped his head up. "Did you report here yet? Please tell me you will not have to be involved in this mess."

"I'm not in active combat. Assigned to provide training in Homs."

"Try to ask for a transfer to Damascus as soon as you can." Marwan handed him a glass of water. "The good news is that you're back. You're healthy. And you have a job." Marwan's face brightened with a huge smile. "And Nadia and I are to be married."

CHAPTER
THIRTY

One year later, 1969

When Omar arrived in Homs, he searched for a rental place away from the garrison. He was in charge of basic training but had the freedom to leave camp when shifts allowed, and he enjoyed normal life in the city. The furnished room atop Um George's house provided enough privacy with its separate entrance, and it fit within his small budget. Most of his paycheck went to Mama Subhia. Shareef never sent money from Kuwait and Omar was left with very little to manage his needs. Yet, he didn't need much.

Like a sponge floating in a bucket of water, his affordable room absorbed noise from downstairs and forced on him lives he had no desire to be part of; he overheard private conversations between Um George and her six sons, discovering secrets worse than his own. His landlady prepared a meal for her sons and their families every Sunday, and she always insisted he join them. He obliged a couple of times out of respect, but he had no place intruding on the tight family, and he stayed in the barracks whatever Sundays he could manage.

Throughout the year, he skipped his monthly breaks, needing the physical distance to keep Nadia out of his thoughts. His efforts accomplished nothing more than making Fatimah angry, and eventually he had to go to Damascus when he had leave.

On his first visit he showed up at her place unannounced. Fatimah hung onto his neck for what seemed like forever and dragged him inside, crying and laughing at the same time.

"Forgive me, but you need to watch what you eat." He bounced his nephew on his knees. "You have grown a bit . . . wider."

Setting a fruit tray on the table in front of him, she straightened with difficulty. "That's because I'm five months pregnant."

He shot to his feet, holding his nephew firm in his arms. "Not again?"

"People usually say congratulations, Omar."

He took her hand and eased her down on the sofa. "Sorry. I'm worried about you. Isn't it too soon?"

"Two years is a good span between children. This is perfect timing. Sit down, relax. Everything is going to work out for the best."

Omar took back his seat. Relax? Did she forget the agony of her first delivery? Was she intent on keeping him worried?

Fatimah peeled oranges. "Shareef left for Kuwait right after his graduation."

"That was the plan." He didn't want to talk about Shareef, and he cared nothing about where he was. His nephew found his watch fascinating, and he let him pound on it with his chubby fingers.

"Yes, but he didn't take Sameera with him."

"It takes time to get her papers ready for a visa. I'm sure Shareef is working on it."

"I'm afraid that's not going to happen." Fatimah took back her son from his lap and handed him a peeled orange. "Shareef divorced her."

Choking on a slice of orange, juice dripped down his chin. "When?"

"Right before he left, apparently. She received her divorce papers from court two weeks after he was gone." Fatimah carried her son to the playpen in the corner. "Her brothers tried to reason with Waleed, thinking he had a say over Shareef to take her back before the divorce was final."

"What did Shareef say?"

"He told Waleed not to call him again." Fatimah returned to her seat. "Shareef didn't pay her dowry."

Omar held back a curse. "If her family pursues this legally, he'll be arrested the instant he tries to come back."

"Waleed asked her brothers to give us time to work things out. I don't know what he has in mind."

"I'll talk to him." Damn Shareef. Let him get arrested and rot in prison. Why were they talking about him? Nadia, what news of Nadia? He couldn't bring himself to ask.

"I can't help but feel sorry for Sameera. She deserved to be punished for trying to ruin Nadia's life. But what Shareef did was wrong."

"She brought it on. And the divorce is legal."

"Yes, but still wrong. A woman should have a say, not get discarded like that without her knowing."

"What makes you think she didn't know?"

Fatimah shrugged. "Shareef is too selfish. I think he didn't want to bother with a wife in his new life in Kuwait. I doubt he did it to avenge Nadia's honor."

Omar chose an apple from the tray and tried to sound nonchalant. "Speaking of Nadia, how is she?"

"I'm worried about her. I know Marwan is your best friend, but please try to keep an open mind."

Keeping a cool facade was almost impossible. To avoid looking at his sister and letting her see the hunger in his eyes, he examined the apple in his hand. "What's going on?"

"I will let her tell you, but I think something is off. Marwan is very traditional, you know?"

"And that's a problem?"

"Small things matter, Omar."

"Like what?"

"Marwan insists on driving Nadia to and from her classes every day, like she is a child going to school, not a university student. And he wants to know where she is at all times." Fatimah plucked a handful of grapes off a vine and dropped them onto his plate. "We never had to ask Uncle Mustafa for permission to go to the market, or to go out with our friends. Not like that, you know? It's difficult for Nadia to accept Marwan's controlling ways." She leaned closer, lowering her voice. "I shouldn't be telling you this, but I doubt Nadia will say anything to you about it." She glanced at her child playing in his pen, making sure he didn't hear her. "Nadia tries her best not to be alone with Marwan. You know what that means?"

His insides twisting like a laundered shirt about to hang on the wire to dry, he shook his head. "I know my friend. Marwan would never try anything indecent."

Fatimah sat back, a triumphant smile on her face. "Exactly."

"You lost me."

"I can't believe I'm having to explain this to you. Look, if a woman is truly drawn to her man, she will create the chance for him to try something. Do you follow me?"

He sprang to his feet, angry heat surging to his face. "They're only engaged. You're not encouraging her to do something disgraceful?"

"Nothing like that. Oh, you poor fellows. You have no idea what women are like." Fatimah gazed at him with the warmth of a loving mother. "Small things matter, remember that. A woman likes to know how desirable she is." She took his hand, pulling him down to his seat. "How could Marwan say or do anything to show his feelings if they are surrounded by children all the time? Nadia drags the girls with her whenever they go out, and she insists he brings his sisters every time he comes over. And that boy, his cousin's son? He's attached to Marwan's hip."

"People talk. Nadia is being careful."

"Too careful. I asked her. She wouldn't allow him to even hold her hand, lay his arm across her shoulders, or get close enough to whisper in her ear, or . . . or anything." Tilting her head to one side, Fatimah squinted. "Little things you fellows try to sneak in. Don't tell me you don't know what I'm talking about?"

Omar stared at his sister, not believing he was having this conversation. "I wouldn't —"

"I won't say more. I'm sure you understand where I'm going with this."

He cleared his throat. "Nadia knows what she's doing."

"She asked Marwan to visit Thursday evenings only, so she could study during the week. She isn't eager for his visits." Fatimah shook her head. "She is not drawn to him, I'm telling you. Not the way a woman is to her soon-to-be husband. Something is not right with them." Fatimah patted his knee. "This engagement will not last. Mark my word."

"It's best to stay out of it. I better go."

"Omar Bakry, you will not leave here before Waleed gets home."

As though Fatimah's words were Aladdin's summoning his Genie, Waleed walked in, his surprise and joy at seeing Omar genuine and heartwarming.

Nadia blew out the nineteenth candle on her birthday cake and struggled to hide the embarrassment brought on by cheers of onlookers at the fine restaurant. Marwan had gone out of his way to arrange the midday celebration. He had asked Mama's permission to bring her to this place on the outskirts of the city without the children. Mama had sent Huda instead.

Nadia's nervousness prevented her from enjoying finely minced kabobs and butter-soft barbequed lamb. Marwan noticed her lack of enthusiasm and kept trying to feed her bites wrapped in pita bread soaking with tomato juices. Despite herself, she cringed every time he extended his hand. Huda kicked her under the table and enticed her to accept Marwan's engaging efforts.

Glad that dessert brought the elaborate meal to an end, Nadia's stomach muscles relaxed enough to let her enjoy cake with big chocolate ribbons on top.

Huda left her chair. "I'm going to the restroom."

Marwan exhaled through a smile. "I thought she would never leave us alone. I kept filling her water glass, hoping she would get the urge sooner."

"You're terrible." Nadia fiddled with her napkin, somewhat amused. Pushing him to resort to that kind of behavior to get her attention wiped the smile off her face. She was the terrible one.

"What's bothering you, Nadia?"

She shook her head. "Nothing." She didn't lie. Nothing in particular was troubling her, but she *was* bothered. She couldn't figure out why. Marwan left no room for criticism in his plans, thought of every little detail, and looked so handsome in his simple white shirt and gray pants. What was it that darkened her surroundings in this daylight and prevented her from enjoying his efforts?

Marwan placed a gift box wrapped in white paper and a satin red ribbon on the table before her. "Happy birthday."

"Oh! I didn't expect this." She fingered the ribbon. "You've already given me too many gifts at home."

"Those were for your mother's benefit. I hope this one is to your personal liking." He crinkled his eyebrows and glanced in the direction of the restrooms. "Will you please open it before Huda comes back?"

Nadia pulled the ribbon free and opened the box. A gold heart studded with small diamonds rested on a red velvet pillow. She lifted the pendant with numb fingers. A gold chain dangled to the table. "This is too much."

"Just the right thing to replace those silver wings you wear all the time, don't you agree?"

Her other hand flew to her necklace. "This is from Omar."

"Someone as beautiful as you should be draped in gold." Marwan took the pendant from her hand and moved to stand behind her. "May I?"

She clutched her wings and froze. A mess of emotions gripped her — embarrassment, disbelief, helplessness, and finally anger. How dare he remove the connection she had to Omar?

"Hmm," Huda cleared her throat. Nadia swung her head to see her sister grab Marwan's hand. "We're in public, Marwan. Something this personal should not be done here."

His face reddened. He mumbled in agreement and returned to his seat.

Huda tucked the pendant in its box. "A fine piece of jewelry. You have exquisite taste."

Nadia rose, stiff and awkward. "I need to wash my hands." She walked away from the table before Marwan could say anything. She should thank Huda for stepping in the way she had. Whether the excuse Huda used to stop Marwan was genuine or not, she didn't care. Her sister had saved her from making a scene in this crowded place. About to trip in her haste, she almost ran to hide in one of the restroom stalls. That unknown presence dimming her world earlier became a bright beacon before her eyes. She cherished Omar's silver wings way more than she did Marwan's diamond-studded golden heart.

CHAPTER
THIRTY-ONE

One year later, 1970

Omar threw himself face down on his bed, exhaustion taking command of his limbs. Noises from downstairs traveled through the thin walls, too loud to let him slip into sleep.

Kicking off his boots, he flipped to his side and checked the calendar hanging on the wall by his bed. Four more days until his scheduled leave. Four more days until he saw Nadia again. Four more days, three hours on a crowded bus, and a long restless night, before he could spend two hours in her company.

When he took his breaks, he caught the last bus to Damascus on Thursday to arrive at Fatimah's house late at night and crash on the spare bed in the baby's room. The few hours he got to see Nadia the next day, before he took the bone-jarring bus trip back, had been pure torture so far. Surrounded by all the family members over a big Friday meal in Mama Subhia's house, he barely squeezed in a word or two to Nadia. And Marwan hovered, his manners gentle and caring, but his eyes fierce, full of possessive pride. Seeing him by Nadia's side did things to his mind, distorting the friendship he used to treasure and causing him to spend precious time gritting his teeth, rejecting Marwan's presence.

His eyelids closed, blocking out his meager surroundings. Fatimah was wrong. The engagement had lasted two years now, and counting. Keeping in mind her analysis of the couple's relationship, he went out of his way to stay at a distance, careful not to utter a word or make a move that would cause friction between Nadia and Marwan. Each time he had seen Nadia, brief and lacking privacy as the encounters were, she grew more and more solemn.

A child screeched from below, and his eyes flew open. What if Fatimah's evaluations were correct? And Nadia, afraid to take action on account of *his* feelings, needed him to intervene on her behalf? Marwan was his best friend, after all.

He sat up. She had been aloof and distant when he visited. Did she hope he would pick up on her dispirited demeanor, giving him a signal? Was he that thick? Nadia was used to speaking her mind to him, and he didn't give her a chance. Self-absorbed and wallowing in self-pity, he didn't see her drowning.

Jumping off the bed, he paced from wall to wall. He must find a way to have a private talk with her on his next visit, see if she was all right. Damn it! He did what he did for her to be happy, not to be all right.

A loud commotion and shouting broke through the walls. Without thinking, he grabbed his pistol and ran downstairs. Whoever scared Um George's family would have to answer to him. Barging in through the front door, he advanced in full combat mode. "Is it a thief? Is he still in the house?"

George blocked his path. "Nothing like that. But, by Our Lord Jesus, it's worse."

Omar blinked. He hid his pistol behind his back, taking in the scene. Everyone in the room was crying, Um George wailing in a corner. "What happened?"

"Jamal Abdul Nasser is dead."

Dragging his feet up the stairs late Thursday night, Omar tried not to land the heels of his heavy military boots on the steps for fear of waking his landlady. Before he reached his room, the door downstairs opened.

"Lieutenant?"

He leaned over the railing. "Sorry to wake you, Um George. I'll try to be more careful next time."

Um George waved her hands. "Come down, please. I need to talk to you."

Omar clenched his jaw. He was dead tired and should have been on the bus by now, heading home. The commanding general of his division had made a surprise inspection this morning, forcing him to cancel his scheduled leave. Something was brewing in the higher ranks, the entire camp put in ready mode. Depression and frustration dominated everywhere he went. News of Nasser's death had hit everyone hard, including those who didn't approve of his policies. Omar felt orphaned again.

Resigning himself to the uselessness of explaining that to the old lady, he headed downstairs. "What can I do for you?"

Um George grabbed his arms and pulled him closer. "Lieutenant, you have lived here long enough to know what kind of family we are." She pulled back and stomped one foot to the ground. "I will not tolerate any wrong doing."

"What's bothering you, Um George?"

"Your visitor at this late hour."

"What visitor?" He pointed above his head. "Did someone stop by?"

"I will not allow it. By Virgin Maryam, this is a decent house."

"What are you talking about?"

Um George stepped into her house, and waved him in. "Come in, and explain yourself."

He went into the foyer and stopped dead in his tracks.

Nadia stood in the middle of the living room, wringing her hands and looking terrified. She threw herself in his arms. "Oh, Omar! *Alhamdullilah.* I was afraid I had the wrong house."

Frozen with fear, he crushed her to his chest. "Fatimah all right?"

"She's fine." Nadia's voice came out muffled and shaky.

"Mama Subhia? The girls?"

"Everyone is fine."

Um George cleared her throat.

He held Nadia by the shoulders and eased her away. "What's wrong? How did you get here?"

"I took the bus." She glanced at Um George. "I need to talk to you."

He let her go. "Does Mama Subhia know you're here?"

Nadia shook her head.

"Huda? Marwan?"

She kept shaking her head, adding tears to her silent answers.

"Nadia, how could you do this? They must be going out of their minds with worry."

"I . . . I can't explain it. I just needed to see you."

Um George crossed her arms over her chest. "I demand an explanation now, Lieutenant. You told me you had no blood relatives other than one older sister, and you are not married or engaged. So what's your relationship to this girl?"

Nadia rounded on the old woman. "I told you, we grew up together."

Omar pushed Nadia behind him and faced his landlady. "In the two years I have lived here, did I ever cause problems?"

"I have to say no. You have proved your good upbringing. That's why I'm upset, Lieutenant. I didn't expect this from you. I hate to be wrong."

"You're not wrong about me. Nadia's mother raised me from infancy. I consider Mama Subhia my mother, too." He had to phrase it that way, unable to bring himself to say the word *sister*. He noticed Nadia didn't say it, either. "If you will allow me to use your phone to call home and let them know Nadia is safe, you will hear it for yourself from Mama Subhia."

Um George held her defiant stance for a heartbeat, then her face crumbled and she threw her hands in the air. "Oh, who am I fooling? I know you're not that kind of man, Lieutenant. I raised six men, myself. And I like to think I'm a good judge of character." She took hold of Nadia's hands and dragged her to a chair. "You should rest, dear. You look like you're about to faint. I'll make you something good to eat." Before she went into the kitchen, she waved her hand to Omar. "You make your calls, Lieutenant. Don't worry about me."

Omar called home, and for the first time in his life, he was relieved to hear Huda's voice. He let her rant for a minute, then suggested she inform Mama Subhia in her own way to ease the sting. His next call went to Marwan.

"I don't understand. Why didn't Nadia tell me?" Marwan's voice sounded calm, and Omar appreciated the effort it must have taken him to keep it that way.

"Haven't had the chance to find out what's going on yet. I wanted to let you know she's here. And she's fine."

"Had she told me she wanted to see you, I would have driven her over. Instead, she got on the bus at night by herself? Why?"

Omar leveled his gaze on Nadia. "You two have a fight?"

"This is foolish. Let me talk to her."

Omar placed his hand on the handset to muffle the sound and pointed it toward Nadia. She shook her head.

He returned the handset to his ear. "Maybe you should wait, Marwan. It's late, and I have to figure out a few things. I'll call you tomorrow."

"If I leave now, I'll be there before dawn."

"Don't. Sorry, man, but let me handle things from here." He heard Marwan breathe into the phone a couple of times, striving for composure no doubt.

"This is wrong, Omar. It will cause trouble, you know that."

"Keep it to yourself, please. Huda will control her end. I'll get back with you tomorrow."

Ending the call, he pinched the bridge of his nose and cursed under his breath. Marwan showed tremendous restraint, going against his deeply traditional nature. He deserved better than this kind of treatment. Nadia must have pushed him to the limit by her careless actions. Why had she done it?

Nadia approached him. "This was a mistake. I should go back."

"How? There are no buses running this late. I can't send you in a taxi by yourself in the middle of the night, and I can't go with you. I have to report to duty in the morning. I can see you're not ready for Marwan to come here, either." He rubbed his tired eyes. "Just what do you expect me to do?"

Um George set a food tray with cheese and cucumbers on the dining table. "Come now. Eat something."

Nadia didn't move. She looked like she was about to crumble on the floor any minute. He held her elbow and guided her to a chair at the table. "I'll spend the night in the barracks. You can take my room. Will that be a problem, Um George?"

312

"She could stay here with me. You should know I'm on call for George's wife, though." Um George shoved a bite of pita bread and cheese in Nadia's face, forcing her to open her mouth and take it. "She's about to have her baby. If George calls, I have to hurry over."

"I'll try to get an emergency leave for the day, but I'm not sure when and if they will give it to me. It wouldn't be right to have Nadia stay in your place while you're away."

"I don't need a babysitter," Nadia whispered.

"Um George has visitors all the time. I don't want anyone stopping by to start asking questions and jump to unnecessary conclusions."

"You're right. It's best she takes your room. No one will bother her there." Um George forced more food on Nadia. "Don't worry, dear. Everything's going to be fine. Whatever problem brought you here, I'm sure it will be resolved in the morning." She lifted her eyes to Omar, still standing by Nadia's side. "Right, Lieutenant?"

"Yeah." He attempted a smile. The woman never called him by his name.

Nadia turned her head away from Um George's extended hand. "No more, please."

Um George walked him and Nadia to the door. "Take her upstairs and get her settled for the night. Come see me before you leave. I will keep the door open."

Omar held Nadia's arm and guided her up the stairs. The moonless night shrouded them in darkness, further depressing the mood. The despondent girl by his side was not his Nadia, his cheerful, bouncy-ponytailed Nadia. God forgive him if he found out Marwan was behind this transformation. Best friend or not, he would pound his face to the ground.

The short sleeves of her dress exposed softness, and he endured an urge to caress warm skin under his fingertips. Her dress hem brushed his uniform at the knees with each step they took, making swooshing sounds loud enough to compare them to his racing heartbeat. Like waves, her flowery scent washed over him with the light breeze, and he held his breath until they reached the top. He let her go and opened the door.

Nadia made a sound somewhere between a sigh and a shallow cough.

"Are you sick? Should I get a doctor?"

"I just need sleep."

Keeping the door open behind them, he walked her in and turned on the lights. Some of his clothes lay scattered on his bed. He collected them and threw them into the laundry bag, picking up a pair of socks off the floor.

"I don't have spare bed sheets. I have used these a couple of days. Um George can lend me a set —"

"It's fine, Omar. Don't bother."

He dug a fresh towel from the closet and draped it over a chair. "New soap bars under the sink in the bathroom. Extra toothbrushes in the medicine cabinet for when I come over. Help yourself. Need anything else?"

314

Nadia's fingers crept to her neckline. "Something to sleep in? I didn't bring anything with me."

Tucked under the collar of her dress, her angel wings now showed, drawing his attention like a magnet. She rested the silver pendant on top of her chest over the smooth fabric. Wings rose and dipped with her quickening breaths. His insides clenched as though someone had punched him in the gut. He willed his eyes to the floor, ashamed he took in a good measure of her fullness. He turned to the closet, pulled out a clean shirt and laid it on the bed. "You can use this. Should I ask Um George for a nightgown instead?"

"The shirt is enough."

He headed outside. "Lock the door behind me. I'll be back as soon as I can tomorrow. Keys on the table here."

CHAPTER
THIRTY-TWO

Nadia leaned her back against the door and let tension drain from her body, taking in details of her surroundings. The room seemed small for a man like Omar. His bed under a window occupied the facing wall, a closet and small bookcase the left wall, and a kitchen sink, a small refrigerator and the bathroom door took the right wall. A small table covered with newspapers and one wooden chair crowded the middle of the room.

One chair? Where did he seat his friends when they visited? He must not have visitors. Was he lonely here? She had her entire family around her, yet without Omar by her side, she felt alone. If she brought herself to say that tomorrow, would he understand?

Her legs trembled and she drew a steadying breath. What had she done? She was in Omar's room, about to sleep in his bed. Leaving campus and getting on the bus earlier, she hadn't thought this far ahead. She had never seen him act this way, abrupt and reserved. All she wanted was to hear him tell her everything would be fine.

The hanging calendar on the wall caught her attention and she pushed away from the door. One weekend was marked with the word *home*. On the sixth of the month, a number was written in red ink. She flipped through previous months. Numbers were scribbled on the sixth of each month indicating an increasing count. What was significant about the sixth?

She hung the calendar back, and opened his closet. Running her hand over his hanging shirts, few and immaculate, she caught a whiff of cologne, a mix of lemon and cedar wood. She hadn't smelled that on him before. When did he start using this cologne? And who ironed his shirts?

Stepping back, she dropped on the bed. She should be ashamed of herself for prying into his things. She headed into the bathroom and washed, resisting the urge to go through his personal items in the medicine cabinet. Ready for bed, she draped her dress over the chair, slipped on Omar's shirt, and hurried under the blanket.

The scent of cedar wood, and a hint of something other than lemon, earthy and sharp, grew dense under the sheets. She buried her face in the pillow and inhaled deeply, inviting a quiver to run through down to her toes. Sleep. She needed sleep to deaden her heightened senses. She would have to face him in the morning, explain herself. Turning off the side lamp, she flipped onto her back and willed her muscles to relax.

Several breaths later, a thought jolted her. Marwan had brought his entourage of men to ask for her hand on the sixth. She fumbled to turn on the light, and reached for the calendar again. The red numbers counted the days since her engagement.

The sun hid behind dark clouds, as if it, too, dreaded the encounter with Omar. Nadia went about the business of getting ready, made the bed and cleaned the bathroom. Having nothing to do while she waited, she went through his books. In addition to a decent literature collection, there were several textbooks checked out from the university library. Their titles centered around topics of law. Buried under that stack, a worn-out book beckoned her. She pulled it out and the binding became loose. Several papers fell onto her lap. Appalled, she hastened to put the book together. Her eyes landed on Omar's picture among the scattered papers. A civil card identified him by a different name.

Approaching footsteps sounded outside. She hurried to tuck the papers back and return the book to its place. Omar's distinctive rapid knock followed. Smoothing the front of her dress, she opened the door.

He had his back to her, his hands clasped.

"Omar?"

He made a slight turn, giving his profile and keeping his eyes to the ground. "I hope I'm not too early."

"I've been ready since sunrise."

"I tried to call Um George to let you know I was on my way. No one answered."

"I heard her leave around four. You want to come in?"

He shook his head. "If you're ready, we better leave. It's almost seven."

"Are we leaving on the bus right away?"

318

He completed the turn and faced her, no smile on his face. "We'll discuss things over breakfast first."

Omar ushered her into a taxi and took his seat in the front. Talking weather with the driver, he didn't give her a chance to say anything. They arrived at a restaurant bustling with people. As soon as they entered, an old man ran over to greet Omar, drawing his lips wide with a smile. The man opened a pathway to a table near an indoor waterfall, separating the crowds with his body.

"Look at those people waiting. You must come here often to get this special treatment."

"It's the uniform. Never been here. One of my friends recommended this place. Hope you're hungry."

Her stomach in knots, she doubted she could keep anything down. Despite her better judgment, she nodded. Perhaps he would stop scowling when he started eating.

Food arrived at the table. Three kinds of hummus casseroles, multiple plates full of cheese pastries, marinated olives, eggs fried with the Armenian spiced meat *sojuk*, fresh mint leaves and onions soaked in ice water. Omar handed her a loaf of pita bread, steaming from the brick oven, and waited for her to start. She delved in, inviting him to do the same. He kept the conversation revolving around the food and seemed to be avoiding the matter at heart. Perplexed, she went along, nerves settling as the bites landed in her stomach. She started to enjoy the meal and searched for other topics to talk about.

"How is it that you have text books from the university library?"

"I enrolled in open classes."

"Can you do that from here? What about attending lectures?"

"Open classes don't require attendance. A friend of mine sends me his notes and I take the exams at the end of the year." He put down his spoon, seeming hesitant to say more.

She nudged him. "So you're going for a law degree?"

"It'll be good to have after I'm discharged from service. I don't plan on staying with the army. Not many opportunities for someone like me to move up the ranks."

"Someone like you? What do you mean?"

"Not a member in the ruling Ba'ath party. *And* I'm a Palestinian."

"Will they let you leave?"

Pushing his plate away, he wiped his mouth with his napkin. "I can resign any time I want. I wasn't drafted. Accepting my resignation depends on the political climate, of course. Too early to think about that. I want to get a degree first."

"I always thought you should be a teacher, remember?"

A mysterious expression swept his face, easing his intimidating scowl. "I remember."

She popped an olive in her mouth to stop from asking about the strange document she had found in his room. Better not spoil his lightened mood. She needed him to stay calm.

A waiter cleared the table and brought Turkish coffee service.

Omar fell silent. He moved breadcrumbs around with his index finger.

"Aren't you going to ask me what I'm doing here, Omar?"

"I figured you would tell me when you're ready."

Now that she had opened the subject, she didn't know how to proceed. She took a sip of coffee. Then another.

"Nadia?" His voice vibrated through her bones.

"If it makes any difference, you should know I accomplished what I came here for."

He stared at her for several seconds. "Would that be pushing your fiancé over the edge?"

She held his stare. There was no going back now. Relief cascaded over her with each breath. He understood. Omar understood everything. He knew her well. "I had to do it."

"You want Marwan to break the engagement, I get it. But why in God's name did you have to be this . . . this —"

"Stupid? Reckless?"

"This cruel, damn it! Marwan deserves better than this. *I* deserve better than this."

"Yes, I know." She tore her eyes away, tears threatening to embarrass them in this crowded place. "Marwan would never go back on his word to you. He would not hurt you like that. I was stuck. No matter what I said or did, he found a way to accept it. And I couldn't damage his reputation by refusing to marry him. His livelihood depends on his good name." She placed both arms on the table, bringing her face closer. "What would people think when they saw me reject him after two years of engagement? I couldn't do that. Not after he went against his family and silenced everyone for my sake." She shook her head. "It has to come from him."

"So you used me to plunge a dagger into his heart?"

"Marwan will not think ill of you."

"He's a man, like any other." A vein next to Omar's right temple pulsed with his words. "I have news for you. I'm a man, too. I guarantee you Marwan's mind went exactly where it should in this situation."

Her lower lip trembled, and she bit it down. "No. He . . . trusts you. I suspect it's too much for him to go against his old-fashioned nature, now that he knows I could be this careless." She nodded once. "In his heart, he will let me go."

Omar leaned toward her. "Why didn't you tell me you wanted out? I could have found a way without risking your reputation."

"No one knows about me spending the night here except Marwan, Huda and Mama. Isn't that right?"

He tapped his chest, snapping his back to the chair. "*I* know. How do you think I could . . . recover from this mess you created? You didn't think it through, Nadia. You didn't think it through at all."

She no longer could hold back the tears, and they flowed with her words. "Maybe I didn't. I was suffocating. I don't have anyone else to turn to but you."

He handed her a napkin. "Please, don't."

She dabbed at her wet face and scanned the crowds, checking to see if she had attracted anyone's attention. Thank God for good food. People were more interested in what was on their plates than what was going on around them. She buried her face in the napkin and tried to get a grip, listening to Omar take deep breaths, attempting to calm himself.

"Everything will be all right, Nadia. I want you to be happy."

The tenderness that poured out with his voice filled her with warmth. She had waited for him to say those words. She placed the napkin on the table and faced him with a hesitant smile.

He rose from his chair. "Come, we'll continue our talk on the way to the bus station."

She remained seated. "Will you not ask me?"

"About what?" He counted bills out of his wallet.

"Ask me when I realized Marwan was not the right man for me."

His hand froze. "When?"

"The day you left."

He plopped back onto his chair.

"On the sixth of the month, almost two years ago," she continued.

He breathed out her name. His lips moved, but no sound came out.

"I know you think of me as a sister, but I have to tell you I don't think —"

He shot his hand to grab hers on the table. "Stop. Just stop." His jaw muscles pumped tense and clear. Withdrawing his hand, he finished paying the bill and rose to his feet again. "I'll find a taxi. Meet me outside."

As soon as he cleared the restaurant doors, Omar gulped for air and waited for his heart to stop slamming against his ribs. Nadia was about to say what he always wanted to hear. When he had thought of this moment, he had imagined it to be different, more intimate, untainted by guilt. He had to stop her. What else could he have done? Nadia grew up, for sure, played women's games. And he, the novice, didn't know all the rules.

Someone grabbed his arm. "Knew I'd find you here when you asked me about this place."

He pulled his arm away. "Commander? What's going on, sir?"

"A disaster." Hand to his back, his commander tried to urge him forward. "A goddamn disaster."

He dug in his heels, looking over his shoulder for Nadia to come out. "You signed my papers for an emergency leave."

"You don't want to be off base right now, Lieutenant." The commander brought his face close, and whispered, "Minister of defense is up to something. Hafez Al Assad's military faction is taking over and it doesn't help we are not members of the ruling party." He held his tongue until a passer-by cleared their area. "Looks like a coup."

Omar froze. "Where does that leave us?"

"Fucked. And unless you get your ass back on base right now, you will be fucked even more. Your timing is going to come out suspicious."

"I'm on leave, sir. It's all on paper."

"They are arresting everyone on top and working their way down. I tore up your leave papers as soon as I heard. You have to assume your command before it's noted. You don't want them to think you were warned."

Omar checked his watch. "You have wheels, sir?"

His commander pointed to a jeep parked at the curb. "We can be on base in five minutes. I scared to death the soldier at the gate. He will not talk."

"I'm ready, Omar." Nadia touched his shoulder.

He sprang around, grabbed her elbow and half-dragged her to the jeep. "We have to make a stop at the central bus station first."

Climbing into the driver's seat, the commander raised his eyebrows at Nadia. "I told the general you were battling a severe case of diarrhea. So act sick."

"Yes, sir."

"What's happening?" Nadia's voice quivered.

"I don't have time to explain." He dug money out of his wallet. "Bus leaves in half an hour. As soon as you get to Damascus, take a taxi. You should be home by noon prayer."

She held on to his arm. "You're not coming with me?"

"I can't. Something major has happened. I have to go back to base."

She tightened her grip. Tears shimmered in her big eyes, screaming disappointment and fear. Her delicate shoulders trembled, the vein in her neck pulsing mad.

He fought the urge to hold her, to reassure her and calm her down. "I'll come as soon as I can." He pried her fingers off his arm and pushed the bills into her hand. "I'll call Marwan to spell things out."

The jeep screeched to a stop in front of the station. About to leave, Nadia touched his hand and stopped him.

"No need to come down. I know what to do." She stepped out and slammed the door. "Go. Don't waste time on me."

His commander floored the gas pedal, jerking him back onto the seat. Needing to lash out before his chest exploded, he slammed his fist into the side door, letting out a stream of curses.

"Who's the beauty?"

"Family."

"I see."

The dubious tone his commander used pushed him over the edge. He scooted forward. "I owe you for today. But to be clear, you say anything about her and you will wish you hadn't." He pulled back, holding the man's gaze. Threatening his superior was not a smart move. He didn't give a shit.

"That kind of family, then?"

"Yes, sir."

"Don't worry. And you don't owe me anything. Men like us have to stick together now. You covered my back when my wife was sick. Let's hope we make it there before the ax starts swinging."

326

CHAPTER
THIRTY-THREE

Nadia heard a knock on the girls' bedroom door. She lifted her face off the damp pillow. Crying non-stop, her voice came out hoarse and weak. "I want to be alone, Mama."

"It's Fatimah. Let me in. I can help you."

"Please go away."

"Omar called me. I have a message for you."

Scurrying off her bed, she unlocked the door. "He called you? When?"

Fatimah walked in, closing the door behind her. "About an hour ago. He's worried about you."

Nadia brushed her cheeks with her palms, trying to seem more composed. With pity clear on Fatimah's face, she knew she failed. "What did he say?"

"He wanted me to meet you at the bus station and come home with you. He was frantic. But I couldn't get the children ready in time. I'm so sorry."

Nadia wiped her nose with her sleeve, not bothering with hygiene or decorum. Fatimah's exaggeratedly sympathetic tone aggravated her. She must have looked as miserable as she felt. "As you can see, I'm capable of taking a taxi on my own," she snapped. If everyone insisted on treating her like a child, then by God, she would act like a child.

Reaching for her hand, Fatimah pulled her toward one of the beds. "Omar didn't want you to come home alone and have to face Huda by yourself."

"Huda is out."

"Mama Subhia is so worried. She told me you locked yourself in here as soon as you arrived and refused to talk to her."

Nadia glanced at the door. "I didn't mean to upset Mama. I just . . . I . . . I don't know what to say to her."

"I brought the children. They will keep her busy and make her feel better, don't worry. I want to understand what's going on with you before Huda comes home." Fatimah crossed her legs and tilted her head to one side. "Huda will not be as patient as I am."

Fatimah's veiled threat threw Nadia into a fit of uncontrolled sobbing. She covered her face with both hands. Why couldn't she hold it together anymore? She had not stopped crying since Omar left her at the bus station in Homs.

"Talk to me, *habibti*. Why did you go see Omar?"

Dropping her hands to her lap, she shrugged. "It doesn't matter."

"Oh, it does. A great deal. Marwan is going to walk in here at any minute. I suggest you have a better answer for him."

"You called him?"

"Omar did. And he asked me not to leave you alone when Marwan gets here." Fatimah brought her voice lower. "What happened?"

Nadia crossed over to the window. She imagined Omar by her side when she faced Marwan. But Omar had better things to do, didn't even give her a chance to explain. He had stopped her, cut her off before she made a bigger fool of herself. At least he sent her an ally.

"I told Omar I don't want to marry Marwan."

"You could have told him that over the telephone. Or written him a letter." Fatimah joined her by the window. "I think I understand why you did it this way. But did my brother?"

"It made him angry. He said I used him to stab his friend in the back."

"You could have come to me. I would have understood. I saw it coming."

"You did?"

Fatimah nodded. "I told Omar the day he returned from his secret assignment, this lid is not for this pot. You and Marwan are not right for each other." Fatimah pulled on Nadia's hands, bringing her face closer. "I think it hurt Omar to know that. He wanted you to be happy."

"Omar gave me what I asked for. But I didn't know what I wanted then." She buried her face in Fatimah's shoulder, using the fabric of her dress to soak fresh tears. "Why did Omar listen to me?"

Sure steps clicked on the tile floor, and she sensed Fatimah stiffen.

"Omar will do anything for you, stupid." Huda's sharp voice slashed through the air like a whip.

Nadia snapped her head out of Fatimah's embrace.

"Whether you deserve it or not, is a different story." Huda slammed the door shut.

Fatimah let go of Nadia. "Why are you so cruel?"

"Oh, please." Huda rolled her eyes. "At least I'm honest. I don't manipulate people like Nadia does."

"I did the best I could with the mess my coward brother and his evil wife threw at me. I didn't manipulate anyone."

"What do you call what you have done, then? First you accepted Marwan, kept him hanging for two years. Then you cast him aside and threw your problem on Omar. They both deserve better." Huda took quick steps closer and lifted her index finger in Nadia's face. "They deserve better than *you*."

"That's what Omar said." Nadia threw herself on the nearest bed and buried her face in the cover, fully absorbed in her misery.

"Huda, please. You're not helping the situation." Fatimah sounded angry, her tone firm. "Can't you see how upset she is? Marwan will arrive soon and we need to have a plan to diffuse the situation, not escalate it."

"Fine. Let's do this." Huda held Nadia's shoulders and forced her to flip on her back. "Do you want to marry Marwan?"

"No."

"Then tell him that straight to his face."

"She can't. It has to come from him." Fatimah gave Huda a little shove, moving her away from Nadia. "Marwan is the one who must end it. At least that's how it should seem to everyone. For his sake."

Huda drew a long breath. "So that's why you went to Omar?" Her voice grew louder. "It's worse than I thought. You used Omar to hurt Marwan? How stupid can you be?"

"Stop calling me stupid." Nadia pushed off the bed. "I tried everything I could think of to show Marwan we aren't suited for each other. Nothing worked."

"And you decided to ruin Omar instead?" Huda threw her hands in the air. "You're right. You're not stupid. You're selfish."

Fatimah grabbed Huda's arm. "What do you mean she ruined Omar?"

"Don't tell me you don't know how your own brother feels about her."

"Of course I know. I would have to be blind not to see it. But she has no idea. And if you hadn't barged in like a thunderstorm, I would have gently opened her eyes."

Nadia stepped between them. "What are you two talking about?"

"It was plain as daylight." Huda tapped Nadia's chest. "The day you said you wanted Marwan, you snuffed Omar's soul out."

"What are you saying?"

"Omar is in love with you, stupid."

The words rang in her ears. A hot wave flashed her cheeks, as if Huda had thrown a cup of tea in her face. Her knees buckled and she dropped on the bed again. A hand touched her shoulder. Fatimah's lips moved, but she heard nothing. Huda snapped her fingers in front of her eyes. She tried to focus. "This can't be," she heard herself say.

"Why do you think Omar didn't request to transfer back here not once during the past two years?" Fatimah smoothed back her hair. "He couldn't handle seeing you together with Marwan."

Feeling behind her, she scooted on the bed until her head touched the windowsill, needing the space to breathe, to comprehend. "He . . . he never mentioned anything."

"How could he?" Fatimah sat beside her. "Marwan is his best friend. And you needed Marwan to silence tongues."

Huda bent forward and placed both hands on Nadia's knees. "You gave Omar no choice but to step aside."

Nadia's heart thumped hard, threatening to jump out of her chest. She started hyperventilating. Her thoughts scanned the past years, replaying events she had experienced with Omar, situations she could have seen in a different way had she known. The patience he had shown Shareef when he demanded his sworn oath, his strange behavior in the kitchen the day he had told her about Marwan's intentions, the emotional way he had bid her goodbye the day of her engagement, his marked calendar counting the days since then. The memories crashed down on her and she feared her heart might stop beating altogether. Fingering her pendant, she whispered, "Why didn't anyone tell me?"

"I had my suspicions for a long time. It's not my place to say anything." Fatimah laid a gentle hand on hers. "He never confided in me or Waleed."

Huda crossed her arms over her chest. "I doubt he confided in anyone."

"It's possible you are wrong, then." They had to be. Life was not that accommodating. Now that she realized the depth of her feelings for Omar, the possibility of him sharing her feelings seemed improbable. She could not be this lucky. No one was. "How can you be so sure?"

"Oh, I'm sure. No matter how hard he tried, he couldn't help his emotions from shining in his eyes when he looked at you." Huda shook her head. "Honestly, it was difficult to watch."

Recalling how awkward Omar had been last night, and how he had cut her off in the restaurant, Nadia sprang to her feet. "Do you think Marwan knows?"

"We will find out soon enough." Huda headed to the door. "I'll see what Mama has in mind before Marwan gets here."

Nadia stumbled after her. "Mama knows about Omar too?"

"She was the first to notice."

An hour crept by. Nadia's bewilderment and self-doubt increased with each ticking second. The anticipation of Marwan's visit drove her mad. She kept to herself in the room, unable to face her mother, her thoughts oscillating like a pendulum between her fulfilling interactions with Omar and her stale time with Marwan. Why hadn't she seen what everyone else saw?

Foretelling possibilities for a future with Omar, relief swept over her like a tide bringing hope and promises.

Lightheaded, she couldn't sit still. She paced the room, suppressing nervous laughter, keeping elation trapped inside her chest. Marwan. She had to address the issue of Marwan. Should she tell him how she felt before he had a chance to say anything, or should she let him get everything out of his system first?

The doorbell rang, and she heard him greet everyone in the living room. Running her fingers through her loose hair, she took a deep breath and stepped out.

Marwan stood to face her, his stance reserved and polite. "Are you all right?"

She nodded, her courage abandoning her, tying her tongue. She took the seat across from where he stood and threw an apologetic glance at her mother, sitting with both her grandchildren on her lap. To her surprise, Mama drew her lips into a soft smile, bolstering her nerves.

Marwan sat on the edge of the sofa and rested his elbows on his knees. "I respected Omar's wishes and waited until now to talk to you. Will you tell me what's going on?"

"Did he not explain things?"

"Omar didn't say much. He has enough to worry about, and you shouldn't have burdened him with our problems."

"What's the matter with Omar?" Mama asked.

"You haven't heard?" Marwan sounded impatient. "A military coup overthrew the government. Hafez Al Assad is in power now."

Fatimah grabbed her youngest before he slipped from Mama's hands. "Is Omar in danger?"

"It shouldn't affect him a great deal. His superiors most likely will change. Assad will instate Ba'ath party members loyal to him in places of power."

"That's why Omar couldn't come with me." How blind and selfish she had been. She hadn't sensed his panic when he dropped her off at the bus station. She had been too absorbed by her predicament. Huda was right. She *was* selfish.

"Omar will be stuck in Homs for a while, until things calm down." Marwan addressed Mama, "Do you mind if I have a word with Nadia in private?"

Mama waved her hand at Huda and Fatimah. "Come. Let them talk."

Fatimah hesitated to follow Mama into her room, trying to honor her promise to Omar not to leave Nadia alone with Marwan.

"Fatimah, the children need to be changed." Mama's tone left no room for argument, and Fatimah complied.

As soon as the door to Mama's room closed, Marwan rounded on Nadia. "How could you do this?"

"Do what?" Nadia tried to sound nonchalant, making it seem she had not a care in the world. If Marwan was looking for a way to accept what she did, then she would have to force his hand.

"You realize your situation is bad right now?"

"According to whom?"

"To me, damn it." His voice remained calm, but his face reddened. "I thought you held me in better regard than this. You are tied to my name. What you did affects my family."

"But your family doesn't know."

He placed his hand on his chest. "*I* know. You went to Omar behind my back. You spent the night . . . outside your home. And don't try this meaningless talk that he is *like* a brother to you. I know better."

She stared at him. So he knew how Omar felt. And like everyone else, he had said nothing. Was she the last to know? Anger boiled under her skin. Perhaps she underestimated Marwan's trust in Omar. "You aren't seriously accusing me or Omar of misconduct."

"Don't insult me." Marwan thrust his face closer. "I know Omar like I know the lines in my palm. I thought I knew you too, but you took me by surprise."

"Maybe I shouldn't have been so impulsive, I give you that. But I don't see how big of a problem that is."

He slammed his hands to his sides. "If you can't feel the weight of what you've done, then I have a *bigger* problem." He held her shoulders and mellowed his tone. "Two years. Two years and you haven't figured out what matters to me?"

"Your family, your cousin's orphan, your commitment to your uncle, your frien —"

"*You.*" His arms shook. "You are more important." His voice spilled out like scorching lava.

Confused by the raw emotion, she let him pull her closer. His facial features morphed with the closeness. Angles of his strong jaw softened and his shaved skin hid his masculine severity. What had she done to this solid man? Though trapped by his strong grip, she felt a power she had not known before. Feminine power putting her ahead of anything else in his life. She swallowed.

He touched his forehead to hers. "Let's get married and end this madness."

The warmth of Marwan's forehead burned her skin; his heavy breathing fanned her cheeks. Her stomach turned like it did every time Mama fried fish in the house. A compelling need to escape outdoors had always overtaken her. Now, she had the same urge to flee. She did not expect this turn. Things had gone in the opposite direction of what she wanted. She misjudged Marwan's feelings for her. All the better reason to let him go. He did deserve better than her. Someone who could love him back with the same intensity, if not more. Someone pure and whole. And she was tainted with the controversy she had created by her actions, a huge part of her soul resting in Omar's hands. She placed her hands on Marwan's chest and pushed. A timid move.

His fingers tightened on her shoulders. "Marry me." His voice but a whisper, he failed at hiding the urgency in his tone. "I will do everything I can to make you happy." His words oozed with emotion, coaxing, shrouding her with new sensations she didn't invite. Why did he make her experience this now?

She shoved him harder, unlocking their bodies. "Are you testing me?"

"What?"

"You want to see if I will allow you indiscretions? Now that you think I act recklessly?"

"Nadia, no." He stumbled backward. The insult colored his face crimson and indignation deepened his dark eyes. "How could you think that of me? I can't help the way I feel about you. I want to marry you despite —"

"Despite what I did? I don't need your charity."

"Despite the fact that you don't love me the same way." He yelled out the words, and his eyes flew to the door of Mama's room. It remained shut. "If that makes me a fool, I don't care."

"What does that make me?"

"My wife." With his defeated tone, the words came out broken. "Why are you doing this? I've done everything you asked of me. With all the pressures I am under, I've done my best to accommodate your wishes." He reached out for her again, and she backed away. "Please tell me what you want. You don't want to take care of my cousin's child? That can be worked out. You want to get your diploma? I will make sure you do. You want a job? Fine by me."

Desperation seeped into his voice and saddened his beautiful eyes, hiding them further behind his long eyelashes. It tore at her heart. Her anger turned to pity, an emotion she never expected to experience toward strong, dignified Marwan. She had to end his downward spiral. But what could she say? She dropped on the sofa. "I cannot marry you."

"Why?" he exploded. "For the sake of all angels, just tell me."

Her tears ran as if a faucet had been turned on. Was that all she could do? She cowered under his piercing gaze, her tongue tied a thousand knots.

"Is there someone else?"

Several seconds passed and she remained silent. She twisted her engagement ring around her finger, hesitant to slide it off while he watched.

He dropped beside her, his knees almost touching hers. "Is that why you went to Omar?"

"He . . . he was very angry." She chanced a glance at Marwan. "He thought I was . . . cruel for using him to hurt you."

He released a ragged breath. "Omar was right."

"Please, you must not blame him. Omar cherishes you."

His jaw muscles clenched several times. "And you . . . love *him*?"

Was there a state deeper than love? Omar was part of her composition. It was like waking up from a coma when she came into his presence. There was no way she would admit her feelings out loud now, to articulate them using simple words for the first time. And to whom? To her fiancé? She hardly breathed.

"You refused to take off his pendant and wore it with mine all the time. No one wears silver and gold necklaces together. Rihab had told me and I thought nothing of it." He placed a hand on her fidgeting fingers, staying them. "I should have known then." He rubbed his thumb over the back of her hand. "Does Omar know?"

"I don't think so. I don't want to ruin your friendship with him."

"You don't give me enough credit. You don't know me at all." He knelt in front of her, took off his ring, and placed it in her hands. "Regardless of what you think of me, I want you to be happy." He brought her hands to his lips and placed a warm kiss.

She watched him leave through the front door, her vision blurred.

The door to Mama's room opened. "Why are you crying?" Mama sounded angry and less forgiving than Nadia had hoped. "Did you expect another outcome after what you did? Isn't this what you wanted?"

Fatimah shoved a couple of tissues into Nadia's hands. "Better it happened now. Better than having her come back to you in a couple of years divorced with a baby in her arms."

Mama took a chair. "What are we going to do now? You have ruined everything!" Her outburst snapped Nadia out of her trance. "People will want to know why Marwan broke the engagement." Mama slammed her palms on her thighs. "What have I done to deserve this?"

Another slap.

"Why did God take Mustafa and leave me to deal with this child alone?"

Slap.

"Now I will have two unmarried daughters under my roof."

Slap.

"Where is my son to relieve my load?"

"Mama, stop wailing like an old woman." Huda stepped in. "Shareef would have made a bigger mess had he been here, so don't pretend he could be the answer to your troubles. And who told you I wanted to be under the mercy of a man, anyway?"

"Stop aggravating the matter." Fatimah pushed past Huda and pulled quiet Nadia off the sofa. "Kiss your mother's hand, *habibti*. Ask for her forgiveness and blessings. We will work everything out."

Nadia grabbed Mama's hands, kissing them and touching them to her forehead three times. Mama remained silent, not uttering the usual forgiving prayers. Desperate, Nadia dropped to her knees and tried to kiss her mother's feet. Mama placed a hand on Nadia's head. "Get up."

The phone rang, startling everyone. Huda picked up the handset, put her hand on the speaker, and mouthed out the words, "Rihab. Marwan's sister."

Mama motioned to talk to Rihab. Huda shook her head, gripping the phone with both hands. She greeted Rihab, and then fell silent. Several minutes passed.

"Of course. Thank you." Huda ended the call.

"Well?" Mama wrung her hands. "What did she say?"

"Rihab apologized on behalf of her brother." Huda stuck an index finger in the air. "Apologized, you see?"

Mama raised her eyebrows. "Apologized?"

"Marwan told her he had to break his commitment to Nadia because his uncle was putting too much pressure on him to marry his cousin's widow. She hoped we could understand Marwan's position. She wants to visit soon to wish Nadia well."

Mama put her palms together under her chin and lifted her eyes to the ceiling. *"Alhamdullilah!"*

"Rihab said Marwan hopes he will be welcome here once Omar returns." Huda shrugged. "I agreed, of

341

course. The noble man proved himself to be of a special caliber." She connected eyes with Nadia. "Makes me reconsider my opinion of men."

An invisible force pulled Nadia's bones out of her body. She no longer could bring herself to her feet, and she fell back on her heels. Fatimah leaned by her side, surrounded her with her arms, and pulled her along to her bed, murmuring soothing words and sucking the guilt out of her soul.

CHAPTER
THIRTY-FOUR

"I did what Nadia wanted. You understand that, right?" Marwan took the chair in Omar's room. "I had no choice. It has nothing to do with . . . with what she did."

Omar kept his eyes on the water kettle, watching boiling bubbles rise to the surface. He didn't know what to say to his friend, who had arrived on his doorstep out of the blue. So much had happened in one day. When he had returned to the base, he had been caught up in the upheaval of the swift rank changes following the coup. His mind had kept straying to Nadia's visit, to her declaration of sorts, and his inability to do a damn thing about it had mounted with his frustrating situation. The world was crumbling around him: the death of Nasser but a month earlier, and now this earthquake of a coup. The superior who had saved his ass in the morning was arrested, no idea what the charge was. Omar had made a quick visit to the man's wife as soon as he was allowed to leave the base, and assured her he would launch a defense for her husband. He had friends who graduated ahead of him and worked at attorney offices all over the country, including the Military Court.

His misery reached its peak when he made it home late at night, exhausted and falling apart. The signs of Nadia's presence bombarded his senses. The shirt she had worn to bed lay folded on top of his blanket, the towel hung on a hook behind the bathroom door. If he closed his eyes, he could smell a hint of her sweet perfume. He had to open the window to be able to function, and thank God he had before Marwan showed up.

He stirred a heaped spoonful of coffee and turned down the flame, using the mundane task of making Turkish coffee as an excuse to keep his back turned.

"After all this time, she wanted me to let her be," Marwan mumbled. "Why didn't she come out and say something, instead of going about it the way she did?"

Omar killed the gas. "She didn't want to embarrass you in front of your family."

"She doesn't want to marry me. I don't think she ever did."

The kettle shook in Omar's hand. "Did she say why?" His voice sounded like it belonged to a mischievous boy about to be caught red-handed.

Marwan exhaled loudly. When he took too long to answer, Omar turned to meet Marwan's piercing gaze. He was no coward. Time to face the storm.

Marwan's lips twisted as he ran his tongue over his teeth, clearly weighing what to say. "She didn't have to."

Omar filled one cup to the rim, splashing coffee on the cup's small saucer.

344

"She changed, you know?" Marwan's voice rumbled low. "Not the naive girl anymore."

"She grew up." Omar abandoned the coffee service, sure his shaking hands would make a bigger mess before he reached the table. Could Marwan hear his drumming heart across the small room?

"At my expense. I'm convinced someone else is in her heart."

Omar held his breath. "Who?"

"She spared me the humiliation of telling me to my face. You have to give her that."

Exhaling in relief, he carried the coffee tray to the table.

Marwan reached for a cup, ignoring the coffee dripping from the bottom. He took quick sips. "If anyone can find out, it would be you."

"What makes you think that?"

"You two are close enough. She . . . misses you." Marwan dug in the paper bag he carried, produced a book, and placed it on the table. "I think this belongs to you."

Omar slid the book to his side to check the title. Lacy ends of a blue and white ribbon dangled from one side. He withdrew his hand and studied his friend.

"She did me a favor, you know?" Marwan pushed the book further away from him. "With all the pressures I'm under from my uncle, I think this might be for the best, after all. I've become very fond of the widow's son. He's already like a son to me."

Omar tried to decode Marwan's words. The man's pride smashed to dust, he needed the charade of his uncle's pressure to save face. Omar would not deprive him of that mask. He gave a curt nod, letting Marwan know he would play along. "You may be right."

Marwan rose to his feet. "Are we good here? You and me?"

Shamed by his secret elation at this development and feeling guilty for subjecting his friend to this treachery, he stuck his hand out. "You're like a brother to me. I don't want this to come between us."

Marwan grasped his hand and stepped into a genuine hug. "Of course it will not."

Two months later, Omar had his first chance to take a weekend leave and go to Damascus. He didn't phone ahead of time, and headed to an electronics store as soon as he stepped off the bus. He wanted to walk in carrying gifts, and he had just the right thing in mind for everyone. He had been saving for it for months.

Balancing the big box between his arms, he climbed the stairs home and used the tip of his boot on the door. He had no idea who opened it at first since he could not see in front of him.

"What is this?" Huda asked.

"Clear the table, will you?" he huffed, the weight getting heavier by the second.

He set the box down and straightened. The little girls ran and threw their arms around his waist. "You're home."

He returned their embrace, soaking up their warmth and unabashed affection. How much he missed that. "Mama Subhia home?"

346

"She went to escort Nadia back from her classes." Huda started stripping the wrapping on top of the box, and the girls let go of him to tear away the rest.

"A television?" Salma shrieked, hopping off the floor.

"What do you mean, escort Nadia?" He tried to concentrate over the girls' jubilations.

"You didn't know?" Huda raised her eyebrows; a controlled measure of interest kept her eyeing the box.

"Know what?"

"Mama doesn't let Nadia go anywhere without her. She even tried to prevent her from attending classes, but Waleed and Fatimah talked her out of it."

"Why?" The question slipped off his lips. He knew the answer, and he shouldn't have asked.

The girls pulled on his hand. "Turn it on so we can watch cartoons like the neighbors."

He tried to lift the television set out of the box but couldn't. He ripped the carton apart, exciting the girls more, and headed to a corner in the living room. Lowering the heavy equipment to the floor, his back and leg muscles hurt. When he straightened, Huda grabbed his arm. "Mama doesn't trust Nadia anymore," she whispered. "You took too long to come. You better fix things now."

It took close to an hour to get a shady signal through the long antenna atop the big box and make the necessary adjustments. The girls fiddled with the knobs when he wasn't looking.

Mama Subhia and Nadia walked in. The volume was at full blast, and he stopped mid-sentence yelling at the girls to quit fooling around. Mama Subhia hurried to take him in her arms. When she pulled back he kissed her hand and touched it to his forehead, overcome by the emotions tightening his throat. He didn't expect her to welcome him so heartedly. Nadia extended her hand like a stranger, avoiding eye contact. The object lodged in his throat grew bigger, and he pretended to check something on the back of the television box to hide his disappointment. A frenzy of gasps and laughter filled the room when a broadcaster's black and white face filled the screen.

"How could you afford this?" Trepidation colored Mama Subhia's voice. "Please tell me you didn't borrow money."

"Don't worry. I saved enough."

"How? You must not have enough left to go by after you send us your salary." Mama Subhia ran her eyes over him from head to toe a couple of times. "You've lost weight. You're not taking care of yourself."

Kissing her head, he tried to reassure her. "I'm fine."

"His room is too small." Nadia bit her lower lip as soon as she uttered the words, regretting the impulse.

Mama Subhia squared her shoulders and drew in a long inhale, indicating she was running out of patience. He had seen that stance before, when she used to deal with Shareef's foolishness. He didn't know what to do or say.

Huda shoved the younger girls ahead of her into the kitchen. "Help me get the meal ready."

Mama Subhia grabbed his hand and pulled him down on the sofa beside her. "Time to put dots on the letters." She motioned for Nadia to take the opposite seat.

Omar relaxed his facial muscles to disguise his growing anxiety. She wanted to do this now? When no one else was around to back him up? Should he ask about Fatimah and Waleed? He glanced at Nadia, her eyes glued to the floor, her face full of an expression he couldn't understand. She took off her jacket. Her dress had a low square neckline, revealing smooth skin below the collarbone. Too much skin. If she bent forward, the top of her chest was sure to show. She went to campus in this dress?

"You heard from Marwan?" Mama Subhia asked.

"He came over the day he . . . finalized things here. It's my understanding his family commitments became too much." He swallowed, hoping Mama Subhia would pick up on his attempt to save Nadia's face in front of him. Playing this game was exhausting.

Mama Subhia narrowed her eyes then nodded. "We understood that much. We . . . wish him well. He left on very good terms. You must know that."

"Marwan is a decent man." He cleared his throat, moving onward. "I wanted to come home sooner but I couldn't."

Mama Subhia patted his knee. "I know. Did things change much for you after the coup?"

"I may end up back in Damascus soon."

Nadia snapped her eyes off the floor to strike his a fraction of a second. It was enough to charge him with hope. She was not as passive as she seemed.

"That's great news. I need you here." Mama Subhia put a hand on her chest. "My health can't take any more trouble. No word from Shareef since he left, the girls are growing up, demanding more attention, and Nadia . . ." She closed her eyes and shook her head in a dramatic show of frustration. "Nadia is not making things easy, given the circumstances."

"Don't worry about Shareef. I have the address of the school where he teaches in Kuwait. I know how to get in touch with him."

"I'm not worried about him." Her voice sank, exposing her lie.

God help him, he was going to make Mama Subhia cry. Of course she was worried about her son. Taking her other hand, he patted it. "Shareef needed time to evaluate things. That's how he has always been, taking his time to act. I think he plans to visit during spring break."

Mama Subhia's eyes lit up. "He can't just forget about us like that. Right?"

He searched for a way to put her mind at ease without further embellishing his fabrication. "Of course not. I'll contact him."

"I want him to bear responsibility."

"Have I fallen short in providing for you and the girls?" He couldn't prevent indignation from seeping into his tone.

Mama Subhia's face reddened. "You need to plan for a family of your own."

"You are my family. Or have things changed?"

350

"Of course not, *habibi*. I'm talking about you getting married. Having children."

"When the time is right."

Nadia jumped to her feet. "Mama, I need to talk to Omar." She tugged at his hand. "In private please."

He had to stand up. Had he stayed seated, Nadia would have remained bent forward and spilled out of her dress right in front of his eyes. Damn!

"I don't know what to do with her anymore." Mama Subhia tilted her head toward the front door. "Go to Fatimah's place. Talk things over and help me out here, Omar."

He snatched Nadia's jacket and followed her out the door. He would talk things over, all right. First things first. He must convince her never to wear this dress again.

Nadia walked side by side with Omar toward Fatimah's apartment. She pulled her jacket tighter and thought of a hundred ways to break the silence, but ended up keeping her mouth shut. He had not said a single word to her since he arrived, talking with Mama as if she weren't there. Now, he matched her quick steps, seeming unwilling to engage her in dialogue. If he didn't care to find out how she had been, she could hold her tongue. He didn't even look at her, keeping his hands in his jacket pockets while he walked.

Fatimah opened her door before they reached it and threw her arms around Omar's neck. "Mama Subhia called. I can't believe you're home and you didn't call me."

Omar laughed, a loud hearty laugh. It sounded like a nervous laugh to Nadia, without due cause and taking too long to fade. So he was not as calm and distant as he seemed.

"Come, come." Fatimah pulled on Nadia's hand and walked them both into her living room. "I'm feeding the children. I'll join you as soon as I can." She took their jackets and left the room, closing the door behind her.

Nadia imagined Fatimah on the other side, her ear to the door. She might get bored waiting. From the way things were going, Omar was bent on giving her a hard time, remaining mute. He took a seat and clasped his hands under his chin. Smoothing the back of her dress, she chose the sofa to his right and crossed her legs, waiting for him to start talking.

Noises drifted in from the busy street outside and interrupted the silence. A car honked a number of times, a vendor's voice called to stock up on diesel fuel for the winter, a couple of men's voices rose in argument, and she sat there, withstanding Omar's quiet stare.

"I like your dress." His voice seemed to come out of his chest, not his lips.

"Fatimah made it, like one of the dresses the actress Sua'ad Husni wore in *The Lost Love*. Did you see the film?"

Omar arched his eyebrows. An incredulous look swept over his face. "Didn't have a chance."

Why had she asked that? He must think her silly and immature. Of course he hadn't seen the film, stuck in his army camp. She adjusted the folds of her skirt, determined to keep the conversation going. "I didn't see it, either. Fatimah went with Waleed and I watched the children. It was her way of saying thank you."

"I wish you would never wear that dress again."

"Excuse me?"

"Not to campus, not on the street, and not in the presence of any man."

Her mouth fell open. If she were anything like that actress, she would respond with a seductive laugh, flicker long eyelashes or something. Instead, she crossed her arms to show her displeasure at his meddling in her choice of clothes. Big mistake. Her bosom lifted over her crossed arms, and she felt cold air on exposed skin where she normally wouldn't. It was enough to send Omar to his feet, giving her his back and mumbling a curse.

Flustered, she pulled her neckline as high as she could. "Is that all you have to say to me, Omar? That my dress is inappropriate?"

He slumped his shoulders with an audible exhale, as if she had thrown a rock at him. "I know it must have been difficult when you faced Marwan, having Huda and Mama Subhia on your back. I wish I had been here for you."

"You are here now."

"You told Mama Subhia you wanted to talk to me." He turned to stare down at her. "So talk."

Holding his stare, she felt sideways for a throw pillow and hugged it to her chest. "Are you still friends with Marwan?"

"Of course."

"And is he . . . well enough with the way things are now?"

"No man is *well* when he is rejected like that."

"I didn't mean to hurt him. I just . . . I expected . . . I wanted . . . to . . . to . . ." God help her, she couldn't find the right words.

He ran a hand through his cropped hair. "What, Nadia? What do you want?"

"I graduate next year."

"I know. You want me to try to convince Mama Subhia to let you go to classes on your own again?" He rubbed the back of his neck. "The way things are going is impractical to say the least."

She drummed her fingers over the pillow. Did he think that was why she had mentioned it? She was free of Marwan, almost done with her studies and ready for the next step. A couple of months' break before another engagement would not be considered too soon by social standards. "Is it true you might transfer to Damascus?"

"So I've been told."

She could tell he was on edge, his feet planted slightly apart, one leg shaking. What held him back? If he truly loved her like Huda and Fatimah said, why would he not come out and tell her? Marwan spoke about his feelings with ease, to the point she became irritated sometimes. The situation was reversed now. She could not let Omar know her desire to be his. It was the man's job to do the pursuing, the asking. "When would you move?"

354

He dropped back on the chair. "Not sure. They tell me to go, and I am gone the next day. I have no control. Why?"

She almost screamed in frustration. Why couldn't he catch on to what she was trying to say? Her words couldn't have been any clearer. "Mama is restricting my movement to punish me for sneaking out of town. If you move to Damascus, I won't need to do that." She swallowed, losing her courage to explain further. "Problem solved."

Several seconds passed. Her heart beating fast, she had to break eye contact and found invisible threads to pick off the pillow.

Omar leaned forward, rested his elbows on his knees and joined his fingers. "If I'm to transfer here, it would be as an attorney understudy in the military court until I earn my diploma. I will get a raise. You know what that means?"

"What?"

"I can get a decent place. An apartment."

Breathless, Nadia tried to follow his thread of thought. What was he trying to say? She touched the back of his hand. "Or you can come home."

He rubbed his thumb over hers. "It wouldn't be right. Not after all that happened."

"Will you find a place close?"

"Close to campus." He unlocked his fingers to grasp her hand. "A short walk between your classes."

What was going on here? He was not suggesting she visit him alone in his apartment on a regular basis. She withdrew her hand.

He leaned closer. "Mama Subhia will probably not —"

The door opened and Omar's oldest nephew ran into his arms. Fatimah followed, carrying her youngest and taking Omar's full attention.

Nadia blinked, trying to shake the thought in her head. If he thought it improper to move back to her house, how could he expect her to go to his? He didn't speak of marriage, or an engagement. Watching him relax with his sister and the children astounded her. Did he think she was on board with this arrangement? No, not Omar. That was not the kind of man he was. She must have missed something.

She remained preoccupied by that thought through the rest of the day, unable to seek clarifications from Omar. The entire family went back to her house to celebrate Omar's visit with food and to watch television. He spent the night at his sister's place, and left the following morning without stopping by.

The heavy weight of disappointment and confusion kept her restless and irritated. Why did things have to be so complicated?

Omar fastened a striped cloth around his hips and dropped his pants and underwear. He hung his clothes on one of the hooks, slipped his feet into a *quipquap* and clanged his way with the wooden shoes on slippery tiles. He went around a big fountain at the center of the reception hall and squeezed through a low opening leading to an inner room. He was late, and hoped he hadn't missed much of the party. It was his first time in a *souk* Turkish bath, his first time participating in the ceremonial washing of a groom on his wedding day.

Marwan called out for him as soon as he walked in. He didn't know how Marwan could see him through the thick steam. Light rays shot down from colored stained glass windows in the domed ceiling. Heat came at him from every direction, radiating off marble walls and floor. Splashing water resonated with every step he took and he resisted the urge to extend his arms ahead to feel his way around men with nothing but wet cloths around their loins. He smelled bay leaves and olive oil in the abundance of soap men lathered over their bodies. They scattered everywhere on the glistening floor around open marble urns, laughing and singing while they bathed.

Of course, Marwan had to be at the far end of the big circular room. By the time Omar reached him, he was breathless and sweaty. "Sorry I'm late." He sat next to Marwan, crossing his legs and holding the hems of his cloth together between his exposed knees. He greeted a couple of mutual friends now that he could distinguish faces. Marwan's face and neck were flushed red from the heat.

"I was worried you weren't going to make it," Marwan said. A man behind him was scrubbing Marwan's back with enough force to rock his body back and forth.

Omar wiped moisture off his forehead and upper lip, salty sweat stinging his eyes. "And miss all this fun?"

"Your first time?" The scrubbing man lifted Marwan's arm and ran his sponge up and down several times.

If Omar had been able to see better, he could swear the man was about to skin Marwan alive with his forceful hands. How dirty could Marwan be?

Marwan chuckled and turned his head toward the man, "Don't mind him. He's Palestinian. They don't follow this tradition." He motioned with his hand to an older man nearby. The older man splashed closer, shook hands with Omar, and squatted behind him. Before Omar could find out who the man was, hot water dumped over his head. He let out a curse, spitting water out.

"Relax." Marwan chuckled again. "Let him take care of you."

"I can bathe myself, thank you sir." Omar snatched the sponge out of the old man's hands. "I'm not the one getting married tonight."

"A massage?" The older man looked insulted, and Omar realized he had just deprived him of a chance to earn his keep. "Yes, thank you." He squeezed the sponge. "When I'm done?"

The older man nodded. "Just call out for me. I'm Abu Musa." He slipped away.

Omar washed, his skin tingling under the hot water and steam. "I found a place."

"Yeah? Where?" Marwan had his eyes closed, the man washing him burying his fingers in his bubble-covered hair.

"Arnous Square. A decent one-bedroom apartment."

"They gave you the go ahead at last? It's been three months since they told you of the move."

"I don't know what the holdup was. They had to clear me on all fronts, I guess."

"I didn't think you were still in danger after this time."

"I wasn't sure they wouldn't throw me in the same cell with my superior officer. But I'm out of the woods now. I'm set." Using a brass bowl, he scooped water out of the urn to his right and poured it over his face and chest. He heard Marwan's loud sigh and wiped his eyes. "What's troubling you?"

Marwan motioned to his attending man that he would take over. The man scurried off to another poor fellow. "A little nervous."

"About marriage? If any man were ever ready for this step, it's you, my friend."

Marwan washed his feet, keeping his voice low. "About *tonight*."

Omar coughed into his closed fist. Oh, no! He was not the one Marwan should be seeking advice from on this matter. Shouldn't he consult with a married man? His uncle? One of his older experienced friends? His brother-in-law? Hell, the old man he dismissed earlier could provide better insight than him. "You'll do fine."

"She's a widow, Omar. And I am . . . not . . . you know."

"It's better this way. You won't be at a complete loss like most of us."

Marwan scanned the crowd. "I think you and I are the only ones left. I heard things from these fellows I don't care to repeat."

"Listen, your wife waited more than two years for you. A young, wealthy woman like her could have chosen any of the men who sought her." He put his hand on Marwan's shoulder. "She wanted you. Concentrate on that, and everything else will follow its natural course." He dropped his hand. A persistent thought that kept him awake many nights toyed with his nerves. He had waited all his life for Nadia. What would their union be like if it ever came to life? He dumped cold water on his head.

Marwan rose and extended his hand. "It's not fair to keep her waiting any longer."

Grasping his hand, he let Marwan pull him to his feet. His cloth, soaking wet, threatened to leave him. He pinched it at his waist and tried to pull his hand out of Marwan's grip.

Before releasing it, Marwan gave him a quick tug. "It's time you step up. I have it on good authority, Nadia turned down a damn good man for you."

Stunned, Omar stared at Marwan. Before he could articulate a response, Marwan's friends surrounded them, as if seeing Marwan on his feet was their signal he was done bathing. They sang traditional chants about the groom's approaching night, causing Marwan's cheeks to flame a deeper red. They wrapped him in dry towels from head to toe and passed around stacks of dry towels for everyone in the circle.

Omar made sure to cover his chest to avoid a colder draft when a small wooden door opened. Caught by the cheerful crowd, he followed everyone to a bright, spacious hall, his mind, stomach and soul all in one big knot. Nadia wanted him. Not in a brotherly way, not due to her innocent emotional closeness to him, and not because she needed him to get rid of her fiancé. Marwan had to spell it out. She wanted him. And he, the obtuse idiot, had let his anger at her actions get in the way. He had given her a hard time before he started to explain his intentions that day in Fatimah's house, and when he had been interrupted, he'd lost his nerve. He had kept her waiting.

Sucking a dry breath, he entered the resting hall, brightened by huge stained glass windows. A big round fountain stood at the center of the marble floor. A continuous raised seat jutted off the wall around the room, covered with colorful rugs and cushions. Everyone found a seat and Omar ended up at the end of the row near the door. It was better this way. He couldn't wait for the ceremony to be over so he could slip away, his core seeking Nadia.

He tried to relax, his body adjusting to the gradual temperature change. Trays with short hot tea glasses were passed around with dessert: crunchy *baklava* stuffed with pine nuts and pistachios, drizzled with sweet syrup.

The men joked while they ate, and from the look on Marwan's face, he seemed to unwind and get used to their jests. He lost some of his clownish coloring, but a serious buzz hung over his bowed head. His hair still wet, his lips glistening with sugary syrup, Marwan radiated with vehement appreciation for the step he was about to take.

Omar closed his eyes. When would it be his turn?

The call for evening prayer resonated from minarets outside the bath walls and got everyone to their feet. The joyful atmosphere shifted to a serious one. Men headed to the dressing hall, a less spacious room with semi-private stalls side by side. Omar left an extra tip for Abu Musa for missing his massage before he left like a sheep following its herd. Everyone dressed and escorted Marwan to his house, cheering him on and declaring to the entire neighborhood that a groom was being prepped.

At the house, Marwan's relatives made a show of dressing the groom in his finest outer layers, splashing him with cologne and making sure he looked his best. The explicit jokes Omar heard in the Turkish bath disappeared, replaced by serious advice and comments about Marwan's duties as a family man.

The procession moved back to the street and headed toward the bride's house. Music and women's voices singing traditional songs spilled out to the street. Before Marwan was allowed in and the men dispersed, Omar reached him through the crowd and shook his hand, wishing him well.

Marwan managed a smile. "May your turn come soon, my friend."

CHAPTER
THIRTY-FIVE

Omar didn't know how he made it to his new apartment, walking through the streets in a daze. Rejuvenated and pumped by Marwan's ceremony, he experienced a severe let down stepping into the unfurnished space, and suffered a restless night alone in his sleeping bag. He had finalized the rental arrangements as soon as he was ordered to take up his new position at the military court, but hadn't told anyone in the family of this place yet. Had he told his sister or Mama Subhia, they would have scrambled to help him furnish the apartment and he didn't want their influence in the decorations. Nadia alone had that right.

The following afternoon, he looked out the window of his living room, snacking on a handful of roasted almonds. He could make out the main campus buildings a couple of streets away. Nadia could walk to her classes from here with ease. She could come home to rest during her breaks, have lunch or take a nap. Her friends and colleagues could visit her, study for exams, or work on papers. And he would get to watch her relax, flutter around happy and content like she used to.

He bit into a bitter almond and winced. About to spit it out, he closed his eyes and continued chewing instead. Uncle Mustafa's pale face appeared behind his eyelids. Bracing himself, he swallowed the bitterness and sent a mental salute to the old man.

He checked his watch. Nadia's last class was about to end and she would soon come out to take the bus home. He must hurry. Walking to campus, he concentrated on the early signs of spring to calm his nerves. Rose buds had started to awaken, hinting at splendid blooms and promising abundance of beauty to come. Perhaps he could be part of the seasonal cycle. Spotting Nadia clear the front gates with a group of students, he picked up his pace.

A gust of wind ruffled the hem of her skirt, and she pressed it down with a book in her hand. She advanced toward him as soon as she saw him, her eyes wide with worry. "What's wrong? Is Mama sick?"

"Everything is fine. I told her I wanted to walk you home today." He scowled at a couple of young men approaching from behind Nadia.

The young men flanked her, standing erect and flexing their arms by their sides. "Can we help you?"

Omar deepened his frown. "No."

Nadia clamped her other hand on her skirt, struggling to keep it from lifting. Flustered, she broke into a shy smile. "These are my friends, Riyad and Kareem."

The tallest of the two stuck his hand out to Omar. "And you are?"

Omar took his hand with a little more force than a handshake required. "Nadia's fiancé."

Nadia inhaled out loud, then bit her lower lip, glaring at him.

Riyad or Kareem, whichever the tallest man's name was, gave an idiotic smile. "Sorry. We thought you might be bothering our Nadia."

Omar clenched his jaw. *Our Nadia?* Who the hell was this guy? He took one step forward to get in his face.

Nadia hooked her arm in Omar's. "Thanks, Kareem. We don't want to be late." She tugged at Omar's arm until he gave in. He let her drag him away, maintaining eye contact with the two men as long as he could.

Once they rounded a corner, Nadia withdrew her hand and hurried onward. "I can't believe you just did that."

This was not a good start to the conversation he had in mind. He fell into step with her. "Would you rather I said I was your brother?"

"Of course not. I don't see why you had to say anything at all."

"The guys were measuring me. I'm not a fool."

"They are my *friends*. And they were looking out for me." Her voice rose. "You think you're the first handsome man to approach me on the street?"

It was his turn to get angry, but he did a double take. She thought him handsome? Now that was a good start. He clung to that. "Slow down, please. I want to talk to you about something important. Let's go to the Toledo café."

Nadia came to an abrupt stop. "Are you serious? The lovely café on Abu Rummaneh Street?"

"About a fifteen minute walk from here." He eyed her stubborn skirt. "Or we could take a taxi."

"I'm starving. Let's go to the falafel stand at the park entrance. It's a beautiful afternoon."

Omar nodded. Falafel stand? Not the refined place he wanted but he would go along. No point irritating her further.

He pushed through the crowd gathered around the falafel stand to place the order, keeping his eyes on Nadia, who waited at a distance. Gathering the hem of her skirt to one side, she examined flowers and followed a couple of butterflies before they flew high, the expression on her face delightful and carefree. He had made the right decision, seeing her unwind, returning to the old Nadia he knew. Carrying the hot sandwiches, he walked her through the park and kept the conversation centered around her studies until he found an empty bench. He motioned for her to take a seat.

Her face sparkling with the excitement of discussing her classes and professors, she bit into her sandwich unreservedly, closing her eyes while she savored the juicy bite.

He ran his fingers over the wrapping of his sandwich. "How come you don't wear your wing necklace anymore?" He cleared his throat. Where did that come from? Why couldn't he jump into what he really wanted to say?

"It reminds me of my engagement to Marwan. He's a married man now."

366

"Right." Omar pointed in the distance. "I rented an apartment in that building over there."

"So close?" A drop of *tahini* danced on her upper lip.

"I told you I would find something near campus."

She licked her fingers. "Furnished?"

"Not yet."

"When do you move?"

"Moved already. I report to military court day after tomorrow."

"That's great news." A tremor seeped into her voice. "Will you attend classes now that you're here? Is that why you decided to be close to campus?"

He shook his head, knowing he was staring at her mouth, unable to take his eyes away from the dancing sesame sauce. "I did it to make it easy for you."

She stopped chewing. Her cheek bulged with her bite, stretching her moist lips further. She swallowed. "I'm not sure I understand."

He handed her a napkin. "Shareef arrives tomorrow."

Her face drained of healthy color fast. "I won't stay home if he is there. But I cannot stay at your place, either. I can't believe you expect me to do that."

Confused by her reasoning, he coughed behind his closed fist. "Of course not. What I'm trying to say is —"

"How did you get Shareef to show his face?"

"I told him Mama Subhia is sick, and he must come see her. It was the one way to get him here."

Setting the remainder of her sandwich by her book on the bench between them, she wiped her mouth. "You had to lie to get him to remember his mother."

"He must take his place in the family."

She frowned. "We're doing just fine without him."

Omar touched his chest. "*I* need him here. Do you know why?"

"Mama will be pleased. You promised her to bring him home."

He put his unwrapped sandwich next to hers. "Shareef is your brother, your one blood male relative, and I have to address him in a matter only he can undertake." He took her hand in his. "If you agree."

"I don't want anything to do with him after what he did to us." Her hand trembled between his fingers. "I will not accept his apology if you think you can get him to do that. And you shouldn't depend on Shareef's ability to take charge —"

Omar clasped his other hand over hers. "Will you be my wife?"

She snatched her hand, rose to her feet, and gave him her back.

He waited a couple of breaths, watching her fight with her skirt, her head bowed. He went to stand behind her. Her hair tied high in a bun, the fine hairs on her nape flitted over smooth skin. Partially hidden under the hairline, a chocolate birthmark the size of a pencil eraser captivated him. He had never noticed it before. What other mysteries did she have?

Trying to keep his voice steady, he dropped it to a whisper, "I don't remember a time in my life when I wasn't in love with you. You must know that."

She remained silent, facing a tree.

"If you agree to marry me, I don't want to wait until you graduate. You could finish your studies from your new home. That's why I chose it so close to your campus."

Her head snapped up, but she didn't utter a sound.

"There's no other woman for me but you, Nadia." He touched her shoulder, dropped his hand when she flinched. "I don't know how else to explain it."

She made a soft sound, a faint moan. If only she would let him see the expression in her eyes. Why was she being difficult?

He released a shaky breath. "You don't have to answer me now. I'm telling you of my intention to ask Shareef for your hand, now that I finally paid off all my debts and can provide a decent life for you." He stepped back. "You can give your answer later if you like. After you have had time to think."

She swung around, and he was struck to see tears running. "Don't you know?" Her lips trembled.

His breath caught in his chest. "What?"

"I was born to be yours, Omar."

Omar stood by Waleed's side, tense and apprehensive, his eyes on arriving passengers. Resisting the need to tap his foot, he turned to Waleed. "You sure everything is set?"

"Relax, man. I worked everything out. The family will receive us."

"They dropped their claim? They know it's for the best, right?"

Waleed nodded. "I spelled everything out. They want this over with. They weren't asking for legal trouble, anyway."

Omar spotted Shareef clearing customs and stayed rooted in his spot, waiting for him to come closer. A border control security officer, one of Omar's acquaintances, escorted pale-faced Shareef through the crowd. The officer made a show of handing Shareef over to First Lieutenant Omar Bakry. Omar nodded acknowledgment to his friend, keeping a straight face. Connections in the right places came in handy in situations like these.

Waleed clasped Shareef's hand. "Welcome home."

Shareef dropped his bag by his feet. "What's going on? Why am I being escorted like a criminal?"

"You would have been dragged to prison had Omar not intervened on your behalf," Waleed explained.

Omar was impressed. Waleed threw up the lie without flinching. He never imagined Shareef's pale face could become more ghostly. It did.

"Prison? What are you talking about?"

"Sameera's father drew a court order reporting your name to border control for not paying her dowry." Omar stretched the deception as long as he could, the first step in his plan achieved. Shareef was scared shitless.

"Why didn't you tell me?" Shareef thrust his chin in Omar's face. "You let me come here to get arrested?"

Omar didn't flinch. "But you aren't arrested, are you? You're coming home with us to see your mother."

"How . . . how is she?"

"Better. You brought money to cover the hospital stay like we discussed?"

370

Shareef patted the chest pocket of his jacket. "Exact amount."

Nodding, Omar turned on his heels. "Let's go then."

Getting into the passenger seat of a taxi, Omar whispered the destination to the driver. During the first thirty minutes of the drive, Shareef asked about Mama Subhia's condition, directing all his questions to Waleed. Once they entered the city, he asked, "Where are we going? This isn't the way home. You said Mother was out of the hospital."

Omar gritted his teeth at the blatant avoidance of his presence. "We're making a quick stop first."

The taxi went down a street. Shareef bolted forward, gripping the back of Omar's seat. "This is Sameera's neighborhood."

"Right." Omar motioned for the driver to stop.

"Wait. What are we doing here?"

Waleed shoved Shareef out of the car. "We're here so you can make things right with Sameera's family. You will pay her dowry and be a man."

"I have to pay the hospital bill."

Omar grabbed Shareef's arm and dragged him onward. "You have to do this if you don't want your mother to visit you in prison."

Stumbling and cursing, Shareef tried to resist. "But the medical bills . . ."

"Mama Subhia didn't go to the hospital. No bills."

"You tricked me, you bastard?"

Omar tightened his hold. "Had to."

Waleed grabbed Shareef's other arm. "Omar saved your ass. You owe him your freedom. So just play along

371

now. You walk in there, ask Sameera's father for forgiveness, hand over the money, and walk out."

They reached the door. Omar let go of Shareef and rang the doorbell. "You will have your life back. And spare your mother a lot of heartache."

The door opened. Omar slid behind Shareef. Step two accomplished.

Walking into Mama Subhia's house an hour later, Omar left the front door open, Waleed and Shareef behind him on the stairs. He called Mama Subhia out of the kitchen and sat her on the sofa. Holding her wrists, he took his time kissing her forehead to check her pulse without her noticing. Satisfied she was relaxed enough, he pulled back. "I have a surprise for you. Someone is here to see you."

Her hands flew to her hair, patting her tight bun in place. "Who?"

Shareef walked in and stopped a couple of steps inside. Mama Subhia's hands froze on top of her head. Waleed nudged Shareef from behind. Dropping his chin to his chest, Shareef shuffled forward until he stood before his mother.

Omar watched the expression on her face shift from eyes-widening surprise, to jaw-dropping disbelief, to brow-furrowing undeniable anger, until it settled in a warm expression, emanating hurt, censure and forgiveness all at once.

He looked away, jealous of the intimate moment. No one but a mother was capable of producing that instinctive look in one heartbeat. He headed to the

372

door, passed Waleed and threw him a satisfied nod. Step three accomplished.

Later that evening, Omar picked up a tray of *kanafeh* dessert from the best sweetshop in town and headed to Mama Subhia's place. Having stayed away the rest of the day to give the family a chance to reunite with their son without his animosity toward Shareef hanging over their heads, he didn't know how Nadia's encounter with Shareef had gone.

Taking a deep breath, he balanced the wrapped tray on one palm and knocked on the door. Fatimah and Waleed should be there by now. At least he would have their support.

Huda let him in, her face more sour than usual. She took his load to the kitchen. Everyone gathered in the living room. Everyone except Nadia. Waleed stood, giving him a warm greeting. Shareef remained seated, lounging further in his chair and glaring at him.

Omar kissed Mama Subhia's head as usual and took a seat by her side. He connected eyes with Fatimah. She motioned with her chin toward the girls' room. His sister understood him well, letting him know Nadia hid. Out of shyness or was she avoiding Shareef's presence? He tilted his head in Mama Subhia's direction, raising his eyebrows. Fatimah nodded twice, giving him the signal she had informed Mama Subhia of the specific reason behind his visit tonight. Not wanting to waste one more minute on superficial pleasantries and small talk, he cleared his throat. "I'm here tonight to ask for Nadia's hand."

Shareef raised one eyebrow.

Omar looked him in the eye. "Nadia and I have talked. With the approval of Mama Subhia, we are ready to settle down."

Before Shareef could utter a sound, Mama Subhia put her hand over her upper lip, wobbled her tongue, and launched into a long, loud *zaghroota*. Fatimah followed suit, and then Huda, as if the women were competing to produce the highest joyful screech. Fatimah ran to get Nadia.

Red-faced and smiling, Nadia received the women's hugs and kisses. Her younger sisters sang something rhyming and silly. She wore a soft blue dress with white frilly lace around its collar and sleeves. Her dark hair cascaded to her shoulders in neat layers and contrasted with the white lace. She didn't just look beautiful and soft, she radiated with feminine appeal. Omar had to check his breathing.

Waleed struck his shoulder. "Finally."

Shareef rose to his feet. "So you all worked it out, huh? And what am I? A chair's leg? A decoration?"

"Your job is waiting for you, son." Mama Subhia patted his chest. "A duty toward your sister when it is time to give Omar her hand."

"You expect me to give my sister to a man of doubtful origins?"

Omar jumped to his feet and roared, "How dare you?"

"I met people in Kuwait." Shareef's voice rose. "Other Palestinian refugees who frequented the British clinic in our village." He thrust his chin forward. "Told

374

me interesting things about your father. Your real father."

Omar grabbed fistfuls of Shareef's shirt. "My father died working his land before I was born. What the hell are you talking about?"

Waleed tried to pull him back. Omar wouldn't budge. Fatimah said something but he registered none of it. He shook Shareef. "Speak, damn you."

"Ever wonder why that . . . that old woman in the neighborhood called you the Englishman?"

"That's enough!" Mama Subhia's voice vibrated throughout the house. She laid a hand on Omar's shoulder, bringing him back from the dark pit he was thrown into. "Let him go."

He released Shareef and took a couple of steps back, the muscles in his arms aching from lack of release. He kept his fists balled.

"You just can't see anyone happy, can you?" Mama Subhia advanced on Shareef. "I don't know where I went wrong with you, son. Seeing you sink this low breaks my heart."

Shareef pointed his hand in Omar's direction. "You never explained why he looks so different from Fatimah. You let him grow up with your children, and you knew all along who he was. What he is."

"What am I, Shareef?" Omar's voice rumbled out like a bear's growl.

Shareef squared his shoulders. "The English doctor's bastard."

He lunged for Shareef, moving on pure instinct, a predator aiming for his prey.

Mama Subhia stepped in his path. She slapped Shareef hard. "Shut your mouth." Her chest heaved up and down with her words. She teetered left and right and sank toward the floor.

Omar caught her under the arms before she hit the floor. Waleed helped him lift her to the sofa. Shareef shrank in the background. Huda and Nadia rushed to tend her.

Omar squatted by Mama Subhia's head, his energy and reasoning draining fast, like a squeezed wound oozing bile and blood. Shareef's words throbbed in his ears. A bastard? He sought his sister.

Fatimah clung to the arms of her chair, her face like a lemon. She shook her head and mouthed, "Not true."

Water splashed on his hands when Nadia sprinkled Mama Subhia's face. He rose and leaned his back to the wall, giving her more room. Did Fatimah see doubt in his eyes? Despite looking so different from her, he had never considered the circumstances of his birth. In the back of his mind, he often saw himself as an outsider, and he had reasoned the thought away for being an orphan. But an illegitimate child of an English doctor? Where did Shareef come up with this information? There was no smoke where there was no fire. And that old woman who gave him his nickname as a boy, how come he never checked to find out why?

Someone tugged at his hands. The younger girls clung to him, crying. He wrapped his arms around them. "Don't worry. Your mother will be all right."

His words penetrated Mama Subhia's mental break, and she came to. "I'm fine. I'm fine." She held on to

Huda's hands and tried to get up. "Help me to my room. I don't want to see his face."

Shareef strutted to the door. "I will leave."

Nadia sprang ahead, beating him to the door. She turned the lock and rested her back to it. "You are not going anywhere." She glared at her brother, eyes clear and intense, dark hair framing her determined face. "I don't care what Omar is, or what name he uses, or who his father was. I don't care if he was a gorilla or an alien from outer space. I love him. I was in love with him before I understood what love meant." She pushed away from the door and moved to stand a step facing Shareef. "You will not leave this house before I am married to Omar." She jabbed his chest with her index finger. "You are going to make it happen. Tonight."

Shareef swatted her finger aside. "The stars above are closer to you, Nadia."

"I am trying to hold on to the last thread between us for Mama's sake." She lifted her chin. "I don't need you. I am old enough to get married without you."

He grabbed a fistful of her hair. "You defy your brother?"

Omar was on Shareef before he could twist his grip. He held Shareef's neck from behind in the crook of his arm, trapping his throat in an iron-clad hold. "Let go."

Shareef freed Nadia's hair and flailed his arms to no use.

Waleed tried to intervene. "This is not the way to solve anything."

"When did you *ever* act like my brother, Shareef?" Nadia screamed. "You were *never* there for me or for

377

anyone in this family. Always watching out for yourself. Just because we don't say anything to your face doesn't mean we are blind." Rubbing her scalp, she scrunched her hair and in the process added a disheveled look to her fierce stance.

Omar had never seen her look more beautiful. He released Shareef with a shove and faced Mama Subhia. "Is there any truth to what he is saying?"

Mama Subhia clasped his face in her palms. "I knew your parents well. Your father's mother was from Jenin. Do you hear me? She had red hair and pale skin with red freckles. We didn't have time to take family portraits from your father's house when we fled."

Omar swallowed with difficulty. "You never mentioned my grandmother before."

"I didn't see a need to." She dropped her hands. "I thought we made you feel like you were one of us."

He kissed her hand and touched it to his forehead. "You did."

"When we made it across the border with the other refugees, I wanted to register you and Fatimah under our family name, as our children. But Mustafa would not have it. He insisted you were the single male survivor of the Bakry family." Mama Subhia held his shoulders with both hands, giving them a gentle squeeze. "Mustafa said you had the responsibility of carrying on your father's family name. Do you think he would have said that if he had any doubt about your origin?"

"You know what I can't figure out?" Huda's tone came out surprisingly, calm and mellow.

Everyone turned toward her.

"I have been tending to the women of this community since forever. And they are refugees like us, many from surrounding villages." She squinted at her brother. "Not one of them mentioned anything about that English doctor you are talking about. And you, in particular, know how women love to gossip. How do you explain that?"

Shareef shifted from foot to foot. "How should I know? Maybe . . . maybe they spared your feelings, they wouldn't say it to your face." He darted his eyes to his mother. "Or maybe they . . . they respected Mother too much for taking him in." He shrugged. "I don't know."

"I have a better explanation." Huda's voice hardened, making the sharp switch more frightening. It matched her dead stare. "You made it all up."

Shareef's face crumbled. "There was a British clinic, wasn't there? I mean, just because women didn't —"

"Stop lying," Huda shot back. "Why are you doing this?"

"Mother always favored Omar over me."

"How old are you? Nine? Mama would never favor anyone over her own son. It's against nature. Don't you understand?"

"She kicked me out of this house!" Shareef yelled, spit flying out of his mouth. "For him!"

"She did it for Nadia's sake, not Omar's." Huda's tone chilled the entire room. "You should be kissing Mother's feet right now for allowing you back after what you did."

"That was Sameera's fault." His voice lost its defiant edge. "She tricked me."

Huda crossed her arms over her chest. "Did Sameera trick you into cutting ties with us? Did she trick you into screaming at your mother? You know Omar shouldered the burden of this family alone. And one more thing, *brother*, Omar never raised his voice in Mama's presence. Not once."

"Stop this." Mama Subhia approached Shareef, giving him that mixed look Omar saw in her eyes before. "You will do what is expected of you now, son. We will leave what happened behind us and never talk about it again."

Shareef opened his mouth to say something, then seemed to change his mind.

Mama Subhia turned to address Waleed. "Go to the mosque and bring the *sheikh* and a couple of witnesses. We will seal this marriage before God tonight, and do the civil registration in the morning. The wedding will be the last Thursday of this month. Almost three weeks from today."

CHAPTER
THIRTY-SIX

Nadia lifted the hem of her wedding dress and took the first step into her new home with her right foot, inviting good luck. She could barely stand, her legs wobbling like rice pudding. The mad rush to get everything ready for the wedding in such a short time had taken its toll. Her feet hurt and she contemplated taking off her shoes, but wouldn't that seem undignified?

Omar closed the front door behind them, undid his tie and opened the collar of his white shirt. "I thought the evening would never end."

"You did well with the band. Everyone seemed to enjoy their music."

"Good. Wish they had wrapped it up a little earlier, though." He draped his suit jacket on the back of the lone chair in the living room. With Omar's tight budget and Fatimah's modest contribution, they were able to buy a decent bedroom set and the necessary kitchen appliances. The rest of the apartment remained nearly empty.

Nadia headed to the bedroom. A couple of pins holding her veil in place had dug like nails in her scalp throughout the wedding ceremony, and she had resisted the need to pull them out as long as she could. She could take the pain no longer, tugging on the veil to loosen the pins. Her heavy locks spilled from their elaborate hairdo, but the stubborn pins didn't budge. Why were her fingers shaking like that?

"Here, let me help you." Omar reached out to unpin her veil. His warm breath brushed her face, and his cedar wood-laced cologne invited a flood of memories. The shaking spread to her entire body. What was happening?

Dropping the veil to the floor, he combed his fingers through her hair until the locks came undone. His breathing deepened, his smile vanished, and a strange expression clouded his face.

The pulsing pressure in her head dissipated with blood rushing to the sore spots. Must be why the room started spinning. Dear God, let her not be the kind of silly girl who fainted on her wedding night. She placed her palms on his chest. "Hold me."

He wrapped his arms around her, tentative and lax at first, then his muscles tightened and his palms spread flat on her back. "God, you are trembling like a leaf. Are you cold?"

She buried her face under his chin. His quickening heart rate pulsed in the vein touching her cheek. She moved her head from side to side to indicate her answer, brushing against his skin, marveling at his increasing warmth.

He made a deep throaty sound. "Do you know how long I have dreamt of this moment? You in my arms?"

She shook her head again, inhaling his masculine scent, unable to speak.

382

"Too long, Nadia. Too long." He dipped his head to brush her ear with his lips. "I wish I could tell you, but I don't know how to say things like that." He nuzzled the tender spot on the side of her neck. "God, you smell good."

A quiver darted to her toes, like a shot of electricity spiking her heartbeat. Under her fingertips, a tremor ran through his chest muscles. Was that her effect on him? She flipped her head to face away, laying her other cheek flat against his shoulder.

Releasing a ragged breath, he moved his hands down her back. "Don't be afraid. It's you and me now."

She was a married woman in the arms of her beloved husband. Only thing, *Omar* was her husband. This was supposed to be the most natural thing in the world. Why did she feel this awkward? She squeezed her eyes shut. "That's the problem."

He stiffened. "I don't understand."

Lifting her head, she kept her eyes on the base of his throat. "I think . . . I need more time. To get used to the idea of . . . you and me." Her voice came out strangled, like a child's, about to cry.

He withdrew his hands and stepped back. "Of course. Take all the time you need." His jaw muscles pumped, his face and neck flushed red.

He seemed hurt, as if she had insulted him. Why had she listened to Huda talk to her about this night? Now she couldn't stop coming out like a frightened fool. She sat on the edge of the bed. "My feet hurt."

A wave of confusion passed over his face before he went down to one knee and slipped off her high heels.

He massaged her feet. Keeping his head down, his forehead almost touched her lap.

She ran ten fingers through his hair to the back of his head, admiring the coarse feeling on her skin. "Your hair is so thick now."

Exhaling loudly, he dropped his forehead between her knees. His warm hands inched up her legs under her gown. No, his hands were not warm. They were hot, searing her skin. He branded her legs, matching his slow progress with her crawling fingers through his hair. Her skin vanished, and her entire body fused into one entwined nerve connecting her legs to a deep spot in her stomach. What feeling was that? How could she put a name to something totally new? Hearing herself pant, she released his hair and placed her palms on her knees to stop his ascending hands.

Lifting his head, he struck her with an intense gaze she had never seen before. His bright blue eyes turned darker, like the ink from her fountain pen, the expression in their depths too foreign. She sucked in a sharp breath.

Withdrawing his hands, he sat back on his heels. "Your feet better?" His voice was deep, and although he asked a caring question, it sounded rugged and edgy.

She swallowed. "Yes, thank you."

He rose, twisting sideways and giving her his back. "I'm thirsty. Want me to get you anything from the kitchen?"

"Fatimah and I ran out of time. We didn't have a chance to unpack the kitchen sets yet."

He moved toward the door while she was talking. Why was he eager to leave? He could not be that thirsty. Maybe he was giving her a chance to change out of this bulky gown. She slid off the bed. "Omar, wait."

He put a hand on the doorjamb. "Yes?"

"Could you . . . please . . ." The letters melted on her tongue, not forming the words she needed.

He faced her again. "What do you need?"

She swept her hair to one side of her neck and turned. "Could you . . . undo my dress, please? I can't reach the zipper." She didn't hear him move for several heartbeats and was about to give up when he came closer. Much closer. If he breathed any deeper, his chest would touch her back. She hung her head, the tense wait making her wish she hadn't asked.

His fingers brushed the base of her neck, lingered on a single spot close to her hairline, then moved to undo her zipper. The dress loosened around her chest and waist. Should she thank him and wait for him to leave? But he didn't move. His body heat radiated through the almost nonexistent space between them, and she sensed it on her exposed back.

"It's not sleeveless," he whispered, as if talking to himself.

"Excuse me?"

"Your dress. I heard you once say you wanted a sleeveless wedding dress." He sounded like he had climbed a flight of steep stairs.

She turned around, holding her top over her chest with both hands before the soft fabric slipped down her shoulders. "Mama wouldn't allow it." Embarrassment

385

gripped her throat, making her voice almost inaudible. She chanced a quick glance at his face. His eyes were fixed on her mouth, not her bare shoulders. He should leave her now to change into a nightgown with some dignity. "Weren't you thirsty?"

His eyes struck hers a fraction of a second before he dipped his head and moistened her lips with his. He broke contact, long enough for her to draw in a breath, shallow and shaky. Then his lips were on hers again, full and eager.

She let him kiss her again and again. Maybe she kissed him back, she wasn't sure. How would she know? Thoughts emptied out of her head like water out of a spilled bucket. Her lips merged with his until she became acquainted with their commands. She may have sighed, or it could have been his deep groans that played music in her ears.

Lost in his embrace, she didn't realize her back had become exposed until his fingers tingled her skin at the small of her back. Still clutching the front of her dress, her hands were trapped at his chest. Her dress started to slip down. A wave of panic hit her. Breaking her mouth free, she managed to choke out, "Wait. Wait."

His lips trailed the side of her neck and continued to sear little spots on her shoulder.

"Omar, wait."

He rested his forehead where his lips were, releasing a long tortured exhale. "Don't do this, please. Don't pull away from me."

"But my dress . . . It's slipping."

"Let it." He moved his hands to her hips and pressed her against him.

She gasped at the poking pressure.

"It's all right, Nadia. This is me."

She risked freeing one hand and pushed his chest. "No, something is wrong."

Swearing under his breath, he let her go and stepped back.

Gathering the sagging fabric higher, she dropped on the bed and glared at him.

He gripped the corner of the dresser, his breathing hard and loud. "I was willing to leave you alone like you asked. But then you called me to undress you." He rubbed his neck. "You have to be clear with me. Do you want us to be together tonight?"

To her shame, she nodded, wanting him to kiss her again, that she was sure of. The rest? Maybe she could skip?

He sat next to her on the bed and held her free hand. "Please tell me you know how this works. Didn't you study this at school or something? Hasn't anyone talked to you about tonight?"

"I know the basics. Huda explained things."

He groaned. "Huda? Didn't your mother say anything? Fatimah?"

"Mama tried, I was too embarrassed, so I told her I already had the talk with Huda. And Fatimah? She said you would know what to do and I shouldn't worry."

He studied their clasped hands in his lap. The skin showing from his open collar glistened with sweat and his chest heaved with every breath. His leg next to hers pumped up and down. Was he impatient? Irritated by her ignorance? Or could he be plain nervous? Perhaps Fatimah was wrong, and now he expected *her* to do something.

She squeezed his hand. "Omar?"

Lifting his gaze, he swept her with those darkened irises, exquisite and all-consuming, speaking a language she couldn't quite grasp. He kissed her naked shoulder. "There's nothing to worry about."

"It isn't going the way it should. Not like Huda explained."

"What the hell did Huda say?"

She pulled her shambled dress tighter. "She said it would be quick. Look at me." She bit her lower lip. "I'm half naked and you have not even taken off your shoes."

He cleared his throat and stood before her. Stepping out of his shoes, he took off his shirt and slid out his belt. His fingers lingered over his fly zipper. "Would you like me to go on?"

She shook her head in denial, but didn't look away, either. Audacious or brazen, she didn't care what Huda thought of her. His tight body was too beautiful not to openly admire. The muscles under his shimmering skin rippled like waves breaking on the shore. "You are shaking?"

"I ache for you, Nadia." He closed the distance. "I want you to be mine." His voice poured like liquid chocolate, like hot syrup blanketing all in its way.

"Huda said it would be painful. I didn't think it would be painful for you too."

388

He cradled her face in his palms and dipped his head. "I can't promise it will not be painful at first, but I can promise you this." He held her mouth captive in his for a long kiss. "I will do my best not to be quick."

She didn't know what that meant.

He took his time explaining.

Acknowledgments

I owe one person my utmost gratitude and respect: my late father, Hasan Taha. I had written this story under his guidance and with his encouragement, engaging him as much as possible on a daily basis, absorbing his thoughts, memories, and the feelings he experienced growing up during the timespan of the book's events. I had hoped he would see how it turned out, but he passed away two months before I signed the publishing contract. My father was the reason I started on this path, and remains the constant power under my wings. I only hope I made him proud.

I have relied on the unconditional love and support of my affectionate mother, Nawal Abu Quara, whom I could never thank enough for all that I am, and ever will be. Her involvement and consistent belief that I would get this story out never wavered. She made me believe in my writing abilities when I suffered serious doubts at times.

I am deeply grateful to my husband, Saad Saleh, who stood by me during all the emotional and time-consuming stages I went through while writing this book. On the road to visit our kids in college, driving back and forth from Houston to Austin too many times to count, he patiently listened to me read out loud chapter by chapter as I developed the story. His feedback was extremely valuable, and his suggestion for the title was the icing on the cake.

My appreciation goes out to my lovely kids, Leila Saleh and Bassel Saleh, who tolerated my absentmindedness and preoccupation with imaginary people on paper. My children's constant smiles and warm embraces helped me get through the complicated process of writing this story, showing me patience and maturity beyond their years.

I am thankful to my brother, Bassel Taha, for his love and cheerful attitude that keep propelling me forward.

I would like to extend my sincere thanks to the Head of English Publishing at Bloomsbury Qatar Foundation Publishing, Thalia Suzuma. From the instant she acquired my manuscript, to the instant it came out, as the book it is, she has been extremely and expertly supportive, seeing with a sharp eye angles and plot threads and suggesting improvements wherever needed. My thanks also go out to the editing team, specifically copy editor Michelle Wallin, and the team of cover artists at BQFP, who worked hard to produce the final book with its jacket.

The following persons have been instrumental with their backing, help, and encouragement: Sana Dabbagh, Manal Broeckelmann, Roger Paulding, Sharon Dotson, Barbara Andrews, Luke Chauvin, Joe Night, Sandra M.

DiGiovanni, Paula Porter, Bob Gregory, Louis Allen Epstein, Julian Kindred, Carol Swiantek and Alexandra Chasse.

UNDER A CORNISH SKY

Liz Fenwick

On the sleeper train down to Cornwall, Demi can't help wondering why everything always goes wrong for her. Having missed out on her dream job, and left with nowhere to stay following her boyfriend's betrayal, pitching up at her grandfather's cottage is her only option . . . Victoria thinks she's finally got what she wanted: Boscawen, the gorgeous Cornish estate her family owned for generations, should now rightfully be hers, following her husband's sudden death. After years of a loveless marriage and many secret affairs of her own, Victoria thinks new widowhood will suit her very well indeed . . . But both women are in for a surprise. Surrounded by orchards, gardens and the sea, Boscawen is about to play an unexpected role in both their lives, as long-buried secrets are uncovered and a battle of wills begins . . .

VIGILANTE

Shelley Harris

Jenny Pepper manages a charity bookshop and looks after her husband and daughter — but it feels like something is missing in her life. An invitation to a fancy dress party sparks her interest, and she decides to go as a female superhero. On her way to the party she stumbles across a woman being mugged, and she intervenes. Feeling an adrenalin rush and a sense of satisfaction, Jenny wants to do it again — to right wrongs and fight for justice. The masked mystery woman catches the imagination of the public and the press; and backed up by self-defence classes and basic common sense, Jenny soon becomes a local legend. But can she incorporate what she has learned into her everyday life, rather than throwing it all away — the good as well as the bad?

SLEEPING ON JUPITER

Anuradha Roy

A train stops at a railway station, and a young woman jumps off. She has wild hair, sloppy clothes, a distracted air. The sudden violence of what happens next leaves the other passengers gasping . . . The train terminates at Jarmuli, a temple town by the sea. Here, among pilgrims, priests and ashrams, three old women disembark — only to encounter the girl once again. What is someone like her doing in this remote place? Over the next five days, the old women live out their long-planned dream of a holiday together; their temple guide finds ecstasy in forbidden love; and the girl is joined by a photographer battling his own demons. As the lives of these disparate people overlap and collide, Jarmuli is revealed as a place with a long, dark past that transforms all who encounter it . . .

THE SUMMER OF BROKEN STORIES

James Wilson

England, 1950s: While out playing in the woods, ten-year-old Mark meets a man living in an old railway carriage. Despite his wild appearance, the stranger, who introduces himself as Aubrey Hillyard, is captivating — an irreverent outsider who is shunned by Mark's fellow villagers, and a writer to boot. Aubrey encourages Mark to tell stories about a novel he is writing — a work of ominous science fiction. As the meddling villagers plot to drive Aubrey out, Mark finds himself caught between two worlds — yet convinced that he must help Aubrey prevail at any cost . . .